OUT OF TIME

PAULINE BAIRD JONES

Hard Shell Word Factory

Copyrright 2006 Pauline Baird Jones
eBook ISBN: 0-7599-4592-6
Published July 2006

Trade Paperback ISBN: 0-7599-4603-5
Published August 2006

Hard Shell Word Factory
PO Box 161
Amherst Jct. WI 54407
books@hardshell.com
www.hardshell.com
Cover art © 2006 Paul Greer

I'd like to dedicate this book to
My dad, Robert N. Baird
And to
My father-in-law. Chester N. Jones

And to the rest of
The Greatest Generation
Thank you for your sacrifices for our freedom.

And to the new generation of heroes,
Fighting for our freedom around the world,
And here at home...

Acknowledgements

I couldn't have written this book without the help of so many people. First, I'd like to thank the Greatest Generation for their faithful service in the wars of the 19th Century. Without their sacrifice, I wouldn't have the freedom to have written this book.

And from the amazing B-17 email list, what can I say to Jim Kissock, Doug Gross, Otis C. Ingebritsen, Lt.Col. USAF Res. (Ret.), Robert W. Livingston; Gene Carson, Paul Roderick, Everett Worrell, Major, USAF Retired, Roy Test, Jerry Hogan, Bob Dun, Earl Pate, Jr., Otis C. Ingebritsen, Jim White, C.W. "Mac" McCauley, Wes Sullivan, Robert Johnson, my father-in-law, Chester N. Jones and my dad, Robert N. Baird. Thank you, thank you, thank you for what you did back then and for all your help now. You're my heroes. ☺

I'd also like to thank the World War II Writer's Research Group on Yahoo, in particular Morag McKendrick Pippin and Maria U. Budzynski. Maria not only provided me with information from the German side, but proved how amazing it can be when enemies become friends.

And my thanks to all the wonderful people in our online group who were so great in sharing references and resources.

I'd like to thank others who took time to answer personal questions: Sandra Parshall and her husband, Tricia McGill and her very kind sister who answered my questions about rationing and what it was like.

And I'd like to thank Christopher A. Ebdon, of the Confederate Air Force, who gave me my tour of a real B-17 and took time to answer my many questions.

And there's my son-in-law, Paul Greer. Thank you for my wonderful cover art. ☺ I'd like to thank Jamie Engle and Diana L. Driver for their help and advice in the writing, editing and polishing this book. And my editor, Diane Kirkle. Thank you for making me look good. ☺

And I'd like to thank my husband, Greg for his patience, my son, Nathan for letting me bounce ideas off him, and my mother, Ann G. Baird for information about the period. I couldn't have done this without any of you either.

And then there's my sister, Marilyn and her husband, David. Thank you for all you do to keep me going. ☺

If I've forgotten anyone, I apologize. This book has been many years—and a couple of computers—in the writing.

Chapter One

Present day

THE C-130 rumbled through the sky, the propellers cutting determinedly into the gradually thinning air. Melanie Morton had been miserable on the ground in her wet suit and gear, but as the plane went up and the temperature dropped she realized she was an amateur in miserable.

She'd done some crazy—and misery-inducing—things for her television magazine segment, Make Mel Cry Uncle, appearing four times a year on *BrightLine Weekly*, but doing a HALO jump with the Navy SEALS was taking crazy thirty thousand feet too high.

Her producer had had to do some heavy duty persuasion before the Navy would allow her to even prepare for the jump, let alone attempt it. They finally agreed, probably because the powers-that-be thought she'd never make it through Hell Week, let alone survive the grueling training regimen that was required prior to the high altitude-low open drop with an actual SEAL team. But here she was, all geared up and only one way to go: down. At one-hundred and twenty miles per hour.

If she'd had any doubts about her sanity, she didn't anymore.

She really was out of her freaking mind.

The sad part, she'd been out of it clear back to when she'd first pitched the idea that had eventually become Make Mel Cry Uncle. Since that time she'd learned to fight various sorts of fires. She'd trained with cops and SWATS, trekked to the Arctic, done a stint with the Coast Guard and another in search-and-rescue, gone swimming with sharks, dived to deep sea wreckage—the list was long and getting longer. Four shows a year for five years. *Dang.* So far she hadn't made it into space, but it wasn't because her producer hadn't tried to talk her into it. There was buzz of going back to the moon, but that was so last century. Maybe if they let her go to Mars...

She shook her head. What was she thinking? She still hadn't gotten her tush out of this plane and she was thinking about Mars? She was worse than freaking insane...whatever that might be.

Of course, she could cry uncle and go home. Show over. SEALS happy. Their charity would be even happier because she'd have to ante up the dough and not them. That was the deal, if she cried she donated to their favorite charity. If she didn't, then they had to donate to hers. So far, her charity had made out like a bandit. They loved her. But all good things had to come to an end sometime. So why wasn't her mouth open and why wasn't she crying uncle like a baby?

Her Gran could have supplied the answer. She'd told Mel almost every day of Mel's life that she was the most stubborn person on the face of the earth. It was probably her biggest character flaw, though it wasn't her only one. However, there came a time to face those flaws and defeat them.

Did it really matter if her SEAL team expected her to fail? Was proving them wrong that big of a deal? So what if they had bets on when she'd cry? They were also betting on when she'd wet her pants. It was probably a guy thing.

She looked down the row of faces, seated on the hard, narrow bench with her. All of them were in full scuba gear and each held an oxygen mask, in anticipation of the moment when the cabin would be depressurized. Hers was probably the only face without the tough-guy expression. This was an experienced team of steely-eyed, professional killers who'd proved their chops in Afghanistan and Iraq. They were honest-to-goodness heroes, like her grandfather and her father. She was proud to be sitting with them, even if they did want her to fail.

It wasn't personal. They liked her, or what they knew of her. Some of them had even offered to get to know her on a more personal level and weren't holding a grudge at being turned down. They just wanted her to fail. Only in the movies could a girl make it as a SEAL. It would make them so happy if she failed. It was probably the patriotic thing to do.

It was a pity the necessary word was stuck in her stubborn throat like a freaking hair ball that wouldn't hack up. Even as she was listing the reasons for crying uncle, another part of her brain was pointing out that it was only a jump. Other than the first step and the velocity, it was really no different from her time with the paratroopers.

So that made her stubborn and delusional.

There was a saying in the SEALS that the only good day was yesterday. This was her last, bad day. Tomorrow she'd be on her way home, with all her SEAL yesterdays behind her. She could go back and kill her producer. Thanks to the SEALS, she now knew about a hundred different ways. Pity she could only use one of them on him.

The aircraft shuddered and then straightened out.

"Three minute warning," Rockman's voice said in her ear piece.

They all donned their oxygen masks and then the rear ramp slowly lowered, depressurizing the hold. Mel had thought it was as cold as it could get.

She was wrong.

"Line up!" Rockman spoke again.

Moving like ungainly gooney birds, the team and Mel formed two lines, on either side of the plane, clutching at hanging straps for balance, their footing made precarious by heavy packs, webbed feet and the bouncing of the plane as it rode the air currents. Mel realized she was hyperventilating into her mask. Would the friction and pure oxygen set her lungs on fire? That thought didn't help. Fear Rockman would notice did.

Rockman got nose to nose with her. He didn't need to. She could hear him just fine in the ear piece. On the other hand, he'd spent the last three months with his face in hers telling her to move her butt somewhere other than where it currently was. It was probably a hard habit to break. Maybe it was even a freaking SEAL rule.

"So, Frog Lady, you ready to cry uncle?"

Frog wasn't actually meant to be an insult, even though everything Rockman said sounded like one. This team were divers, hence the frog appellation. Over his shoulder, Mel could see Henry, her rather green-about-the-gills cameraman, recording the moment. It was also his job to record her exit from the plane, or her ignominious defeat. If she did make the jump, then her free-fall would be recorded by mini-cams affixed to the team's head gear. Her *Mel-cam* was so that her viewers could have the illusion of seeing it from her point of view.

So this was it. Decision time. And she needed to pee. No question someone was going to win at least one bet, with the cold lining up against her sphincters. If she was going to be in for a pee, might as well go for the pound. Or in this case, in for the jump.

"Sir, I'm going to jump, sir!" She shouted, because shouting was the only tone Rockman could hear, based on past experience.

He nodded sharply, even as his brown eyes told her he didn't believe her. Mel tried to focus on her instructions, rather than the increasing pressure on her bladder. If she wet her pants now it would probably turn to ice inside her suit. Hopefully it wouldn't form into stalagmites in there. Or was that stalactites? Either was sure to be painful.

"Ladies first." Rockman gave her a sardonic look.

Great, now he decides to be a gentleman. She looked at the ramp hanging over thirty thousand feet of atmosphere and ocean and her sphincters gave up the unfair battle, releasing in a warm, wet rush. It wasn't that bad. And it was as much encouragement as she was going to get on this plane.

"Hoo-yah!" She ran forward and leapt off the ramp into nothing. Six guys who owed her charity money followed her out. She just hoped they weren't bitter about the money. She had a long way to fall with them.

December 6, 1942
Somewhere over Occupied France

JACK HAMILTON RUBBED at the ice collecting around the edges of his oxygen mask and then made a minute adjustment in his course. Everyone on board the Time Machine was tense, because of the pasting they'd taken on their last outing, but so far it had been a smooth ride. No fighters. No flak. Fourth time they'd been alerted for the Lille mission, only this time it hadn't been scrubbed. The briefing was 0345, but they didn't get airborne until 0900. Now they were about fifteen minutes from their target. No one expected it to stay easy, but after St. Nazaire, well, he was learning to be grateful for the small mercies.

At least it was a short run, just two hours to get over the target, dump their bombs and head back. Almost imperceptibly, he relaxed his shoulders. That's when he heard it.

"Bandits! Ten o'clock!"

Jack heard the shots and then saw the silver trails from their guns tracking out ahead of them, toward the diving FW's. One of the bandits kept coming right at them. Red bloomed on the end of its guns again and again.

Jack held his course and kept his eyes open, though neither was easy. At the last moment the FW turned aside.

"Beginning bomb run," he called out, over the crew chatter in the intercom. Now Jack turned the plane over to the Ram and the automatic bombardier correction instrument as they went in for the run. After that it was almost a cake walk to "bombs away." The crew cheered as they made the turn that meant they were heading home.

Present day

MEL TURNED HER SUV into the driveway of her little house. Despite its rather forlorn air, the house welcomed her as it always had, stretching back in time to when it had been her Gran's house and Mel the newly orphaned granddaughter.

Halloween was over, but a few dejected bats and ghosts still fluttered in the trees next door and the occasional candy wrapper mingled with fallen leaves the breeze had piled up against all available obstacles. Fall had done its work here, stripping leaves from the trees and turning green to brown. She climbed out and stretched, welcoming the feeling of freedom from MRE's and shouted orders. The air she inhaled was cold and smoky. And free—as free as she was for six wonderful weeks. The upcoming holidays tried to intrude into her thoughts, but she pushed them firmly away. Usually she preferred to be working during the holidays, but she hadn't been able to manage it this year. The SEAL gig had run long, as had editing it for the broadcast. Then she'd had to close the New York apartment. But finally she was here. *Home*. Despite the looming holidays, she was glad to be here.

She looked around, her gaze filtered through a lens of weary nostalgia. Her neighborhood sometimes seemed lost in the past. It always looked the same, except for the changing seasons sweeping through. Most of the houses were pre-World War II. Gran had come to this one as a bride, lived in it most of her life as a widow, and left it six years ago for the long-delayed reunion with her Norm, the grandfather Mel never met. Despite the sorrows it had seen, it was a cheerful, hopeful place, like her Gran, whose personality had been, and still was, the shaping force both inside and out. Mel wasn't around enough to make many changes, and as the only survivor of the family line, she liked coming home to the familiar and unchanged. Her father had died in Viet Nam and her mother had faded from life not long after, leaving Mel to Gran's care. Mel didn't remember either of her parents, though Gran had made sure she knew of them, and Norm, through stories and pictures.

Mel wasn't sure if Gran were a natural biographer or had been forced into it by events. Whatever the reason, she'd written her own life story, Norm's, and that of their son and his wife, before beginning to work on the story of Norm's military service for the remaining crew of *The Time Machine*, their B-17 bomber. She hadn't finished that before she died, so Mel was trying to finish it for her.

Gran probably wouldn't have approved of Mel's career choice. It was dangerous work and it made romance an uphill job for even the most optimistic of suitors. Before her death, Gran had pestered Mel about her lack of romantic entanglements. Mel didn't have an explanation then, or one now, other than a deep-seated realization that she hadn't yet met the right man.

Mel felt vaguely guilty as she unlocked the door and pushed it hard enough to dislodge the piles of mail that would be heaped on the floor under the mail slot of the shabby, white door. It would mostly be junk mail. Of necessity, Mel had her bills sent to her financial manager. Otherwise, she'd have to get her utilities turned on again every time she came home—and those ever increasing deposits.

She found the light switch and flipped it. The old fashioned lamps flared to life, pushing back the dim. At least her manager hadn't absconded with her money while she was doing time with the SEALs. She dropped her duffle and hand-bag on the floor just past the mail mess and headed for the bathroom. As usual, she needed to pee.

THOUGH THE HOUSE had gone through some updating, it was essentially unchanged from the way it had been when Norm, carried his bride across the threshold. It was a straightforward, unpretentious rectangle with two bedrooms to the left of the front door, both connected by a long closet and the bathroom. A living room and a fairly generous kitchen took up the right side of the structure. Under it all was a slightly damp basement with another bedroom behind a storeroom. All the fixtures, except for the refrigerator, were original, including a claw-foot tub hogging most of the bathroom.

Inside the fridge she found several cans of Diet Dr. Pepper, grabbed a glass, added ice and then soda. It hissed and bubbled in the glass. The first drink was always the best. All those chemicals bit pleasurably into her tongue and throat. As the caffeine entered her bloodstream, it temporarily kicked out the jet lag.

Mel turned back toward the living room, leaning a shoulder against the jam as she took another drink. To Mel's left, Gran's chair anchored the space, the imprint of her body still there in the sagging cushion. Her glasses rested on the open book she'd been reading the day before she went into the hospital that last time. Her footstool was pushed slightly to the side, so she could get up. Mel had never been able to take possession of that chair.

She kept expecting Gran to come out of her bedroom and settle there, before looking up at Mel with a smile of welcome. Across from Gran's chair was the chair that was Norm's. If he was also haunting the house, he was a kindly ghost. Sometimes, just as the last of the light was fading from the sky, Mel imagined she could see them both in their chairs, young again and smiling at each other with all the delight of young love. If she didn't move, sometimes she'd also smell Gran's powder and Norm's aftershave. If she closed her eyes, she could feel Gran's arms close around her, feel the cool softness of Gran's dress against her cheek and Gran's hand stroking her hair again and telling her it would be all right.

This night there were no friendly ghosts to welcome her home and the air in the room was resolutely stale from being closed for so long. She put her soda can down on a coaster near the computer and went to open some windows, passing the split couch in a pale blue-green. The two halves squatted in front of the windows that looked out on the enclosed porch, and had always been separated by a vintage table. Neither couch was even remotely comfortable, but Mel usually sat there anyway. It was her *spot*, and had been since she moved in.

"Pretty sad, aren't I?" she said to the silence. Only ghosts for company, but how was she supposed to make and keep friends when she was never around? It didn't help that, on this street, the residents were dropping like flies. She'd noticed a couple of kids toys left out as she drove by. Eventually the street would become young again, but the attrition was slow, albeit steady.

Mel probably should have cleaned up all Gran's stuff and given it away or at least put it in storage, but Gran's spirit and memory were the only things that welcomed her home. A pet would have been nice for her, but not for the pet.

On the dining room table was the only truly modern touch in the house, a computer set-up with all the bells and whistles. Gran had taken to computing like a Navy SEAL to water. She particularly loved the scanner. It made working with the old, fragile photographs from World War II so much easier.

Those pictures and all the other stuff she'd collected from the men who'd served with Norm, were now scattered across the top of the dining room table and the side buffet. Mel remembered a time when the kitchen table had been the staging area, since Gran liked to keep the mess out of sight of company, but when Mel brought her the computer, the move was inevitable. And there, at the end, company was almost nonexistent.

Mel still worked on her project, at first from a feeling of obligation, but eventually had found the stories of the men of *The Time Machine*, and the other bomber groups' stories, as fascinating as Gran clearly had.

The survivors were happy to let Mel continue as their recorder. She'd been going to their reunions since she was little and they all treated her like one of them, though they weren't going to be around much longer either. The Greatest Generation was dying.

That reality had given her a sense of urgency and she'd actually made a lot of progress the last time she was home. That's when she'd realized there was no picture of plane and crew all together. Before she left for the SEAL gig, she'd put out a call for anyone with a picture. She looked at the pile of mail. Well, there was only one way to find out if she'd gotten an answer.

One hour later, she had the mail sorted into the stuff she wanted to keep, the stuff to shred and the junk headed for the trash heap. There were several promising looking offerings from her WWII sources, including an intriguing one marked *private* and *urgent*.

These she took to the dining room table. She turned on the computer, then, while it went through the tedious booting up process, picked up a letter opener and slid it under the flap of the private and urgent envelope. Once containment was breached, she pulled out a single eight-by-ten photograph with a business card clipped to one corner.

Jack Hamilton. No address. Just a phone number and his name. Talk about a blast from the past. The only member of the surviving crew she'd never met—and the one she'd most wanted to meet.

She examined the photo, wondering if it really was the complete crew. That was certainly *The Time Machine*. She could see the name on the nose of the fuselage behind the crew, integrated with the nose art, a tornado-looking object—something Mel had always found puzzling. What did a tornado have to do with time travel?

Most of the pilots at the time had named their planes for their girl or a sexy movie star, but not Jack. He was an HG Wells fan to his toenails. Because of him, she'd read the books, too. Where in the post-war world had he gone? She looked at the card. At least he wasn't dead yet.

Mel picked up a magnifying glass and studied the photo. Norm, the radio operator, was in the back row of five, between Jack and his co-pilot, Ric Bramwell. Gran had always said Norm wasn't one to put himself forward, Mel recalled with a smile. His face was as familiar to her as her own, since Gran had pictures of him all over the house, but she still felt a sense of loss at not knowing him. The other five filling out the usual complement for a B-17, knelt in front. Slightly off to one side, a woman stood partly in shadow. That was odd. She applied the magnifying glass to that area and a face, curiously like her own, jumped out at her.

She pulled back. Okay, that was...weird. She applied the glass again. They even had the same, cropped, flyaway hair. It wasn't a typical hair-do for the time.

She leaned back in her chair, studying the photograph again, a feeling of unease in her middle that she couldn't begin to explain. Finally she lifted the top on the scanner, put the photograph face down and hit start.

In a few minutes she had a graphic image to work with on the screen. Even though she was consumed with curiosity about the woman, she still paused a moment to admire Jack when his face filled her screen. Okay, she'd seen other photos of him, but not this one. And he was always worth examining. The photograph was a bit grainy, but it didn't stop her from noting that his thick, dark hair tumbled across a high, aristocratic brow. His eyes were set deep under jutting brows. The black and white picture didn't give away the color, but Mel was sure they had to be a deep and sincere blue. His face was long and narrow, with high, sharp cheek bones and a straight nose. His smile, cutting across his face, the miles and the years, curled her toes inside her shoes every time she saw it, today being no exception.

Dang, he was cute. Why, she wondered, when she looked at his picture, did she feel like she'd been born sixty years too late? Not that she had any desire to live in the forties. Her feet were planted firmly in the twenty-first century and happy to be there, if only for the comfort of the shoes. But he could have come to one of the crew reunions. Only he hadn't and no one seemed to know why.

With a sigh, she adjusted the picture until she could isolate the part with the woman's face, then selected it and copied it to its own file. The image she had to work with was still large, but fuzzy. Luckily she had a good program for clearing up problems. She tinkered with it, watching with interest until a face came slowly into view.

The girl could be her twin. She backed off the image a bit, bringing more than the face into view. She was dressed like the crew, which was even stranger, considering the highly chauvinistic times. She backed off some more. That's when she got her second shock. On the wrist that the woman held up to shield her eyes from the sun was a small tattoo that looked a lot like the temporary tattoo presently fading on the inside of her wrist. The SEAL team had insisted she commemorate her jump with a miniature Uncle Sam. She backed off some more and worked on that area, bringing it into better focus. Then she only had to hold her wrist up to the screen to see they matched perfectly.

Okay, Jack was clearly pulling her chain.

She picked up the card and studied the phone number. It was long distance, but there was no indication of a time zone. She looked at her watch. It was after midnight. And what would she say to him? *Why is my arm in an old WWII photo?*

At that moment, her phone rang. She jumped, looked at it suspiciously as it rang two more times. This time of night, it was probably obscene. She lifted the receiver.

"Mel?" The voice was male and strong, though there was an aged quality to it she couldn't quite put her finger on.

"Who is this?" Mel had a policy of only being polite to people she knew. It cut down on solicitations calls—or at least shortened them.

"Jack. Jack Hamilton."

Shock held her silent for a long moment.

"Jack Hamilton." She felt winded and for no reason she could think of her heart was thumping in her chest.

"That's right."

She wanted to ask him if he knew what time it was, but she was pretty sure he did. And somehow, he'd known she'd be up.

"Your SEAL segment was your best yet," he said into her silence. "I really wondered if you were going to jump."

She'd wondered the same thing.

"Thanks." Jeez, did she have to be so lame? She talked for a freaking living, for Pete's sake! "How are you?" *Oh, that's good, take yourself beyond lame. Be a freaking loser.*

He chuckled. "I'm eighty-four."

It surprised her when she heard herself chuckle.

Then he said, "We need to meet. We're almost out of time."

What did he mean by that? "O...kay...when..."

"Tomorrow. I'll be there at ten hundred." There was a pause. "Good-night, Mel."

"Good...night..." She didn't know what to call him. Inside her head, she'd called him Jack her whole life, but he was an elder and, according to Gran, should be treated with respect. The only problem, calling him "Mr. Hamilton" sounded all wrong. Before she could decide, the line went dead. She stared at it. Maybe she dreamed the call. Maybe she was in bed right now and didn't know it. Maybe she should go to bed.

She saved her work, turned off the computer and headed for her bedroom, wondering why Jack had called after all these years. And what she was going to wear for her first meeting with the mysterious and elusive ex-captain. She may not cry uncle, but she was still a girl.

Chapter Two

WHEN THE SUN fell across Mel's face the next morning, she woke with a jerk. For a moment she was disoriented, until she remembered she was home. With that realization, all her questions about Jack jumped her. Why was he coming to see her? Why had he sent that photo? Was it some practical joke planned by the remnants of the bomber group who liked to tease her about her interest in Jack? Maybe it wasn't even Jack who called. That made a lot of sense, but how had they gotten a picture of her arm and the temp tattoo? Maybe one of the SEALS took the picture? That would be it. They were in on it. Jack or the guys, probably still had contacts in the military.

Relieved and yet somehow not, Mel prepared herself for the visit. She looked around her, painfully aware of what her surroundings gave away about her life. Maybe they could have their meeting on the porch? It wasn't as pathetic.

She changed clothes several times before settling on a pair of jeans and a simple, long-sleeved tee shirt. The sexy black dress she'd considered wearing might kill the old man and it was hardly typical day wear. She had to keep reminding herself he was old, no longer the dashing captain of the photos. For some reason, the more she thought about what he'd said, and what he hadn't said, the more nervous she got.

Almost ten-hundred. She got up and peered down the street, wondering what kind of car he drove. Then she heard a distant clack-clack. She knew that sound. She'd heard it often enough. It was a helicopter. But the only place something like that could land around here was the field behind Gran's house. She stepped outside and shielded her eyes, straining to see into the rising sun. It was a helicopter all right. It clacked toward her until it was right over her house, the blades stirring up the air, and the dead leaves. Neighbors came out into their front yards—the ones not suffering heart attacks from the shock.

Someone in the passenger seat pointed toward the rear, and then the chopper moved that way. Mel went through the house and out the back door. If this was a joke, it was a pretty elaborate one. Across the yard and through the fence, she saw the chopper land in the clearing, the noise slowly fading as the motor shut down. The pilot went around to the other side and helped someone out of the cockpit. Mel crossed slowly to the gate, feeling nervous and curious...and hopeful it really was Jack leaning lightly on a cane as he came toward her out of the rising sun.

He was tall enough to be Jack and though he moved slowly, he held himself rigorously erect, as if rejecting his own aging process. He was close enough now for her to see that his hair was white and still full, and his features were familiar, though time had blurred and softened the edges. His eyes were as intense now as they were in his pictures and, to her delight, undiminished blue.

"Hi." She still didn't know what to call him or what to say to him and, to tell the truth, the sight of him took her breath away. She'd always figured that younger women were interested in older men for their money. She could have been wrong about that. He may be in his eighties but he still had some serious babe factor to bring to the table. She'd bet money he still caused a stir at the nursing home, or where ever it was he'd emerged from.

Surprise gave her some protection from the intensity of his gaze, but it did nothing to dilute the delight she felt at this long delayed meeting. She had the odd feeling that they'd known each other before, and that this meeting was important.

"Hello, Mel." He stopped on the other side of the gate and grinned at her with unabashed pleasure. His voice was stronger and clearer in real life and his grin was as engaging as the one in the pictures, despite the wrinkles around the edges.

She realized he was waiting for her to stop hanging on the gate and let him in. Feeling like an awkward thirteen year old, she stepped back and unlatched the gate. It felt like she was letting him into more than her yard. He stopped and looked at the quiescent shrubbery.

"I'll bet it's beautiful in the spring with the lilacs in bloom."

Mel felt a smile flicker across her face. "It is...sir." His white brows arched. "Oh, dear. You make me feel a hundred years old. Please, call me Jack."

This time her smile stayed. "Jack."

He smiled down at her, crinkling the edges of his eyes and deepening their blue.

Mel drew a shaky breath. "So, where you been all my life?"

Jack chuckled, and then gestured toward the house, a sober and unsettling insistence muting his gaze. "Can we talk inside?"

"Sure." Let's go inside and you can see my total lack of a life, she added to herself as she led the way toward the back door. "Can you manage the stairs?" Mel turned to ask.

It was a short flight up to back porch that boasted a washer and dryer and the door to the kitchen.

Jack held up the cane. "You're worried about this? I just use it as a chick magnet."

Mel chuckled. But she noticed he used the railing and took the four steps slowly. Gran used to say she didn't feel as old as she looked. Maybe it was the same with Jack. Or maybe it was a case of a boy being a boy.

Whatever it was, she liked it. She liked him, even though he made her uneasy.

Inside the kitchen, she turned, managing to avoid looking at him as his gaze moved around the old-fashioned room. The antique countertops were a homely green and set low. She'd loved them as a child, because they weren't too high for her to reach. The sink was set low, too, and had a single basin and old fashioned taps. The table was built into a space behind the cabinets, with two long benches for seating. All in all, it was like going back in time, if she took out the refrigerator, which she was glad she didn't have to do. It kept her Diet Dr. Pepper cold.

When Jack's gaze finally made it back to her she heard herself say, "I'm not here a lot."

His smile was slow and sweet. "I like it." He hesitated. "Norm used to talk about being here. Snow outside, fresh bread smell from the oven and a pot of chili on the stove. Shut away from the world with his Elaine. He wasn't like some of the other married guys, you know. He never strayed. He fought for her, lived for when he could come home to her."

"But he didn't." Mel's voice was flat, hiding the emotion his words had stirred. It was odd to miss someone you'd never met, but Mel did. The rift, the sense of loss wasn't huge, but it was always with her. The really weird part, she didn't have that same feeling about her own dad. She wished she'd known him, of course, but it wasn't the same.

"He shouldn't have died," Jack said, putting into words the feeling Mel had never let herself think, let alone say out loud. He suddenly looked drawn and tired—and every inch his eighty-four years.

"You should sit down," she said. It was easier to focus on that than what he'd said. "The living room is through there."

"Can't we sit there?" he asked, nodding toward the kitchen table.

"Of course." Mel started toward the table, but stopped abruptly.

"Would you like something to drink?" Did she have anything but soda to offer him? She hadn't had time to get to the store and restock.

"Diet Dr. Pepper would be fine," he said, as if she'd spoken out loud. "In the can."

She got them both a cold one, her thoughts tumbling uselessly in all directions. She slid onto the opposite bench. She was a tall girl, but he sat taller than she did and their knees bumped slightly under the table.

He took a drink, then lowered the can to the table top. His gaze seemed to bore into her, laying bare her soul. Mel looked down, away from his gaze, remembering a time when that table had been Gran's biography assembly area, before the move to the dining room. In her mind, the surface was covered again with pictures and the pages of Norm's biography that were half written in Gran's spidery handwriting. For a moment the pain of missing her was as sharp as if Gran had died yesterday. Grief was like that, she'd learned. It would retreat for a time, then return when least expected.

"You still miss her," Jack said. It wasn't a question.

Mel looked up and nodded, a lump clogging her throat.

"You shouldn't have to."

She shrugged. "Gran always said life isn't for wimps."

Jack smiled. "She nailed it."

Mel could have sat there smiling at him all morning, but curiosity was a virus inside her head, even if it did kill the cat. "That was a neat trick you pulled with that picture. How did you get a picture of my temporary tattoo? Did Rockman get it for you? I never did trust that guy."

Instead of answering her, Jack slid his hand in the inside pocket of his expensive looking, dark suit and pulled out an envelope. He slid it toward her.

With one swift, wary glance at him, Mel opened it and pulled out a series of snapshots. They were all of her forties twin in a variety of poses. In one, she was with the captain of the famous Memphis Belle, and in another, she was behind the wheel of a Jeep. All the photos were in black and white and clearly aged.

"Who is she?" Mel set the photos down. "She could be my twin." She could be me, she thought, wanting to laugh at the thought, but for some reason she couldn't.

"She..." he stopped. He ran a hand through his hair, the gesture oddly familiar and endearing. He looked at her ruefully. It was a cute look on him. "I've had sixty years to think about it and now that I'm here, I don't know where to begin."

"Usually it's best to begin at the beginning," Mel suggested.

"The beginning. If only I knew what it was," he said, so softly, she almost missed it.

"Is there something you wanted to tell me about Norm?" she asked, hoping to prompt him. Curiosity was a very uncomfortable emotion.

He looked at her then. "Yes, it's about Norm. And you and me and what we did sixty years ago...what we shouldn't have done."

"What could you and Norm do then that would affect me now?"

"Not me and Norm." He hesitated, as if at the edge of a dive, and then said in a rush, "You and I."

Mel blinked. She couldn't have heard him right. "I wasn't born sixty years ago." It was stating the obvious, but she felt it still needed to be said.

For some reason, this appeared to help him relax. His shoulders rose and fell in a quick sigh. He looked apologetic.

"I can't believe I'm muffing this, but there just isn't a good way to explain. It's so unbelievable."

Jack seemed to be a few marbles short of a full complement. "What is?"

He held up one of the photos. "This isn't your twin, Mel. This is you."

Mel blinked again. It wasn't particularly useful, but it was something to do. Make that more than a few marbles. She was, she realized distantly, alone in the house with a loony tune.

"Norm shouldn't have died fifty years ago. You...we...changed history and now we have to change it back. Actually, you have to change it back."

Mel swallowed, trying to wet a suddenly dry throat. He didn't look dangerous and she could kick his butt, but she didn't want to beat up an old man, even if he was insane.

"And you know this because..."

"You told me sixty years ago. I sent you back to tell me and...you told me."

Funny he didn't look insane, but what does insane look like? Humoring him seemed like the best course to take for now. "Really? That's very...interesting."

Jack grinned, as if he knew what she was thinking.

"You don't remember it, of course, because for you, our meeting hasn't happened yet. The past is still in your future."

"I suppose that would...explain it." The next question, the obvious one was how she told him all this, but she already knew. He'd named his freaking plane *The Time Machine* and Gran hadn't raised a total fool, though Jack clearly thought differently. He looked so serious, so sincere. A pity he was nuts. Who let him out?

His expression turned rueful again.

"When you told me you were from the future, I didn't believe you either at first."

Okay, humoring him wasn't working for her. She needed a new plan, but what?

"I went before I left the plane," he said.

"People can't really—what did you say?"

"I went before I left the plane."

Her stomach dropped, not just to her feet, but to China, at least. "How did you know I wet my pants up there?" She hadn't told anyone she wet her pants before she left the plane.

"Is that what you meant? You never told me that part." Jack grinned.

Maybe her new plan should involve keeping her mouth shut.

"You said it was a sure way I could make you believe that I do have a time machine and that I can, and did, send you back in time, if I needed to." He leaned forward, his expression urgent. "We did things and your family got wiped out. When I met you in the past, you had a large, happy family." He looked around. "Not this."

She stared at him, trying to process what he was saying. It couldn't be true...and yet...he started to move away from her. A dark tunnel formed around her and began to close in. She heard him exclaim sharply and he jumped up. She felt his hands turning her so he could push her head down between her legs.

"Deep breaths," he said. He sounded a long way away.

The only problem, there was no way to get her head down far enough or breathe deep enough to clear it of this.

December 12, 1942
Thirty thousand feet above Paris, France

THEY'D LEFT AT 1215 hours, heading across the channel toward Romilly-Sur-Seine. No problems reaching the target, but it was obscured by cloud cover, so they turned back toward Paris and some rail yards, their target of last resort. *The Time Machine* was one of only six planes that actually dropped their bombs, because even this target was partially obscured. They weren't sure if they hit anything useful. Enemy planes sighted, but they made a pass at them, got shot at, a couple got knocked out of the sky and they took their toys and went home. The chatter was cheerful and profane. Relief was as palpable as their breath in the cold air.

It was luck, not skill today. The formation had been ragged to non-existent and most were returning to base with their bombs. Colonel Wray wasn't going to be happy. Jack could see more drills, more training ahead.

He sighed silently. The Ram claimed he got a glimpse of the Eiffel Tower through the bomb sight. Maybe he had. Jack hoped it would still be there when this was all over. Not the way he'd hoped to see France. He'd wanted to stroll Paris streets, talk to Paris people, not bomb it to oblivion with the 500 lb bombs in *The Time Machine's* belly.

Jack didn't waste a lot of time thinking about why he was here. He knew that. In the month since their Group went operational, he'd quickly learned it didn't pay to think a lot about the deep stuff. His life, his death, all that was out of his hands, no matter how well he flew his bird. Better pilots than him had already gone down, worse ones than he were still around. Jack figured God already knew the outcome and the survivors, so no sense worrying about when and where. He needed to just do his job until he couldn't anymore.

It was actually fairly easy to not think too deep in the cockpit of a Fort. There was so much annoying little crap to think about. The leg room was non-existent. His heated suit only heated him in the heat of battle when he didn't need it. Then it held pooled sweat against his body until he could get back to the station and strip it off. On the up side, the deep cold did numb his legs and a body aching desperately from the vibration of the Fort's four engines. His arms trembled from the effort of keeping the huge plane level and in formation. She had a mind of her own and fought him coming and going.

Despite the misery of the vibration, Jack was glad all four engines were running. That painful vibration meant they stayed in the sky. If he focused on being grateful, he could almost forget the metal and rubber smell from his oxygen mask and the ice that quickly formed around the edges from the moisture of his own breath. Hey, that ice meant he was still breathing, also a good thing and he only saw his *raccoon mouth* from ice burn when he looked in the mirror.

Nothing in the Fort had been designed for their comfort. It served one purpose: to rain a lot of bombs on a target. It bristled with guns in an attempt to keep the crew alive long enough to keep them trying to fulfill their purpose. It wasn't called the Flying Fortress for its size, though it was a big mother.

"There's the coast," his co-pilot and best friend, Ric Bramwell said. They'd joined together, learned together and now they served together–and they would probably die together. Ric didn't ever think about stuff, deep or little. His thoughts were filled up with girls, which left room for little else in there–barely enough for him to help out with the flying. "Get this bucket on the ground. I've got a date."

"You've always got a date," Jack said, his gaze reaching past the haze-shrouded coast to the landing field. Now exhaustion hit him, and in a mean twist, numbness fled, leaving behind snarls of pain to gnaw at the edges of his concentration.

"You could have one, too. She's got a friend."

"She's always got a friend." Jack made a slight course correction as the formation loosened up even more in sheer relief. And the friend always wished she was with Ric, not Jack. It didn't make for a fun date.

"So many girls, so little time. Why waste any of it?"

It wasn't that Ric thought he was going to die. He just thought the war wouldn't last forever and he might fall short of his goal to kiss every pretty girl in England and possibly France. If he survived, he'd probably make it. While Jack wasn't an expert on the male attraction factor, he'd been in position to observe considerable empirical evidence that Ric had plenty of it. Jack was a great believer in empirical evidence.

For a moment he was tempted to take Ric up on his offer. Be nice to put his arm around someone soft and sweet-smelling and think about something besides killing the enemy and breaking things. All those years spent observing Ric and he still didn't know how to take it casual. Ric was always telling him he was too serious, too intense. Always thinking he was responsible. Luckily Ric didn't know that much of what went on inside Jack's head. He probably thought Jack thought the same thoughts Ric did. He sure as heck didn't know about Jack's fascination with the science of time. They'd all teased him plenty when he named their Fort for his favorite novel, but they didn't know he didn't just believe in time travel, he knew how to do it. And if he had his way, they never would. Trouble was, when you thought about time too much, it changed the way you looked at every day. Made it hard to live right now. Ric had no trouble with right now and most days, couldn't remember yesterday. Or pretended he couldn't when it wasn't convenient.

Jack should let him take over more, but he felt the wave of discontent from the crew when he did. Ric took too many risks, particularly when they were headed home. He was too eager to get on the ground. It meant Jack got back feeling like he'd been stretched on the rack.

In the distance, he saw the field, with the planes ahead of him already lined up and going in. They'd made it. They'd all live one more day.

Present day

MEL DIDN'T LOSE consciousness, but it was a near thing. When the stars cleared and the blackness retreated, clarity of thought remained stubbornly elusive. Had he really said she'd traveled back in time? He was senile. He had to be.

Only he didn't look even slightly senile. And if he was living a delusion, how did he know her embarrassing secret? She hadn't told anyone, only according to Jack, she'd shared it with him twice.

"I'm sorry, Mel. I'm sorry we have to do this again, but we have to fix what we did. You need your family back and I," he stopped, shaking his head slowly, sadly, "I thought I was helping Ric, but all I managed to do is ruin him.

"Ric?" Mel frowned. "He's dead." Jack's co-pilot aboard *The Time Machine* had died in a car accident a couple of years ago, while under the influence of a lot of alcohol. Took a family of four with him to the next life. Norm would have made better use of his life, but Norm had died. Only according to Jack, he wasn't meant to die. He was supposed to be alive. No, not Jack. Her. She'd told Jack that. In the future past.

She felt a headache start behind her right eye.

"Can we talk while you pack?" Jack asked. "We really are almost out of time. Your SEAL gig ran long."

He wouldn't get an argument out of her on that point. Her producer had been hiding from her since she got back. He smiled and she found herself smiling back. What was she doing? Her smile faded.

"What am I supposed to be packing?"

"Some of your grandmother's clothes from the late thirties, and some of your own stuff. Enough to last until you jump."

"Jump?" Her brain latched on that word like glue. "The one thing the SEAL gig taught me is that I don't like jumping. It's too much like falling."

"I know. I'm sorry."

Mel's eyes widened. "You want me to go on that last mission, the one where you got shot down! You want me to jump into Occupied France with you?"

"Yes." He looked sorry, but there was also an "and" hanging in the air between them.

"What?" she asked with suspicion. What could be worse than jumping into Occupied France?

"You also have to jump out of a plane at high altitude again. Into the vortex my machine will create. Time travel requires velocity, you see."

She didn't see, and yet, in an awful way, she did. "Velocity? And how do I achieve this velocity?"

"By jumping into the vortex without a parachute."

Mel felt her jaw drop and heard something rather whimper-like come out the opening, as her thoughts spun into one clear certainty. When her head was down, she should have kissed her tush goodbye.

Chapter Three

December 17, 1942
Basingbourne Airdrome

JACK HAD BEEN right. Colonel Wray wasn't happy with their performance outside of Paris. They'd dropped some bombs, but it wasn't clear if they'd actually done any damage to anything. Shooting down a couple of enemy planes didn't earn them any praise either. They were, according to Wray, lucky the enemy hadn't pressed their attack. They couldn't rely on luck. It wouldn't always be on their side. They needed to maintain the formation. The formation was everything. The formation was their only chance of surviving.

And so they practiced staying in that formation every day the weather was clear enough for flying, but not optimum for a mission. When they couldn't fly, they did time in ground school and practiced in the link trainer. That carnival ride training device at least took energy and focus. The classes were mind-numbingly dull.

Jack knew that a lot depended on the success of this very dangerous experiment. The Brits only flew at night. Trouble with that, you can't see where you're dropping your bombs so their success rate was dismal. The Yanks aimed to bloody the enemies' nose with daytime missions. Those in charge figured the well-armed B-17's, flying at or above twenty thousand feet and fitted with the Nordan bomb sight, were just the ticket for taking the war directly to the enemy, while the generals worked on plans for an invasion. They needed to impair the German's war production, too, or an eventual invasion would be impossible.

They'd been lucky so far, but no one expected it to last, not after St. Nazaire. As soon as the weather cleared, they'd be back up again. Flying over the continent, looking down on what the Germans controlled, and seeing their war machine come up to greet them with a hail of lead, well, it was hard to believe they'd ever be able to contain them, let alone invade and win.

We won last time, he reminded himself, but this was different. The guy in charge over there was different. And they were fighting on two fronts, trying to play catch-up with two enemies who'd prepared themselves well for battle. There were lessons to be learned here...if they survived to remember them.

Norm nudged Jack out of his reverie. "Time for grub, Jack."

Jack was glad for the distraction. Of course they'd win. They had to. Jack got up and shrugged on his jacket, huddling into it as they emerged from the Quonset hut into the cold, English wind. A damp chill cut through all his layers like they weren't there.

"You going to Cambridge tonight?" Norm asked, as they paused in a sheltered spot to light up.

"I don't know," Jack said, inhaling the smoke deep into his lungs. He'd only started smoking since he joined up, but it did calm the nerves. "You?"

"Wouldn't mind a break," Norm said, leaning close so he could use Jack's match to light his cig.

"Everybody's stir crazy," Jack said. They were all going through the motions. Everyone had some kind of practice area rigged up. Even Fitz, their ball turret gunner, had to spend hours in the stand-alone ball, spinning and aiming until his brains were thoroughly scrambled. Jack shook his head. With Fitz, it might be more accurate to say they were getting unscrambled. And their gunners were sick of shooting every day on the butts. They all felt like they were pedaling in place. At least a trip into Cambridge would be a change of scene. He tossed his cig down and ground it out with his foot. "Let's do it. I wouldn't mind a break either."

At least Norm wouldn't try to set him up with anyone. His heart, and all the parts connected to said heart, belonged to his wife, Elaine.

With shoulders hunched against the cold, they headed for the mess.

Present day, four weeks later

ONCE AGAIN MEL found herself sitting on a hard bench in an airplane preparing to do something she'd rather not, only this time without the option to cry uncle. It was a pity, because now she was more than ready to do it. Luckily she was still freaking stubborn or maybe it was pride that kept her from crying like a baby. And Jack. What was it about him that kept her from wimping out?

She couldn't pinpoint the moment when she started to actually believe Jack really could hurl her through time. Or maybe it wasn't time travel she believed in, but the man. He had plenty of confidence layered over a soul-deep sadness.

She huddled deeper in the vintage coat that went with the rather sassy, and also vintage, nineteen thirties suit of Gran's. Neither was up to the task of keeping her warm in the cargo plane, not with the hatch open. The suit's colors were sober, and terribly uncomfortable, but they weren't the worst things she had on. No, the top honors in awfulness had to go to what she was wearing under Gran's clothes. There was the evil and unrelenting girdle that held up her cotton stockings. If she made it back she'd never curse her panty hose again. The bra was, amazingly enough, worse than cotton hose and a girdle. No wonder her mother's generation had burned them.

So they wouldn't get lost during the buffeting from the vortex, Mel had commandeered one of Gran's old, large and ugly, clutch bags and tucked in it Gran's sassy little matching hat, along with Gran's *sophisticated street shoes*, according to an old catalog had Jack showed her during her prep period, and as many other necessaries as it would hold, all hideous and time-line contamination proof—with a few exceptions she felt guilty about. The catalog claimed the shoes were comfortable, but Mel's feet vehemently disagreed, the one time she'd tried them on. The toes were too narrow and Mel hadn't worn high heels since her brain returned to her body at the end of puberty.

Despite her dislike of the shoes, she was hoping she'd be able to hold on to the bag during the jump through time. If she couldn't, she'd end up in the past, shoeless and hatless—and without a change of underwear. Her Doc Martens and backpack would have made it just fine, but apparently the time line couldn't survive the contamination. It could survive her presence, but not that of comfortable shoes. Clearly men were in charge of the op.

Important documents, like her identity papers, American and British money, ration card and the orders that would get her on the base, were in a money belt strapped tightly around her middle. Arriving without those would doom the mission.

She was also carrying a computer chip, though not in her gear. No, it had been surgically implanted in the fleshy part of her tush. It was her ticket home. Apparently returning was easier than going. The vortex would home in on her tush and suck her up like a vacuum cleaner. The ride, Jack had informed her, would be a bit rough, but she wouldn't feel the landing, just re-emerge in her own life at some point. And if something went wrong, the chip was designed to destroy itself.

With acid. Unless the vortex vacuumed her up. A great thing to have in your tush.

It was, however, a good match for her *vintage* wrist watch.

As soon as she'd arrived at Jack's secure facility, they'd started bombarding her photographic memory with photos and information about the war. Faces of who was friendly, who wasn't.

"You need to know the players, so you don't impact the time line again," Jack told her, when she asked him why.

"You're sending me to the Germans with my head stuffed full of everything they'd need to change the course of the war. That can't be a good thing," she'd felt driven to point out.

"We did think of that."

Something in Jack's expression had worried her. Amazing. And just when she'd thought she was fully saturated with worry. He'd produced the watch. Mel had examined it, but found nothing about it that impressed her. It looked old, like her clothes and harmless. She shook it. It ticked back at her, unperturbed.

"What?"

"It's a dead man's watch," he said. "If it's not removed properly, a needle will inject you with cyanide." Jack caught the watch as it slipped from her fingers. "We'll wait to put it on until just before your jump. And we'll show you how to remove it safely."

"Good idea," she'd muttered. A really good thing she couldn't forget how to take it off. But what if it suddenly malfunctioned? She shivered. If it did, she'd only know it for a couple of seconds.

"Cold?" Jack asked, drawing her back to the present. He sat across from her in the belly of the plane, buried in enough expensive clothes to keep his old bones comfortably warm. She'd never asked him where his money came from or who had funded the time travel research. Or if they knew about the mission. Or how it all worked. It wasn't need-to-know when she had a brain that couldn't forget. And she'd had plenty of other stuff to think about instead.

"A little." Scared out of her mind is what she actually was. The past weeks had passed in a breath-stealing rush, while still managing to be oddly slow. How ironic to have, both too much, and too little, time on her hands.

Not surprisingly, some events from the past few weeks were burned into her brain.

For instance, there was the day Jack went over the time line of events with her, starting a month prior to the last mission. He showed her map of the places in London that had been bombed, so she could avoid those and gave her some suggestions about places she might find lodging. She loved that might.

He didn't have to tell her that that would be only one of many challenges. War-time London had been a crazy place.

"You shouldn't go to the base until a day or two before the mission."

"Why not?" Mel asked.

For the second time since their first meeting, he avoided her gaze. "You didn't fit in." A sort of smile flickered across his face. "I was suspicious of you back then. I expect I will be again."

"But, isn't all this stuff supposed to help me fit in?" She gestured toward the piles of papers she'd been scanning into her memory and the period clothing.

Now he grinned. "Clothes may make the woman, but they can't change who you are and when you were born. Women were...different back then, Mel. Even the way you walk gives you away."

"What's wrong with the way I walk?" Mel shifted her hips slightly and Jack laughed.

"Nothing." He looked wry and reflective. "Nothing at all. But it's nothing like women walked back then. For one thing, you've still got that SEAL edge. It challenges. Not something women did a lot–at least not in an "I can take you," kind of walk."

"Oh." Mel smiled slowly. "Well, I can. Can't change that now."

Something sparked in his eyes. "Wouldn't want you to. It's one of the things that makes you so well suited to this mission."

The mission. She'd wanted to know what drove people like her father and grandfather. People like Jack. Soldiers and cops. People who put themselves in danger for the benefit of others. The question had propelled her into her career as she sought to understand her grandfather, in hopes it would mend that rift in her heart.

Now she knew how little she'd gotten *it*. Going through the training, all of it had still only put her on the edges of the fire. The view was good, better than turning a blind eye. But in the end, the only way to know about something was to do it. Like the Garth Brooks song, she'd stood outside the fire.

Now she was getting ready to jump into it.

Without a parachute.

And with the growing feeling there was something in the past that Jack hadn't told her. She hadn't been able to put her finger on where the feeling was coming from. Jack had been friendly, but distant. Brisk and professional. Informative–but not. And all through the prep and briefing, she'd felt his eyes on her, known the minute he looked away. It was as if they were connected by an invisible line of tension.

It was weird and unsettling to meet that gaze and see knowledge in them that she didn't yet have. One night at dinner in the cozy, very masculine dining room that made up part of his living quarters in the complex, she asked him flat out what it was.

"What do you mean?" His face closed like a book and became excessively polite in the subdued lighting that reflected gold off the rich wood of the table. The good smells of great food lingered in the air between them and almost made her forget why she was here. Almost.

"What aren't you telling me?" All she'd learned, all she'd felt began to come together in her head. She picked up the cut crystal glass and took a sip of water. "We screwed up the time line, but more than that is driving you, isn't it?" When he didn't answer, she added impatiently, "Jack, I have to know. Or it could happen again."

He looked at her then, and for a moment, his eyes opened to hers, giving her glimpse of hell before he shuttered those windows. She could see him consider and decide, but until he spoke, she didn't know what he'd decided.

"Your last...visit...ended badly," he admitted. She arched her brows and he added, "Your mission was to save Ric and you did...but..." he hesitated, his gaze leaving hers briefly before returning to give her another glimpse into his personal hell. "You...died."

She stared at him. Died? I died? Her brain couldn't process it. How could she be dead when she was alive?

"And now here you are," he said.

Mel was quiet for a moment, processing this new information, or at least trying to. "Wouldn't it be better if I didn't go back again? Wouldn't my not going change things without intervention?" She really liked that idea.

"Don't you think I haven't thought of that? And everything else I could in the last fifty years." He shoved his hands through his hair, wreaking charming havoc. "You already went. We met. You died in France. It happened. It's done. It's already your future." He pushed back his chair and stood up, pacing away from her to the window that overlooked the paved inner yard of the compound, before turning to face her. "If we do nothing, it's entirely probable that who you are now, will cease to exist when who you were returns to the future. In the future, in the past, you jumped today. And three weeks from now, on Christmas Day is when you'll return. Unless you change the outcome."

"How can I guarantee I won't be killed again? I'm going to a freaking war."

"You can't, entirely, but you died when you tried to save us. If you don't do that again, if you let events play out the way they're meant to, you should be all right."

He came back and sat down, taking a seat closer to her. His straight back was reflected in the mirror over the side board behind him. Despite the obvious disintegration of his body, she warmed at his proximity. He smelled good, wonderful actually, and there was a fineness, an honor about him, that was more potent than youth. And if all went well, she was going to meet him in his youth, in his prime. Oh my.

"I was going to talk to you, but closer to the jump. I was trying to find a way..." He hesitated, shaking his head. "It's not easy to tell someone they died sixty years ago."

It wasn't easy hearing it. It erased the warmth like a candle snuffed out. "Is there anything else? Any more surprises?"

He hesitated. "I've tried to figure out the best way to handle...well, me. Last time you told me the mission. Maybe that was a mistake, but I don't want to tie your hands either. I am—I was a suspicious bugger. If you can...keep your distance and let events play out. If you can't, well, don't tell me until you absolutely have to. Or more than you have to."

Mel frowned. There was a flaw there if she could just feel her way toward it. Then she had it. "What's to stop you from trying to build your machine and save Ric again, Jack? I don't think I want to spend my life replaying this same scene over and over again."

Jack sighed. "In both time lines, I've acted out of guilt, first because Ric took a bullet for me, then because you died. If you can stay alive, and take Ric out of the guilt equation, I won't have any incentive to mess with your time line."

"And how do we take Ric out of the equation? Do you want him off the plane—"

"No." Jack's tone was almost sharp. "It needs to play out as close to the original time line as possible." He rubbed his face, and then looked up, his expression rueful. "I didn't want to see Ric the way he was. I'm not even sure why. Maybe it's one of those guy things. If you help me put my friendship with him in proper perspective, I'll be able to deal with his death and resist the urge to meddle with time."

Mel frowned. "But...if you don't create time travel...how will I get back to the future?"

He sighed again. "It's all theory, Mel. We don't know what will happen. We just have theories..."

"And your theories tell you...what?"

"It may be that this time line won't change until after you return to the future and it will be as if none of this happened. You'll wake up at home, with your life restored and no memory of me or traveling through time. I'll just be someone your grandfather flew with, someone he knew in the war."

"Or?" She knew there was an *or* waiting out there. A big one. It was practically an orb throbbing in the air between them.

"You could become a time orphan. Stuck in the past, lost in time."

"Stuck in Occupied France, you mean and about to get captured by the Germans—with your dead man's watch as my only recourse."

He met her gaze steadily. "That's right."

"I...see."

He seemed to shrink a bit and for the first time, Mel realized how old he was. She covered his hand with hers, felt it shake slightly at her touch. Close up, she could feel the waning of his strength, feel his life force slipping away.

"You're dying, aren't you?"

"We're all dying, Mel." He smiled, his expression almost relieved. "But I won't go before your send off."

"I," she wanted to say something, but she didn't even know what.

"I know," he said. "Just...don't fail."

Her smile wavered. "You know how stubborn I am."

He'd smiled at her then, the cocky one that curled her toes in her shoes and suddenly he didn't look old at all. Her body warmed as his confidence in her washed through her.

And brought her to this place, this time, what she was about to do. She blinked away the past, which was ironic, since she was getting ready to head into it. This was not only going to be hard, it was going to be confusing.

The plane rumbled as it banked, then straightened. The technicians traveling with them jumped up and started fiddling with the dials on the time machine. It was small and very space-age looking and hanging above the hatch where the vortex was supposed to form.

"It's almost time," Jack said. He looked at her as if he were trying to memorize the moment. Meeting his gaze, she felt isolated from the sudden burst of activity. They were two people caught in a bubble. His eyes tried to tell her something, while at the same time trying to hide it from her. She wanted to solve the puzzle, but there wasn't time. There was only time now for the mission.

She stood up. As hard as her SEAL gear had been, in some ways it was easier than the late thirties get-up, though the stocking clad feet were easier than the webs, except for the punishing cold. Toes could dig into the metal floor, but the clothing felt odd and constrictive. She actually missed her fatigues. As she made her way toward the open hatch with Jack's time machine hanging over it, hanging over her, and hanging on to the clutch bag, the final briefing played in her head.

"You'll feel yourself falling, and then spinning. The buffeting will be considerable and fairly prolonged. Then you'll integrate into the past. You'll be a part of it. They tell me you won't even feel a jolt. You're just there."

That's why they'd targeted London. She wouldn't be as noticeable appearing there. They hoped. That was assuming she didn't end up splattered all over present day London.

One of the techs reached out to help steady her as she stopped by the hatch. She looked down. Clouds obscured the city below. She had only their word London was down there. For all she knew, they were dropping her into the ocean. It was truly a jump into the unknown.

So now she knew, or at least she was starting to understand what drove people to face unknown danger. Or even known danger. It wasn't about being excessively brave or a longing to do deeds of valor. Because she wasn't feeling either of those things right now. Not even slightly. It was about the people she loved, keeping home and hearth safe. She didn't know the family their meddling had cost her. She didn't know what impact, what ripples in time their actions had caused. She may never know. She did know Gran and through her, Norm. If she could find a way to bring them back together, well, that was worth risking everything for.

Someone was shouting the countdown.

"Five...four...three..."

She looked over her shoulder. If she succeeded, she'd never see Jack again. If she didn't, she still wouldn't see him again. He knew it, too. Their gazes met, clung, and then he smiled and gave her a thumbs up. She didn't have a free hand, but she could nod. She even managed a smile for him.

"...two...one. Go...go...go," the tech shouted.

She looked down and wished she hadn't. The clouds were gone, replaced by what looked like a spinning, shining tornado. Oh, crap. She closed her eyes and stepped off the edge.

Chapter Four

1942
London

DUSK MADE ITS way across the horizon, spreading a modest glow across a scene that was both familiar and stunningly alien. In the past weeks, she'd watched hours and hours of footage of war-time London, seen the vintage cars and clothing in a city in which many of the buildings were not terribly different from modern London. But most of that footage had been in black and white and all of it slightly grainy in texture. Even the color film had been degraded in quality. Now, in the midst of a thousand impressions her mind struggled to cope with, what stood out the most was the color. Vibrant, rich, alive, and sharply clear.

The street she'd arrived on was a quiet one and could be any street in England. The stone facades gleamed gold as the sun's last rays tracked up them on the way to the other side of the world. The cars parked in front of her were straight out of a colorized Mrs. Miniver.

She turned slowly in a circle. The city had settled into night mode. Down the street, an older man carrying a briefcase let himself into one of the houses with his key. Across from her, a woman straight out of a forties movie stood on her stoop, smoking a cigarette with an air of waiting for something or someone. An ambulance rumbled past, an ancient precursor to the modern-day van with its square and clunky lines. The cross on the side was blood-red in a field of dirty white, giving it a worn, dispirited air. Mel caught a glimpse of weary, soot-covered faces in the front seat, before it rounded a corner. The acrid smell of smoke drifted in the chilly air. She'd never smelled death, but at a primal level she recognized its scent in the air, too.

Mel looked higher, above the buildings, so old, so interesting, so postcard English. Against the skyline were ominous columns of smoke rising past thousands of barrage balloons, the helium-filled *blimps* suspended on cables above the city in a mostly futile effort to deter enemy aircraft. In the semi-silence she heard the rumble of many engines. She turned toward the sound and saw a sky that seemed filled with aircraft.

At first she wondered if it were the B-17s returning from the continent, but the silhouettes was wrong. With a sharp chill, she realized they were fighter craft, most likely heading toward the coast to intercept the enemy. What had been an intellectual exercise, thrilling tales of past glory, was now an ugly reality.

Holy, freaking crap. She was in wartime London. Jack had done it. He'd hurled her into the past.

Mel looked around and found the cigarette-smoking woman staring at her curiously. Mel ran a hand across her wildly tousled hair. Nothing like a spinning vortex to give a girl a bad hair day. It must look pretty odd to the forties lady. She'd cut it short for her stint with the SEALS. No way to make it look forties in the short interval she'd had to prep for this...adventure in time. She smoothed down her clothes and gave the woman an over bright smile that she hoped looked friendly.

"What day is it, please ma'am?"

"You're American," the woman said, as if that explained everything. For her, maybe it did.

"Yes, yes I am," Mel agreed. "It's December, right?"

"It's the seventeenth, Thursday the seventeenth." The woman looked suspiciously at Mel as she started to turn away.

Mel didn't blame her. "Thank you, thank you very much." Three days until she had to fall out of the sky again. It wasn't enough time and it was too much.

The woman paused, her expression softening slightly. "You should get some shoes on those feet before you catch your death, love."

"I'll do that, thanks." Mel could only imagine what the woman thought she'd been up to without her shoes. Now that it had been pointed out to her that she was shoeless, she couldn't get at her shoes fast enough. She sat on a near by step and dug them out of the bag she'd managed to hang on to. The suede of Gran's old shoes was soft, but the shape and feel were odd and alien—perfect for her current reality. She tried standing up. Luckily the heels were square, but they were also higher than she was used to wearing. Her feet were happy not to be bare, but that probably wouldn't last.

She found her hat next and gave it a shake to restore the shape, at least that's what she hoped she did. She found the tag and then carefully settled it on her hair. She looked in the side window of a parked saloon car to see how she looked. The hat did make her look a bit less wild, but she had no clue if she looked *right*. Hats, other than the *gimme* variety were way outside her experience.

In the fading light, with her face blurred by the glass, she could have been Gran looking out at her from an old photograph. With a jolt of shock, Mel realized that Gran was alive back in the States, and not just alive, but a young bride with a new son: Mel's father.

"Whoa, that's way too *Back to the Future*." That's when reality whacked her upside the head again. She was in the past. Her legs went weak and she had to lean on the saloon car she'd used as a mirror. The surface was cool, smooth and firm under her hand. It was real, amazingly real.

"Oh, I say, I just polished her," a male voice said behind her.

Mel jumped and turned. "I'm so sorry."

He was young and very British. Blonde and upscale, wearing civvies and leaning on a cane. His annoyed expression turned into pleased. "Sorry. Didn't mean to startle you. It's just bloody hard keeping her clean, what with all the bloody bombing."

It was a downside of bombing she hadn't considered.

"She's lovely." Mel used the sleeve of Gran's coat to rub away her fingerprints. "I am sorry."

"You're American." His eyes opened wider. They were brown and very nice. His upper lip softened into a friendly, interested smile. Some things didn't change. It was sort of comforting.

"Yes. And I'm afraid I'm turned around. Can you tell me which way the tube is from here?"

"I'll show you," he said. Mel opened her mouth to protest and he added, "I'm heading that way myself. No petrol to run the old girl. Rationing and all that." He gallantly offered her his arm. Good manners required her to take it. Mel fell into step beside him, feeling very Greer Garson, only without the accent. Proximity and a slight evening breeze brought his aftershave, or whatever the British equivalent was, to her nostrils. It was clean and crisp and made a nice change from the other smells in the air.

"What brings you here?" he asked, as he steered her around a corner, listing slightly from his limp. Now she could see the tube entrance ahead of them, surrounded by sand bags. Across from it was an anti-aircraft gun, also surrounded by sand bags and buckets. She had to quell an impulse to ask him to take her picture in front of it. She wasn't a freaking time tourist, well, she kind of was, but that didn't mean she had to act like one.

"I'm a reporter," Mel said, falling naturally into her cover story. It was, after all, true. "I'm here to do some stories on our troops and how they are adjusting to English life and the war."

"Always wanted to visit the colonies," her companion said, with a wicked grin.

Mel laughed, as she turned and held out her hand. "Thanks so much for showing me the way."

He took her proffered hand, but didn't let go. "How about a spot of supper? You Yanks eat, don't you?"

Mel hesitated, but she was hungry. As if to help her make up her mind, her stomach rumbled. She started to agree, but before she could, the sirens went off." Well," he said, lifting his gaze to the horizon, "that's bloody annoying."

"Bloody," Mel echoed as the anti-aircraft guns started up in the distance.

INSIDE THE TUBE station, families were already there, setting up for the night. There were double-decker bunks fixed along the walls and floor space was disappearing fast as people could claim it. Women knitted or handed out food to children. Old men read books that looked both serious and important. There were no young men, except for the ones in uniform, or injured, like Mel's companion. There were American uniforms mingled with the Brits waiting for the train. It was all orderly, no rushing or pushing. It had the feel of a familiar routine. They'd had plenty of time to get used to it.

"This your first?" he asked Mel, as they found a bit of wall to lean against.

Mel nodded.

"It's a bloody nuisance, but you grow accustomed to it." He shifted slightly. "Here, I don't know your name. Rodney Stanfield. Formerly Captain, RAF." He thrust out his hand.

"Melanie Milburn." Mel stumbled a bit over the last name. It felt odd to be incognito, but she could hardly arrive at the base bearing Norm's nom de plume.

"Cheers, Melanie." He made a point of shaking her hand, and held on to it when the shaking was over.

Mel didn't mind. She needed something to hang on to as she listened to the ominous rumble of approaching aircraft. *The enemy.* There was the rat-a-tat from planes defending London and the pop of the anti-aircraft guns. Those made the ground under their feet tremble. Mel looked up, even though there was only concrete to see. It just seemed easier to hear that way.

"The first is the hardest," Rodney said. His upper lip had stiffened up nicely now.

Mel had done live fire exercises with the SEALS. Dangerous, without a doubt, but she'd had some control over the outcome. This was different, very different.

"I expect it's more satisfying to be up there shooting at them." Mel was proud of how steady her voice sounded, though she had to raise the volume to be heard. Apparently stiff upper lips were catching.

He nodded. "Too bloody right."

In her mind's eye, Mel saw the flak tracking skyward in black and white. She'd never seen it in color. As she strained to sort out the sounds, there came the distinctive whine of a bomb following gravity's pull toward the braced and waiting city. The whole group paused. Hands stilled, pages weren't turned, toys weren't played with, and drinks weren't taken. Mel didn't even breathe. It felt like forever until contact.

There was a boom. The ground wrenched one direction, then the other. Dust from the ceiling sifted down on them. A baby started to cry. Mel tasted grit in her mouth as she looked at Rodney with eyes that felt wide and dry.

"Close." He sounded like he was talking about horse shoes or basketball shots. Then she couldn't hear him anymore. There was only the sound of falling bombs and the wrenching of the earth when they hit. How had anyone survived this? How was it they weren't all gibbering idiots? Other than that first pause for the first bomb, no one seemed to notice bombs were falling out there. A young mother played a finger game with her child. Another passed around a canteen for her kids to drink from. An old man turned a page in his book as if he were in his own study by a comfortable fire.

This was a different kind of war, a different kind of courage than she'd observed in Iraq. The outcome was still very much in the balance. And there was no precision, no care for civilian casualties. Just raw, ugly destruction as each side tried to kill more people than the other side. She'd never liked thunderstorms and this was one on steroids. There was no time to recover between concussions. Conversation was impossible.

She wanted to cower against the dirty floor, but how could she in the presence of such bravery? She caught some of their courage and felt stiffening flow up her spine. Maybe she caught it from her bluffing upper lip. She realized she was gripping Rodney's hand and relaxed her fingers. They felt stiff and cold. She noticed he flexed his.

"Sorry," she mouthed, because there was no way he could hear her. It was hard to keep on her feet. The ground heaved again and again. There was no escape for it or them. And then, just as quickly as it began, it stopped. The bombs first, then more slowly, the flak batteries.

The silence filled with the rustle of the living, the soft cry of a child, the waning drone of the attackers and defenders. The distant, and different, wail of the ambulances rushing to give aid and comfort. Fire engines, too. In her mind, she could see it playing out from the films she'd seen. She couldn't hear the crackle of the fires, but she knew they were there. She looked at her watch, her dead man's watch, but she didn't know what time the attack started, so there was no way to know how long it lasted. And she hadn't adjusted it to local time either. After a bit, the all-clear sounded.

"Should be a train along shortly," Rodney said, taking her arm and steering her past the huddles of people to the edge of the platform.

Mel was almost afraid to try out her voice. "Is it like that all night?"

He shrugged. "Depends on the weather. Better than previously when it lasted all day, too."

Mel nodded. She knew all the stats, all the facts and figures, but there'd been no way to know this without being here. And this was just the beginning. In three days, she had to go up into the sky and get shot down.

"Is it this bad up there?" Mel asked. "In battle?"

"Pretty much, only you can shoot back." Rodney's grin was wry and edged with bravado.

"Have you ever had to bail out?"

Rodney looked surprised. "Several times. Twice into the Channel. I was lucky."

Indeed. Clearly Mel needed to pick his brain. She had a feeling that her HALO drop was very different from this kind of bailing out. She was a reporter, just one without a place to sell her stories. Pity. She had a feeling she was going to run into some doozies.

A series of whistles suddenly broke through the crowd noise behind them. Mel, and everyone around her, turned and saw a man roughly pushing his way toward them. He passed under a light and she realized she'd seen his face in one of the newspaper stories from this time.

"He's a spy," Mel said, involuntarily. The story had been about him eluding capture by jumping down onto the tube tracks.

The man roughly pushed a pregnant girl out of his way and then he was heading directly for Mel. She didn't plan to intervene. Her plan was to restore the time line, not mess it up even more. If he hadn't touched her, she wouldn't have touched him. But he did and so she did.

The SEALS had trained her well. As soon as his hand connected with her shoulder, she grabbed it, popped him in the chin with her elbow, and then used his own forward momentum to flip him on his surprised posterior. It felt good to hit back.

Two Bobbies ran up, and then stopped in surprise, looking from the prone spy to Rodney, and then finally at Mel.

Mel shrugged. "He pushed me. I pushed back."

The crowd around her took a step back, leaving her semi-alone. Rodney looked impressed. And surprised. But more impressed than surprised.

"She's an American," he said. A sort of "ah" sound emerged from the circle around them. He looked at her.

"I'll remember not to push you," he said. "How did you know he's a spy?"

She opened her mouth, but there was nothing to come out it except an unbelievable truth. Luckily, a train arrived just then.

"Oh, look," she said. "Our train."

She could feel Rodney watching her, as they boarded the train, leaving behind the Bobbies hustling the spy to his feet. She rubbed her face. Jeez, no wonder she ended up dead last time.

SO FAR, MEL wasn't enjoying her adventures in time travel all that much. All the *oooh* had worn off, leaving only the *ugh*. She was tired. She was homesick. She was homeless. Her feet—there wasn't even a word to describe what her feet felt. And her body, well, it was beginning to identify the sore spots from the vortex buffeting. There were a lot of them. And that was just the personal stuff.

First, she'd had to cross London by tube to catch her train to Cambridge. After long stops in the dark while bombs fell overhead, they finally arrived. Rodney fed her, as promised, and her stomach was still bitter about that. She'd asked him what it was and he told her it was better not to know. At least she'd been able to pee at the railway station upon arrival in Cambridge. At the moment, her bladder was her only happy body part.

It was dark on the platform, but a kindly air warden had offered to help her find her way to her destination. She could have come down in the morning and probably should have, but quite frankly, she wasn't sure she had the guts to spend the night in London, even knowing where the bombs would fall. Three hours were more than enough.

Of course, her other reason was curiosity. She knew the men had liberty busses into Cambridge. She didn't know if Jack or Norm took one this night, but there was a chance she could observe them prior to her arrival at the base, if they had.

So she'd made her way like a weary lemming, not sure if she'd ever get used to being when, let alone where. London, the train, even Cambridge seemed to be littered with American servicemen. Bright, confident, interested in everything, but especially interested in English girls, they stood in stark contrast to the British soldiers and citizenry, who'd been at war so much longer and were weary of it. Most of the soldiers were delighted to meet an American, even the Yanks, but Mel tried to stay a moving target, still shaken by the possibility she'd altered the time line. But now she was more than ready to be a stationary target—even for a bomb. It would be a mercy killing.

She looked at the pub, rising stocky and anciently solid in the deep dark. The pub appeared to be Tudor, though Mel wasn't really up on her architecture, so had no way to know that in a city blacked out by war. She thanked the warden and watched his hooded flashlight vanish into the blackout as he moved away.

The door of the pub opened, loosing the cheerful sound of many voices and the enticing smell of food, but still no light. It surprised her how much she missed street lights and head lights and windows spilling bright and heedless into the night. Mars would have been easier to face than this hunkered down, dark world.

Before the door could close, Mel slipped through it, then through the blackout curtains that separated the door from the rest of the pub. The inside was brightly lit and as cheerful as it sounded, despite dark wood walls. The floor of the lobby was wooden and ahead she saw a staircase that she hoped led to a room she could stay in tonight. She briefly considered trying for that room now, but the longing to sit down trumped everything.

She followed the sound to the bar and found a mix of locals, RAF and a small cluster of Air Force pilots. The room was sharply divided, since the RAF didn't like the Yanks and the Yanks didn't like not being liked. There were a couple of women with the American boys and none with the RAF—another reason why no one was getting along.

She didn't see Jack or Norm among the faces that turned briefly her direction. She made her way to an empty stool at the end of the rustic bar, aware that multiple gazes followed her to her destination. The relief of finally sitting down trumped any self-consciousness though. Mel didn't hesitate to pull off the hat that had grown tighter around her head with each hour. She kicked off her shoes and rubbed her aching feet together.

"What'll you have, luv?" the bar maid asked, her gaze openly curious.

Mel probably needed food, but her stomach was still muttering bitterly about her last meal. Jack hadn't briefed her on pubs. Did they stock soft drinks? Surely they'd have tea or coffee? Even if she'd been a consumer of alcohol, Jack had warned her not to imbibe. Alcohol didn't mix well with a recently time-traveled bod. She did know chocolate was rare by this time. For sure there'd be no Diet Dr. Pepper. War really was hell.

"Something hot. I'm so cold." Mel didn't like either, so couldn't bring herself to commit to one.

"You're American."

"Yes." Did they all think she didn't know?

The girl looked curious, but there were other calls on her time. "Right then."

Mel smiled her thanks, tucked her hat in her purse, and tucked the purse down against the wall, glad to be sitting. When a cup appeared in front of her, she wrapped her cold hands around it and let the steam drift up to warm her face. Her insides still quivered from the shock of her first air raid and she was vaguely aware she was suffering from what Jack had told her was *time shock*. She felt sluggish, alien and intensely homesick—to the point she thought she might throw up. And possibly a bit paranoid. She desperately needed something familiar to hook her brain into, so she stared into her cup, as if it had the answer to all of life's questions.

She took a cautious sip of the dark liquid, hoping it would settle her stomach. It did help some and, even better, warmed her insides a bit.

She felt cold air swirl around her legs and looked toward the doorway where she saw a cluster of men, more Yanks judging by their uniforms.

With a jolt, she recognized Norm among them, his cheeks ruddy with cold and his eyes bright with interest. He looked exactly like the photos of him in his uniform, except he was all color and vitality. And he was alive. Stocky and cheerful, the blue of his uniform lifted him into the realm of handsome, something he'd never really be to unbiased eyes. But his eyes were good-natured, kind and direct. Yes, she could see why Gran had lost her heart. He was perfect for her.

I wonder what he'd do if I said, *Hi, gramps*, Mel thought with an inward grin.

He moved to one side, and Mel found herself staring at Jack. Also like his photographs, none of them–or the meeting with Jack's older self–had prepared her for the vibrant reality of Jack in his prime. The uniform suited him disturbingly well, but even without it, he'd draw attention with his thick, dark thatch of hair and bright, blue eyes.

The bar maid approached him, her hip action sassy and inviting, drawing a quick, potent grin from him, one similar to the one from his pictures, but this live version stole her breath and made her heart contract in her chest.

As if he felt her gaze, he glanced around and saw her. For a long moment, he stared at her. She stared back at him. She might have stopped breathing. It was possible her heart stopped beating. It felt like even time halted in its tracks. Now she knew what Jack hadn't told her, why he'd looked at her the way he did. It felt like she was in an electric current. Or a Star Trek plasma conduit.

He wasn't looking at her like he had—or was that would? Instead he looked puzzled and a bit intrigued. Did he see recognition in her eyes? Norm nudged him, said something with a grin. Jack laughed, but it didn't look entirely natural. When he started toward her, easing his way between the clusters of customers drifting back to their tables, she inhaled shakily. *He should have warned me...*

Jack stopped in front of her. She had to stop herself from saying his name.

"I know it sounds like a corny line, but have we met before?"

"It does rather sound like a line." Without being told, her lips curved up in a smile. "And I wondered the same thing."

"You're American." His delight seemed a bit out of proportion to her...American-ness.

"So everyone keeps telling me."

He indicated the empty stool next to her. "May I join you?"

In lieu of an answer, she scooted her chair over a few inches. This time she wasn't surprised to find him sitting taller than her. His shoulder brushed against hers as he straddled the stool. There were other things to surprise and delight her, such as his vigor and vitality. And his...vigor. She gave a mental shake. She probably shouldn't spend too much time pondering his...vigor. It wasn't part of her mission brief. Though the side benefit of that pondering was a nice warming of her insides. It was the first time she'd felt warm since her unorthodox arrival in the past.

"Name's, Jack," he said. "Jack Hamilton."

"Mel," she managed. "My friends call me Mel."

"No last name?" His blues eyes lit with humor.

Still lost in their deep, blue depths, she knew she had a faux one, but for the first time in her life, she couldn't remember something.

Chapter Five

"CAN I BUY YOU a drink?" Jack still didn't know how he got from the doorway to sitting on the stool next to her. It felt like his body had been taken over by someone very like Ric. He was even dishing out Ric's lame lines. It should have been embarrassing, but for some reason it wasn't. He studied her upturned face and found it a pleasant field of study.

Her hair was blond, though he'd never seen hair that looked quite like hers. It couldn't seem to make up its mind which direction to go, but it suited her, framing her sassy, cleanly featured face and directing attention to her wide, purple eyes framed by thick, dark lashes. He'd never seen eyes that color either, so he stared at them for a bit, until the edges crinkled up in a smile that twisted his gut into a knot. Her clothes were wartime drab, she was a bit on the thin side, and she had an icy cool; but it was wrapped around a luminous core that both puzzled and intrigued him.

It was hard to put his finger on, but there was some quality, something in her bearing, in the tilt of her chin and the look in her eyes that was seemed almost...alien. A table became free and he jumped up and claimed it, holding a chair for her, before settling in across from her. Mel. What kind of name was that?

"It's short for Melanie," she said, as if she could read his mind. "But I never felt like a Melanie, so I shortened it."

"What does a Melanie feel like?"

"Girly. Giggly." She sounded demure. "Silly."

Definitely a bit odd, but a nice odd, an interesting odd. And with those legs, those eyes and that mouth, she was definitely a girl. His discreetly examined the legs, following them down to her feet. "You lose your shoes?"

"I'd like to, but they're my only pair." Jack must have looked as startled as he felt, because she added, "They're evil—and there by my chair with my bag."

He retrieved her things, while his thoughts worked at figuring her out. Ric would have considered it a waste of thought, but Jack couldn't help himself. At his core, he was a scientist and puzzles were the life blood of a scientist.

Mel slid her shoes back on, with an obvious reluctance that made Jack grin, and then she hung the bag from the back of her chair. When he had her attention again, her calm, steady gaze met his without...guile. And yet he had the feeling she was holding back. Or perhaps it she was reserving judgment?

"Will I pass?" The words were flirty, but the tone was matter of fact.

"Pass what?" Jack didn't know what to say, so he punted.

"Muster." She propped her elbows on the table between them. "Have I passed your muster?"

It was in moments like these that he wished he had just a bit of Ric's glibness. It was the perfect moment for a compliment of some kind. He could even think of several. What he couldn't imagine was any of them coming out of his mouth. To his relief, the waitress stepped between them.

"What are you drinking?" he asked Mel.

"Tea, please."

"Same for both of us," Jack said.

"You take a vow of sobriety?" Norm asked. Without waiting for an invitation, he snagged a nearby chair and joined them.

Jack saw Mel's gaze leave him for Norm. Her eyes were wide and interested.

"He's married," Jack said and then wished he hadn't. Norm choked back a snicker. Mel's lips twitched twice.

"I'll have a pint and he's paying for it," Norm told the waitress. When she left, Norm held out a hand to Mel. "Norm Morton."

"And I'm Mel."

She looked delighted as they shook on it, but it was a friendly delight. Jack looked at Norm, trying to figure out why. Norm was...Norm. Straight forward, compulsively honest and enduringly loyal to his wife, his country and his group—in that order.

"You're American." It was Norm's turn to look pleased.

"I did know that," Mel said. "Does it stick out a mile?"

Norm grinned. "Further than that around here."

"What brings you here?" Jack asked, when what he really wanted to ask her was, who are you? Why do you puzzle me?

"I'm a reporter, here to do some stories on our soldiers, how they are coping with life in England, things like that. I'm starting with bomber crews, like you two."

Jack frowned. "How did you know we are part of a bomber crew?"

Mel arched her brows. "Well, duh. Your uniforms? And the raccoon mouth thing you've got going there."

Duh? Jack touched the marks left by his oxygen mask and the extreme cold. It was inevitable and unavoidable flying at high altitude. "Raccoon mouth, huh."

Mel shrugged, but humor glittered in her unusual eyes.

She didn't fit here, but then who of them did? What was his problem? He'd been wishing he had a girl to spend the evening with and here one was. And what was he doing? Looking a gift horse in the mouth. Duh, indeed. He pushed suspicion to the back of his head and smiled at her instead.

"How long have you been covering the war?"

Her lashes hid her gaze for a moment. "Actually, this is my first serious news story."

He heard her words, but he couldn't say he comprehended them. He wished for music, so they could dance. He wanted to invite her to the base dance on Saturday, but glib still eluded him.

"Usually I cover fashion, hair styles, make-up and crap like that."

That he understood. Had he ever heard a girl say crap? He didn't think so, but then he lacked Ric's experience with the fairer sex.

"Sorry." Mel looked rueful, but not really repentant. "My Gran used to wash my mouth out with soap for saying crap."

Jack had a feeling that wasn't the only word she'd been punished for using.

"She sounds like Elaine, my wife," Norm said. He smiled, but his eyes showed thoughts that had winged home. "She's always after me about my language."

"Do you have a picture of her?" Mel asked.

Of course he did. Jack looked at the two of them, shoulder to shoulder, studying the picture. He had an odd feeling he was missing something important, but whatever it was stayed just out of his reach.

"She's beautiful." Mel sounded soft and kind of sad.

Did she have someone at home she was missing? Or someone in the service?

"And this is my son, Norm, Jr. I just got that picture in the mail bag yesterday."

Mel looked at that photo for what seemed like a long time to Jack. It was a baby, for Pete's sake.

"He's...wonderful," she said. "You must be so proud."

Was that a catch in her voice? Jack waited for her to look up and when she did, it did seem as if her eyes shimmered a bit. Jack added this to his mental summary of Mel, but it didn't clear anything up.

"Yeah," Norm said. "I hope—"

Norm stopped. Jack knew why. He hoped to meet his son, but didn't believe he would.

Mel covered his hand with hers. "You will see your son, Norm. I know it."

Norm looked up, half disbelief, half hope, in his eyes. "You sound very sure."

"I am completely sure."

"How..." Jack began. He stopped. Why tear down the hope lifting Norm's spirits? If anyone deserved that hope, it was Norm.

It was easy to forget why they were here, easy to lose touch with the families they were fighting to defend. The face of his mother and father, his little sister, had faded to the shadows of his memory, trumped by the obscenity of war. He'd almost lost them, but somehow Mel had connected him to them again. Home. He closed his eyes and he could see them both waving good-bye...

Now he remembered why he tried to, not forget, but just keep it distant and not too real. It was less painful that way. He looked down at his coffee, wishing he'd ordered ale. It did take the edge off.

He lifted the cup, tossed back what was left. When he lowered his hand, Mel covered it with hers. He looked up and met her gaze. The war receded into a distant sound and fury. Tomorrow it might be harder, but tonight he didn't care. It was enough to be alive, to be here with a pretty girl.

"Do you want to dance?" he heard himself ask.

She smiled. "There's no music."

"I can try to play something," Norm said.

For the first time, Mel noticed an old upright in the shadows to one side.

Without taking his gaze off Mel, Jack said, "Something slow."

He pulled Mel up from her seat and into his arms, stopping just short of full body contact. Some part of him warned against getting too close, against getting in too deep. With one hand on her waist, the other loosely clasping her hand, he waited for Norm to begin without looking at her. It didn't help that much, since he could smell her now that she was close enough to push back the pub smells. The scientist in him made a half-hearted attempt at analyzing it, but the rest of him just inhaled and enjoyed.

A soft, slow melody flowed out into the room from the piano. They started to move with it, an inch in one direction, and an inch in the other. It couldn't quite drown out the clatter of mugs and pub talk, but it did push it to the point of distant background.

The foreground was Mel. She swayed with him, her body occasionally brushing against his.

"I never asked if you had someone waiting for you at home."

"No." She seemed to hesitate, then said again, more firmly. "No. It's just...complicated."

"The war." Jack sighed, his hold tightening infinitesimally. Someone tapped him on the shoulder. He was aware of it, but distantly. Not enough to react.

"Cutting in," a voice said, tapping him hard now.

Jack turned toward the voice. And looked up. And up. And up some more. It wasn't often he met someone taller than him. Why did it have to happen tonight? He finally found the beefy face at the top of the even beefier body. Two angry eyes were buried deep in his fleshy face. The smell of ale came out of every pore in his body. A drunken leer formed on his mouth as he shoved Jack to one side and started toward Mel.

Jack struggled to recover from the shove, but just when he thought he had, a chair caught the back of his legs and he went down with a mighty crash. He blinked and missed something key, because now the drunk was bent over clutching himself. This brought his chin down to Mel's level. Jack didn't miss what happened next. Mel turned and lifted her elbow sharply. It connected with the fleshy jaw. The drunk's head snapped back. His eyes rolled back into his fleshy sockets. He swayed like a mighty oak in a heavy wind, while all bodies behind him scattered for their lives—or least for the integrity of their bones.

At the calm center of the storm, Mel stood studying her work with a pleased look. Then she reached out with her index finger and pushed. The *mighty oak* went down, taking a table and two chairs with him.

Mel looked at her finger. "Cool." She flexed her elbow experimentally, and then looked at Jack. "Are you all right?"

The ring of faces looking down at him were clearly conflicted about what to do first, laugh at him for being saved by a girl or look impressed and/or awed at the girl. It did some strange things to their faces.

Jack scrambled upright. His dignity stayed down there somewhere. It would probably be in hiding for months. He wished he could join it.

"I'm fine." He looked at the drunk. He looked at Mel.

Her eyes widened. "He touched me."

Almost as one, the circle of onlookers took a step back from her. Jack had to grin.

"I touched you."

She nodded thoughtfully. "Yes, you did," she said, "but you did ask first."

Jack looked at the fallen and gigantic drunk again. "How—"

Mel shrugged. "Leverage. After a well-placed knee, of course."

"Of course." Jack rubbed his face. She looked, well, like a bit of fluff, he thought, cribbing from Ric. Blonde and cute, with a bit of sass, not some tough butt kicker. He moved his elbow in modified mimic of her movement.

"Leverage?"

"That's right. Kind of like physics," she said vaguely, her expression getting even more blonde and vacant. "Isn't it physics that's about leverage?"

"Physics. Right." He thought for a moment. "Could you do it again?"

She shrugged, but something in her eyes told him she could do it again. And again, if necessary.

"Truck's here," Norm said. "Time to go." Norm looked like a man who'd won a prize. Jack just wished he wasn't that prize.

Jack turned to Mel, trying to think of something to say.

Mel smiled demurely. "I'm not the one who knocked you down, you know."

"No, you just knocked him down." She looked at him, one brow elegantly elevated. He wished he could put his arms around her again. Already he missed her. "You going to be in the area for a while?"

He tried to sound casual, like he didn't care. He wasn't sure if he succeeded. Something in her eyes softened.

"Until I get my...story."

Norm tugged on his arm. "We've got to go."

"You'd better book," Mel said.

"Book?"

"Go. You should go." Her gaze shifted from Jack to Norm. "Bye, Norm."

There was an odd note in her voice as she shook hands with him. Then her gaze swung back his direction.

"I could walk with you to the truck."

Jack shook his head. "It's not safe.

"Air raids?"

"Men," Jack said.

"Oh." She thought for a moment. "I wouldn't hurt them."

He laughed. He sobered, reaching out to lightly brush the curve of her cheek. "Bye. I'll see you again if—" He stopped.

"We will meet again, Jack."

She spoke with such certainty, it made him grin. What did it really hurt to pretend to be sure? "We're having a dance on the base tomorrow night. Anyone can come."

"I'll check and see if I'm anyone."

Maybe that's what made her different, that air of serenity. She must be the only person on the earth who felt sure of anything in these times. Before he could consider it further, Norm pulled at his arm, dragging him toward the door. Jack looked back until he couldn't anymore. She didn't turn away, just watched him leave with a look that was sort of wistful and wry.

Norm shook his head as they settled on the hard bench of the truck. "I don't know if I'd want to date a girl who could knock me down."

Jack rubbed his face ruefully. Norm had a point, though thinking about Mel, she might just be worth it.

Chapter Six

December 18, 1942

MEL FOUND IT strange to the point of disorienting to walk down a street she'd walked down—or was that would be walking down?—sixty-plus years in the future. The buildings of Cambridge stood, as they always had, familiar, but somehow not. On that first occasion, she'd felt suspended between past and present, wondering if she was walking where her grandfather had walked, wondering what he'd thought about, wondering about the kind of man he was.

Now she kind of knew. Here she was strolling past timeless buildings on a narrow, cobblestone sidewalk fronting a street filled with period cars and period people. Only she was the period piece, not them. And if this weren't weird enough, she probably knew more about them than they knew themselves—and yet she knew almost nothing. She knew the outcome of the war, who lived and who died, but not the small details of daily life in 1942. It was the small things that could trip her up—like the way she talked. And now she understood what Jack meant about the way she walked. It was just...wrong. And she couldn't fix it, at least not without a lobotomy.

Added to the general weirdness of it, there was what Jack called *time disorientation*, caused by knowing what was going to happen and trying to keep it all sorted out. The flash of a face in a crowd and her mind would be filled with pictures and information about them. And if that person happened to be, say, a German spy, she had to resist the impulse to knock him on his tush.

She had no way of knowing what changes she'd caused by her first contact in the tube. Jack said that because the past was her future, time would be fluid until she reconnected with her future timeline. He didn't know why it happened or why her memories didn't update with each change. There were things they just didn't know about time travel and may never know.

In Mel's opinion, it would have been better not to engage in behavior they didn't understand, but no one had asked her and now here she was, the unblendable person trying to blend in.

"It's better not to think too much about the paradoxes of time travel, I'm told," Jack had told her. "Try to stay focused on specific tasks. Set goals for each day."

She didn't know if it was good advice or not and since she didn't know, all she could do was try to do it and see if it did help. Her present goal was to locate the bus stop, purchase a ticket for said bus, board it and then disembark at the base. Jack wanted her to stay away from the base, but sightseeing wasn't going to do it for her. Her brain insisted on action or it would continue to worry at the problem. And besides, it fitted her cover story better to arrive at the base and at least pretend to be a reporter. Also, it felt like she could do less damage there than left to her own devices in larger England. It was Friday. From the Group's dailies, she knew there'd be an orchestra concert tonight. On Saturday, there'd be some practice formation flying and then the dance Jack had invited her to attend. And on Sunday, crash and burn day...

No, don't go there. Don't think. Just do.

She paused at a crossing with a small crowd of people, waiting for clear passage across the street. Little snippets of conversation pecked at her introspection. Mel realized one woman was talking about a recent letter from her soldier son. Relief colored the woman's voice. For the time being she could believe her boy was alive.

The emotion of being here was almost as hard to deal with as the time paradoxes. These people were fighting for their lives, working against their own grief and fear to do it. They managed to find a middle ground, but Mel hadn't located it yet.

There was too much time before the next bus left, so Mel slipped into a shop, needing a break from feeling so much, if that were possible.

"Can I help you, luv?" the shopkeeper asked.

What might be a reasonable request? "Stockings? I need some...stockings."

"You're an American."

Mel bit back a sigh and nodded.

"Haven't had stockings for a long time."

"I suppose not. Is it all right if I browse a bit?" Surely browsing was typical in any generation or time?

She wasn't sure she could buy anything anyway. She had a few clothing coupons, but she didn't know if she could or should use them. She sighed a bit. A dance tomorrow night and she, quite literally, had nothing to wear but the clothes on her back. She was going to be real sick of this suit by the time she got out of it.

She pushed through a rack of clothes and found a red, party dress.

It wasn't exactly her style, and it was really, really red. At least sixty years out of date in her world, but it was...charming. It had a flared skirt and a wide, boat neck. It was even her size. She pulled it out and held it up to her, studying herself in the rather spotty mirror affixed to the wall. With a sigh, she put it back on the rack and turned to go. It was better to flee temptation, particularly when she hadn't the power to give into it anyway.

"Why don't you try it on, luv? It suits you a fair treat." She looked around, and then lowered her voice. "I'm sure we could come to an agreeable...arrangement." Mel's surprise probably showed on her face, because she added, "Not like my lot can afford the coupons for glad rags like that."

She had a point. "How much?"

The amount wasn't unreasonable, even in American dollars, and a deal was made. There were even shoes to match. In short order, it was wrapped and the package stowed in Mel's capacious bag, just in time for her to catch the bus.

MEL STARED OUT of Colonel Stanley Wray's office window. The view wasn't that deserving of her attention. It was in fact, rather bleak. She just thought it a good idea to let the Colonel absorb her cover story unobserved for a few moments. The last thing he wanted on one of his planes was a reporter and for that reporter to be a female...Of course he thought she was out of her mind. That he was correct was beside the point.

His choleric color only added to the oddity of seeing him like this, in the vibrant prime of his life. She had a vague sort of memory of him from a Group reunion just before he died. She'd been young, maybe six or thereabouts. Other than that, she'd only seen him in the inevitable black and white photographs from the period. Talk about your dead man walking.

Okay, getting disoriented again. Mel gave a mental shake and turned around. Wray was standing pretty much the way she'd left him. The only movement was in the region of his mouth, though no sound emerged. He was probably giving silent voice to his opinion of whoever had cut her orders. His formerly dropped jaw was square and classic and he had a straight, unapologetic gaze that cut through bull like a razor—when the playing field was level. Mel was glad she didn't have to try out her real reason for going on the mission with Jack.

Normally he was straightforward and very determined. His Group had originally been detailed to Kimbolten, but he hadn't like the accommodations and the runways couldn't handle the Forts, so he'd picked up and moved here, informing the powers that be after the fact. Clearly his sense of outrage was at war with his notion of how a gentleman behaved in the presence of a lady, not to mention the respect due those in command over him. It didn't help that he thought she really was a reporter, either. As Mel had cause to know, being on the record was a bit inhibiting. She'd bitten back a lot on her many adventures in not crying uncle.

She tried to look sympathetic and harmless, while projecting an aura of competence for the task. It was not a compatible mix, if the look on the Colonel's face was an indication. She thought about bringing on the charm, but something in his eyes made her discard that approach, too. She would, she realized a bit sadly, have liked his respect, but was not likely to get it.

"I'm not here to expose or betray your group, Colonel. My purpose is to make a record. My...article most likely won't even appear in print until after the war." *Sixty years after, if ever.*

"That's the biggest line of..." he stopped, clearly trying to find an alternative acceptable for the presence of a lady.

Mel met his gaze squarely, trying to look serious and honest. "You're right. And I wish I could tell you why I need to be on that plane, but I can't. I give you my word, though, that my presence is not, and will not, be a danger to your plane or your crew."

"And what if they are a danger to you, young lady? What if you go down in France? What then?"

Young lady. Mel had to bite back a smile. He was kind of cute and gallant in a gruff, I'd-like-to-spank-you-and-send-you-home kind of way.

"I'm fluent in both French and German, sir, and have received ample training. I won't be a burden to them." His men could be so lucky to have her training. "I just need to be on a plane...the next time you fly." She'd almost slipped there, dang, it was hard not to reveal what she knew. When he still didn't say anything, she asked, "Are you going to help me, sir?"

He waved her papers at her. "These don't leave me much choice, young lady." His hard gaze still bored into her. His fingers beat an impatient tattoo against the side of his leg.

It wasn't easy to meet that gaze. She wasn't used to being drilled for character by such an expert. Usually her looks worked for her. It was better if people didn't think she could do the job and underestimated her. This time it was a pain in the posterior.

"I'm not as young as you think I am, sir." She smiled just a bit, careful not to cross the line into impertinence. "Would you feel better if I kicked someone's... bottom...for you?" She added a bit of demure to her smile. "I promise you I can."

This time he looked at her like he was seeing something more than a young lady standing before him. A slight frown pulled his brows together as he studied her, before the frown faded into a reluctant, though, a bit parsimonious smile. "So I hear. Corporal Stymes has a bruised tail bone."

"He was...intoxicated, sir," Mel felt bound to point out. "And belligerent."

"He often is," Wray said. His smile got slightly less parsimonious. He tapped the papers with one hand. "What made you decide on Hamilton to fly with?"

She had no good answer for that and fell automatically back on basic reporting technique: deflecting awkward questions with a question of her own.

"Is there a problem with him?"

Wray shook his head. "He's a fine pilot. His copilot is...less than one, though. I could have him replaced for the mission."

Mel stiffened slightly, and then made her self relax. "I think it would be better if everything looks...and goes...as normal, sir."

She could tell he was still troubled, but other than flipping him on his tush, she didn't know what else to do.

"Combat is no place for a woman," he said.

"With all due respect, sir, this war affects everyone. All any of us can do is our best—and what we're asked." She tried to look older and serious.

He sighed and nodded slowly and she knew she'd won. "What do you need from me, young lady?"

"If you have some spare gear I could use, it would be helpful. I think it would be best if I blended in with the crew as much as possible. And then just let me on that plane when the time comes."

"The gear shouldn't be a problem, but I can't control the weather." He looked out at the gray, grumbling sky.

Mel looked, too. "I have a feeling it will clear up soon, sir."

He looked at her, his gaze sober and serious, then out at the overcast sky. "I have the same feeling."

MEL, FEELING MUCH more comfortable in her recently issued Air Force fatigues, stood on the tower next to Colonel Wray with her hand shading her eyes. The chill wind whipped through her clothes and hair as she looked up at the approaching Forts tracking white contrails across the gray sky like clouds of glory. It was amazing to see them all together like that. Before it was over, so many of those planes, and the men flying them, would be gone. What she knew, it haunted her. It felt as if she walked and talked with ghosts, but they were the ones who were real to this time, to now. She was the ghost, the one who was out of time.

Despite her doubts, she was almost glad to be here and see this in real time, to be where men fought grimly to free the world from tyranny and were honored for it by those who benefited, not castigated by the clueless. They didn't know that someday they'd be called the Greatest Generation, that they'd have changed the world, that it was a better place, that their sacrifice had meant something. They were just doing their duty. She thought about the odds against them. *Dang rough duty.*

The formation looked pretty good to her, but Colonel Wray snorted in disgust.

"We'll do it again tomorrow, unless—" He stopped, but they all knew what he meant.

He strode away, leaving her to watch the Forts roar in for their landing. It was an amazing sight as one by one they touched down. The roaring of their engines filled the air and the ground shook beneath her. When they were all down, Mel turned and headed down. It was lunch time. She'd find Jack and Norm in the general region of mess tent looking for a late lunch.

JACK AND NORM paused outside the mess to light up. Cigarettes helped blunt the taste of the food. He also needed some wind-down time before plunging into the chaos of the mess. His shoulders ached from wrestling to keep the Fort in tight formation. His legs would hurt, too, when the feeling returned to them. He was cold all the way to his bones and hungry enough to face whatever food horror was waiting for him inside, but he needed a spot of quiet first. Time alone was one of the things he missed the most.

As he inhaled the smoke, his thoughts drifted in Mel's direction...

"Don't you know those things can kill you?" A voice very like Mel's came from behind them.

Jack spun around, his match burning down to his fingers as he stared at the girl who went with the voice. He cussed sharply and dropped the match to the ground. She was standing where the wind could whip her hair to a sexy tangle. In Air Force blue fatigues she looked more comfortable than she had last night. She faced him with her hands shoved deep into the pockets of her flight jacket, her shoulders at a don't-mess-with-me angle and her booted feet planted.

Jack struggled to organize a response with his thoughts tangled up in pleasure. Finally he managed a slow grin and nodded in the direction of the flight line.

"Those can kill us, too, ma'am."

Mel chuckled. "Point to you, Captain, but I'll bet your Fort doesn't stink as much as that cig."

"You'd lose that bet," Norm said, but Jack noticed he put the unlit cig back in his pocket.

"Well, I guess I'll soon find out," Mel said, strolling forward, her walk as relaxed as a guy's.

Jack didn't like the sound of that.

"The colonel's letting you go up on a practice run?"

Luckily, Norm asked the question because Jack couldn't. Just who was she and what was she really doing here? The Colonel might give a reporter a joy ride, if the brass were pressuring him, but a woman?

"I don't believe it," Jack said flatly. Only...why had she been outfitted like one of them? "He'd never let a woman up there."

Mel didn't look offended. "Brave talk from a guy who was saved by a girl last night." She grinned. "Maybe I used my feminine wiles on him."

"Not bloody likely," Jack said.

"That I have feminine wiles or that he'd be influenced by them?"

Jack didn't have an answer that didn't put him at risk for a...physics lesson.

Mel's look of amusement deepened. "If it's not likely to happen, then why are we talking about it?" Mel asked.

Jack didn't know, so he tried a subject change. "What are you doing on the base?"

"Working on my story." She looked at the line of men flowing into the mess. "I was going to join you for lunch, but I caught sight of it and lost my appetite." She shuddered delicately. "Would you like to comment on the chow—for the record?"

Jack knew an amused Norm watched and listened. Jack was determined not to give him any more tales to tell. "No."

"Fair enough." She held up a small, box camera. "I think I'll go take some pictures, talk to some of the guys. Maybe they'll be more willing to share their feelings."

No doubt about that, Jack thought grimly, but they might not be the ones she expected.

"I'll go with you," Jack said. Her brows arched in a question. "To show you around."

"Why thank you, Captain."

The words were respectful, but the tone...

Norm choked back a laugh, tried to turn into a cough, but couldn't quite manage it.

"Good, you can be my photographer. The magazine wouldn't spring for one. Cheap ba—buggers."

Norm snorted this time.

"Do you suppose your crew would assemble for a picture? With your Fort? And me? That would be so cool."

"Cool?" It wasn't exactly hot.

"Neat." She emphasized the "t" at the end. "Actually, it would be really neat." She grinned again.

"We could probably manage something," Jack said, wondering what was funny about it and why he wanted to smile with her. It wouldn't be hard to get them to all show up to meet her. They'd been teasing him unmercifully about Mel since last night and they'd love meeting her. It would make the story that much better.

Norm nodded. "I'll see who I can round up and meet you on the flight line. Want me to bring you something to eat?"

Jack shook his head slowly, not taking his gaze off Mel.

Mel smiled at Norm. "I'll see you later then."

Night came early this time of year, so the light was already turning that deep, afternoon gold as they started toward the flight line. It made the place look slightly less bleak than usual, though it had never been, and never would be, a comfortable scene. Its purpose was to wage war, not charm the eyes.

As they emerged from the huddle of buildings at the edge of the flight line, Mel stopped, her gaze making a slow one-eighty. He knew what she was seeing, it was as familiar to him as the back of his own hand, but in his mind, he could see it the way it looked from the air as he was coming in. The base lay in a shallow valley, with the main runway tracking along the length of the patchwork valley. The hard standing dispersals sites jutted out at angles into the countryside. The taxi strip made an uneven circle around the main runway, and then appeared to bleed off into the buildings huddled to one side. It wasn't a pretty sight coming home, but it was a welcome one. This evening, though, it did look pretty inhospitable.

She inhaled deeply, then let it slowly out. "Oh my."

Jack wondered what she was thinking. Her gaze looked open, and yet managed to reveal so little.

"So this was better than Kimbolten?"

He chuckled, lifting his hat and smoothing his hair back before replacing it. "Yeah, it is. Marginally."

"Which way is *The Time Machine*?"

"How did you know what it's called?"

Her lips curved enigmatically. She shrugged. "I'm a reporter, Captain."

She walked away from him and directly toward the hard standing dispersal site where his fort was parked. She seemed to know her way around.

"Why are you really here?" he asked, easily catching up with her.

She looked at him again, her gaze suddenly serious. "To do my job, Captain."

Chapter Seven

IN THE LATE afternoon light, this small city of ugly necessity was pretty bleak. Mel knew its history. Bassingbourne had been an RAF base until Colonel Wray co-opted it for his *Ragged Irregulars* in October, though they weren't too ragged yet. That was for the future she needed to try to not think about.

As they crossed the main runway, then turned toward the hard standing where Jack's plane would be, Mel mentally adjusted the layout with how she'd seen this area the spring she'd come over for the memorial service. Then the areas between what was left of the runways had been green and vibrant. Many of the original buildings had survived and were still in use to service the small, but modern air strip that also hosted a small museum as a tribute to this past.

Inside her head was all the information Jack could give or find for her about this base, but none of it could have prepared her for the reality of it. How could pictures give her sense of the textures, the colors, the smells, the sounds of living history—or how incredibly, coldly inhospitable it all looked to homesick eyes.

The knowledge of just how far from home she really was swept over her, almost taking her to her knees. She stopped to catch her breath as panic attempted a coup.

"What?" Jack, who had walked with her, casting the occasionally questioning glance in her direction, turned to face her.

She fought an internal battle, until she was sure she could keep her voice steady.

"How do you do this? How do you go up there? And come back to...this? How do you...bear it?"

He started to reach for his packet of cigarettes, but then stopped and shoved his hands in the pockets of his flight jacket. The chill wind tugged at them both. It alternately brought and removed the smell of the food from the mess. There were other smells, metallic ones and human ones. Wood burning somewhere, maybe, from a fire or bombs. She didn't know enough to sort them out.

"You can smoke if you need to," Mel said. "Does it help with all this?"

He shifted his shoulders, as if to shrug off the implication he needed to smoke. "Just something to do with my hands."

"So what does help?" she asked.

Jack's expression turned as bleak as his surroundings. "Is this for your article?" Mel shook her head. He shrugged. "Nothing helps."

He took out his pack and shook out a cigarette. Mel had the feeling he didn't even know he was doing it. Mel watched him light it up and inhale the smoke. It was awful to watch, knowing what she knew about them. She wanted to tell him, but she'd promised Jack she'd only tell him the truth as a last resort.

She turned away. It would have helped to talk to him about it all. He was the only person here who would understand or believe her— eventually anyway. And that's the danger, she realized. Sharing it would lead...some place they had no right to go. This is why Jack had wanted her to stay away. Shared danger, shared burdens could only result in stirring the feelings simmering beneath the surface, feelings that couldn't be. The cheese stands alone. So...very...alone...

"What is it, Mel?" Jack stepped toward her, breaking into her bleak thoughts. Concern made his blue eyes even more tempting. "What's wrong?"

Mel lowered her lashes, counted to ten and managed to produce a shaky smile. "Home suddenly felt...far away." She took a deep breath. "I guess I'm just a girl after all."

"I don't think there was ever any doubt about that," Jack said, a sudden grin blazed with warmth she wanted to lean in to. His shoulders were nicely broad for burdens in need of sharing.

"So how do you keep it all...in balance?" she asked, as much to distract herself as get information from him.

He was quiet for a moment, the cigarette in his hand sending a curl of smoke up his side, until the wind whisked it away. "Everybody has their own way of coping, I guess. Some of the guys drink. Ric chases girls." He grinned slightly, then tossed the cigarette down and ground it out with his foot.

"And you? How do you deal?"

"I try to stay focused on my job. At first, I took it a day at a time, then that got too long. Now, I work in hours. Sometimes I break it down into minutes." His tone was light, but his expression wasn't.

So she had one hundred and twenty hours to get through, give or take a few. The math on the minutes was a bit beyond her at the moment. It didn't help that she knew most of what was going to happen in most of those hours. Jack had briefed her very thoroughly, despite the obvious gaps, up until the time she was killed. What had happened after that, she wondered, not for the first time? The survivors had spent the rest of the war in prison camps, but what had Jack done? If she'd talked to him freely the last time, if he knew some of the future, the one thing he couldn't do is fall into German hands.

It was a light bulb that should have gone off in her sooner. He'd had to survive to undo what they'd done. It must have been terrible. Alone, with no one to talk to, no one who would or could understand. And even after, how to explain where he'd been and why? No wonder he'd avoided the Group reunions and stayed off the radar. It had isolated him for his whole life, in many ways. So, he'd tried to tell her, without telling her, to stay away, to keep the truth to herself. He didn't want to bind her too tightly or make the burden too heavy on her, but he wanted his past back, too. How could he not? He was only human.

And because he was a gentleman, and maybe because they'd fallen in love in his past, he'd hoped she wouldn't figure it all out. He knew this was going to be hard and he didn't want the weight of his past on her shoulders, too.

So much for hope. She'd managed to figure it out and add it on top of the pile.

For just a moment, panic almost won again as the weight of everyone's need tried to crush her. Somehow she fought it back, or at least got it at bay. What was the big deal anyway? She just had to keep her secrets, crash in Occupied France, evade the German army, make sure Jack's best friend died and Norm didn't and not fall in love with the only guy she'd ever wanted to fall in love with. Hey, if she made it home, there was always Eharmony.com.

Like Jack said, it was all about focus. And not thinking too far ahead. She'd start with seconds and work her way up to minutes. It was how she'd gotten through the last five years and it was how she'd get through the next five days. *Or die trying.*

Oh, that was a happy thought.

"I'm a good listener," Jack said. "My mom always said a trouble shared is a trouble halved."

Mel wanted to tell him not to be nice to her, to not trust her, because he was too darned tempting when he was nice. But she couldn't tell him that either. The list of what she couldn't do was getting way too long.

"Captain Hamilton!" Mel turned away from temptation with relief, and toward the voice. It was the Colonel's aide approaching them. "The Colonel would like to see you, sir, in his office."

Jack looked at Mel. She avoided his gaze, producing a facsimile of a smile. "I'll wait for you by *The Time Machine*."

He looked about to say something, but for whatever reason didn't. He nodded and turned away, leaving her with an easy, determined stride, that had only a hint of arrogance to it. Men in uniform, she'd learned, all walked that way. She half smiled at the sight. Of course, her smile faded, they needed that arrogance to survive all this. Maybe she could get an infusion of it? Or catch it?

She heard the roar of trucks and saw the crews for the next round of practice flights starting to arrive. Captain Morgan of the *Memphis Belle* hopped out of one of them and walked passed her. Mel couldn't help but gawk like a groupie. He'd died just this spring and yet here he was in all his youthful...glory. Dang.

Without thinking about it, Mel followed him until the *Belle* came into view. She'd seen her, of course, in the future, but now the *Belle* was as young as her Captain. Mel walked up, her head tipping back further and further, the closer she got.

"Wow." She grabbed a passing ground crewman. "Could you take my picture with her?" This wasn't being a groupie, exactly. Last time she'd had her picture taken with the *Belle* and her captain...

"Sure." He looked startled, until it dawned on him she was a girl in crew's clothing. He smiled broadly.

"I want it here, by the nose art." She looked up, wondering if she could mimic the Belle's pose for the picture, but before she could decide, Bob Morgan himself came up, looked her up and down, and then slid an arm around her waist.

"Who are you?" he asked, smiling down at her as the crewman snapped off a couple of shots.

"Just a reporter." She slid clear of his hold, wondering if he'd remember her the next time he saw her. That thought made her eye want to twitch. She reached up and patted the *Belle*. "That's a lucky plane you have there, Captain. She'll bring you safely home."

He looked at her for a long moment. "You really believe that, don't you?"

"Thanks for the picture." She smiled and turned around to find Jack watching her. That had been quick, almost too quick. He was smoking like a volcano about to erupt, too. It should have made him less cute, but it didn't. "It was lovely to meet you, Captain. Give my best to your other *Belle*."

He tipped his hat at her, gave Jack a grin that was definitely designed to provoke and strolled away. Jack looked like he might get pulled off the scent of what was really steaming him, but then he managed to shake it off.

"Are you out of your mind?" he hissed for her ears only. "Is a story really worth risking your life for?"

Once again she was saved by an interruption. Several voices called out to them. It was the crew, waiting for them by *The Time Machine*. Jack muttered an expletive.

"This isn't finished. We're talking later."

"Sure." But for once, Mel wasn't looking at him. She was looking at his plane, at his crew. "So that's it."

"It looks just like the *Belle*," Jack pointed out.

"No, it doesn't. Yours has a—" Mel stopped, staring at the nose art.

Ric came up, smiling and smoking. "If she'd been mine to name, she sure as shooting wouldn't have a tornado on the cone."

Mel looked at him, as her thoughts did a spin. "It's not a tornado." It was a vortex. A freaking vortex. She needed to think about it, but there wasn't time. They were all crowding around her. She had to focus on them, not Jack's vortex. *His freaking vortex.*

Ric stared at her like she was dim. "That's not a tornado?"

"No, it's..." She hesitated and then it came to her. She smiled at him coolly. "It's a flux capacitor."

"A what?"

Mel could see Norm biting his lip, trying not to laugh. She shouldn't take it any further, but she did. "Well, double duh, it's written right on the side of the plane. It's a time machine."

The charm faltered as Ric turned to look at the nose cone. "Oh, right. A flux capacitor. I guess it could be. It's not like Jack is an artist. But I can see it. Sure."

Mel looked at Norm and winked. She shouldn't have done that either, but she'd always had trouble with impulse control. Just past Norm, Jack was looking startled and a bit alarmed. He should have told her this, too, and she wouldn't have been startled. Did he think she wouldn't recognize it after jumping into the freaking thing?

Added to that were his orders to help him put Ric in perspective. This seemed a perfect opportunity to help him see the light. But perhaps she should pull back a bit now that she'd made her point. Didn't want him to figure out that she knew about his vortex. As the crew, hats in hand, jostled into a ragged line for introductions, she leaned close to Jack and whispered, "I think it's a very good tornado. Very artistic, but what made you choose it as a symbol for time travel?"

His expression cleared part of the way, but there wasn't time for more. The crew was waiting. Jack's crew, Norm's buddies.

The moment was both portentous and pedestrian. She knew them all so well, and in some cases, had actually met the survivors. *Don't think about that now*, she cautioned herself sternly. *Focus, girl. They're alive now. That's all that matters.*

First up was the crew chief, Sam Gabay. He was a big, dour man, so it was inevitable they'd call him Gaby. His hand engulfed about half her arm, the shake was short and oily. He apologized and wiped it away with a quiet charm, despite the cigar clenched between his teeth. He drifted naturally into the place he'd stand in the photo Jack had sent her. Or would send her. Or something like that.

Next was the Ram, also known as John Ramsey. He was a big man, too. As bombardier, he folded himself into that terrifying, exposed space in the nose of the Fort and directed the bomb run while getting shot at by diving FWs. In later model B17's they added a gun sight to the position, but not soon enough for a lot of bombardiers. When he wasn't looking through a Nordan bomb sight, he was a schoolteacher. English, with a particular love of for the romance period.

Harry and Roy were the waist gunners and such a matched set that most people thought they were brothers. Both medium in height, weight and coloring, they weren't related and couldn't have come from more different backgrounds. Mel always thought of them as rich man, poor man.

Lours and Fitz were tail and ball turret gunners. Their small statures had predestined them for these low life-expectancy positions. They occupied them with amazing good humor. The navigator, Hal Larsen, looked like an escaped shoe store clerk. Narrow wire rim glasses circled pale gray eyes and his light brown hair was already retreating across his scalp. He pushed them up with a finger, before shaking her hand and mumbling a greeting. Despite his mild-mannered exterior, he was a good navigator.

After Hal came Bennie, the top turret gunner, being jostled to hurry by Ric. Bennie was the comic relief of the group. He talked fast and funny and he looked goofy, too.

Ric, well, Ric was the glamour boy. Blonde and certain, he was beautiful. Actually, he was beautiful, being in the full flush of his manhood. He probably rocked a lot of girls back on their heels just by smiling at them. Mel didn't rock or blink or blush. She knew too much to about him to be dazzled, or even impressed. She couldn't look at him without seeing his future face superimposed over this one, a face raddled by alcoholism.

This self-centered man was the flash point of her and Jack's personal history, and the propellant for two trips into the past. Today he looked like a charming, shallow pool being slightly ruffled by the winds of war. Looking into his handsome face, creased by a smoky smile, it was hard to believe he'd ever died for Jack or for anyone else. There must be more to him than could be seen. Jack definitely needed a wake-up call about the nature of their so-called friendship.

Ric lifted her hand and pressed a kiss to the chilly back of it. "So you're Jack's Amazon, his mystery girl."

He smiled confidently at her, his fingers stroking the palm of the hand he'd just kissed. It was creepy. She'd like to have tossed him on his tush, but she didn't. Instead she gave him one of her wide-eyed, dumb blonde looks.

"I'm from, like, Wyoming, like, not the Amazon," she pointed out, blinking a couple of times for effect. "That's, like, a river or country, isn't it? And where's, like, the mystery in a pub pick up? I hear it happens to you, like, all the time."

"I think it's the physics lesson he's referring to," Norm said, with a broad grin.

"Would you like, like me to show, like, you how I did it?" Mel opened her eyes even wider and slow-blinked some more. "It only, like, hurts when you, like, land, but they tell me the trip is, like, well, a trip."

The crew got a kick out of this, even if they didn't get the Valley Girl connection, but Ric looked like he was in a play with the wrong script. His smile was still there, but was a bit uncertain. It was almost too easy. She'd have stopped, if it weren't for the memory of the family he'd killed. If this was the only way to erase that event...

"Give it a try, Captain, you'd be pretty—" Gaby drew the word out, as he rocked on his heels with barely suppressed amusement, "—flying through the air."

Ric seemed to realize it was a joke and his smile widened. "If it weren't for the landing, doll—" He leaned close to Mel, automatic seduction back on. "—you could flip me to the moon. Or we could just hit a pub?"

Mel widened her eyes. "The pub? That's, like, so, like, last night." She looked at Jack. No surprise he was having trouble keeping up, too. "Besides, Colonel Wray, like, invited me to the concert tonight. A colonel so, like, trumps a captain, don't you, like, think?"

Ric's smile faltered and he blinked a couple of times. "So you don't have a date with Jack tonight?"

"No." Jeeze... "So you can, like, quit trying to beat his time and we can, like, get a picture."

Ric laughed heartily. Not even a glancing blow as the shot went past him. How on earth had he managed to get his mind off himself long enough to save Jack's life? And how did an intelligent guy like Jack delude himself into thinking this waste of space was his friend? Clearly, men were, like, so from Mars.

Mel looked past Ric to Jack, letting her eyes clearly ask him, "Who is this guy?"

He looked a bit defensive, but she could tell her shot hadn't gone past him. He turned from her. "Form two rows," Jack said, "front row kneeling."

As she moved to her predetermined place, she felt his gaze probing her, too. Thank goodness she was from Venus. She pasted on a deflective smile, but perverse Mother Nature sent a last bit of sun through the gray cloud canopy and right across Jack, lighting him from behind. It was like putting the cherry on top of the sundae. Thank you for making this even harder. She'd had, she realized a bit ruefully, a crush on his memory, so it wasn't that surprising she'd bring it into this skewed reality. But crushes could be gotten over—particularly when the parties involved were separated by sixty, freaking years. She repeated the sixty, freaking years part to double their impact, but Jack still looked good enough to eat. And her heart was still doing a willful pit-a-pat.

Stupid heart. Didn't it know that in a couple of days, she'd be stranded in Occupied France with the survivors of this bunch? The poor *Time Machine* would be a broken wreck in a foreign field. And Gran would get a telegram informing her Norm was missing in action. If Mel failed, it would eventually be followed by the official notification of his death. Both telegrams were pasted at the end of the biography Gran had written for her husband. Mel knew them word for word, as well as the letter of condolence that Colonel Wray had written. Her only chance of succeeding was to keep her mind on the job so that Norm could emerge from a prisoner of war camp to the life he was supposed to have.

Or she and Jack would have to do this all over again. And again, until they got it right. The only way out of this Jack-induced causality loop was to do it right this time.

Mel turned away from the temptation of Jack, taking her place with the guys and raising her arm to expose her Uncle Sam tattoo—just in case history needed to repeat itself—and forced her lips into a brave smile.

"Now we should get some with each of us alone with Mel," Ric said, cutting Mel neatly from the herd. Clearly Mister Charm-in-the-box had wound himself up for another try. His arm snaked around her waist and his hand started to slide down her tush. She grabbed the hand, turning herself—and him—using their combined momentum to flip him on his tush instead. She twisted his arm slightly and lifted her foot to rest lightly on his chest, just shy of his throat.

"You must have missed the part of the story where I don't like to be touched, Captain Bramwell." She applied just a bit of pressure to his throat, enough to make him gasp, then eased it up. "Do you really want another picture with me?"

His eyes wide, Ric shook his head.

"Good answer." Mel stepped back from him. Ram and Gaby stepped forward to help him, even assisting with dusting him off. The rest were hiding grins. Ric, to his credit, realized it and looked at Mel with a laugh that didn't reach his eyes. Clearly she'd penetrated his ego this time.

"So that's physics? Well, I was never that good at math, but I can tell time. Don't want to miss the liberty bus." With a half salute, he sauntered off toward the barracks, his dignity a bit tattered, but the patch work on his ego already under way—like the Borg. In his mind, resistance was futile, apparently.

"I don't think he likes you anymore," Norm said.

"That's fair. I don't like him either." At least Ric was deep enough to get ticked off at her.

Norm's brows arched. "That was quick. It usually takes longer to hate him—some longer than others." His gaze found Jack and bounced back to Mel.

Mel almost said something, but the look on Jack's face stopped her.

"Was that necessary?" Jack's voice was low, but angry.

"A guy puts his uninvited hand on my bu—tush, he's lucky he's still got it swinging from the end of his arm." Mel tipped her head to the side. "I figured he might need it to help you fly the Fort—if he does help you? I mean, he's not a total waste of space, is he?"

Jack's face whitened, but she couldn't stop for Jack's—or her—own good.

"What's your problem with Ric? He's okay."

"Okay? Only if your definition of okay is slime of the universe." She looked at the men clustered around them, clearly enjoying the deconstruction of Ric. "Am I right?"

"She does have a point, Jack," Norm said. "And he was trying to cut you out."

Jack opened his mouth, but Mel cut him off. "It doesn't matter whether I'm your girl or not. He thought I was and he hit on me right in front of you."

"It's just his way..."

"Exactly my point. His way was to put his hand on my butt." This time Mel didn't censor her self. "And I'd like to know why you didn't knock him on his? Or isn't that your way?" It wasn't a fair question. She hadn't given him time to react, but he'd made her mad and a temper was another one of those faults she should be working on instead of trying to fix his freaking mess in time.

Jack stared at her for a long moment, then turned and stalked away. Temper faded as quickly as it rose. Mel looked at Norm. "I guess I was a bit harsh?"

Norm shrugged. "The truth is harsh." He looked at Jack's retreating back for a moment, and added, "Maybe he'll even hear it this time."

Mel grinned in relief. Her grandpa was pretty cool. She looked at what was left of the crew. "Anyone else want to take a picture with me?"

They all took a step back. Mel grinned at them. "Now you're all being harsh."

JACK STOOD BETWEEN sets of blackout curtains, watching Mel ask questions of the men clustered a respectful distance around her. They were the right questions, but something was wrong with the picture, something was missing. Then he got it. Another guy in the room got it, too.

"How come you don't take notes?" he asked her.

Mel stared at him for what seemed a long time.

"I have a photographic memory," she said, slowly, then added more quickly, "That's one reason the...magazine let me come. They knew I wouldn't exacerbate the paper shortage."

"Photographic memory?" Another guy looked puzzled.

"I can't forget," Mel added.

"Anything?" Someone else asked, looking a bit horrified at the idea.

"A woman who can't forget?" The original questioner shook his head. "Now that's just wrong."

Jack grinned, but it didn't last. Mel was a puzzle and he'd never been able to resist puzzles. Had she really been tweaking Ric with her comments about the nose cone art? When she'd first seen his vortex, she'd looked like she recognized it. And she'd called it a time machine. She'd made light of it, but he still felt uneasy. She was the first person who'd ever made a connection between the name of his plane and the vortex as an instrument of time travel.

And then there was her altercation with Ric. Ric was still steaming about it, but the worst part was, she was right. Ric was a jerk. So why did he keep making excuses for him? When had they stopped being friends and why hadn't Jack noticed that Ric was just a habit, and a bad one at that? Jack could handle being wrong, it was being stupid that was hard to swallow. Why had he let it go on so long? It was bad enough Jack had done it to himself, but it didn't just affect him. Ric was a lousy pilot and if Jack were injured, the crew would be at risk because Jack had put his loyalty to a jerk before their lives. He'd failed as a leader of his crew. And he should have knocked Ric down when he grabbed Mel. And all the other times he'd made a play for any girl Jack showed the slightest interest.

He made sure the inside curtains were in place and slipped back outside. The black out was more intense, with all the cloud cover, and the air was thick and damp. He hunched his shoulders irritably, wanting a cigarette, but Mel had spoiled that, too. He pulled the pack out of his pocket, looked at it for a few seconds, and then crumpled it up and tossed it into the trash barrel.

"Giving it up?" Mel asked.

She was standing just outside the doorway. Could she see in the dark, too?

"What?" he stalled. Already he wished the pack back.

"They're pretty addictive, besides turning your lungs, like, totally black. Like this night." She looked up. "Blackout's a pain, isn't it?"

That surprised a laugh out of him. "Yes, it is." He wanted to tell her she was right, but the words stuck in his throat. His mom always said, climbing down was hard.

"I'm sorry about...Captain Bramwell, Ja—Captain Hamilton—"

"Jack. My friends call me Jack," he cut in. Tension left, his throat came unstuck. "Gaby was right, he did look pretty—" He drew it out like Gaby. "—flying through the air."

Mel's chuckle sounded relieved. "I always like the landing the best. The look of surprise, when they realize a girl just took them down."

"Is it so hard being a girl?" Jack was rather glad she was one, but he didn't have to live with it.

"Despite the shoes, the bras, and clueless guys, it has its moments."

Jack almost choked. "Bras?" In his world, bras were mystical items to be removed, not instruments of torture—and generally not a topic of conversation between the sexes.

"I can't seem to help being indelicate. Sorry, but if you had to wear one—"

Jack chuckled, pushing his hands into his pockets as the urge for a smoke swept him again. He hadn't realized how much he used them to distract himself, or give himself something to do when—he stopped, then reluctantly let his brain finish the thought: while he decided if—or how—to make a move. There wasn't really an *if* in there, though. Want was already there. He'd had her in his arms once when they danced. He'd held her hands and looked into her purple eyes. Now he wanted to kiss her more than he wanted a cig.

"Would you like to—" He couldn't ask her that, so he compromised. "—to take a walk?"

She hesitated long enough for his gut to clench, before saying, "Sure."

They turned together, walking, inevitably, toward the flight line. It was the only place to be alone. To distract himself from his preoccupation with kissing, he cast about for something else to talk about, but all he came up with was her flux capacitor. She was a reporter. What would she think of a pilot who not only believed in time travel, but knew how to make it happen? He couldn't even explain how he knew. He just did. Oh, he had years of research ahead of him to actually make it happen, assuming he actually survived the war and he could find the energy source required to create his vortex, but he knew how to do it. It was all there, inside his head. Putting it on the nose cone of his plane had probably been a mistake, or perhaps it was an exercise in arrogance, an impulse he couldn't resist, a sort of hint, if he did die, to some future kid with an inquiring mind. Some kid like he'd been, one who read H.G. Wells and saw beyond the story to the possibilities. Now he realized it would look odder not to ask.

"So exactly what is a flux capacitor?"

Mel chuckled, the sound rich and warm in the chill of the night. "It's just a funny word I heard somewhere."

"I thought you can't forget?"

Mel was quiet for a moment, her boots hitting the ground twice as often as his did. He wished he could see her expression, but that wasn't possible.

"Not everything I remember comes with a definition, you know. Unless I get curious and do the research, it's just a word I can't forget. Which is not always a blessing. Boy, when I get a song stuck in my head—" Her teeth put a slice of white in her face, indicating a grin.

He stopped in the shadow of a Fort's wing, grabbed her arm and turned her to face him.

"Ric was right about one thing," he said, as much to him self as to her, "you are a mystery."

"While I hate to disillusion you any more about Ric," Mel said, "that's not exactly a news flash. Most women are a mystery to men—and the reverse."

He chuckled, the sound oddly husky in the quiet of night. He inhaled deeply, trying to suck enough chilly air into his lungs to clear his head. While the air was frosty, it was also filled with her scent. It wasn't perfume, in fact she smelled of standard issue soap, but beneath it was the...the...essential Mel. Kind of crisp, like her, with a touch of humor and whatever it was that drew men to women and had since the beginning. Working with the chill, this only sharpened his longing to explore the mystery posed by her mouth.

Mel lifted her chin, examining the horizon with the air of a connoisseur. "Cloudy again. I don't expect there'll be an alert tonight. I'll bet it doesn't clear before Sunday. That means drills, drills and more drills."

Jack didn't care about drills. He slid his hands up the sides of her arms, stopping at her shoulders for any sign his touch was unwelcome. He really hoped she didn't toss him, but was willing to take that chance. He didn't mind taking flight if the reason were good enough.

For a moment she stiffened slightly. He might have missed it if he hadn't been waiting for it, then she sighed and he felt her body relax, not against him, but not away from him either.

In the deep dark, he could only sense where his target was. There was no radar to help him here. And, not unlike their missions, he missed the first time, his mouth landing lightly on the curve of her cheek. Her skin was soft and cold and slightly sweet. He lingered there for a moment, just savoring the sensations of this first contact. Almost reluctantly, he cupped her face with his hands. His hands liked the feel of her skin as much as his mouth did. They spread across the soft silken surface and felt warmth bloom there. He tilted her head slightly and moved in again. This time he was right on target.

Her lips were supple and even sweeter than the first contact. They welcomed him, though with a slight reserve. Despite that, he was inclined to linger, to find the passion he felt waiting to join them, to erase the reserve, but it didn't seem wise, so he slowly, very slowly, backed off. He felt her sigh again and echoed it. He pulled her gently against him and just held her. It felt right. He felt...at peace for the first time since he left home. Part of him knew it wouldn't, it couldn't last, but he was content to linger there for now. Even the promise of passion in the kiss they'd exchanged couldn't lure him out. One thing he'd learned in the military, get your priorities right the first time. Passion was easy to find in war time, but peace, even if fleeting, was a gift.

She didn't speak and he was glad for it. He had no idea what she'd say. In the distance, he heard faint strains of music. The concert. The colonel.

"You're late for...the concert," he murmured.

"I said I'd been invited, not that I accepted." Her voice was soft and lightly lit with laughter. Something broke inside him. He hoped it wasn't his heart.

Now passion tried to struggle up from his gut. He fought it back. He needed to think and that wasn't possible with his arms around her. His brain sent an order to step back. His body was slow to respond, but eventually the night chill flowed between them again.

"What now, Jack?"

He couldn't see her face and her voice gave him no cues to follow. What did he really expect from her? He was a pilot with the life expectancy of a bug. She had everything to lose and he...cared too much to put her through that. He took another step back.

"The concert?"

Mel laughed softly. "As...enticing as that sounds, I don't think so. It's been a really, long day. I think I'll just...turn in."

Jack nodded, but realized she probably couldn't see it. "I'll walk you to your quarters then. Don't want any of the guys to get hurt."

"It would be unfortunate." There was a pause, and then she added, "I'm bunking with the nurses, from the hospital. I suspect the Colonel is also concerned about the safety of his men."

"That would be this way," Jack said, touching her arm only long enough to steer her in the right direction. And that almost undermined his resolve. He wanted to curse the war, but what good would that do? You could only work with the hand you're dealt. It might be a good idea to keep his distance, though. He needed to keep his focus, to remember why he was here.

Chapter Eight

JACK WAITED OUTSIDE until he saw a light go on in one of the rooms. Only then did he start toward his own quarters. Like Mel, he felt disinclined for company.

"I thought you'd gotten lost," Norm said, walking out of the shadows to meet him. "Where's Mel?"

"She spun off." Automatically he patted his pockets for his cigs, until he remembered what he'd done with them. "She's tired."

"She's ruined cigs for me, too" Norm confessed ruefully. "She's an odd one, but likable. Interesting."

Jack grinned ruefully. "She's going with us." He had to tell someone and he knew Norm was a safe repository. "I don't know how she did it, but the Colonel gave her permission."

"For a practice run?"

"No, our next mission."

"No." Norm's eyes opened wide. "He wouldn't."

"Well, he did. Said the orders came from Washington. That it was good PR for the group and the daylight bombing."

"Well," Norm cleared his throat a couple of times. "Well."

"I know." What else was there to say? They walked a few minutes in silence. "Good news in your sugar report?"

Norm's face lit up. "Yeah, the baby's gaining weight and Elaine's happy she's losing it."

"Good, good." Jake was quiet a bit longer. "When did you know, you know, that she was the one?"

If Norm knew why Jack was asking, he didn't let on. "I knew right away and it scared the crap out of me. It was like she knew me, inside and out. I felt all exposed and...awkward. I wanted to hide. But..."

Jack waited for him to go on, and when he didn't, gave him a verbal nudge. "But...what?"

"Well, I got over it."

"How?"

"After a while I realized that it didn't matter if she knew me. She liked me. And she wouldn't hurt me, at least not deliberately. See, I knew her, too." He grinned. "Balance restored, I guess." He hesitated.

"It was well worth it. Ric thinks he's got it made, but he's got nothing worth having, Jack. He'll never be satisfied and will probably never know why not."

Jack's first instinct was to defend Ric, a habit he needed to get over. He'd probably always known Ric was weak and basically selfish. He'd gotten so used to it, he'd quit seeing it. He had so much and made so little of it. His easy charm hid it for now, but he couldn't hide behind it forever. Not here, not now. This place stripped away pretence and left you facing who you really were. He'd stayed with Ric, Jack realized, to protect him from that moment, but he couldn't protect him and he shouldn't. Jack was denying him a rite of passage into manhood, if he had the guts and wits to take it.

"I know." Jack sighed.

Norm's eyes were kind. "If you'd had a wife, she'd have helped you figure it out sooner. They're good at peeling off undesirable friends."

"Don't tell me you ever had anything but good judgment?"

Norm chuckled. "We all start out young and then our wives raise us—if we're lucky." Norm hesitated. "You going to the concert?"

Jack shook his head. "I think I'll turn in."

At least Ric had gone on the liberty bus. Jack wanted to punch him, which wasn't exactly fair. It wasn't Ric's fault that Jack had been stupid about him. But if they were flying practice drills tomorrow, well, he knew a way to begin the education of Ric.

MEL LOOKED AROUND the spare room she'd been assigned. It didn't look any better in the dim light of the single, naked bulb hanging from the ceiling, than it had in daytime. Resolutely cold, the predominant odor was stale body smell, with even more stale perfume coming in a close second. The only color besides drab was the painfully red dress she'd bought for the dance she really shouldn't even think of attending. Looking around her, Mel wondered if she'd have the guts to put it on. Against the wall, it looked like a blood stain.

Mel poked the bed experimentally. Her finger bent. The bed didn't. Great. It wasn't that she couldn't deal with an uncomfortable bed. None of her gigs had provided one star accommodations. Actually most hadn't provided half star. Sleeping rough went with the gig more often than not. It was just that this time she hadn't had enough down time, she was years from home, and had no clue if she would make it back. Ahead were dark and dangerous days. It would have been nice to wind down with some HGTV or Food Channel. Now, with the feel of

Jack's kiss lingering on her mouth, would not be a good time for a vintage romance on TCM.

She rubbed a finger across her lips and sighed. Jack really, really should have told her about...this. She was reluctant to give it a name and elevate its importance even more. How involved had they been the last time? Had he hoped to keep it from happening? If he had, it wasn't working.

She'd never met anyone like him...except him, of course—which made her head hurt just thinking about it—and was amazing, because she'd met a lot of men in her various adventures in not crying uncle. And these weren't your average, run-of-the-mill men. These were the risk-takers and heroes of her generation, the ones not afraid to put themselves between the world and danger. And still, Jack was the only who made her heart speed up and her knees go soft. Maybe it was some commitment phobia that had her panting for the one man she could never, ever have? And if that wasn't a freaking, depressing thought, she didn't know what was.

She sank onto the unforgiving bed and bent to remove her shoes. The flight boots were slightly better than Gran's shoes, but still firmly in the clunky zone. She wriggled her toes inside the thick socks and sighed with relief. She tried to plump up the pillow. That didn't work. She tried doubling it, and then again. She studied its lumpy indifference. She could be wrong, but it seemed flatter than before. She tried to focus on her fluffy, feather pillows, but Jack's face kept getting in the way. Face it, he'd been in the way since her hormones started kicking up a fuss.

And he thought she was the mystery, with all the secrets rattling in his closet? She traced the vortex pattern on the rough surface of the blanket. He'd looked uneasy when she'd said the "flux capacitor" was a time machine. Did that mean he knew, here and now, how to do it? It was rather mind boggling—even to a brain pretty thoroughly boggled already. She'd just assumed that he'd believed in time travel and pursued it out of guilt, but the vortex seemed to indicate he'd known how to do it now. Of course, knowing how to do something and actually doing were two different things. But, wow, he must be some kind of genius and the Air Force, in its infinite wisdom, had thrown him into the meat grinder over the skies of Europe. And lost him. It was interesting to contemplate what might have been different if they'd realized his potential. Maybe Jack didn't know how smart he was? In any case, it wasn't her job to enlighten them. Her job was to restore the timeline, not further corrupt it.

She rubbed her lips again, studying the red dress. Jack had left the dance out of the briefing. If she were smart, she'd leave her dress hanging there and avoid the dance—and Jack. Of course, if she were smart...she wouldn't be sitting in 1941 with no HGTV.

December 19, 1942

TO JACK'S RELIEF, weather conditions had improved enough for practice flights. It got them out of ground school and gave him a chance to prove he could command his crew—all of it. When Jack came to face to face with Mel waiting by *The Time Machine*, he almost didn't recognize her. She was geared up like the rest of the crew, her flyaway hair hidden beneath a standard issue flying hat. Jack almost objected, but stopped himself. If she was going to fly into battle with them, she needed to know enough to stay out of the way.

Ric had staggered in late last night and now he looked hung over as he joined them. As they clambered into the Fort and made their way to the cockpit, he grumbled about the practice and his headache and Mel, in between bragging about his evening. He settled into his seat and closed his eyes, clearly preparing to sleep through the run.

"You take the controls," Jack said.

"I've got a hell of a head, Jack—" Ric began, in his easy, careless way.

"You need the practice," Jack cut him off.

"Jack..." Now Ric brought out his surprised, slightly hurt voice.

It surprised him how clearly he recognized all of Ric's dodges, now that the blinders were off his eyes. Jack turned at met his gaze directly. "Do you have a problem with flying this plane, Captain? Because if you don't take off, fly this plane in formation and land her, I will ground you. This crew needs a co they can count on in an emergency. Either get eager or get off my plane."

Ric didn't have an expression for this situation. It had never happened before. He stared at Jack, the veins in his eyes so red, they looked like a map of the London underground. But Jack knew he wouldn't want to lose his wings. The ladies loved them.

"You're serious?"

"You will address me as, sir, when we're in this cockpit. And you will follow my orders."

Ric's jaw dropped. He closed his mouth. Opened it. Finally he shrugged.

"Yes, sir," he said. He turned to the controls, looking at them like he'd never seen them before.

Jack had a feeling Ric had tried to sound bitter, but he just sounded whiny. The silence over the intercom was deafening.

"Take us through pre-flight," Jack ordered.

Ric managed to stumble his way through the checklist. He got them in the air, but his formation flying earned them some scathing rebukes from the Colonel over the radio. By the time they were back on the ground, Ric's face was sweat soaked and his arms trembled from the workout. The Colonel was waiting for them on the ground. He glared at Ric.

"Get some food and report back here. You'll fly again until you get it right."

When Ric had left, his bravado dragging, the Colonel turned to Jack. Jack braced for a trimming, but all he said was, "Eat. You're going back up again in an hour." His gaze tracked past Jack to the crew. "Don't need a full complement. Your crew can practice on the ground."

"Yes, sir." Jack hesitated. "Sorry, sir."

"Took you long enough." Without another word, the Colonel strode impatiently away.

Jack turned to his crew and Mel, waiting by a jeep. Two of the guys were playing craps in the meager shelter the jeep offered them, while the rest watched. Jack knew some of them would be making side bets on the players. He joined them, feeling a bit awkward after his exchange with Ric.

They all looked up at him, and then started to get up. He shook his head. "Finish your game." He leaned against the jeep and almost reached for a cigarette until he remembered. Lours offered one of his, but Jack shook his head. Only then did he allow himself to glance casually at Mel. He hadn't spoken to her, except to exchange greetings before take off. "So, ma'am, what did you think of your first flight?"

Mel appeared to consider. She pulled off the cap and ruffled her hair carelessly. She shook her head slowly. She sighed once, and then said in a kind of sexy drawl, "Dang."

Jack was surprised into a chuckle. The wind swept through her hair, ruffling it even more. Her face was scrubbed clean and the color in her cheeks was clearly from the cold. She didn't even have lipstick on, he realized. What was even more amazing, she didn't appear to mind. She seemed happy to be as nature made her and why shouldn't she? Nature had done a fine job.

"Are we going up again, Jack?" Ram asked, holding the dice

lightly.

"Just Ric and I. Colonel wants you all to practice your stuff, though." Jack looked at Mel. "You should probably get some instruction in bailing out."

He could tell she was thinking about this and wondered why.

"I already know how to bail," she finally admitted.

What reporter gets that kind of training? Nothing about her seemed to add up to a sum he recognized. Nor could he see what possible end game she might have. What was the point of going on a dangerous mission with them? The Colonel had assured him that she wasn't there to expose or spy on them. She was just to observe. He was used to collecting data and being able to organize it neatly, but even taking into account she was a woman—and therefore resistant to neat cataloging—there was something just...wrong about her.

"Do I have a smut on my nose, Captain?" Mel asked, with a meekness Jack suspected was assumed. There was nothing meek in the purple depths of her eyes.

"Your nose...is fine, ma'am," Jack said. "I'm going to go eat. Unlike the rest of you, I have to go up again." *And possibly again.*

Gaby produced the jeep's keys, but Jack shook his head. "I'll walk. Need to stretch my legs."

"Mind if I join you, Captain?" Mel asked.

He should mind, but he didn't. Even with the guys watching him, clearly amused, he didn't mind. He shook his head. He started to turn and stopped.

"You should all eat." He looked up. Felt the chill of someone walking across his grave. "I have a feeling we'll soon be going out again."

To his relief, Mel didn't talk as they walked down the flight line toward the mess. The wind was steady and cold, but not so stiff they couldn't fly. As they walked, the ground under them rumbled as the next group took off for their practice run.

He watched the Group rise into the air and had that feeling again. Some of the guys had claimed they felt it coming, that they knew when they wouldn't be coming back. Evidence suggested they were right, but did they cause it because they felt it? Or did they feel it because it was true? Either way, he didn't want Mel there.

"Mel, please don't fly with...us," Jack said. "Wait for the next mission. Or go with someone else."

Mel was quiet for several paces.

"Jack, you have to do your duty and I have to do mine. Please believe me, please trust me when I say, it's important I be on your plane to—when you fly again."

He hadn't missed that small hesitation or the correction.

"What if we get shot down?" Or worse, he wanted to add.

"I know you don't believe me, but I can take care of myself."

Jack had the feeling she'd meant to say more, but stopped her self. It wasn't his imagination. She was hiding something or holding back. The Colonel had assured him she wasn't a threat to their Group, but her so-called mission was a joke—or a smoke screen for something else. But what? What could she possibly need to do that was worth risking her life for? It was like trying to see through a London fog. Everything kept shifting and changing. He'd think he saw something and then it was gone again. So why did he feel like he should know? She was giving off clues, if only he could assemble them into something recognizable and logical.

It wasn't hard to figure out what the interrupted word should be. To—morrow. She believed they would be flying tomorrow. It was a good guess, but it was almost as if she weren't guessing. It sounded as if she...knew. But that wasn't possible.

When you rule out the possible, you're left with the impossible.

He'd heard that somewhere. What was the possible? She could be a reporter. She could have some hidden mission that made sense to someone. She had inside info on the upcoming mission. Okay, if she were getting it from Command, why? Someone high level had gotten her on his Fort, but again he came back to, why? What possible purpose could it serve to put a reporter, if she was a reporter, on his plane and send her over Europe with them?

And even if she did have inside information, even Command didn't know they'd be flying tomorrow. Until they left the ground, no mission was a sure thing. So, did she know, or did she know? Just what question was he asking? And did he really want to know the answer to that question?

"Are you all right?" Mel's voice broke into his thoughts.

It was a welcome interruption. He felt...uneasy with the direction his thoughts were—or was it his instinct that was—trying to take him?

Jack gave himself a shake. "I'm fine." He sounded curt. He hesitated. "If you could, would you tell me why you're doing this?"

Mel's whole body seemed to hesitate. "Yes."

She looked at him. There was an odd look in her eyes as she met his gaze. There was nothing flirtatious about her or the situation, but Jack felt tension slowly begin to build between them again. There was a...connection...between them. He admitted it with some reluctance. His mind told him not to trust her, but his...instincts ignored reason and logic. He wasn't ready to admit that some other body part might be involved. In the midst of a war, what good did it do?

"Don't give up hope, Jack," Mel said, not looking at him now. "You're out manned, out gunned...out...almost everything, but the tide will turn."

"How do you know?" Jack watched her, but all he saw was the wind lifting the soft strands of her hair, then releasing them to brush against her skin.

She didn't speak for a moment. She stopped and turned back to the flight line. She shivered, shoving her hands deep into the pockets of her flight jacket.

"I know because of who and what you all are. You'd rather be home, but you're here, pitting your hope and determination against a war machine fueled by fear and Hitler's lust for power. It may take a while, but hope will prevail." She turned to face him and the wind whipped her hair off her face, leaving each line and curve completely exposed. "What you're doing here, it matters—" Her eyes filled with sadness. "—it matters more than...anything else you could be doing right now."

More than their lives, that's what she meant. "I...know."

Even as Jack felt the truth of her words isolate him and harden his resolve, he wondered what it was about it that seemed...odd. It was like trying to look through a lens that wouldn't focus. It wasn't the best analogy, when she stood there outlined and back lit by the pale winter sun straining for supremacy over the cloud cover. He was sharply aware of how the wind smelled, how cold the air was, and the warmth spreading from his gut because she was there. Because of her he wanted to live and he was probably going to die tomorrow. It was a...pity.

He turned from her and started walking again. He was tired of thinking, tired of feeling. He just wanted to get on with it.

MEL WAS GETTING some strange vibes from Jack. His gaze was seriously penetrating, while giving nothing away. She'd had him off balance, which gave her a bit of an edge, but the balance had shifted a bit, removing what edge she'd had in what was turning out to be a battle of wills? Or was it a battle of the sexes? Maybe anything else wasn't possible between a gal and guy and truth be told, she was enjoying striking sparks off Jack. Seeing him now, knowing the man he was to become...Mel pushed a piece of unidentified meat around the metal edges of her plate...dang.

Norm dropped into the seat next to her, and across from Jack, his bright gaze scanning each, before turning his attention to his food.

"What do we have here?" he asked, breaking the silence, to Mel's relief.

Mel loved a good romance novel, but sometimes she wondered about all those intense emotions. Why couldn't they just control themselves, she'd wondered? She was starting to understand both the intensity of attraction and the discomfort. And despite that, she kind of liked it. Way weird.

Mel smiled at him. She was finding she could enjoy this...dance with Jack, but didn't mind a break either.

"I think its mystery meat, with a side of anonymous veggies. This," she poked at something orange in one of the smaller dividers, "might be fruit, but if it is, I expect it's too humiliated to admit it." She looked at Norm. "I thought the fliers got the best food?"

Norm's eyes widened. "If this is the best...He grinned. "Dang."

Mel chuckled, looked at her food and sighed. "Yeah."

"You'll save me a dance tonight, won't you?" Norm's gaze flicked Jack's way, full of mischief. "All the guys want one, actually. I told them I'd put in our reservation."

"My feet just flinched, but consider them reserved."

"I guess Jack's already got the first one lined up?"

Mel shook her head slowly. "Actually, no. My dance card is wide open. I think he's afraid I'll step on his toes—or toss him on his tush."

"Is that true? Is the big, bad captain afraid of the little, bitty girl?" Norm asked.

Did Jack sigh? It was hardly flattering, but for some reason Mel wasn't offended.

"The Captain would very much like to reserve a...couple of dances with you ma'am, if that would be agreeable to you?"

"Should I give the big, bad captain two, whole dances, Norm?"

Norm pretended to think about it, as annoyance did a slow build in Jack's eyes.

"It would be an act of kindness, ma'am," he said, finally. "He needs the practice."

"Oh." Mel looked at Jack. "Despite a dissenting vote from my toes, I'll add you to my dance card, kind sir."

"Make sure you save the last dance for him, Mel," Norm said. "The slow ones are...safe."

"Are they?" she shook her head slowly. "Well, I'll save a later dance for him. If you get alerted, there won't be a last dance."

"Have you heard something?" Norm asked, turning serious.

Mel shook her head. "Just a feeling."

"Well, I hope you're right. I'm ready for something besides ground school and drills. Even getting shot at is starting to look good."

Mel met Jack's gaze across the table. He held it for a moment, and then pushed away from the table. "I've got to meet Ric for round two. If he doesn't get it together, we may not have a plane to be shot at."

"Not going up this time?" Norm asked.

Mel smiled. "I'm still waiting for my bones to quit vibrating from this morning. How do you do that without teeth guards?" Mel poked at the food. "Is that why the food is so...soggy? Because they know you all have to gum it?"

Norm laughed. "You kind of remind me of Elaine, my wife. I never know what she's going to say either."

Mel felt a secret delight at the thought of being like Gran. Gran had told her ways she was like Norm, but there wasn't anyone to compare her to Gran. Mel leaned her elbows on the gnarly table. "Tell me about her. How did you meet? When did you know she was the one?"

Mel had heard Gran's side of the story, read it in her autobiography, too, but she wanted a peek inside his head now.

Norm smiled ruefully. "I saw her before she saw me. She was sitting in front of me at the movies. I knew the seat she was in was broken, so I put my foot under it and tipped it forward just enough so that she kept sliding forward all through the movie. My foot finally got tired and I had to let it drop back. She realized it and oh, was she mad at me." He grinned at the memory. "Tore a strip off me and almost slapped my face when I asked her out."

Gran had left this part out of her story.

"And then?" Mel prompted him. When she got back she was so going to—Mel stopped the thought and examined it. She'd thought when, not if. Interesting.

"She started to leave, then turned and ordered me to pick her up at seven the next day. Said I owed her a movie."

Mel laughed. "She..." Mel pulled her self up. She'd almost let out something she shouldn't have. "She sounds spunky."

"Oh yeah. She's got spunk. In spades" He sobered. "She'll be all right."

"And she'll cry when you come home to her and never let you

leave her again."

Norm looked up. "Yeah, sure."

"Norm." Mel held his gaze. "You are going home. Believe it." She smiled. "I'll bet Elaine believes it."

Norm grinned. "She is that stubborn." He looked thoughtful. "It's odd..."

"What?"

He looked uncomfortable. "Nothing."

"I like you, too, Norm, as a...friend. I'm not threat to your Elaine, I promise."

He looked at her. "I know. It's just...different. Oh well." He grabbed his plate. "Ground school waits."

Mel watched him walk away, moving easily between the tables and people. She knew what he found strange. Gran used to say that blood spoke to blood. Perhaps their mutual blood was trying to talk. If he'd lived, what would she have called him? Gramps? Grandpa? Neither seemed quite right. Gran had done a great job raising her, but it would have been nice to have Norm there, too.

Someone blocked her view, taking the seat Norm had left. It was Ric.

"I suppose you think you're pretty smart?"

Mel thought of, and discarded, several replies before settling on a neutral, "Aren't you supposed to be airborne?"

"Oh, I'm going. A word of advice first. Don't mess with me. I make a bad enemy."

"You're a bad friend, too."

He jumped up, his fists clenched. Mel wasn't sure if it was a remnant of decency or his very real fear she could take him that kept him from hitting her.

"Just stay out of my way." He stalked off.

Dale Carnegie wouldn't be happy with her. She hadn't made a friend, though she might be able to make a case for influencing him— into a really pissy mood. She only hoped it wouldn't have an adverse affect on the time line she was supposed to be fixing.

Chapter Nine

MEL ALMOST DIDN'T wear the red dress, but one of the off-duty nurses, who was also going to the dance, persuaded her—not by words, but by her open envy. It was the only thing about Mel that had engendered envy in this time, she realized rather ruefully. Their barely disguised contempt for her hair, lack of make-up and clothes swept Mel back to the days of high school peer pressure. Mel couldn't help but feel some satisfaction about the dress envy. Judging by their clothes, her dress was fairly conservative in cut, but oh, the color. The war had turned the fashion world a bit drab, so it wasn't their fault, but...Mel smiled, she was just glad that for tonight she got to be the windshield and not the bug. And she wished she could see herself in a mirror. A pity there was only the warped and spotted mirror above the sink in the bathroom. In that, she looked like a speckled-faced, scarlet blob.

She wasn't used to feeling this separated from other women. She'd always played well with others. It wasn't just the surface stuff, it was her century and the way she looked at the world and interacted with it. And she hadn't even started walking on these heels yet. Or dancing. In this day and time, couples actually moved their feet. And they did twirly things while wearing pointy-toed, stiletto heels that were harder to walk in than stilts.

It was ironic. She could flip a man three times her size on his tush or kill him with her feet or hands, but she didn't know how to dance. She tried a couple of steps with the heels. Okay, how was she going to walk in these shoes, let alone dance? This could get really embarrassing.

She walked around the room until she was dizzy—and could do it without her ankles wobbling...noticeably. Though how they made her walk explained a great deal about why women walked the way they did in this time zone. They forced her hips into that side to side thing, whether they wanted to or not. Maybe that's where *the walk* started?

The covetous nurse poked her head in the room. "You coming, ma'am?"

Mel hid a grin. It was probably meant to make her feel old. At twenty-seven, she probably was old in their eyes—though technically she was younger than all of them. In fact, her age was in the negative digits at the moment, so if she decided to cry like a baby, she was perfectly justified. Mel quit hiding the grin.

"Sure." Mel slipped her vintage coat. It didn't go with her dress, but it was all she had, unless she wanted to wear her flight jacket, and she had no intention of freezing for fashion. She followed the nurse down the hall, glad the girl wasn't looking back at her. Running an obstacle course had been easier than these stupid shoes.

"You want to borrow some lipstick?" One of the other nurses asked her, looking doubtfully at her face.

"Thanks, but I think the dress is enough red for one night." It might have been better to blend into the background, but it was too late for that now—unless she wanted to further humiliate herself by turning tail and wobbling back the way she'd come.

The wind caught them in a cold embrace as they exited the building. With a touch of the smug, Mel noticed the wind wreaked havoc on their stylized hair-dos, despite an armored coating of hair spray. Jeeps were waiting for them, which caused further acts of aggression to be visited on their hair. Upon arrival at the senior officer's club, the disheveled nurses peeled off to the ladies' room to effect repairs and bond. Mel felt a bit bereft, knowing she wasn't welcome at the session. She'd learned the truly important female things in the ladies room and she could have used some pointers tonight. Oh well. She ran her hand through her hair, so that ruffling was in several directions and not just the one, and then looked around her.

The music was straight out of a thirties movie, or so it seemed to her. It was dreamy and smooth, with lots of orchestra and a bit of singing. It reminded her of some of the stuff Gran used to play while she worked on Norm's biography. She wondered if the tempo would pick up later. Her toe almost tapped, but her arches told her, don't even think about it. A cough called her attention to an NCO waiting to take her coat.

Mel's first reaction was to pull said coat tighter around her. Under the coat she could feel the dress hugging her curves like they hadn't been hugged for a long time. She'd worn swim suits and briefer clothes than this decade's fashion. So why did she feel more self-conscious?

She undid the buttons slowly, hoping for an air raid or something to save her. It was silly. She'd been on freaking television covered in mud and humiliation and jumped out of a plane at thirty thousand feet and wet her pants, even if it wasn't generally known. And here she was, afraid of a red dress and a dance with a bunch of horny fliers.

Okay, put that way, her fear actually made a lot of sense.

The last button separated from the hole. Mel pulled on one sleeve, then the other. The NCO grabbed the lapels and eased it back. The air felt chill as it hit her arms, bare to just below the elbows. Cool air took full advantage of the boat neckline, also seeking out any other exposed skin, setting off waves of goose bumps and shivers. Marilyn always smoothed her dress down, but Mel couldn't do it. It didn't come natural. She turned slowly, managing to face the NCO without falling on her face, and found him staring at her with what might have been a look of admiration slackening his jaw.

"Do I get a check or something?" Mel asked him, after a short pause.

He blinked twice. Finally he nodded. More seconds ticked by until he produced a check stub and handed it to her.

"Thanks." She took a deep, steadying breath and realized that didn't help his situation. But it was nice to know she could breathe. She was, she realized, used to being cute, but not...sexy. Maybe it was the heels? She felt taller and more...fragile. Actually, in one sense, she was fragile. If she fell off these heels, something would break and what price her mission then?

It didn't look like the NCO was going to move away from her, so Mel left him. There was only one way to do this shindig—she had to go in like she went out of the SEAL plane, with her chin up and her bravado flying—only minus the pants wetting part.

She followed the sound of the music and the smell of food and drink. Mel recalled from the dailies that this party was a mix of locals, nurses and military personnel. A good—though somewhat sedate—time had been had...would be had, she corrected herself, until the alert.

Colonel Wray saw her and indicated she should join him. He introduced her to his group. The mayor of a near by town gallantly asked her to dance. Mel smiled her assent and let him lead her out onto the floor, hoping she wouldn't be a blight to continued positive diplomatic relations—and that her superior height wouldn't be a problem in this partnership.

Mel quickly realized what it meant to be lead in a dance. It wasn't as hard as she'd thought. Her partner seemed to prefer stately progress to the energetic, perhaps because of his girth. He made gentle, British accented small talk and even twirled her once. When the music ended, Mel felt a cautious optimism. She thanked him demurely and turned, hoping for a break. But behind her back a line had formed. The only up side, the presence of the dignitaries seemed to be keeping the music well inside the sedate zone.

An eager lieutenant stepped forward, his hand reaching for hers.

"I'm not sure—" Mel began. She never got to tell him what she wasn't sure about. It was her last, semi-coherent, albeit incomplete, sentence until the band took a break. Now she thanked her partner and tried not to limp toward the refreshments. Norm intercepted her with a glass of punch. Mel took the cup and drained it. "More," she croaked.

"We thought you might say that," Ram said, handing her two more.

Mel drained those, too. As she lowered her arm, Norm caught it, turning the wrist up and exposing her Uncle Sam.

"What's that?" He looked surprised. Nice girls probably didn't have tattoos in this decade.

"It's a temporary tat," Mel said, hoping it would at least partially restore her niceness.

"Tat?" Ram looked less than enlightened. "What's a temporary tat?"

"Tattoo. A temporary tattoo. It's already faded quite a bit from when I applied it."

"Oh." Norm appeared to ponder this. "I've never heard of that. Where did you get it?"

"From...a box of breakfast cereal. It's just a piece of waxy paper with ink in the pattern and you rub it on..." If they bought that one, they'd be easy targets for a Brooklyn Bridge salesman. And if they asked her what brand cereal, she'd be in huge trouble, because she didn't know what brands were available here and now. A distraction seemed in order. "Do you think anyone would notice if I took off my shoes?"

Mel looked at the other women, some with shoes that looked higher and pointier than hers. If their feet hurt, they weren't showing it. How did they manage it? It was interesting studying them. Some of them looked more like tableau participants, than moving, breathing people. Mel mentally compared the scene to the cocktail parties of her time. No surprise that there were significant differences. For one thing, their postures were better. Mel straightened her back and put one hand on her hip, trying to duplicate the standard issue provocative stance. She raised her glass to shoulder height and lifted her chin, giving her hair a sort of toss. It wasn't quite right. Maybe a little more arch to the back...okay, that hurt. And it was unnatural.

"What are you doing, ma'am?" Norm asked. He sounded amused.

Mel looked at him. "Oh...just some...research."

Ram and Norm turned to look at the object of Mel's study. The young woman was a pretty little thing, so it probably wasn't that painful for them.

"What is it you are...researching, ma'am?" Ram asked. He sounded amused.

"Body language." Mel rubbed the small of her back. "But I think I'll stop. I don't think this body was meant to speak hers."

Ram's gaze swept her, down and then up. "I don't see why you feel the need, ma'am. Your...language is just fine."

Mel chuckled, but before she could respond, Ric popped up at her side, his arm snaked around the cinched in waist of a pretty, young nurse. His looked at Mel, then to either side of her.

"Jack stand you up?" His voice had a slight slur to it. Clearly he had access to more than the resolutely bland punch.

Mel sighed. "If we were dating," Mel used her fingers to make quotes in the air. "—I'd probably be upset, but we're not dating. I'm not even sure we're friends yet." She enunciated slowly and carefully, as if he were stupid, which she kind of thought he was, actually.

Ric gave an unconvincing laugh. "What's your beef with me anyway?" His gaze did an insolent survey of Mel's assets. "Did I forget we...spent some time together?"

The nurse pressed against him tittered, the sound both silly and painfully high pitched.

Mel tried to look bored, but she had a feeling her eye twitched. "Well, I know you're completely forgettable, but I doubt we spent any time together. You're just a boy. I prefer my men to, well, be men."

It took him a minute to sort through this. He scowled. Mel wasn't sure who looked more put out, him or his nurse. She leaned close to the girl. "And just so you know, honey, if he didn't care what I thought, he wouldn't be standing here trying to taunt me. Think about it."

She did. So did Ric. Her tiny back straightened. She pushed Ric away. "Well!" She stalked off, her incredibly high heels hitting the floor like infuriated mallets.

"How does she do that?" Mel muttered.

"What?" Norm's voice was thick with unexpressed laughter.

"The heels. It's like they aren't even there."

"You have a real thing about shoes, don't you?" Ram said.

"Until you've walked a mile in these shoes, you're not entitled to comment," Mel said, softening the words with a grin.

Ric glared at Mel, then turned and followed his date. "Cissy! Baby!"

"Got 'em both," Ram said, admiringly. "Good shooting, ma'am."

"I try to be an equal opportunity offender, whenever possible," Mel said and got blank looks from both of them. It made for a tough room, when all her jokes were time sensitive. She looked around. "So..."

And then she saw Jack. He was wearing his dress uniform and...dang. She actually felt a bit light-headed and her heart was pounding like it was going to jump out of her chest and flop at his feet. She was sort of aware that both Norm and Ram were deriving considerable amusement from her predicament, but this didn't help her get over it.

"He's pretty, ain't he?" Norm said, provocatively.

Enough to eat, she thought, but was wise enough not to share. Jack had that look in his eyes again, the one that said he was still trying to figure her out. He didn't know how much she wished she could help him. She shivered slightly as the chill of her isolation from the here, from the friendly camaraderie surrounding, swept over her. She was out of her time. It was a fact. And there was nothing she could do that would close the distance between her and Jack. Not here and not in the future. It just wasn't meant to be. If she kept repeating this, maybe she could quit hankering for something she couldn't have.

More than anything she wanted to go back to her room and hide as much of her head as would fit under her lame excuse for a pillow. She looked at her dead man's watch. Ten o'clock. In an hour the alert would come. The party would be over. Boy, would it be over.

Jack joined them as the band made warming up sounds indicating their break was concluding. Mel flexed her toes, which had curled in her shoes, and not just from pain.

"My dance, I think," Jack said, holding out his hand. They were playing Norm and Gran's "song" Faithful Forever.

Mel eyed his attractive digits for a moment, before taking his hand. His fingers closed warmly over hers, pulling her back into the moment. It was an illusion, but she didn't care. Even her feet seemed resigned to their fate as his other hand settled lightly on her waist. She hoped he didn't feel the slight shiver that spread out from the spot, before dancing lightly down her spine.

Jack was a good, though conservative dancer, something Mel was grateful for. The words of the song slipped into her brain, mingling with her longing for Jack to have faith in her, as they moved slowly around a small portion of the floor in silence. Jack didn't talk and Mel didn't know what to say. Around them, like leaves in a whirlwind, chatter rose in waves. It was bright and brittle and brave.

Someone tapped Jack's shoulder, separating them. Mel saw him dancing with some of the local women, some nurses, slowly working his way toward her as the clock ticked closer and closer to eleven, when they'd all turn into pumpkins.

In a brief pause between songs, Mel found herself thinking about one of her favorite songs, *I Will Remember You.* Just like the song, the past wasn't letting her choose. And though he'd given her light he couldn't give her love. She hoped he would remember. She hoped she'd remember. Someone should.

As *I'll Never Love Again* started, Jack waited for her. She was grateful for his steadying hand, even though he was the one making her knees wobbly. Luckily her ankles wobbled opposite her knees, giving the impression she was steady on her pins.

She glanced at her watch as Jack once again took her in his arms. The last dance. The music felt like it kept time with the clock and their steps got slower and slower and slower until Jack paused as an aide approached the Colonel. He signaled for the music to stop, but Jack already knew. He looked down at Mel.

"We're being alerted."

Mel nodded.

"Party's over."

"Yes."

"You could still change your mind."

Mel looked at him without answering.

"I've been wondering what mission you could have worth risking your life for and I just can't come up with anything that makes any sense."

"No?" Mel looked at him. There was a look on his face she hadn't seen before.

"When you rule out the possible..." He hesitated for a moment. "When were you born, Mel? What year?"

Mel's eyes widened. Did he actually suspect she was a time traveler? "Excuse me?" Panic could easily be mistaken for outrage, thank goodness, providing stall time while she tried to do the math. And she'd always had trouble with one's and seven's. Forty-one minus twenty-seven? That was almost thirty years, which would put it in the teen's, wouldn't it? Nineteen-fourteen?

"You told Ric you were twenty-seven. So that would make you born in..."

"Nineteen...fourteen." She tried to look confident. Why did her super memory have trouble with simple adding and subtracting? "I was born in nineteen-fourteen." Jeeze-Louise that seemed old. She might be older than her own grandmother. She knew she was older than Norm, even though technically she was actually about forty years younger. She hadn't done the math on that either, mostly because she didn't want to know. "What year were you born?"

He didn't hesitate. He didn't have to. "Nineteen-sixteen."

"So I'm older than you." Even she could do that math. "Is that a problem for you?"

"No. That's not my problem."

Mel stared at him, debating the wisdom of asking the obvious, when she already knew, but Colonel Wray rescued her.

"Sorry to break things up, Captain, but you are both flying in the morning."

Jack stepped back. "Yes, sir."

The colonel looked at Mel. "My aide is standing by to drive you back to your quarters, young lady."

Mel looked in the direction he'd indicated and saw the young man standing nervously at the door, cap in hand.

"Oh."

"Try not to break him," the Colonel said, giving a grimace that might have been a smile.

"Sir, if I might have one minute—" Jack began.

"I'll just say goodnight and let you have your minute, sir and sir." Mel smiled blandly at Jack. She started away from them and realized her feet had had it. She bent and slipped off her shoes, picked them up and started forward again. Her feet flattened out against the floor. They cramped a bit, resisting straightening as vigorously as they'd resisted the heels, but it was still an improvement. Each step got easier. Maybe her walk wasn't as sexy or hippy, but at least it was almost her walk again.

Mel collected her coat and headed outside. The cold tarmac felt wonderful against the soles of her aching feet. She stopped, letting the cold do its healing thing.

"The jeep is this way, ma'am," her escort said, bashfully.

Mel handed him the shoes. "Get rid of them, would you?"

"Yes, ma'am." He tried to salute, but couldn't with a shoe in each hand. Finally he pointed toward the jeep with one of the shoes.

The cold was starting to get intense, so Mel legged it to the jeep, hopping in and pulling her legs up under the coat for warmth—though careful to make sure she didn't semi-moon anyone in the process. Her escort looked at the shoes uncertainly. Mel took pity on him, retrieved them...and tossed them over her shoulder. There was a sort of exclamation and she looked back. Jack was holding one. And a proper Prince Charming, he looked, too. As they pulled away, Mel didn't face forward until he was lost in the blackout darkness of the night. She sighed. She'd never wanted to be Cinderella... until now.

IF YOU TAKE away the possible...

He'd never met any woman like Mel, but that was hardly the scientific proof he'd need to believe she was from...somewhere else. There was one other possibility he hadn't considered. What if he hadn't been as cagey as he thought he was? What if Mel were part of an elaborate joke dreamed up by his ever loving crew?

It wasn't that he couldn't believe Mel was a...time traveler. Jack's brain wrapped reluctantly around this thought. If he really believed in time travel, then it was reasonable to expect his future self to send someone back in time. What wasn't reasonable was to believe that he'd send a woman to do it. The world couldn't have changed that much.

But even if he assumed the world had changed, and he had chosen Mel, then why didn't she tell him? And what if he had a good reason for her not to tell him about himself? He gave himself a slight shake. It was making his head ache to think about it. He had to face a hard truth. Maybe the only reason he wanted to believe Mel was out of her time was it would mean he survived—which made his conclusions highly suspect by reason of bias. He rubbed his face and sighed. And it didn't mean that tomorrow was going to go well.

Earlier he'd wished they could get on with the job, but now he wished for more time.

"Do you think we'll actually go this time?" Norm asked.

Jack lifted his head. The sky above had cleared enough to give glimpses of the distant stars. "Yeah, we're going."

As he and Norm walked toward their quarters, Jack was quiet, his mind worrying at the puzzle that was Mel.One moment it seemed logical to wonder how far back in time she'd come from and the next to wonder if he should ground him self and ask to be committed. What really was his evidence? She walked and talked a bit different. A few almost slips of the tongue and eyes that seemed to know things about him and others. What he knew wouldn't stand up in court—or mean any thing in a lab. It was the illogical that made it seem...logical to believe the impossible. Her so-called mission was the biggest incongruity. If the plan was something his future self had cooked up...would cook up...then he was crazy—or he would be. And if it was a joke? They'd be sorry.

"You all right, Jack?" Norm's voice broke into his confused thoughts.

It was actually a relief to be pulled out of the mental morass.

"I'm fine, Norm. Get some rest."

Norm nodded, and left him, his footsteps fading into the deep darkness.

"You going to tell me what's eating you?" Ric asked, pushing away from a wall in the shadows and tossing away his cigarette.

Jack sighed. It would be easier to smooth things over. He was tired. They had to fly in the morning. "Do we have to do this tonight? We've been alerted."

"We're friends, Jack. Why you letting that..." He hesitated. "...reporter mess up our friendship? Women come and go, Jack, but friends..." He hesitated again and then looped an arm around Jack's shoulder. "Best friends, Jack. Right?"

Jack eased Ric's arm off his shoulder. "Down here, we're friends, Ric." It was a compromise. If they made it back tomorrow, he'd talk the colonel about changing Ric out of their crew. "Up there, we're officers with a job to do." He grabbed Ric's shoulders, frustrated at the wasted potential that was Ric. "This is serious. Figure it out before you get us all killed."

Jack stepped back, facing Ric, hoping for something, though he wasn't sure what, when it was clear Ric had had a few tonight.

"You've changed, Jack." It wasn't a compliment.

"And you haven't changed enough. Go to bed."

Jack turned away from him, striding quickly off into the dark. He couldn't face their shared quarters until he was sure Ric was out. The night was cold, the sky clearer than it had been for a long time. There were people around. He could hear murmured conversations and footsteps crunching softly as the camp shut down. Soft laughter, doors shutting, the firing of a motor car in the distance as the locals headed home, but with the black out, he was essentially alone. He couldn't see them and they couldn't see him.

He wanted a smoke bad. He wanted to talk to Mel. But what would he say? Are you from the future? Did I send you here? Why? Why would I do that? Why would I send you? Or are you a joke and couldn't you call it off now that we're, well, almost friends? Only a joke didn't explain how she had Washington level approval to fly with them. Unless the joke was an add-on and separate from that?

He really hated to think she would be party to a cheap joke. She couldn't know how much it mattered to him, but he still felt she should. Not fair, but no one said he had to be fair in his thoughts.

The night gave him back no answers or solutions, or if it did, he wasn't hearing anything but the wind moving across the base, stirring things unseen to creak or groan. Slowly he made his way to *The Time Machine*. He leaned against the fuselage. It was crazy to be out. It was cold, he was tired and he had to fly in a few hours. But he didn't move, just huddled deeper in his coat, his hands dug into the pockets looking for warmth they wouldn't find.

Slowly he realized the footsteps crunching softly against the tarmac were coming closer, not moving away. After a while, he saw a shadowy figure. Whoever it was, they were huddled in a coat in much the same way as Jack. He didn't move, hoping whoever it was wouldn't see him there. They stopped up by the nose and he knew, he didn't know how, that it was Mel.

"What are you doing out here?"

She didn't seem surprised either. "I couldn't sleep." She walked along the side of the plane until she was close enough that they could sort of see each other.

"Nervous about tomorrow?"

"About flying into enemy territory and getting shot at? Well, yeah."

Her tone made him smile. "No one would think less of you if you changed your mind."

A pause. "I would." He heard her sigh. "I double dared myself. I hate it when I do that."

Jack sensed a story—or several. "Sounds like you should stop."

"That's the plan—after this one."

This sounded more and more like a set-up. Jack felt...disappointed when he should be relieved. A joke meant he wasn't crazy.

She stamped her feet. "You're freaking crazy to be out here in the cold, Jack. Jeeze."

"If I'm crazy to be out here, what does that make you?"

"I thought we'd already established that I'm freaking crazy."

"If I had any doubts, you've managed to erase them." Jack could hear the smile in her voice. He couldn't help asking, "Freaking?"

"Fricking? Frigging? They're all less...objectionable than the original."

"I guess they are." He should ask her where she picked them up, but he wished he could do it where he could see her face, see her eyes. The silence stretched out, oddly companionable as he tried to decide if he really wanted to know. Maybe it was better not to know.

"Now what's your problem?"

She did have an uncanny knack for mind-reading. But since she asked...

"Did the guys put you up to this? What I can't figure out is how you persuaded the Colonel to let you fly? Unless that wasn't part of the joke? You're just pulling my chain as an extra thrill?" The questions came out more hostile than he'd planned.

She was quiet for a moment. He felt her surprise.

"Joke? I think I missed a beat somewhere?"

Jack hesitated. If she wouldn't come clean, was he prepared to admit that he'd considered her a time traveler—even if not that seriously?

"I think you know what I mean. Or are you going to try to convince me that you've never met any of my crew before?"

"I have the...odd feeling that no matter what I say, you won't believe me." He thought she sighed, but it might have been the wind. "I wish..."

Mel straightened now, turning fully to face him. He could feel her gaze on him, but the darkness and her bulky clothes, defeated his efforts to see her eyes. The silence seemed to stretch long, but oddly enough, it wasn't uncomfortable. He'd vented and felt better, no matter what she said now.

"What do you wish?" His voice was low and he wondered if she could hear him.

"I wish that you could...trust me. I wish you could know that I'm not your enemy. They're out there somewhere, but tonight, you're with a...friend."

It wasn't about trust, he wanted to tell her, well, maybe it was. He didn't know anymore. Like her he just wished...for something more.

"I expect it will be a rough one tomorrow."

He didn't want to, but he accepted the change of subject. He didn't blame her for the distance in her voice either, since he hadn't responded.

"Yeah." He was quiet for a moment. "We should turn in."

Mel nodded. "Jack, would you do something for me?"

"If I can." He felt his gut tighten.

"Tomorrow...just don't...worry about me. I know it's probably against your programming, but your crew, your mission has to come first. I'll be fine. My Gran used to say I'm luckier than I deserve to be."

It seemed straightforward, but there was just enough ambiguity to make him wonder if she knew...something. She sounded so sure.

"I don't have much choice about that, Mel," he finally said. He hoped her Gran was right. They could all use a bit of that luck. "You should turn in."

"So should you."

"Yeah."

"The mission or Ric?"

"What?" Jack frowned.

"That's keeping you out here. Because he's probably sleeping it off by now."

"You're not a fortune teller, are you?" He was only half joking. It was another impossible option—and actually made as much sense as time travel.

Mel giggled. There was no doubt about it. It was a giggle. No other word for it.

"What's the joke?"

"Did anyone tell you that you're kind of paranoid?"

"And you weren't spanked enough as a child." Jack realized he was grinning, possibly like an idiot. Thank goodness it was dark. "I'll walk you back to your quarters."

"Yes, sir!" She didn't salute that he could see, but it was implicit in her tone.

She turned and walked quietly beside him, but her essence...giggled all the way. He could feel it. He wanted to spank her. He wanted to kiss her. He was careful not to touch her. Outside her quarters, she stopped.

"Thank you for the...safe passage, sir." Her voice was provocatively demure.

He pushed back another spanking urge and then almost choked on it when she placed a hand lightly on his chest, stood up on her toes and gently brushed her lips across his cheek, leaving a streak of warm on his chilled skin. He wanted to grab her and hold on. He didn't.

"Good night, Jack."

"Good night, Mel."

He didn't wait for her light to come on this time. He already had some to take away with him.

Chapter Ten

December 20, 1942

IT WAS OFFICIALLY morning, though dawn was still hovering below the horizon. The darkness was deep, but not as unrelenting as the cold, because dark would be pushed out by light—which is why it was called daylight bombing. Inside the veil of pre-dawn darkness, the base was alive with activity in preparation for the mission. Mel lay in her unfriendly bed, listening to distant, discordant sounds as planes were readied for the upcoming mission. Out there somewhere bombs were being armed and then trundled towards bomb bays. Some of them would have to-the-point messages to Hitler scrawled on the sides before loading. Soon the pilots and co-pilots would be shaken awake for breakfast prior to the briefing. Maybe they were already awake?

Mel lay there for a while, hoping sleep would win out over cold reality and the knot of fear in her stomach, but no such luck. She tensed before flipping back the blankets. Her flesh tried to shrink away from the cold and failed miserably. There was no escape. She scrambled into her shoes and then scampered down the hall to a loo that wasn't as primitive as it could have been, but wasn't as great as she would have liked. The shower was lukewarm and so, after more miserable scampering, this time to the mess, was her breakfast.

Her stomach didn't want food, but she made herself eat a slice of toast. It helped to settle her stomach, as did the inevitable tea. She went easy on the liquids, though. Bathroom facilities were nonexistent in the air—for girls. Men, curse their sorry hides, could go anywhere they could point. Everyone around her was still sleepy and quiet. They didn't know that the mission would be a go. Too many times this month, they'd sat in their planes to the point of annoying before standing down. Why should they worry about something that might not happen?

She fingered the roll of film from her camera, tucked snugly into a pocket. In the last time line, she'd given it to Jack, but Jack had been in on everything. It felt wrong to carry it with her to France. She looked around and spotted Norm. He saw her and waved, waiting for her to join him.

"I was wondering if I could store my film in your foot locker. I don't have anything that locks." Mel knew it would be sent to Gran when Norm was reported missing. It would be safe there and Norm was happy to help her out. When he opened the lid, Mel was swept back to her childhood and Gran, who'd showed her the contents many times, as she helped her granddaughter get to know her grandfather. Maybe someday she'd see her photographs in that album and remember this time spent with honest to goodness heroes—and her grandfather. Maybe.

If anything could give her the incentive to get on that plane, it was standing by that locker looking at Gran's face smiling at her out of the frame of the photograph above Norm's cot. She couldn't fail. She just couldn't.

"Thanks, Norm."

The briefing had started just before 0445 hours. Mel would have liked to have been one of those who had to attend, even though she knew the drill as well as they did. It would have been interesting to see it live, though.

In her mind's eye, she saw them grouped in the crowded hut, getting their target: Romilly-Sur-Seine, an air depot outside Paris that they'd tried to get to on the seventeenth. Next, the group intelligence officer would brief them on any intelligence they'd managed to collect. This would be followed by a weather report, which would be followed by the formation lineup. This was chalked on a blackboard. Who would be high, who would be low, and who got the lucky and more protected center. The lights would go down and using an epidiascope, they'd study a reflection of the aerial maps of their primary and backup targets on the wall.

While the briefing continued inside, outside, trucks and jeeps collected, waiting to transport the men to their planes. To escape the tension coiling in her gut, Mel slipped outside, where the pre-flight growl of the engines was louder. The ground under her feet rumbled because of it, and the passage of large trucks. No one appeared to notice her as they went about their appointed tasks. She was a spectator, not a participant.

The process wasn't as smooth as it would become, but it was still amazing to see. These boys, because they were still boys, all knew their jobs and did them pretty well. She felt awed and privileged to see them—even as she wished she were anywhere but here, heading anywhere but where she was heading. One of the songs from last night started to play in her head. *I'll be seeing you in all the old familiar places...*

Would she see Jack like that? Jack had said that no one really knew how time paradoxes worked, which was why they were called paradoxes. She wished she'd gotten a picture with just her and Jack, though, to remember him by. She saw him emerge from the briefing hut and her heart clutched. He deserved to be remembered.

The men joked and talked as they filtered out of the briefing in Jack's wake. Was it because they didn't yet know how bad it was going to be? Or just the natural resilience of youth? As if they had a sixth sense for it, the rest of the crew appeared and the groups began piling onto and into anything moved. It was a long walk to the dispersal areas, Mel knew, having done it a couple of times now. And if she felt any inclination to walk, she had only to remind herself that she'd get plenty of exercise in France.

They didn't have to jockey for transport, though. Because of Mel, Jack's crew had a semi-reserved truck to take them out to *The Time Machine*. There was room in the truck for more than their crew and it didn't take long for the leftover space to fill up. With the sky barely beginning to lighten in the east, she felt almost invisible as she waited for the truck to move out. The winter sun was slow to appear. It had good reason. What fun was it to light up a world at war?

Mel wished she'd looked at her watch when she had the chance. They were due to leave around ten. The lucky ones would return a bit before three this afternoon. Suddenly the bleak base seemed very dear and almost beautiful. She didn't want to leave it. Actually, she wanted to cling to it and cry like a baby. This stiff upper lip stuff wasn't all that great—though in her current situation, she wasn't sure anyone would hear her whimper or cry uncle.

Crammed against Jack on one side and Norm on the other, with a crewman huddled on the floor between her feet, and the roar of the truck all around her, Mel could barely hear herself think. With a jerk they were in motion. Sort of. Either the huge tires were square or the road was rougher than it looked. Maybe it was a good thing to be packed in so tightly as they bounced slowly in what she assumed was a forward direction. The faces around her were still indistinct in the murky light, which was probably a good thing, since she knew which of them would die today...or later.

She was intensely aware of Jack pressed hard against her side. She'd tried sorting through what he'd said, and not said, last night, but she still wasn't sure what he suspected and what he didn't. Nothing added up to a good reason to take him into her confidence, which left her still isolated and still alone. And actually a bit grumpy about it. She'd never been great in the morning and this wasn't a great morning.

The truck stopped with an extended lurch that snapped her neck one direction, then another. Everyone scrambled out into the gathering dawn. Jack jumped out ahead of her, before turning to help her down. This marked her as different and a pool of silence formed, getting wider and deeper as she followed Jack and his crew to where *The Time Machine* waited.

In that silence, Mel joined the crew in donning the heavy flying clothes that were supposed to help them cope with the extreme cold, but mostly didn't. She'd cheated a bit and felt guilty about it, but not enough to take off the thermal underwear and Thinsulate socks she'd smuggled into the past with her. It wasn't like they helped her with the fear generated chill, she pointed out to the guilt, and it mostly subsided. Over her electrically heated flying suit, she added her parachute and life vest. She was tempted to bag the life vest, since she knew they weren't facing a ditching in the Channel, but it would have looked odd. She collected her portable oxygen tank and found herself a spot out of the wind whipping across the dispersal area.

Why is it that the wind always seemed to blow at airports, she wondered, mostly to keep from thinking about what came next. The crew was unusually silent as they formed a circle around Jack for their briefing and pep talk.

All of them were young and, with their faces pinched with the cold, looked it, but not one of them looked nervous. Even Ric just looked bored as Jack outlined their objectives and went over ditching procedures once more.

"And guys," Jack finished up, "please keep the chat down over the intercom. Let's keep our focus, get this done and get home, because—"

"Bramwell's got a date," everyone, but Ric chanted.

Ric grinned. "Well, yeah."

Mel had to admit to minor respect for Ric. He looked cool and unconcerned. Was it bravery or just cluelessness? If things went as badly as they were supposed to, she was going to find out.

She huddled inside her flight clothes as the wind tugged at her from every direction, trying to find any opening it could burrow into. On the positive side, it did sweep away the acrid scent of sweat and fuel that hung around the assembly point.

The pep talk over, everyone did a token dispersal for a last pee. Mel found a spot to do her business in the thinning darkness off to the side, hoping no one saw her pale *moon* rising. She didn't enjoy it much with the wind stinging past her bare tush—and it made it harder to pee. Her sphincters clearly didn't know when something was for their own good.

As she walked back to the Fort, she was struck again by its sheer size. Their sortie today would be relatively small. In the next few years, thousands of these monsters would fly over Europe before the war would end. As Churchill had pointed out at the end of the Battle of Britain, this wasn't the beginning of end, or even the end of the beginning, but it was the start of something amazing...and tragic.

Jack, Ric, Ram and, the navigator, Hal Larsen, climbed in through a front hatch. She'd read that some pilots preferred the rear hatch to the nose cone. They didn't like navigating the claustrophobic tunnel that led to the upper flight deck, but clearly Jack wasn't one of them. Each man reached up, swung his feet up and in, then arched the rest of their body inside. Larsen, the last man in that way, handed up their gear, and clambered inside.

Mel followed the rest of the crew to the rear hatch. The Fort might look enormous, it might even be enormous on the outside, but the inside was cramped and hostile to the human body. No one had thought to insulate it for high altitude flying. After the waist guns were readied and the windows opened, the temperature inside the plane quickly dropped as low as fifty below zero. They were all outfitted with electrically heated suits, but they didn't always work. Frost-bite was a big problem, almost as big a problem as bullet holes—though getting frozen was still better than getting shot out of the air.

Lours Kennedy turned right and crawled down the narrow rear end of the Fort, and over the rear wheel well, to his position as tail gunner, dragging his gear with him. It was a lousy position and somewhat isolated from the rest of the crew. Sometimes the tail gunners would pass out from a lack of oxygen, if the oxygen lines clogged or froze up, and would die before anyone realized it. And if that weren't bad enough, there was also the problem of basically being in the Fort's tush, a favorite target of fighter pilots, second only to the nose cone.

No adult person stood upright in a Fort except the top gunner and that wasn't exactly a blessing, since it involved shooting and being shot at—and no sitting. That was Bennie Heavener's position, just across the bomb bay. The waist gunners, Harry and Roy, had to stand half-bent, with the freezing wind blowing in, to fire their weapons. But even they agreed ball turret gunner, Fitz's position was the worse, hands down, no argument.

Statistically, it had proved to be the worst, too. The small, spinning space didn't allow for a parachute and Fitz spent the flight with his knees up by his ears. If the plane got in trouble, he had to get out of the hatch and don his parachute. It was tough to do one of those things when a plane was spinning earthward, let alone both of them. Centrifugal force was a bear. The ball was also exposed, hanging down from the belly of the Fort like, well—Mel figured it hadn't got its name just because it was round.

No matter where they were headed, they all had to crouch or crawl to get there. Mel chose a hybrid of both as she followed Norm to the radio room, positioned rear side of the bomb bay. Compared to everyone else, it wasn't a bad spot, if one didn't think too much about how easy it was for bullets to penetrate the sides. Norm had a chair and even a smaller gun he could fire when needed. There was a small, uncomfortable chair across from him where Mel planted her tush. She could fit her legs in between it and wall—just, but how could a guy manage it? Had any one of the designers of this craft had one thought for the real men who had to use it? Had any normal sized person actually sat in any of the positions before it went into mass production?

The two waist gunners started preparing their guns and Mel, if she looked across the bomb bay, could see Ben working on his gun, too. He was also the flight engineer. It was his job to make sure the plane stayed in the air long enough to drop their bombs and make it home. From his top position, he had the best view of anyone, including the pilots. He could see forward and aft and often directed fire during battle.

In the radio room, Norm quickly donned his head phones and began alternately listening and chatting, as Jack and Ric, up in the cockpit, went through their pre-flight routines. Ram and Hal Larson would be setting up for business in their plastic bubble in the nose cone of the Fort. They had a great view, but it wasn't exactly a bennie either, since that view usually included diving FW's. The Ram had been lobbying for a nose gun of some sort. He didn't like being a sitting duck up there with no way to fight back. Mel could have told him that cheek guns were coming, but it wouldn't help Ram or Hal. For this mission, *The Time Machine* had been assigned to the much more dangerous outside edge of the combat square and the outside edge of the total formation, where the covering fire wasn't as good.

Jack was right about the smell inside the Fort. It was almost as stinky as cigarettes. The acrid *aroma* of fresh sweat mingled with that of old sweat, the old gun powder, new fuel and cold metal. It wouldn't be warm inside the plane until summer, so Mel found her spot to plug in her suit and connect to the intercom. Then she checked her oxygen flow. Both seemed to be in working order. She also had portable oxygen, in case she had to move around. That was pretty much all she needed to do before take-off.

She fidgeted restlessly. The tiny seat wasn't particularly comfortable, but it was better than most of the other positions. She wouldn't have minded sitting in as co-pilot, but she hadn't told anyone she could. And even if she had, well, something hot would probably have to freeze over twice before anyone let her fly a plane.

The fuel had been topped off and now, one by one, the engines started, creating a slowly building vibration in every part of the plane. Her body remembered this part and starting sending protests to her brain. Mel rubbed her temples and wished she were in a galaxy far, far away.

She should have gone straight to bed last night, instead of chatting with Jack. It's not like she'd been sleeping all that well since she arrived in the past. Tiredness tugged at the edges of her mind, stealing concentration and starting the tendrils of a headache inside her head, not helped by sitting on a vibrating metal stool. This was a bad time to be off her game. Assuming it was possible to be on her game in this place and time.

She recognized what she was feeling. It was a regular feature in her gigs, the moment just before stubborn kicked in, when morose ruled. It was a hazy, miserable place. All she could think about was getting out, getting away. This was the place where she wanted to cry uncle. It was a real bummer that she didn't even have the option. She was much better at overcoming adversity when she had a choice. That's when stubborn kicked started. What if it couldn't or wouldn't this time? What if she stayed in this...this...daze of misery and yes, self pity? What chance the mission then?

Mel kept waiting for her mental whining to hit rock bottom, but before she did, the engine rotations increased, coincidentally increasing the misery factor. Mel cranked her neck to a position where she could see out the window, as the big Fort turned off the dispersal hard stands and onto the taxi way that circled the main runway.

She felt a touch on her shoulder and turned around. Norm was looking at her with a frown of worry pulling his somewhat shaggy brows together.

"Are you all right?" His mouth shaped words she hadn't a hope of hearing off the intercom.

There were a lot of things she would have told him, if she could have shared them at a volume less than shouting. I'm not all right. I'm scared to my toenails. I want my Gran. But as she looked into his steady gaze, she felt her lips curving into something that might have been a smile. Her head nodded. And stubborn started to stir in her gut. Her shoulders hadn't drooped. The chair wouldn't let her droop, but she felt stiffening flow into her spine again.

She managed to bend her hand into a sort of thumbs up. When his gaze left her, she said for her ears only, "Hoo yah."

She almost laughed. Who knew that not leaping out of a plane would be the hard thing? Perspective really was everything.

"Ma'am?" It was Jack's voice over the intercom. "You can come forward and look out the top turret if you'd like."

"Cool." It was a relief to get off the vibrating stool, though standing on the vibrating floor wasn't a whole lot better, particularly with the plane in lumbering motion. She unplugged herself from the intercom, leaving her oxygen tank behind. They wouldn't start the serious climb until they reached the coast.

Through the hatch to the cockpit, Mel could see the narrow ramp across the bomb bay. The monster bombs filled the space on either side of the extremely narrow metal walkway. Dang, it was narrow. Has she mentioned it was narrow? It mattered because below were the bomb bay doors. If she slipped and fell, they wouldn't catch her. They were designed to open if anything over one hundred pounds hit them, in case a bomb shook loose during flight. She was definitely more than that, though she declined to do the mental math to figure just how far more. She might be a glutton for punishment, but she didn't have to veer over into masochism.

It was particularly unnerving to contemplate that ramp with the plane randomly bouncing along the runway. She took a deep breath and stepped into a spot between the massive, five hundred pound bombs. On one someone had scrawled an obscene message for Hitler. If all went as planned, he'd get it.

Bennie was waiting for her with a big grin creasing his freckled face, his legs braced against the unwieldy movements of the plane. The plane hit a bump, throwing her against him and the grin widened. Mel righted her self, but didn't hurry. No reason to be stingy.

Behind him she could see Jack and Ric at the controls, the nose of the Fort stretching out ahead of them. Through the wind screen, she caught a glimpse a few other B-17s in the Group. They were sending up seventeen planes today, but two would fall out of the formation before they joined up with the other groups from other bases. Mel eased into Bennie's position and straightened up into the cramped space, grabbing the gun for leverage. Ben plugged her into the intercom, so she could listen.

She turned around, catching her breath at the sight of the first planes beginning their take off from the main runway. On the ground, the Fort was a clumsy beast, ungainly and hard to maneuver, but they achieved a sort of grace as the air seemed to catch them in its embrace and help them rise.

The whine of the engines got louder as they began their turn. The Fort began to pick up speed. The bouncing and vibration got worse. She tried to look forward and look back, tried to see it all. The Fort's rear wheels lifted off first, then pulled the nose of the plane up. The plane seemed to hesitate, grabbed hold of the currents, and rose slowly into the air. The checkerboard English countryside fell away behind them, its colors dimmed by the winter season, but not erased. Thirty seconds behind them, the next Fort took off, following them into the wild, blue yonder. It was almost exactly ten-fifteen.

Looking past the tail, the base looked smaller and smaller. Already it felt colder inside the plane, and they weren't anywhere near battle altitude. Was that really her hands wrapped about the gun handles? Surely it couldn't be her feet weren't braced against this shuddering ascension? She leaned forward until her head touched the cold metal of Ben's machine gun. The enormity of what she needed to do, compressed her lungs, it dragged her whole body, her whole soul down. She'd messed things up, even if technically she hadn't actually messed anything yet. Oh, those time paradoxes.

"Hoo yah," she said it again, silently, defiantly, but inside her head it sounded a lot like "uncle." With a sigh, she crouched down, unplugged, mouthed a silent thank you to Ben, and traded places with him. To her left, she could see Jack at the controls, Ric next to him, taking them on the last flight of *The Time Machine*. For her, there was only one direction she could go, only one way to go to get out of this. At the moment, going forward meant going back...to the radio room.

She climbed back down to the bomb bay ramp. Her feet on it, she stopped for one last look back at the cockpit, but the plane hit an air pocket, lifting her feet briefly off the ramp. When she landed, she couldn't get back into the radio room, and her hard, cold stool, fast enough. Those romantic looks back played a lot better on the screen than in real life.

The Fort banked, rising slowly, but steadily, the engines pulling the plane through the gradually thinning air. Gravity didn't like losing. Mel could feel it fighting to hang on. She recognized it. It was how she felt about Jack.

Dawn had made its appearance a couple of hours ago, but it wasn't a dazzling entrance. The winter light was cool and thin, as if aware it was a limited engagement. England was spread out below them, stamped into quaint, irregular patterns. Wisps of clouds flowed past the window like strands of furtive cotton. It was cold and getting colder. She was really glad for the SEAL underwear, though she felt obliged to feel a bit guilty about it.

She'd heard that the flights were periods of boredom broken by sheer terror. They were in the boring part and would be until they were feet dry over France. She twisted around until she was semi-comfortable again and closed her eyes, trying to relax. In a few hours she would be on the ground in hostile territory. It would be wise to rest while she had the chance.

Chapter Eleven

English Channel

MEL JERKED AWAKE, startled by the sound of gunfire. For a moment, she thought she was back with the SEALs and then she saw Norm. His mouth moved, but she couldn't hear him. Had she gone deaf? He pointed to her suit and then held up his intercom cord. Right. She'd forgotten to plug in after her trip across the bomb bay. Not deaf yet, though the Fort's engines were making serious inroads in that direction. She corrected the omission and found herself in the 1940's equivalent of the chat room. The waist gunners fired again, sending silver tracers to dance along the surface of the water.

"They're test firing the guns," Norm said. "We're over the Channel."

"Feet wet," Mel said, wondering why she felt surprised. She knew they were heading this way, but, dang...feet wet over the English Channel. Occupied France dead...straight ahead.

"Feet what?" someone asked.

The various voices sounded different over the intercom and Mel hadn't had time to sort them out.

"It's just an expression for leaving land and being over water." She really needed to think before she spoke. And maybe count to ten. Or one hundred. "You know, feet wet and then...feet dry when you're over land again."

Silence as ten men processed this.

"Is there one for feet dry with flak?" someone finally said. Mel thought it might be Ben. He was quick on the humor.

"Feet...fried?" Mel proffered. This earned her what sounded like a universal laugh.

"Well, it won't be long for that, so check your oxygen. We're going up."

Mel put her mask on and inhaled. So far it was still working. The rest of the crew checked in, giving her a chance to put voices with names.

Even though they were still over the channel and had Spitfires escorting them, she could feel the tension inside the plane beginning to build as they approached the French coast. It was, she discovered, catching. Her stomach tightened and she glad there was only toast and tea in there. Anything else would have been packing attitude—or worse, unpacking itself. There were so many ways to be embarrassed in this decade. The Greatest Generation should all be in therapy instead of Florida.

She peered out the window. The sky above them was a clean, clear, insipid blue. Ahead, pale gold stabbed at the horizon, peeking through the fitful cloud cover screening the coast from view. It was an oddly hopeful sight, in the circumstances.

"Holy freaking cow." She forgot she could be heard through the intercom.

There was sort of a collective chuckle in varying degrees of deep. She peeked over her shoulder at Norm. He was fiddling with his dials, a bit of a grin curling up his mouth. Her grandfather. How she wanted to tell him who she was. A pity he wouldn't believe her. She was living it and she didn't believe it.

She looked back, toward England, noting the white contrails from the engines being painted across the sky behind them. They were an amazing sight, but dangerous. Might as well hang up a *here we are* sign for the Luftwaffe. Mel pressed her nose against the window, trying to see below them, but her exhale fogged it over. She drew a smiley face with her finger, feeling like a bored child instead of an intrepid adventurer.

She could feel the Fort continuing its battle with gravity as it climbed toward combat altitude. She couldn't see it, but she could feel the coast grow closer and closer. It was like being slowly lowered into ice as the temperature dropped. The cloud cover intensified, too, now giving her only the occasional glimpse of the green and brown and gray.

"Almost feet dry," she said, as much to herself as the crew. Just a guess, but an educated one, that this was the part where the sheer terror phase began. Outside the Spitfires bird dogging them, waggled their wings for good luck, then peeled off and headed back to England. Mel knew a plane couldn't look relieved, but...

Through the hatch opening, she could see Roy Smith and Harry Morrison scanning the sky through the waist gunner openings. The wind howled through those windows, swirling around her feet and lifting dirt off the floor in eddies. Norm fiddled with his dials and suddenly Mel heard French music.

"Feet fry coming up," Ram said, his voice punctuated by a

muffled explosion. Ahead tell-tale puffs of white marked the flak line as the first of the Forts crossed the coastline. The puffs looked harmless, but they weren't. The shells were propelled to a pre-set altitude where they exploded, sending metal splinters in all directions. The shrapnel were essentially needles with the Forts playing the role of pin cushions. There was no way to defend against flak. They went in and hoped they came out the other side—where the Focke Wulf's waited for their shot—literally—at the incoming bombers.

There was no question about when they made feet fry. From hearing the flak explode, now she felt it and heard it. The concussions turned the air currents into rough seas to cross. The Fort lurched and bounced across shock waves. Mel flew up. And then came down—onto the floor with a bone rattling thump. Well, she had a new hobby, courtesy of this mission: collecting bruises.

The noise was freaking unbelievable. It was not only all around, it felt like it was inside her. She scrambled back into her seat, this time managing to hang on. It didn't stop her bouncing, or wrenching effect on her shoulders, but at least it kept flight to a bare minimum. At first all the explosions were below them, but then the batteries got their altitude. That was not a good thing. In what seemed like slow motion, a flak shell rose off their left side, rising to a height just above the Fort. Mel just had time to duck and brace for it. First there was the bang. This was followed almost immediately by multiple thumps against the side of the Fort. It rocked violently, almost tearing her fingers free of their grip.

"We've been hit!" Harry shouted.

Mel lifted her head up from the protective, kissing-my-tush-good-by position and peered out the window. Immediately she wished she hadn't. There was a freaking huge hole in the wing. That mother was at least a foot across, the sides of it bent out like the petals of a metal flower. She knew that was nothing to the sturdy fortress, but it was still disturbing, particularly when she was looking at it through another hole in the skin—at about the height her head had been. Norm. He'd been seriously injured on their way to the target. She slowly turned toward him...

...and found him clasping an arm welling deep, red blood. While distinctly disturbing, it didn't look life threatening. She grabbed the first aid kit. "Are you hurt anywhere else?"

"Who's hurt?" Jack asked sharply.

"Norm." She spoke tersely as she rummaged through the kit until she found some disinfectant and bandages. She thought about offering the standard, this might hurt, but there wasn't any *might* about it. She opened and poured. As it stung into the wound, she got a glimpse of the extent of it.

"It's just a graze." She heard surprise in her voice and hoped no one else had. Jack hadn't mentioned an early wound in the briefing, she thought, uneasily. She bandaged it decently, thanks to her stint on search and rescue, while her thoughts sped out in crazy tangents. Things were pretty crazy now...and Jack's memories were sixty years old...but he hadn't mentioned the hole in the wing either...

"I'm hit!" Another scared voice on the intercom. It was Kennedy in the Fort's tush.

Norm started to get up, but Mel stopped him with a sharp shake of her head. "You're needed here. I'm just excess baggage. Let me go." Norm looked dubious, but Mel ignored him, quickly repacking the kit. At least it was something useful to do. Cringing might feel useful, but it wasn't.

"Go where?" Jack asked sharply. Mel ignored him.

She switched to her portable oxygen and unplugged from the intercom. The silence was, well, deafening, but she missed the connection to the crew. Once she was sure the oxygen was working—by not passing out—she headed for the rear, grabbing whatever she could find to keep from being tossed on her tush. It didn't always work. More bruises for the collection. Finally she gave walking up as a bad job and started crawling. It wasn't great for the knees, but her tush was happier.

Outside the hatch door, the ball turret was spinning slowly. Fitz had the best, or possibly worst, seat in the house for this show. He could look down and see the flak coming up at them. At least he seemed to be all right. She edged past, a sudden lurch almost throwing her onto the top of it. She managed to halt mid-fling and reach the other side, only to face another obstacle.

It was the narrow, icy part of the fuselage where the waist gunners waited tensely, bent awkwardly over their guns. Here there was no protection at all from noise or from the wind—or flying shrapnel for that matter. The only way to get past them was by crawling, so she did, alternately dragging and shoving her oxygen and the first aid kit. They'd be out of the flak screen soon. She wanted to be out of the tail before then. She'd have felt silly if it all weren't so freaking serious. Still on her hands and knees she made her way along the narrow trough that ran down the floor toward the wheel well. Each explosion would lift her off the floor and then drop her down again. Gravity didn't like losing its grip for more than a second or two. It was lucky her knees were numb with cold. She could see Kennedy on the other side of the wheel well, but couldn't tell how badly he was injured.

The rumble of the engines crawled up the floor through her body. It was actually reassuring, though not comfortable. The rear wheel was folded up in to the well, stolidly in her way. There was clearance, but not a lot. She worked her way half around, and half over it, both helped and hindered in this by the bouncing and rocking. As she passed over the top, she looked straight down to the ground twenty thousand feet below.

"Holy freaking crap."

She tumbled onto the other side, helped by another lurch, landing at Kennedy's feet. He was holding his upper leg as blood flowed over his hands and dripped onto the floor. There was enough of it splashed around to make the tail section suitable for inclusion in a freaking horror movie. But it wasn't pumping out between his fingers. That was a good sign. It hadn't hit an artery. At least she didn't think so.

Working as fast as her shaking hands would let her, she dug through the kit again. Over Kennedy's shoulder, she was looking right down his gun sight. It was a bit unnerving. Wrap, wrap. Boom. Boom. Tape, tape. Life flash before her eyes...several times. Repent for some of it, okay a lot of it. Pray, pray. Make promises. Make lots of promises. Even some she could keep.

With a final lurch, the Fort cleared the flak screen. As if it had been waiting for this moment, she saw an FW burst out of the clouds, high and to the right. It appeared to be diving right at her.

JACK DIDN'T HAVE time to worry about what Mel was doing. It took all he had to keep the plane semi-level and in formation as they were buffeted by the exploding flak. It was black and thick enough to walk across, with some of the tracers were coming up red, purple and green. He felt like a duck in a carnival shooting gallery as shrapnel pelted the plane. There were reports of holes and hits from almost every crew member. Something struck the window in front of Ric, cracking out from the point of impact until it ran into the frame. A shell rose up right in front of them. For three, long heart beats he stared at it, before it fell out of his view again. Amazingly, it didn't explode. It felt like forever, but it was only about six, very long minutes, that flak buffeted the plane, and then they were through it—flying right into the waiting guns of the FW's. Queued up like school girls, they dove at the formation, peeling off in separate directions. Two picked them out for special attention, raking bullets down each side.

His were ears full of crew chatter and the sound of their guns firing back. Someone yelled he'd got one, but Jack couldn't tell who. He tried to ask about Mel, but the noise level was insane. No one was misusing the system, so he couldn't complain.

Out of the chatter he heard Ben yell, "Kennedy, you got one coming right at you!"

It sounded like Kennedy cursed, but Jack wasn't sure.

"What's happening back there?" he yelled. He couldn't spare a glance at Ric. "Check on it, will you, Ric?" Check on her, he didn't say, but that's what he meant, though he wondered why he bothered. Right now, it didn't seem possible any of them could survive.

MEL SAW KENNEDY'S eyes widen. Maybe someone on the intercom had warned him about the incoming. He made a move, as if to turn around, but there wasn't time or space for it. Mel pushed his head down and partially sprawled across his body as she grabbed for the gun handles. She swung the sight up until it was over the FW. She didn't close her eyes, but she wanted to. She pulled the trigger. Big mistake. Her whole body jolted like Raggedy Ann being shaken by a two year old. Bullets tracked out the end. The track was a bit erratic. It felt like forever. It took two beats of her heart. The FW passed out of sight and she had no idea if she'd even grazed it.

She heard firing below and to the side. She scrambled off Kennedy. He lifted his head. They both patted themselves down, looking for holes. Gave each other brief, relieved smiles. His eyes widened again. He made it around this time and grabbed his gun handles. He was just in time.

Mel dove for the floor. Spent shells casings pelted her head and shoulders. At least that's what she hoped it was. The sound of bullets leaving the barrel filled the small space, using up all available sound waves. Inside the oxygen mask, she could smell her own fear. It wasn't pretty. The firing stopped. It started again. It wasn't going to stop any time soon. She had to get out of here.

Mel lifted her head cautiously. Kennedy had his back to her. His shoulders bunched. Tracers tracked out from his gun. Stopping. Starting. Like a bizarre dance. When another FW started to dive toward the tail, discretion seemed the better part of valor. She backed as quickly as she could dragging oxygen and kit, mostly by instinct. It was too soon for it to be a habit. Adrenaline helped. She didn't stop to sightsee over the wheel well and actually, didn't remember crossing it.

On the other side, Harry and Roy were still crouched over their guns, alternately firing and looking for something to fire at. Harry had the worst of it. He was on the side that was on the outside edge of the formation. Spent shells rolled around the floor, some with wisps of steam drifting off them as hot metal and cold air met for a brief dance. Mel glanced up, half expecting a weather system to form. No clouds, but the Fort appeared to have picked up a few more holes while she was in the tail. She could see sky and bits of the Fort above them.

Across the ball turret, Ric half crouched, gripping both sides of the radio room hatch. If he had a question for Mel, there was no way for her to know what it was. Clearly future Jack hadn't known as much about what had gone on during the flight as he'd indicated. There were as many information holes in her briefing as in the plane.

Roy scrambled to get his gun around, giving her glimpse of sky and a nearby Fort, flying high and to their right. It took a hit. Jumped and rocked violently from the impact. Dark smoke flowed from two engines on one side. The wing fell off. It shuddered again, and turned in a slow, horrifying cartwheel toward them.

Was this how they went down? Mel grabbed something and got to her knees. From the tiny window of the hatch door, she saw some parachutes bloom in the air around the tumbling Fort, but not enough. Not nearly enough. The falling Fort exploded. Their Fort rocked violently.

She sank back on her knees and closed her eyes. She didn't want to see anymore. But she'd already seen too much. The scene played over and over against her closed lids. There was a yell, jolting her out of the visual causality loop.

Harry was on his knees. There was blood spurted and spurting around on the floor by him. Lots of it. She could smell it, sickly and sweet, despite the roar if air coming in the openings. She could almost taste it. She couldn't tell the source. He staggered up to fire at an oncoming FW, but quickly sagged to his knees again, when the momentary danger was past. Mel looked at Ric. He didn't move, just stared at Harry, his eyes wide and shocked above his oxygen mask.

This was the guy who was going to take a bullet for Jack? Mel crawled over to Harry. Shells whistled past her head. She shoved the first aid kit at him, pushed him aside and gripped the gun triggers. Adrenaline helped bring her to the semi-upright position she needed. She braced her feet and pulled on the trigger. Short, sharp bursts. Don't use up all the ammo. She could hear the guys' voices inside her head, talking about battle in the future as it played out in front of her eyes now. Her shoulders protested this new round of abuse. She ignored them and the other unhappy parts of her body. At least there was a consensus.

If the Forts were a canopy of approaching carnage, the FWs were swarms of angry bees. They spun and dived, spitting angry fire in short, stinging bursts. One headed toward her. She fired a short burst. It kept coming. Mel braced for the collision. At the last moment it pulled up, exposing its belly. Mel fired into it. Heard the top turret pick up where she left off. After a moment, she saw it tumble back, spewing black smoke. She might have cheered. No figure came out. No parachute appeared. Someone had just died, possibly with her help, but he wasn't real to her. He didn't have a face like the men around her. Someone else would have to mourn his loss. There wasn't really time to think or feel anything. There was barely time to act.

She'd read about this in accounts from the time, this severing of emotion in the midst of heavy action, but it still sort of surprised her to feel it, too as she did what had to be done.

She wasn't plugged into the intercom, so she couldn't hear the chatter of the battle, only the sound of gunfire, either leaving the plane or heading for it. Her ears quickly learned to tell what position was firing. This helped her know where to look for trouble. Even so she had to scan the sky, back and forth, up and down. Keep firing as they took fire.

Spent shell casings littered the floor. She slipped on them as she moved, trying to keep her side of the sky covered. The plane bounced and jerked. Somehow she managed to stay on her feet. She didn't know how.

There was almost a rhythm to the way the firing moved around the plane. Waist, ball, top, tail, back to waist, back to her. Norm's forty cal sounded slightly different as it entered the mix. The firing sounded continuous. It wasn't. Thank goodness. Her whole body shook with the effort of keeping her end up. She swung around, tracking an incoming. Almost slipped and fell. Gave a short burst. The FW veered off.

Someone grabbed her. Harry was on his feet again. He'd managed to roughly bandage his leg. She gave way for him, felt pain flare up in her shoulders as adrenaline faded. She scrambled to the other side of the ball turret and looked at her watch.

Norm. It was almost time for his injury...

RIC CLIMBED BACK in his seat. Jack didn't look at him. There wasn't time. "Is she, is everyone all right?" Ric didn't answer. "Is Mel all right?"

"She's fine."

Something wasn't right, but Jack didn't have time to figure out what. It was time to start the bomb run. His hand hovered above the switch for the automatic bombardier correction instrument.

"Ram, you ready?"

"Ready."

"You have control. Take us in." Jack hated this moment, but it was also a relief. Now he could look at Ric. "What's going on back there?"

Ric didn't look at him. "Harry took a hit, but he's still on his feet."

Why did he sound so odd? "You sure you're all right?"

"I'm fine." He looked up. "Got one coming in on our nose!"

"I got it!" Ben yelled.

Jack heard the top turret gun open fire.

Ram was right. They needed some guns in the nose. He looked at Ric again. Something wasn't right.

"I'm going back to the radio room. Take charge here."

Ric didn't look at him. He just nodded.

MEL CRAWLED AROUND the spinning ball turret. Her legs were too shaky for walking. And her arms weren't doing that great either. Her muscles felt rubbery and almost fluid. She actually missed being busy. She took another quick look at her watch. Jack hadn't known exactly when Norm was injured, but he did know when they dumped him out, hoping the Germans would give him medical care. It was almost that time now.

She tumbled through the hatch, helped by a sudden course correction. She'd been "helped" to a lot of bruises in a very short time. Her collection might soon overwhelm any non-bruised skin. She landed at Norm's feet and looked up. He was still at his position. He made a move to help her, but she shook her head. She managed to get back into her seat on her own. It wasn't really a blessing. It felt like that moment in Jurassic Park when the car fell out of the tree on Sam Neill and the kid.

"We're back in the car," the kid had said. That's how she felt, like she'd come full circle without really getting anywhere.

She looked at her watch again and then gave it a shake. Was it still working? If it was broken, it wasn't completely, because she was still breathing. Even if it was wrong, how wrong could it be? No matter how she parsed it, Norm was late for his injury. And if that wasn't a freaking, weird thought, she didn't know what a freaking weird thought was.

She plugged back into the intercom and crew chatter exploded in her ears.

"Bandit at six o'clock!"

"Look out, got one coming in high and right!"

"Kennedy, watch it back there!"

And the calm voice of Ram, running through it. "Steady, steady. We're going in."

They'd started their bomb run, which meant they were going back into the flak zone again. Great.

"Jack?" Norm's voice broke into the battle chatter and Mel's thoughts.

She looked up and there was Jack, standing in the hatch. He looked tired. Actually everyone looked tired. She knew she felt tired, so she was probably part of "everyone."

"Are you all right?" He had to shout and she still almost didn't hear him.

She wasn't all right and never would be again, but she nodded. It was easier.

Jack's gaze punched into hers, but she was too tried to care. "What happened back here?"

Mel covered the microphone at her chin, not sure what he was asking her. "Kennedy got it in the leg, so did Harry. Different legs, I think. Norm was...grazed. Lots of...holes back there." She looked at one by her head. "And in here." She wondered if she sounded dazed. She felt dazed.

"You've got gun powder on your face."

She had a feeling he wouldn't like knowing she manned a gun...twice. "I played medic."

He looked...odd. "I've got to get back."

It wasn't a news flash. Why had he come back? What did he want?

"Stay..." He looked like he didn't know how to finish the sentence, but finally added, "... where you are."

Where did he think she could go, for freaking Pete's sake? Mel looked at her new window again and then back at him. "Okay."

He might have tried to grin at her. His eyes crinkled in a grinnish sort of way. He hesitated a moment, then turned away, scrambling across the ramp just as the doors opened beneath him. He didn't even look down. Mel didn't realize she was holding her breath until he made it and she exhaled explosively. This place wasn't for wimps. So what was she doing here? She didn't know it before, but she knew it now. She was definitely a wimp.

She looked at Norm, who was definitely a non-wimp, and as she did, time seemed to slow down. She felt fluid and almost formless, as if there were no more fixed points she could use to navigate this freakish reality. She'd lost her...mooring somehow.

What did it mean? Her body felt slow, too, as if only her mind were running at normal speed. She turned toward the hole. It seemed to take forever until she could look out. The wind streamed past her face. She didn't feel the cold. She knew there was air streaming past her face, but didn't feel it either.

Outside the FW's were falling back. Ahead the flak was waiting. Far, far below, she saw the first bombs from the lead groups hitting the ground. Flashes of orange, then smoke billowed up and out from the points of contact, growing and growing into darkly ominous clouds that obscured the ground below. Could she hear the explosions or did it just feel like she could? Their plane followed their squadron leader into the flak screen. This time the altitude was right on the mark. There was a sharp cry.

"Bennie's been hit." It was Ric on the intercom. "He's down."

"Mel?" The crackle of the intercom couldn't obscure the reluctance in Jack's voice. "Could you see...?"

"Sure." No problem. Just because their bomb bay doors were open and she was a total wimp, didn't mean she couldn't cross that ramp again. She did the unhook intercom, hook oxygen thing again. *Just don't think about it and whatever you do, don't look down.*

So what was the first thing she did? She looked down. She'd done some freaking stupid things in her short time on earth, but this was hands down, the stupidest.

"Uncle," she whispered, but the distant ground continued to pass beneath her. And if she didn't hurry, Ram would drop their bombs. She did not want to be in there then. She closed her eyes, realigned them higher and opened them again. Straight across the ramp, she could see Ben's crumpled figure.

She grabbed the sides. She stepped on the ramp. Another step, then grab the support. More steps, grab the wall, and she was across. She stepped over him. She didn't have to guts to crouch with her back to an open bomb bay.

He didn't move, but she could see blood pumping sluggishly from a wound in his chest. She pulled off a glove and found a thready pulse before the feeling in her hand started to go. She shoved her hand back in the glove. He was going into shock. She managed to unbuckle his parachute. Once it was free of his body, she eased his head down, and tucked the parachute under his feet to raise them above his head. It wasn't much, but it was something.

She took his hand and gripped it, trying to make him feel her grip through both layers of their gloves. To her surprise, he opened his eyes. Mel leaned forward, so he could see her, so he'd know he wasn't alone. His lips moved. She couldn't hear...she found an intercom plug and used it. His voice was hard to pick out of the other sounds.

"Not...going to make it..."

Mel hesitated, and then slowly shook her head.

She felt him struggle against inexorable death and without considering it, began to recite the twenty-third Psalm.

"The Lord is my Shepard; I shall not want..."

He managed a slight smile and crew chatter ceased. Slowly, very slowly he began to relax and before she was done, he was gone.

Only then could Mel consider the impact of his death on what she'd known of the time line. He'd died before, but he hadn't been the first.

"How is he?" In her ear, Jack sounded sharp and tired.

"He's gone." Mel eased her hands free of Ben's and closed his eyes. She felt old and tired as she struggled upright and made her way back to the radio room without even pausing to look down. She didn't sit down, but, after a pause to plug into the intercom again, she grabbed the sides of the hatch and stared at the ball turret spinning slowly in a circle, first left, and then right, the movements gentle because there was nothing to shoot at right now. Every few moments, she caught a glimpse of the top of Fitz's head, Fitz who should have been the first. Harry and Roy were still at their guns, but also scanning the sky as they all waited for bombs away. Kennedy seemed to be all right, too, though it was hard to be sure from here.

"He's dead?" Ric sounded flat and strained, like he was finally figuring out that this war was more than his personal dating game.

Again she had that sense of time slowing down. Unease prickled down her spine like melting ice. Mel gripped the sides of the hatch as the Fort lurched its way across the flak turbulent air. To her toes she could feel it. She'd changed the future all right, but not the way Jack had intended. It was fluid and...hidden. She didn't know anything anymore. She didn't know who would live and who would die. She didn't know when they'd get shot down. She didn't know where. She didn't even know if. She didn't know how.

She didn't know.

JACK COULDN'T DECIDE which was worse, FW's or flak. They both had their down side and no upside, except that you only got them one at a time. The down side of this flak screen was the need to keep in their bomb run until they delivered their eggs to the target, which made them an easier target, since they couldn't avoid problems coming at them.

"Bombs away," Ram said calmly, sounding almost bored.

The Fort shuddered, and the nose jinked up as the eggs tumbled free of the nest, and the Fort lost a lot of weight. Instinctively Jack made the needed adjustments to get the Fort back where it was supposed to be. Still following the leader, he made the wide turn away from the target area. Time to go home.

"Did we hit our target?" he asked.

"Ninety-nine percent sure we delivered the goods," Ram said. The intercom couldn't fuzz out the self-satisfaction.

At least Bennie hadn't died for nothing. He just hoped it was enough. Jack saw the edge of the flak screen just ahead. Shells still exploded around them. The lighter plane rocked and bounced across the disturbed air, handling differently now. He was tired, but his body produced just enough adrenaline to keep him at it, that and hope now that they could head back.

He heard Fitz shout something and tensed for a hit. He didn't tense enough. The heavy Fort felt like it took a hit from a giant tennis racket. It felt like they flew sideways and up at least a hundred feet. Crew chatter exploded in his ear.

"Ball hit! Ball hit!"

Even as he struggled to regain control, they took another one.

"Radio room—" The words were cut off as the intercom went dead.

"Anyone hurt?" Worry about the crew warred with worry about where they were in the sky. How far out of the formation were they? How close to other planes?

"Ric, where are we? Be my eyes!" He expected to see a Fort come through the windshield, but amazingly, they continued forward. They might have been alone in the sky. With a final shudder, they cleared the flak screen.

Chapter Twelve

MEL'S EARS RANG from the force and proximity of the explosion. She wasn't sure if she'd been thrown, or dived into the next compartment and landed on the top of the ball turret. There were new painful places, but they could be the result of her position. She tried out her arms, then her legs. They were unhappy, but still seemed to work. She thought about getting up, but her eyes felt like they were spinning in the sockets, since she was pretty sure the plane wasn't—at least she hoped it wasn't.

"Are you all right?" Norm's mouth formed the words she couldn't hear. The wind, howling through the new holes in the Fort, ripped his words away almost as he said them.

She tried to answer him, but the explosion had also knocked the wind out of her lungs. She nodded. It hurt, but at least her eyes had quit revolving. She started to get up and Norm jumped to help her. That's when she saw what was left of the radio station over his shoulder.

His Forty cal was a gone-pecan. The pieces of the radio that were still there were a tangle of wires and deformed, still smoking metal. How had he survived it? She looked him over. He had a new wound above his right eye and she thought she saw other rips in various places of his gear, but he was clearly better than what was left of his chair. He had to have moved before the explosion. It was the only explanation.

"We have to get to Fitz!" Norm shouted.

Mel nodded again. It took too much energy to shout. She added her strength to Norm's. If they could get the hatch turned up to where they could open it...

"The hydraulics are gone!" Now she had to shout. If they had a lever...or more help...but Harry and Roy needed to man their guns. They were already down two guns, three if you counted Norm's. Once they saw the smoke from the damaged engines, the FW's would be on them like wolves on a wounded deer, trying to cut them out of the herd.

Norm still struggled desperately to move the turret around.

"Is he still alive?" Norm didn't answer. "Norm!" She grabbed his arm. "Is he alive?"

Norm slumped slightly. "I don't know." For the first time, he looked around and saw what was left of his station. His face went white. She didn't have to tell him what he'd escaped. How many more hits, how many more holes could they get, and stay airborne?

Mel found a gap in the turret. "Fitz! Fitz!" He didn't move. His head sagged forward, but it was his chest that made her stomach lurch. Mel sat back. "It looks like his chest is gone." She looked at Norm. "I think he's gone."

"You're bleeding." Norm touched a spot above her eye. At least that is what she thought he did. She couldn't feel anything anymore.

"So are you." For a long moment they stared at each other, as sorrow was replaced with...puzzled.

"What's wrong?"

Before he could answer, the plane vibrated and lurched, not from a blast, though. It sounded more like engine trouble. Now Mel realized that she couldn't hear the crew. Did she forget to plug in again? She pulled on the line and realized it was still connected.

"I think the intercom is down."

No one was shooting at them. The flak was gone, but no FW's either. And why was she wondering what it meant instead of giving thanks for small mercies?

"I'm going to go to the cockpit. Jack needs to know what's going on." She hesitated. "Someone should check on Kennedy. He's cut off without an intercom." How long would the FW's hold off?

Norm nodded and started toward the tail, moving like an old man. She didn't like being separated from him, but she didn't know what else to do.

Mel forced her self to turn back to the radio room. It wasn't a pretty sight. The hole was big enough to fall through. Not fun with the plane still inclined to lurch unexpectedly, but there wasn't an alternate route. She identified hand holds, got on her knees and started across. A sudden jerk tumbled her toward the hole. She flailed about for several panicked heartbeats, and managed to grab the edge of the table, followed by the edge of the hatch. Inside the bomb bay, it seemed almost benign with out the bombs, though they'd found another use for one of the racks. Someone had lifted Ben there. His arm hung limply down, swinging slightly as she passed by him. At least they'd closed the doors.

She reached Ben's position, and tried not see the splashes of blood turning from red to brown. For some reason brown didn't reduce the gruesome level that much. Mel gave silent thanks for gloves and stepped forward, slipped and fell in it, smearing her clothes with the still damp blood. Above her, the turret was shattered, the gun gone. She could see straight up. Just off center was another plane in the formation. It looked like their ball turret was out of commission, too.

She could see the cockpit, but decided to check on Ram and Larsen first. They both gave her a quick thumbs up and she retreated, this time not stopping until she was crouched behind Jack. To his left, Ric sat staring straight ahead. There was something odd about his stillness, but Mel didn't have time to worry about him. Jack was still trying to raise them over the intercom. She thumped his shoulder.

"The intercom is out. So's the radio. Fitz is dead. Norm is checking on Kennedy. Harry and Roy were okay a few minutes ago. Ram and Larsen are fine, too." Which was a massive overstatement, actually. No one was fine. Not after their baptism by blood and fire. And it was just the beginning...well, it was supposed to be the beginning. What if they made it back to England? She shouldn't be so happy about that, but then, she really shouldn't be here.

"We've lost an engine and will probably lose another soon." Jack rubbed tiredly at his goggles. "We're going to fall out of the formation before long. We won't be able to keep up."

Mel eased forward until she was between the two men. She could see blood on Jack's clothes. So he'd helped moved Ben. Jack glanced briefly at her. She couldn't tell if or what he was thinking.

"If we could make feet wet," was that a brief smile over the term? "But once we fall behind..."

He didn't have to spell it out for her.

"When they see our turrets gone, the other guys will try to cover as long as they can, but if anyone stays with us, we'll just endanger them, too." He stared straight ahead. "You should have..."

Mel cut him off. "There's no time for that."

"Yeah, well..."

"Tell me what I can do to help."

"Keep your head down. Once we drop out—"

She looked at Ric. He'd been awfully quiet. He hadn't even looked at her. Oh well... she started to back out, she wanted to check on Norm...and then she saw it.

Blood. Fresh and red and dripping off the edge of his seat.

There was a first aid kit up here. Mel found it.

"Where are you hit?"

Ric slowly turned his head her direction, but didn't speak. Jack couldn't help. She felt his frustration, heard it, too, when he asked, "How bad is it?"

"I don't know." She bent down, trying to find where the blood trail began. After some probing, she found a spot low down on his back. She leaned around and found the place where it had gone in. This was way beyond the scope of a kit—or her.

"I can't feel my legs," Ric said. He didn't sound upset, just surprised.

"It's the cold," Mel said. "You're just cold."

"Cold," he repeated. He frowned. "Am I dying? I have a date tonight."

Mel wadded some bandaging together and shoved in to the hole in his back, then repeated this for the front. It wasn't much, but she wasn't a surgeon, which is what he needed. Was fate redressing some balance by giving Norm's injuries to Ric? What—or who—would be required in that moment when Ric was supposed to take a bullet for Jack?

"He needs medical care," Mel said. "He needs—"

"No." Ric straightened suddenly and it seemed the fog in his eyes cleared a bit. "No." A note of pleading entered his voice. "Don't write me off, Jack. Not yet." He tried to smile. It was a dismal failure. "I have a date." This time he sounded more like himself.

"Well," Mel tried to match his light tone, "we can't let her down then." She hesitated. "Are you in pain?"

Ric looked almost startled, and then pleased. "No. I'm not. That's good, right?"

"Yeah," Mel gave him the first real smile she'd ever given him. "That's real good, Ric."

His cocky grin was a shadow of its former glory. "I knew you couldn't resist me."

"No," Mel said, steadily, "I couldn't." Where Ric couldn't see, Mel reached out, found Jack's arm and gripped it. "No girl can resist you, Ric."

"That's right..." His voice and gaze blurred and again, and he closed his eyes. "Let me know when you need me, Jack. Team...player..."

It was all wrong, but she didn't care. She didn't have time to care. She leaned her head against Jack's shoulder and drew strength from the contact. It wasn't like falling apart was an available option, but that didn't stop her from wanting to. She lifted her head.

"I should check on the guys."

Jack managed a quick look and a nod. Worry had dug deep lines into his face, but his mouth was set in a firm line.

"Keep your head down, Mel."

"I will if you will." She leaned forward and lightly kissed a small, very cold bare spot, then turned and left him, clinging to one frail hope: so far no one had died who hadn't died before. It wasn't a happy thought to know she was on the list of those who didn't make it, but she wasn't supposed to be here, so that should help...somehow...she hoped...

She scrambled back the way she'd come, half ran across the ramp, not even looking down at the doors. There wasn't time to worry about anything but getting to Norm. In the radio room, he had the signal lamp out, letting the formation know their situation. It blinked and blinked. A lot of words when two would have done: we're toast.

"What can I do?"

"Look for bandits."

She nodded and chose a spot straddling the hatch between the radio room and the inert ball turret. She could see Harry and Roy tensely scanning the sky. Past them, just barely visible over the tucked up wheel, Kennedy was still in his spot. These were all good men and she was proud to be there with. Freaking scared, but so very proud.

She glanced at her watch. Jack didn't remember exactly what time they'd been shot down. He'd been too busy to look at his watch, but he knew when they landed in hostile territory. It was almost that time now. It looked like they were going to miss that appointment, too.

ON THE GROUND, the Oberleutnant lifted his binoculars and scanned the sky for chutes, theirs and American ones. Radio traffic claimed multiple hits, but so far the bombers were air borne and heading for the coast. *Herr* Oberst Thorhaus had sent patrols out as soon as the bombers passed through the flak batteries on the coast. It wasn't easy to cover so much ground where fliers could come down, but they would do their best. Eventually they would find them all. Any locals inclined to give aid and comfort would pay a heavy price, as they well knew. A few fools still tried. He relaxed for a moment, lowered the glasses and flexed his fingers. The cold made them stiff and awkward.

It seemed like one of the planes in the formation was lagging a bit. He lifted binoculars and scanned the sky again, but unheeded, unbothered, the formation flew on. He watched for a few more minutes, until he was sure, yes, it was definitely falling out of the formation. It looked like it might be losing altitude, as well. He called it in. He probably wouldn't be the only one, but *Herr* Oberst Thorhaus wouldn't fault them for the repetition. He did, however, dislike inattention.

THEY PASSED THE other time line's crash point with the FW's still

MIA. There was no question that they would go down, they were still too far from the coast to have a chance; the only question was when? With each moment the FW's didn't appear, it only made the tension worse. Mel felt it when they lost their second engine, felt the sputter and the slowing as their air speed was reduced. She couldn't see it, but she knew they would start falling out of the formation now. They were losing altitude, too. Jack was probably still hoping to make it to feet wet. Splashing down in the channel wasn't a get-out-of-German-hands card, but it did give them a chance of getting picked up by a sub or patrol boat if they didn't freeze to death first.

Every nerve in Mel's body was pulled tight, her senses stretched out past their normal limits as she waited for the next attack wave and wondered why it didn't come. Each minute that passed took them closer to the coast. Would fate try to stop them or could they cheat it? Had she so altered the time line that they had a chance of making it out of here? And if she did, what impact would it have on her family's time line if Norm had to go into battle again?

She didn't have answers—or the ability to do anything about any of it. If the future had changed, it seemed like she should remember the change, but she didn't. It seemed that Jack's theory that when time was in flux, a time traveler was buffered from the changes until the period of flux was over was true. That could be what was happening, though she didn't feel that buffered. What she felt was battered, actually.

Since no one could hear her thoughts but herself, Mel admitted that she wasn't averse to making it back to England. If being up here and getting shot at was this bad, how much worse would it be, down there being chased by an occupying force? She hadn't, she realized, really thought about what it would be like to be in hostile territory, hunted and hungry. And without access to a bathroom. Just thinking it made her realize she needed to pee. Jeeze-Louise, shouldn't it be frozen or scared dry? Weren't things bad enough without that?

Two engines down and still they flew toward the coast. She'd been so focused on the preliminary tasks of her mission and absorbing as much information as quickly as possible, she had run out of time to worry about the parachuting into Occupied France part. Now she had some time on her hands, she moved from uneasy to terrified without passing scared. It was bad enough that she had to do the jump, but now they would be jumping into the unknown. Jack hadn't just briefed her on their target area. She'd been briefed on all of Europe, but not with as much detail. She knew a lot about the underground, the friendlys and unfriendlys in the whole of France, but that would still require her to figure out where they were and who could help them. Or hurt them.

She hated feeling helpless. Surely there was something she could do? She needed a plan, a strategy...or at least a vain hope to focus on until the brown stuff hit the fan. She saw a dark speck emerge from a distant cloud and head toward them. A moving brown speck...

She surged to her feet. "Bandit! Bandit!" She pointed and yelled and saw the action ripple down the plane. The FW's were back.

THE EXCHANGE OF fire began again. Maybe it was getting shot at that rattled some thoughts free. Mel wasn't sure. She just suddenly realized there was one person on this plane who might know where they were, and where they were likely to be, if she could just get to him before he got shot. Mel scrambled forward and clambered down the narrow tunnel to the bombardier position. The first thing she saw was the Plexiglas bubble straight ahead—or what was left of it. Through the cracks and holes she could see an FW coming straight at them and not a thing she could do about it. It was like having a front row seat in hell.

Mel knew she should crawl back up the ladder. A pity her muscles and joints were frozen solid, her hands locked around the ladder. She could see the bright flashes from the FW's guns. She heard bullets hit the Fort, punching into the metal like the wrath of God. She saw bullets strike various spots inside the bubble, tracking steadily in her direction. She was wondering if it would hurt, when someone grabbed her arm and pulled her to the floor. Then the FW passed to their right, focusing on a different part of the ship.

She wanted to leave, but where could she go? While time was fluxing around her, there was no safe place on this plane for her or anyone else.

"We need to get out of here." It was Ram who'd pulled her down. Now he helped her up, urging her back up the tunnel with polite insistence. It was harder going up, than it had been coming down. The plane was shuddering like it had the flu. Her foot slipped on a rung and she almost fell. Ram steadied her and then she was back up on the flight deck, with Ram and Larsen crouched beside her.

"She's not going to stay up much longer," Ram shouted.

"How far are we from the coast?" Mel asked, looking at Larsen.

"Maybe half an hour."

Even as he spoke, there was a lurch and a noticeable slowing, as if a giant hand had grabbed the Fort and was trying to pull it out of the sky.

"We're going down." Larsen said the same way one might

comment on the color of the sky.

They all ducked down, as the FW's took them on again, two of them raking down both sides with obvious delight.

Mel scrambled forward until she was by Jack again. Now she could see dark smoke streaming from their failed engines. The Fort wobbled from side to side as the one engine strained to keep the heavy Fort in the air.

Ric was still conscious, but he looked bad. The pool of blood under his seat had grown larger while she was gone. Now she could see the formation flying steadily away from them.

"Tell everyone to start bailing," Jack managed to gasp out. Sweat poured down his face and then froze in thin strands. "I'll try to keep her level until everyone is out."

When a Fort started to spin in, the centrifugal force made it almost impossible to bail out. But if their gunners bailed, the Fort would be a sitting duck for the FW's.

Mel shouted the order to Ram and Larsen, but didn't move.

"Get going, that's an order."

Mel thought about pointing out she wasn't under his command, but she wasn't sure she could squeeze the words past the ball of fear in her throat. How could she explain to him that he had to stay with him and Ric, no matter what? Their fortunes were tied together, for good or ill.

"We could try for Spain," Ric managed to gasp out.

"We've got to bail, buddy. Mel, help him out of his seat—"

Ric shook his head almost violently. He looked at Mel for a moment and she was struck by the look of peace in his normally restless gaze. "I'm done for. We both know it. You get out. I'll keep her in the air. But...hurry."

An FW made a run at their nose. Bullets slammed into the fuselage on his side. He flinched, but held on. They were low enough now, that Jack ripped off his oxygen mask. Mel did, too, relieved to be free of it. At least getting shot down had one upside.

"Ric..." Jack began.

"There's no time" He half grinned. "Get out of here."

Jack started to object again.

"Go! I'm done for. Make me...a hero."

Mel grabbed his arm.

"Let him do this, Jack. He's earned it." Mel stared into his agonized gaze, trying to will him to understand when she didn't. "Let him go.

She must have succeeded, because he nodded and scrambled out of his seat. The plane wobbled wildly, until Ric managed to bring it back under tenuous control.

"Hurry."

Mel saw his blue lips shape the words and echoed them to Jack. But still he stopped for a moment, gripping Ric's shoulder, before silently moving past her, then pulling her toward the rear. The hatch past the waist gunners was the best spot for bailing, though there was also that big hole where the radio had been, as an exit of last resort.

Jack towed her across the bomb bay like it was a mile-wide path, but checked at the radio room. He looked back at her, his eyes wide and shocked. She shrugged, surprised she and Norm were still alive, too.

As they passed the gap, Mel saw parachutes bloom from those who had already bailed. One, two, three, four...there should have been six. Who wasn't there? They were halfway across the radio room when the engines cut out. The vibration just stopped.

"There's no time," Jack said. "We've got to go now."

Mel didn't want to leave without knowing who else was being left behind, but they'd run out of options. And time. This was it. Larsen suddenly stumbled around the ball turret.

"Everyone is out." He hesitated. "Kennedy didn't make it."

It was awful to be relieved, but he'd died before. It was his time.

Larsen dived out the more than man-sized hole. Soon after his parachute bloomed. Mel grabbed Jack's arm. "Wait to pull your rip cord. Maybe they'll think we're dead and not track us as closely." Jack's brows arched. She smiled. "It'll work."

He nodded sharply, and then steered her closer to the hole. She hesitated and the plane began to list to one side, the prelim to a spin. No time to think or feel or time to wet her pants.

"Hoo yah!" She dove through the hole, careful to aim low so her chute would clear the jagged metal petals around the edges.

She did a couple of cartwheels, then managed to assume the classic sky diving position. Now she could look for Jack. He was above her. She brought her arms to her side and shot up next to him, then assumed the position again.

Logic told her they were hurtling toward the ground but it felt like flying, not falling. And as they fell, *The Time Machine* cart-wheeled past them, spinning once, then again, before hitting the ground with stunning force, and exploding. It seemed that the smoke reached up towards them, before the wind whisked it sideways.

Jack looked grim. And worried. He signaled to pull and she shook her head sharply. The ground was closer now. She could see more detail. Off in the distance, the others had landed and were gathering in their chutes. She found her rip cord, her gaze bouncing between terra firma and Jack.

"Now!" She shouted.

She pulled her cord and felt the jerk as the parachute yanked her upwards. She bounced a few times, before it finally settled into a gently swinging drift towards earth. She and Jack were so close their parachutes almost touched, but as they got closer to the ground, the wind caught them, trying to pull them apart.

Mel worked the cords, attempting to stay as close to Jack as possible. The countryside looked rural and mostly deserted. That was good, since they had a few hours until dark. She could see roads cutting through hedges and in the distance, the square tower of a church. An army truck rolled into view a couple of hills away. Most likely a patrol looking for them.

She called out to Jack, "Bend your knees as you hit. Let them absorb the impact. It won't hurt as much." Most of the crews of the B-17's didn't even practice their jumps and broken limbs were a nasty result.

She thought he understood, hoped he did anyway. The ground came at them in a sudden rush. Mel bent her knees, hit, absorbed the blow, and then rolled with it. Her shoulders dug into soft mud and then she bounced upright, quickly pressing the release as her parachute tried to drag her along the ground. A nearly perfect landing. Rockman would have been proud of her. The field where they'd landed was mostly muddy, with a few patches of snow, and surrounded by high hedges, possibly the famous Normandy hedgerows? It smelled of earth and cold and something burning in the distance. She wasn't sure if it was their plane or a fireplace. Not yet anyway.

Mel pulled on the cords and began bundling the parachute. Larsen already had his under control and was prowling the perimeter of the field as Jack worked on subduing his.

She drew a deep, unsteady breath. They were on the ground in enemy territory. Not good.

"We've got company," Larsen called, from the far edge of the field.

Mel looked around. There wasn't even a weed high enough to hide behind.

Jack arched a brow in her direction. "I guess you'll get a chance to try out your German."

HERR OBERST EUGEN Thorhaus sat in the front of his command vehicle, trying not to shiver as his men inspected the wreckage of the fallen American bomber—and wondering what had possessed him to supervise the search today. His office was warm and coffee was delivered at regular intervals, even if it were Ersatzkaffee made from grain, not beans, it was at least warm. Yes, there was paperwork, but there was always paperwork. It was as inevitable as—he looked soberly at the body tumbled partly in, partly outside the wreckage—as death in war.

It would have been good to get their hands on one of the new bomb sites, rumored to be very accurate, but his aide-de-camp, Leutnant Kass, shook his head as he approached. He had a hard, cold face and barked orders at the men like the Fuehrer.

Thorhaus sighed. It was because of Kass that he'd decided to observe the search. Kass was more Nazi than soldier. He had no respect for the men under him, and less than that for their adversary. His POW's always arrived bruised and sometimes broken—injuries Kass blandly claimed happened prior to their apprehension.

He didn't like Kass and Kass didn't like him. At least they agreed on something in this war. Thorhaus was a soldier and he hated this war. True soldiers did not glory in war. They did their duty, served their country, learned to fight effectively, and hoped they wouldn't have to fight. True soldiers respected all soldiers, even the ones who fought for the other side. All had to do their duty. Only fate and borders determined which side you fought on.

These were not popular ideas in the Third Reich. They stayed inside his head and he wasn't sure that thinking them was safe. He knew the Gestapo commandant didn't trust him. So far Thorhaus had managed to appear to be rigorously enforcing the ridiculous rules of occupation, without crossing the line into brutality. He recognized that *Herr* Werner Ullstein's patience was going to wear out before the war ended.

He wouldn't be marching home from this war, but he hoped he died with honor. His only real sorrow was for his wife. She'd already lost one son during the invasion of France. The other was still too young to fight, but if the war dragged on too long, could catch him, too. It was not fair for his Maria to lose everything, but Hitler and his New Germany didn't care about the heart and soul of the German people.

He noticed one of his men carrying a piece of the plane away from the site and clambered out. "What are you doing?"

He didn't sound particularly harsh, but the soldier dropped the piece of fuselage on the ground and snapped to attention. The artwork on the metal drew his attention.

"*The Time Machine*," Thorhaus read the English words, translating them to German automatically. Next to the words was a shining, silver object that he supposed would be spinning if it were real. "What do you suppose that is?"

"It does not look like a machine," the man said doubtfully. Behind him, Kass shifted irritably.

"We have reports of downed fliers not far from here *Herr* Oberst. Our glorious Luftwaffe reports seven chutes scattered across the fields between here and Lisiex." With clear satisfaction, he added, "They appear to be trapped in the hedgerows."

With some reluctance, Thorhaus looked at his aide. Kass did not like the hedgerows and had once suggested they be cut down. In his opinion, they hid and anything that hid or concealed was necessarily bad for the Germans and good for the French.

"If we split the patrol, we should be able to get them all, *mein Herr*."

Thorhaus shook his head. "If they are caught in the hedgerows, where will they go?"

He looked at the piece of fuselage again. In the Luftwaffe, the pilots also painted things of meaning on the fuselage of their planes. Thorhaus had read the novel of the same name, but could not understand what this would mean to a pilot.

"Why did you want this?" Thorhaus asked the man.

He shrugged, unable or unwilling to explain. For some reason the art intrigued him. "Put it in the trunk," he ordered his driver. He avoided looking at the man. It was unlike him to pilfer, let alone pilfer from his men.

With an impatient snort, Kass spread his map on the hood of Thorhaus's command car. "Four of them are trying to get out of a field about here. The other three were just coming down around this area. I don't think these daylight bombings will prove as successful as the Americans hoped."

"No," Thorhaus agreed, because it wasn't wise not to, even when the evidence of his own eyes said otherwise. Only two planes down out of how many? And they'd all reached the target and unloaded their bombs. A failure indeed, he thought wryly. With a last, oddly regretful look at the remains of the plane, Thorhaus turned to Kass. "Let's move out."

THORHAUS STOOD ON the running board of his command vehicle and scanned the horizon with his binoculars. With men spreading out in all directions, his participation was redundant, but it was better than sitting and shivering in the cold vehicle. He was glad for his heavy greatcoat and the scarf his Maria had knitted for him, as the wind was both cold and clever. Above them the FW wagged its wings and then sped off in the direction of the base, its work done for the moment.

As he scanned the winter barren countryside, he found himself wondering what it must be like for the three fliers still unaccounted for. He'd hunted game in pre-war Germany, but this was hardly sporting. There was no refuge for them, no place to go to ground in a country mostly pacified by terror and oppression. And yet still they tried. Where did they think they could hide? If it were him, what would he do?

Standing here, surrounded by his heavily armed men, it wasn't easy to put himself in their place. Maria claimed he had no imagination. In these times, that was probably a good thing, he thought wryly, as his visual survey brought him back to where Kass stood, his hands on his hips and, as usual, shouting orders. He seemed to think the whole world were deaf and dumb.

"What's the problem, Kass?" Thorhaus took quiet satisfaction in cutting into the diatribe.

Kass spun around and snapped out an exaggerated salute. "There is no sign of the fliers, *Herr* Oberst."

That was interesting. "Is this the right field?" He was quite sure it was, but the game must be played, the questions asked.

Kass looked annoyed, though not overtly so. "I believed so, *Herr* Oberst." He didn't say he was wrong. In the Third Reich, one didn't.

Thorhaus lifted the glasses again and studied the field. "And yet they are not here. Perhaps you should broaden your search to near by fields." He held Kass's cold gaze with his, knowing his words infuriated him. Just about everything did. He was only happy when he was kicking someone around.

The men around Kass were stamping their feet, white clouds of expelled air almost obscuring their chilled faces as they waited for new orders.

"Of course, *Herr* Oberst," Kass gritted out, then spun on his heels and took his spleen out on the cold patrol. They looked happy enough to leave Kass's immediate vicinity. Thorhaus wished he could, too, and was granted his wish when Kass took a small group of men down the road, his voice sounding harsh even when the words could no longer be distinguished.

Suddenly semi-isolated from his men, Thorhaus studied the field again. He was sure this was the field the FW pilot had tried to mark. Where could they have gone so quickly? Had it taken them longer than it seemed to arrive here? He saw the church spire in the distance. In the old times, a church was considered sanctuary. If they'd made it that far, they'd find this wasn't the old times. The old priest might want to help them, but the church wanted them to remain neutral. Thorhaus sometimes stopped by for a visit with the old man. He was interesting, polite and...peaceful. Yes, that was the main attraction. He expected nothing and if he judged, it was well hidden.

The missing fliers could, he supposed, have gotten other help. Despite Kass's assertion that no local would dare, Thorhaus knew there was an active underground in the region. So far the group hadn't managed to do much and the Gestapo was slowly arresting the members, thanks to a strategically placed informant. If the men had gotten help from a local, they'd find it only delayed their inevitable capture.

He stepped down from the running board and his driver quickly opened the door for him. The inside gave him some protection from the wind, but not from the cold. He directed his driver to follow Kass's course. It would be wise to keep an eye on the man. As they pulled out, the car bumping over the rough ground, he found himself wondering again, where would he hide if he were the one out there?

AFTER THE SOUND of the truck faded slowly into the distance, Jack made himself count to one hundred before cautiously lifting the edge of the parachute.

"Wait here," he ordered, careful to keep his voice low. Moving stiffly from the cold, he crouched beside the low, snow-filled ditch, listening intently, but there was nothing to hear, except the distant sounds of the search moving away from them.

That had to be a bunch of unhappy Jerries. Jack grinned. Clever idea of Mel's, using their white parachutes as cover. Lucky for them some snow still lingered in the shallow ditch. Neither he nor Larsen thought it would work, but since they had nothing better to offer, they gave it a try. If the Jerries had come close...but they didn't and for now they were free—if being down in enemy territory, and surrounded by said enemy, was freedom.

Keeping low and trying to move quietly, Jack made his way to the edge of the field. The narrow, dirt road was empty in both directions, though he couldn't see a long way. From what he remembered of the area, coming down, the whole area was criss-crossed with these narrow lanes. And there'd been a church spire off to the southwest. What they needed was a barn...he looked up...and the sun to go down.

He quietly crunched his way back to Mel and Larsen.

"It's all clear for the moment." He kept his voice to a low murmur and it still sounded loud in the intense quiet. The edge of the parachute folded back.

"I think I'm frozen," Mel muttered. Jack held out his hand and she took it with a brief smile of thanks.

Once she was upright, she tried out her various limbs. She was a muddy, bedraggled sight and her bulky clothing showed nothing of her figure. So why did he feel his blood warm at the sight of her? He mentally shook his head. He didn't have time to ponder all the things he wondered about Mel.

Now she turned in a slow circle, examining their surroundings like a tourist at the Grand Canyon.

"So...this is...France."

She didn't sound impressed. Jack grinned.

"No one is their best in the cold," he said. Larsen choked back a laugh. Jack looked at Mel and found her looking at him. Something in her eyes made him wonder if she'd caught his veiled joke. Her lips twitched and he knew she had—a pointed reminder that he underestimated her at his peril.

Larsen fingered his chute. "Hate to leave it. I have a feeling we're going to need cover again."

"It's a bit bulky," Mel said, also shedding her life vest. She tucked it under her chute, then weighted it all with rocks. "So, what do we do now? We've still got an hour or so until dusk."

The shadows in the field were long, but not long enough for comfort. Still, his instincts told him the Jerries would be back. Their *disappearance* had to be puzzling. Someone might even figure out where they'd hidden, if they had time to think about it.

"I think we should keep hiding," Larsen said

"No," Jack said. "We need to go."

"It's still light, we'll be spotted," Larsen objected.

"They'll be back," Mel said, matter-of-factly. "They knew this was the field. The shouter wasn't at all happy about our disappearance. It's better if he doesn't find us."

Jack had the same thought about the shouter, even if he hadn't understood him.

"So," Mel said, "which way do we want to go? Spain is that way." She pointed south. "Switzerland is a long way that way." She pointed in its general direction.

"What's that way?" Jack asked, pointing west, though he already knew.

"England," Mel said, her tone neutral, but a slight smile pulling at the edges of her mobile mouth.

"Then we go west," Jack said, without hesitating.

Her smile went from slight to full blown and almost rocked him back on his heels.

"I like the way you think, Captain...most of the time." She wiped her gloved hands down the sides of her cold suit. "Let's go west, young men. And keep your eyes peeled for an...outhouse. I really need to pee—powder my nose."

For the first time since they landed, Larsen grinned.

"I saw a farm that direction, as I was coming down." It was more in the direction of Spain, but that might be a good thing, since the Germans were presently between them and England.

"Slight course correction for Mel's...nose," Jack said. "Larsen, you take point and I'll bring up the rear."

"I guess I'll occupy the middle," Mel said. At the gate, she paused. "Do you think we'll see the Eiffel Tower this trip?"

"That's toward Switzerland, too" Larsen said, a bit glumly.

"Oh." Mel met Jack's gaze blandly. "I was never that good with geography."

Jack didn't believe her. He had a feeling there wasn't much she wasn't good at. "Up and over, ma'am."

"Yes, sir." She vaulted it lightly, then fell in behind Larsen.

There were, Jack decided as he studied Mel's easy, graceful movements to toward the West, definite advantages to bringing up the rear.

Chapter Thirteen

THORHAUS STOOD BY the ditch, fingering the white silk that had hid the quarry from his sight, a slight smile curling his mouth. He wasn't sure why he'd come back, other than the feeling he'd missed something. Had his subconscious mind noticed the silk rippling in the wind? It was a possibility.

It hadn't taken him long to discover the only possible cover in the empty field or the abandoned parachutes.

At least one of the three fliers was both clever and inventive. He could admire this kind of initiative—and wish he didn't have to hunt him down. He would like to meet him, though. He dropped the parachute, using his foot to tuck it back into the ditch. He had to do his job, but he didn't have to tell Kass about this. Let him flail about, like the angry bull he was.

Thorhaus wished he had more imagination. This hunt would require it, not brute force. One might say it was more logical for the enemy to accept reality and surrender, but if Thorhaus were in this position, he would, he knew, be surrendering to a far different enemy. He couldn't say it out loud, but his thoughts were still his own and he could think and feel shame at what he was forced to do to these soldiers doing their duty. The Fuehrer had invaded this country. He had behaved without honor and he elevated men who were like him to positions of power. Thorhaus did his duty, because he had no choice. If he were the one out there, being pursued by someone like Kass, he'd do everything in his power to escape, too.

He paced slowly back to his car. Well, it was mostly out of his hands. If they didn't catch the fliers, the Gestapo most likely would. Either they would get help, which would lead to discovery, or they wouldn't get help and discovery would be inevitable.

It was a pity, though. He'd like to talk with a man who could think so fast on his feet. And perhaps, play chess with him.

AFTER PLAYING IT coy for an inordinate amount of time, the sun abruptly faded into the horizon, leaving Mel stumbling, as quietly as possible, in the deep and unrelenting dark of the blacked out countryside. This was probably the longest she'd ever gone without speaking and it was killing her to keep suppressing some really good material, or at least what seemed like good material. Tired might be impairing her judgment. She quickly and silently passed over the other reason she liked to talk: relieving stress. There was no help for it, so why dwell on it?

Here she was in France and she had no clue where they were or even what it looked like, other than that it had trees and mud. Lots of mud. She'd used some of it on her face, getting some interesting looks from the two men, until she'd explained it wasn't for her complexion.

The first time they almost stumbled into the arms of a German patrol, Jack had moved into point, leaving Mel to cover their six. It was all very gallant and Mel couldn't tell them it was also not the best use of their resources. This would have been a lot easier if she could just tell Jack the truth. Well, not a lot easier, but maybe slightly easier. But not for Jack, she had to keep reminding herself.

There was good reason to break her silence, now that time had shifted and changed so drastically. They weren't where they'd been or with who they should have been with. Ric was already a dead hero. Only Larsen was left to take his place and Mel had no idea if he would. Mel had her doubts about him. He wasn't a bad guy, but he didn't have the connection to Jack that Ric had had.

Their present journey through the night was an all too ironic metaphor for Mel's present circumstances, though it had at least provided her with the privacy to pee. Larsen's memory wasn't as good as Mel's and the farm had, for the present, eluded them.

As they stumbled through the darkness, Mel was also feeling her way through the unknown present, hoping to restore a future that was also lost to her in a fluid, ever-changing mist. It would have been such a relief to share the burden with Jack, but they didn't exactly have a place, or the privacy, for a cozy chat, even if she could have squared it with her conscience.

Thanks to Hell Week with the SEALS, Mel knew she could be this tired and cold and keep moving, but at least the SEALS had fed her. She'd stuffed extra candy bars in her pockets, but a shared bar didn't go far. The brief sugar buzz had faded with the sun. Jack wanted to press on until close to dawn. The plan was to hide during the day and travel at night. And, hopefully, make contact with the underground and get help in getting back to England. It was, unfortunately, the same plan they'd had last time.

Maybe it would go better this time.

Jack stopped suddenly, signaling for them to get down. Mel crouched close to the cold earth, her heart beating so loud, for a moment she couldn't hear anything but that. Slowly other sounds entered her brain's cue for sorting. Mel moved cautiously up to Jack

"They're French," Mel murmured, not sure what to feel about that. It didn't exactly clear up the whole *friend or foe* issue. She tried to pull words out of the murmured sound, but caught only the occasional word. "I think they are arguing about something...us, maybe?"

Jack was quiet, Mel could almost feel him thinking.

"Let's sit tight for now." His voice was a soft thread of sound, but Mel was glad for it. It warmed cold muscles. It shouldn't, but hey, since it was...

"Why don't we ask them for help?" Larsen shifted restlessly.

"Not until we know more," Jack said, allowing a hint of sharp to edge into his whisper.

They were waiting for someone, Mel realized. Only one of them didn't want to wait. They had to be underground. They were out after curfew and clearly trying to keep a low profile, but still she hesitated. If she could see their faces, she'd feel better.

She leaned close to Larsen. "Where do you think we are? What town did we come down close to? Do you know?" There were some underground cells, cells that had been infiltrated, in that future Jack had warned her about.

"You are in France," a soft, French-accented voice said, quietly from behind them. "Please to raise your arms and make not to move.'

December 20, 1942

THE CELLAR THEY were escorted to was dank, dark and quite possibly colder than it had been outside. It smelled of wine and dirt and some things Mel didn't recognize. She caught a brief glimpse of barrels and wooden crates, before their guard removed the candle and left them. They'd made sure no one saw their faces, which strengthened Mel's conviction they were part of the underground. They'd traveled in silence through darkened roads and fields, stopping once or twice to allow a German patrol to pass by. Each time silence was enforced with a knife to the throat.

"What do you think they are doing?" Larsen spoke nervously in the dark to Mel's right.

"Debating whether to turn us in or help us or—" Jack's voice came from her left.

Mel edged in that direction, exploring the floor until she found him. At her touch, his hand closed over hers, his strength passing easily through the layers of their gloves. She wanted to lean against him and refill her courage well but she didn't. She wanted to huddle against him for warmth, but she didn't do that either. She needed to think of a plan, if this went south, but she couldn't. Despite it all, she was just too tired. She pulled her knees up in an attempt to maximize any warmth still lingering in her body and rested her chin on her knees.

"Or?" Larsen's voice was off to her right.

Mel felt Jack hesitate. She knew what he wasn't saying.

"Or they may...eliminate us," Mel said. "It's probably the easiest solution for them."

"Sorry I asked," Larsen said, suddenly sounding like the scared kid he actually was.

Mel was sorry she told him. She felt like the bad news bear. She waved her free hand in front of her face, but all she felt was the movement of the air. The darkness was complete. If she'd been alone with Jack, they might have talked...or something, so it was probably a good thing they weren't alone. Her thoughts tangled and drifted as she felt herself leaning toward Jack. His shoulder was strong and comforting and almost warm...

She must have drifted off to sleep because she found herself back with the SEALS. She was cold and wet and tired and standing on the beach with Rockman yelling something at her. Part of her knew it was a dream and was irritated about it. If she had to dream, why couldn't she go home...

The sound of the door creaking open jerked back to a reality that was only slightly better. No one was yelling at her. Yet.

One of three men held a lantern in front of them. The light cut into her pupils. Closing her eyes wasn't enough. She covered them with her hand, pulling her other hand free from Jack just before the circle of light found them. She hated feeling so disoriented and at a disadvantage. She managed to get her feet under her and stood up, swaying slightly as the blood rushed from her head. Her empty stomach wasn't much help either. She noticed a crate behind her and used it to steady herself.

The three people who'd entered the cellar kept the light directed toward them and made sure they stayed in the flickering shadows. One of them rolled three barrels to the bottom of the stairs, one at a time, then they sat down, with the light between them and the three of them.

She didn't look at Jack or Larsen, though it wasn't without a struggle.

"I'm Captain Jack Hamilton, United States Air Force," Jack finally said into the waiting silence.

The three figures shifted slightly and it seemed they exchanged glances. Mel remembered reading about an underground group that was infiltrated and betrayed. All the men and boys in the village were executed by a...Leutnant Kass. He'd been under orders from the Gestapo in the area. Kass had been the name mentioned by the German commander where they landed. If this were that group, then this must be Romilliy sur Brouere.

"They're afraid we might be German infiltrators," Mel said.

Her words made the men shift again.

"How do we prove we're not?" Jack asked.

Mel could think of one way. Give them the real infiltrator, Rene Bouchard. He'd disappeared sometime before the end of war, either killed in retribution or removed by the Germans when he was no longer useful to them. The question she couldn't answer, was he one of the three men facing them? They appeared to be at a bit of an impasse.

"They know there are three missing fliers. They can't believe we escaped capture," Mel said, feeling the truth of her words as they left her mouth. "So they figure we're fakes. But if they turn us in, then the Germans will know they violated curfew. They are probably planning on killing us, but they want to be sure."

Two of the figures looked toward the middle one and he spoke rapidly, but too softly for her to catch more than a few words.

"Hey, look here—" Larsen began, but Jack cut him off.

"Perhaps you should introduce yourself, Mel."

Of course, the Germans wouldn't have anticipated a woman being on board. She was too tired. Somehow she needed to get her head clear or they wouldn't just lose their lives here. They'd lose the future, too.

Mel straightened and knew the three men stiffened. She pulled off her hat and fluffed her flattened hair, hoping it didn't look as bad as it felt like it looked. She took a step closer to the lantern, stopping at a sharp word from one of the men. She didn't move back, but instead undid her heavy flak jacket, working her way through the layers of clothing until she reached her borrowed uniform, which was filled out in ways it wasn't meant to. She shivered in the increased cold, but made herself look around, like a tourist.

"So, this is France" she said again, in French. "It's...not what I expected."

One of the men muttered something that might have been a curse.

She thought another crossed himself. She was sure one of them stifled a chuckle.

Mel continued in French. "I'm an American newspaper reporter. I was doing a story when we were shot down." She pulled out her most charming smile, though she wasn't sure it would work in a dirty face, and added, "My friends call me Mel."

"You expect us to believe that a woman would be on an American plane?" The voice was charming, even loaded with disbelief and a hint of humor.

"Is it easier to believe the Germans planted me here?"

"American women are weak," another man said, his voice rich with contempt.

Mel smiled. "Really?" She widened her stance, shifting slightly to find her footing on the uneven floor. She wiggled her gloved fingers invitingly, hoping the movement was visible to the eye. The gloves were a bit large. "Try and take me." She almost dared him, but managed to stop herself. "Unless you're afraid of being beaten by a girl."

Okay so that was sort of a dare, but she hadn't actually said it. If he took it that way, it wasn't her fault.

The man who'd mocked her hesitated, then got up. The way he approached her was casual and downright cocky. That lasted until Mel flipped him. They all did the same thing, came at her the same way, never giving her a chance to show her other cool moves.

Mel kept a wary eye on the winded Frenchman. He looked like he wanted to try again. While Mel didn't mind strutting her stuff, she didn't want to break him. He scrambled up, his meaty hands curling into impressive fists. He tried to hit her this time, but, even with a variation on the theme, the end result was the same.

"I received some specialized training from my...newspaper for this assignment." Did that sound as lame to them, as it did to her? Mel held out her hand to help him to his feet. After a wary moment, he took it and jumped upright. Instead of mad, he looked interested now.

"To fight Germans?" The man who seemed to be the leader of the group spoke.

"To fight off American soldiers." Mel hoped her frozen mouth was smiling. She couldn't exactly see them, but there was something in the way they sat that told her they doubted that. "I look better when I'm clean, they tell me." She rubbed at the mud on one cheek, like that would help.

Her words surprised an unstifled chuckle out of at least one of the men. There was one who still seemed to have a problem with her, it seemed.

"Your French is...excellent." His voice was thick with suspicion and his accent was slightly different from the other two men. Not that she blamed him. This was definitely the worst of times.

"So's my German, actually, but my English is better than either and you can't beat my American. It's flawless, being my native language." If only she could be sure this was the Romilliy sur Brouere cell.

The silence from that side of the room was hip deep and stifling. She could almost feel them thinking, or one of them thinking and the other two waiting for him to cease thinking and start acting. Just past the light, she heard a shuffle of feet and realized they were standing. She tensed, and slowly realized it was a manners thing, because she was a girl. How sweet. Three, shadowy bows were directed toward her. Mel might have smiled at their gallantry, but she already was smiling. Her mouth was probably permanently frozen in a smile. One of the men stepped around the lantern and took her hand and, bowing once again, with great charm and clumsy grace, he kissed her hand.

"What my friends call me, it is better not to know," he said. The light fell full upon his face. He was darkly handsome and oozed charm. He was also the infiltrator.

Without missing a beat, Mel jerked him toward her, using the side of her arm to chop him across the throat, then she moved to end his shocked pain with another chop to the back of the neck. He dropped to the floor with an ungentle thud.

His two companions, after a moment of shock, pulled their knives. While Mel figured she could take them, she didn't really want to. They were allies, after all.

"He's a German infiltrator," Mel said, still in French. "Check his body for identity papers. They are probably secured to his chest or back. He'd need them on him if he got picked up."

One of the men ordered her to move away from the fallen man. Mel stepped back toward Jack.

"I don't think the guests are supposed to beat up the hosts," Jack said. "Didn't you like how he kissed your hand?"

"He's a German infiltrator," Mel said, this time in English. "He would have betrayed us all."

"How do you know that?" Larsen asked.

It was a fair question. "I saw him talking to one of the patrols we saw today," Mel said. Larsen bought it, but she could tell Jack didn't.

He shouldn't. She was a bad liar. If they ever ended up alone, she'd have some explaining to do.

One of the men doing the search gave a sharp exclamation. He'd found something. Mel exchanged a quick look with Jack as the man ripped it open, read it once, then again, this time more slowly. Finally he looked up, his expression grim.

Now that she could see him, she saw an older man, possibly in his late fifties or early sixties. She recognized his face from the photos of the men who were executed one month from today. He'd been one of the leaders of the local underground. Francois Mouy. A farmer. A hero.

And she'd just changed the future again.

His companion stood up. "He came to us from Illiers, he said. He came, he claimed, to work with his cousin. Perhaps he is also a traitor?"

He wasn't, Mel knew, but he was on his own for the moment. Almost hazily she thought, he died anyway...but what a bummer...

"Our problems began after he arrived, Pierre. But we will make sure." He stood up, wiping his hands on this clothing with obvious distaste. "Secure him. We will deal with him later." He turned to Mel. "We owe you our thanks, mademoiselle."

What Mel found odd, he didn't look all that thrilled or that grateful. In fact, he looked chagrined. Had he already known? Or was something else troubling him?

"We're allies, sir," Mel answered him in French. "Did you already know? Did I complicate things for you?"

He hesitated again, then shrugged, the movement totally Gaelic. "He is the only one of us who spoke acceptable German. It is a...complication."

Mel couldn't really see how, since the reason he spoke it was because he was a freaking traitor. Clearly she'd compromised a plan, but wouldn't it have already been compromised? She realized he was looking at her...assessingly. It took her tired brain a moment to realize why. Her first reaction was to shake her head. She had only one mission to accomplish, but an odd frisson twisted down her spine. For some reason, that she didn't, couldn't, wouldn't know for right now, she had to help them.

"As I said, I speak German," she said, meeting his gaze without flinching. These men would have no problem using a woman, not after so many years of occupation and hardship.

He gave a half nod and said, "Perhaps we will talk later."

Now that the mini trust crisis appeared to be past, Mel swayed slightly as exhaustion and hunger took over from adrenaline.

"When you are rested. We apologize for your rough treatment." He hesitated and then shrugged again. "It is safer for you to stay here for tonight, but we will endeavor to make you more comfortable. I expect you are also hungry?"

"Yes..." Mel drew the word out, hesitated, but then shrugged. "It would really make me comfortable if I could use your...facilities. I never learned to point and shoot. It's a girl thing."

He looked at her for a long moment, quite possibly trying to process her comments, and then he smiled at her, his dark eyes sparking with amusement. "Of course. It is not far from the house."

An outhouse. It figured.

THORHAUS STUDIED KASS through lowered lids. It amused him to stay silent while his aide waited, red slowly suffusing his face. Kass looked what he was, the worst that Germany had to offer. His features were as coarse as his soul—if he had one. He was a thug with too much power. In this battle of wills, Thorhaus knew he must lose. The thugs were winning all the battles these days, but still he fought—in secret, doing what he could. Always he had to balance what he could do against the safety of his family. Germany would lose this war and when they did, it was his hope that his son would live on to rebuild Germany in a better, finer way.

Kass shifted irritably. "What do you want me to do, *Herr* Oberst?"

With an effort Thorhaus focused his thoughts on their conversation. He arched his brows and made his voice cold. Bullies only responded to perceived strength.

"We wait."

"Wait? But *mein, Herr*—"

"Try to use your wits, Kass." Thorhaus stood up. "Have you never hunted game?" But of course he hadn't. He was born of the city, jumped up out of the slums of Berlin. "Our prey has gone to ground. We beat the bushes, they stay there. But we appear to have lost interest, we let them think they have fooled us, and they will emerge. We catch them and anyone who has helped them." He strode over to the window and pulled the shade back. "Where do you think they can go? They are deep in enemy territory."

"The underground..."

...is defanged, Thorhaus could have told him, but the information wasn't general knowledge and Kass was the type to brag. Ullstein, might not like or trust Thorhaus, but the Gestapo man didn't like or trust anyone. So, however, reluctantly, he'd briefed Thorhaus on the infiltrator, though not his identity. Thorhaus had already informed Ullstein about the missing fliers and he'd agreed to contact his man.

"...will not be able to save them," Thorhaus said firmly, turning back to his desk and the pile of paperwork waiting him. He sat down and picked up his pen, but Kass didn't move. "Was there something else?"

"Yes, *Herr* Oberst. There has been an accident, a farm laborer named," Kass consulted his notebook, "Rene Bouchard has died. He is not local. Arrived in the area a few months ago to work on his cousin's farm. His cousin, one Francois Bouchard, has requested the body be released for burial."

Thorhaus frowned, feeling uneasy for no good reason. "An accident?"

"He appears to have been driving his wagon while drunk and overturned it. Broken neck. He was out after curfew. Might have been underground. I could interrogate his cousin?" Kass perked up.

"If either is suspected of underground involvement, *Herr* Ullstein will deal with them. I will speak with him before we release the body. Inform the cousin. I'd like to speak with one of the fliers we captured yesterday. Have someone see to it, and make sure they don't pick up additional...injury on their way from the holding cells to my office."

"They are the enemy, mien *Herr*," Kass said sulkily.

"They are soldiers, doing their duty. We fight, we don't..." he tried to think of an example the man would understand and knew he couldn't. "We treat them how we hoped to be treated in like circumstances," he said finally, and he knew, futilely.

"I will never be a prisoner," Kass said, his ugly eyes narrowing.

Of course he wouldn't. He was no where near the enemy. Thorhaus rose again.

"But you will obey my orders, *Herr* Leutnant." He held his pig eyed gaze for a long, cold moment, not blinking until Kass looked away.

"Yes, sir." He turned sharply and marched out, closing the door quietly, but with emphasis, none the less.

If Kass weren't already his enemy, this would have assured it, Thorhaus thought wearily. He rubbed his eyes, then picked up his pen again, but a light knock at the door had him lying it down again. Surely Kass couldn't be delivering the prisoners already.

"Enter."

It was his clerk.

"*Herr* Ullstein to see you, sir."

Thorhaus felt the familiar clutch in his gut. Every time the man came around, Thorhaus wondered if this would be the end.

"Send him in."

Thorhaus rose, waiting for Ullstein to come in. He'd come alone and shut the door behind him. So this wasn't his time, Thorhaus thought, both relieved and...not. In some ways, it would be a relief to get it over. For him, a soldier, it would be a short walk and a firing squad. There'd be no trial for a soldier. Too risky.

"*Herr* Oberst." Ullstein gave him the short, sharp new salute. Thorhaus echoed it, his distaste well buried.

"Please, sit down."

All his movements were brisk and jerky. He was a small man, with a ferret face and cruel eyes. He sat, but sharply, as if everything had a point, on the edge of the chair.

"I understand you have the body of Rene Bouchard?"

"That's correct. I was holding it until we spoke. Kass wonders if he was involved with the underground. He was out after curfew when the accident occurred."

"Are you certain it was an accident?"

"There doesn't seem to be any doubt of it," Thorhaus said slowly. "I have not, personally examined the body." Ullstein's eyes shifted from side to side. Bouchard was his infiltrator, Thorhaus realized. Was he going to share that info, he wondered and then knew he wouldn't. Ullstein would consider it a weakness. "I can turn it over to you if you suspect foul play."

"An overturned wagon could cover up much," Ullstein said slowly, frowning. It was clear to Thorhaus he didn't know what to do.

"Then he was underground," Thorhaus played along. "Is there a chance your infiltrator killed him to protect himself?"

Ullstein's gaze flicked his direction, then down again. "It is possible." Ullstein stood up. "Under the circumstances, it will be difficult to contact him for a time, but I can give you a couple of leads of where your missing fliers might be hiding." He handed Thorhaus a piece of paper with a couple of names and addresses on it. "If you do catch them, I'd like to interrogate them about any underground contacts."

"Of course." Poor buggers. Whether they had help or not, they were in for it now. He had to comply or he would be shot for sure. When Ullstein was gone, he sat down. Again he was interrupted.

"The first prisoner, sir."

The man who entered looked somewhat worse for wear, Thorhaus noted, though his wounds had been treated, as per his standing orders.

"Your name," Thorhaus asked.

"You speak English?" The soldier stiffened again, saluting briskly, though it must have cost him something in pain and closed his lips firmly together.

Thorhaus sighed. Why did they have to make it so difficult?

December 21, 1942

IF MEL EVER got a chance to write about how she spent her 2005 Christmas vacation—in 1942's Occupied France—it wouldn't be long article. In fact, she could sum it up in three words: it was dark. If she'd known her only view of daytime France was going to be while dangling from a parachute, she's have looked around more. She couldn't even describe the outhouse, other than by scent. Gross. Maybe she could call her adventures "How I Smelled My Christmas Vacation."

It worked on at least two levels. She sniffed her arm pit cautiously. Oh yeah, she was definitely getting ripe. She hadn't gone this long without a bath since she was little and tried to fake Gran out by pretending she'd bathed.

Despite the change in relations with their hosts, the cellar remained their accommodations. They did try to make it less noisome, but their own, normal living conditions probably weren't that great. The three of them got blankets, some warm soup that was mostly water and access to the outhouse after dark, and that was about it. The upside, they were so tired, they slept the whole day. Mel woke, stiff and sore, when the farmer's wife opened the door, bearing more bland soup, water to wash with, a piece of rough, lye soap and a small lantern that bit painfully into Mel's pupils. She felt like a mole as she squinted and grimaced in the general direction of their hostess.

The water was icy cold, when Mel plunged her hands into it and splashed it on her still muddy face. She was surprised to see traces of blood mixed with the mud, until she remembered the explosion aboard *The Time Machine.*

"Oh yes, that's waking me up," she managed to gasp out. The lye soap was harsh and burned into her scratches and cuts without mercy. They all had to use the same water, so Mel was grateful to get first shot at it, even if she was taking the cold edge off it for the next in line.

While Jack took his turn at the bowl, Mel faced her breakfast. France's reputation in the cuisine arena was taking a hit, too, she decided, after sipping at her bowl of what was called soup—for want of a better description. They probably had a carrot they swirled in it to give it flavor and then removed to use again. At least it was warm and fooled her stomach into thinking it had been fed...for a few moments.

"It's wonderful, thank you," Mel said, in French, smiling at the woman, and thinking of the abundance of the life she hoped to return to soon. There'd be no relief for this woman for three more years—and still she shared with them—and at great risk to her life and her family, if she had any. It was one thing to read tales of the French Underground, but something else entirely to look into the face of someone risking their life for you.

"Thank you," Mel said again. She covered the woman's worn and gnarled hand with her cold and red one. She could almost feel the rough skin as the feeling returned slowly. "Merci."

She hoped the woman understood what she wasn't saying. A tired smile briefly broke the morose surface of her weather beaten face and her eyes showed her curiosity about Mel and her presence in France. Then morose returned and she left, moving as stiffly as Mel felt. At least she left the modest lantern for them, though it only sent its glow out a few inches. When they were alone, Larsen shared his feelings about the food.

"I don't know how they can call this soup, it's just warmed water." He didn't push his bowl away, Mel noted, nor did he avail himself of a wash.

"They share what they have," Jack pointed out, "and have the less for it. Not to mention risking their lives for us. If you think you can do better out there, by all means, leave."

Larsen didn't answer. He finished his soup, then crawled back into his blankets, turning his back to them. In a few seconds, he started to snore, the sound soft but still somehow annoying.

Mel finished drinking her breakfast, but was reluctant to continue to dull her senses with anymore sleep. If Rockman were here, he'd so be yelling at her. On the upside, since he wasn't here, she could start slowly. She began with some easy stretches, but they weren't easy, not with a million plus bruises in a million plus places.

She felt Jack watching her, then to her surprise, he joined her, trying to mimic her movements.

"That's not as easy as it looks," he said. "But I am getting warmer."

Mel was, too. As her muscles warmed, the easy stretches got marginally easier, so she took it to the next level. At least she could still touch her toes and it did feel good to feel warm again. Her clothes were constricting. She shrugged her jacket off and that helped some. Who knew she'd actually miss gnarly sweats? There was nothing quite like suffering and danger to focus your thoughts on what was important.

She longed to talk to Jack, more than she wanted more food. She could still feel the...flux-ness of time around her, if there were such a word. Or a state. And mixed with that was the conflicting pull between her family and her feelings for Jack. It helped not at all to know she could never have him in her life. She didn't belong here and he was old and dying where she did belong. And still the heart wanted what it wanted.

It was a greedy heart, too, because it wanted her family. It wanted it all. And right now, she didn't know if she was going to get any of it. She remembered how it had been, but had no clue how it would be, or what she'd changed.

And if that weren't enough to confuse her thinking, there was Mouy.

What did the resistance fighter hope she could do for his group? And could they get it done before her date with vortex on Christmas Day? Assuming, of course, that she still had that date. She rubbed the still painful spot on her tush. At least that hadn't changed.

Jack was panting from the effort, but he managed to ask, "Do you know if they are going to help us get to the coast?"

"They didn't say anything about that," Mel said. In the other time lines, they'd lingered in the area until Christmas because it wasn't safe to move around. "I expect the hunt will be hot for us for a few days anyway. And the Germans may be looking for their snitch." Another new twist to the timeline, thanks to Mel's acting before thinking. But what else could she have done? He was a threat to them, not just to the Underground. "We might be better off sitting tight for now."

Luckily said snitch was French and not German. If he'd been the real deal, that would have meant reprisals. If they were smart, the underground would arrange an accident that would annoy the Gestapo, and might even make them suspicious, but without certain knowledge of foul play, even they'd have a hard time finding someone to punish for it.

"I wonder how compromised their cell is?" Jack asked grimly. "If they know about this place we could be sitting ducks—"

As if his words had given impetus to action, the cellar door opened. It was the woman again. Behind her was Mouy.

"You have to leave. Now." His voice was flat, but Mel heard the urgency buried in that flatness. "Bring your blankets. You'll need them."

Jack must have felt it, too. He shook Larsen awake as Mel grabbed her discarded gear. She looked around, to make sure they hadn't left anything incriminating, then followed Mouy to the doorway. He hissed them to silence and extinguished the light.

A thin line of moonlight appeared in the deep darkness, slowly growing into a door-like shape. Mel felt like a bow string stretched to the limit as she stained to hear anything—or feel any danger—in the peaceful quiet of the night. Mel had the odd sensation that they were all linked together in the intensity of the moment. The air, now flowing around them from the opening, was cold and smoky and a wonderfully fresh relief from the stuffy basement and their own stench.

Mel closed her eyes, trying to pierce the night, not just with ears and smell, but with her gut. That was one lesson shared by all the men in her various adventures: listen to your gut. While the reading wasn't clear, she did feel like they needed to get moving.

Apparently Mouy agreed. He stepped out, not into the moonlight, but into the shadow of the eaves and began edging along the side of the building. Mel noticed their hostess went the other direction, possibly toward the house. Mel felt a chill as the old woman faded into the shadows and from their lives. There was no romance in this grim fight for life and for liberty. As she stumbled toward the tree line with the others, her feet sticking in the mud, she heard the distant sound of heavy trucks approaching.

All three of them froze Jack half turned back toward the farm house.

"No," Mouy ordered softly. "You can not help her. And if you get caught here..."

He didn't have to finish it. They all moved forward, more quickly now as the sound of the trucks drowned out their movements. Mel made the protection of the trees as the first headlights cut into the dark yard of the farm house. It gave Mel the only glimpse she'd have of where they'd been. She saw the line of a classic farmhouse, a glimpse of an oaken door, then ducked down as the lights tracked in their direction. The roar of engines now combined with the harsh sound of voices, sent them scrabbling through the scrub and undergrowth in a desperate dash away from the danger. There was the sound of a sharp cry cut off abruptly. Then a shot. As Mel stumbled forward, her face was too cold to feel the tears running down her face, but they blurred her vision. She felt Jack grab her arm to steady her more than once.

Mel heard a harsh order for silence and echoed it for them. Mel was sure the Germans must hear their wildly beating hearts or feel their fear. She'd stopped awkwardly and felt herself sway, knew she was going to fall, when Jack grabbed and gripped her arm. She looked his direction and saw a flash of white smile break the terrifying darkness.

I love him, she realized, with more shock and awe then she'd felt over the bombing of Baghdad. I like him, I'm attracted to him, but this is more than that. *I love him*. Perhaps I've always loved the idea of him, but now, knowing him, I love the man.

Carefully, slowly, she reached over and put her hand on his and held on. She was so cold and scared, she could barely feel anything, and yet, they might have been holding each others' bare hands, so acutely did she feel the contact. Her heart beat wildly, with joy and fear. She wanted to tell him, but luckily for them both, she couldn't.

Finally, when she thought she must move or scream or do something, do anything, a cool, cultured voice broke the silence. "Perhaps, Kass, you should have waited until after questioning the old woman to shoot her."

Mel recognized that voice. He'd directed the search back where they landed. And Kass, that was the name of a brutal Nazi.

"Did she have any other family?"

Kass's answer was too faint to be heard.

"Inform the priest of the...accident. Have your men search the house and barn, but I think even we can agree that if they were here, they have gone."

"We should search the area, mien *Herr*." This time Mel could hear the harsh voice of Kass.

"If you wish to stumble about in the dark, be my guest. The rest of us are going to eat our supper."

Mel had to smile, even though her legs were killing her. The noise of the search was loud enough now, to cover their retreat, though Mel paused to smear more mud on her face. The rest of them followed suit, Mouy with a slight, briefly visible smile. They moved more cautiously now. Mouy would move ahead and wait, while one by one, they joined him. Then it started again. Each patch of snow was avoided. As was each patch of light. They clung to the shadows as to dearest friends. It was cold, but fear kept her warm enough for her nerve endings to keep sending complaints through to her brain.

They couldn't talk. In the deep silence of the night, their movements sounded like clanging bells. Had she ever kept her mouth shut so long? She didn't know, but didn't think so. She was a reporter, a television reporter. Words were her trade and the silence was almost as painful as the cold.

One thing the long walk was doing for her, it was giving cold reason a chance to douse her girlish longings for a happy ending with harsh reality. So many emotions swept through her during the long walk. Guilt over the old woman's death. A deep longing for her own free and ordered world, a determination to do more with it if she ever got home. And through it all an unreasoning, singing joy at having time with Jack. She would love and lose, but she couldn't regret it. Well, she looked around her at the dark and hostile land, if she were honest, and she tried to be, maybe she regretted it a little.

Chapter Fourteen

THORHAUS WAS CONVINCED the escaped fliers had been at that farmhouse. He even wondered if they'd watched from the dark as they flailed around in the dark looking for them. Did he imagine he'd felt their fear during the silence? It was a whimsy quite unlike him. He felt odd, almost disconnected since that plane had come down in his territory. Each decision felt...more important somehow.

He looked at his dinner, hot and inviting, and then out the window. The wind had come up, bringing a few wisps of snow to dance in the light falling across the sodden ground. It was a cold night to be outside and hungry. He hoped they'd found new shelter.

He tried to push away the fellow-feeling he had for them. They weren't alike...or were they? They were in the dark, he in the light, but both were afraid, neither free to do what they liked. How had Germany lost her freedom? How had she so lost her way?

He took a few bites of food, but it turned to ashes and dust in his mouth. What good was plenty without freedom? Why did he suspect the three fliers were more at peace, even hungry and cold, than he was right now?

Kass would be wondering why he pulled back on the search. But it would have been silly to flail around in the dark. It wasn't just caprice. So much they did now was silly...silly and wrong.

Right and wrong. He'd never had to think much about it. As a soldier, his job was to do his duty, to follow orders. It was...comforting to know what he was supposed to do at any given moment...or it used to be. Now it was all hollow, all sound and fury, all noise and death.

It was treason, but he was didn't want to find them. He really didn't want to turn them over to Ullstein. But it was his duty. He must do it. He had to do his duty. Didn't he? The truth was, he didn't know how to do anything else.

AS JACK ONCE more took up the rear, right behind Mel, he found himself wishing Larsen had landed elsewhere, not because he was annoying—though he was—but because his constant presence kept him from asking Mel the questions trying to burst free of his throat—no, they weren't questions anymore, but certainties he'd like confirmed for his own peace of mind. The dangers of talking about who and what she was here, in this place, in Occupied France, had not escaped him. It should be enough to quiet his brain and make the dangerous thoughts go away. Only it wasn't.

She'd known about the infiltrator, not because of any patrol. She'd said she had a photographic memory. If he'd sent her here from the future, he'd been, well, he was going to be, incredibly irresponsible. Someday. No question Mel was a remarkable woman, but she was a woman. What had he, what would he be thinking. To send her here and put her in such danger? If only he knew what was at stake.

But he knew himself, Jack realized. The stakes had to be high or he wouldn't have done it. Well, he wouldn't do it in the future. Dang, this was confusing. How did Mel keep it all straight?

As they continued their jerky progress along some path that only the Frenchman seemed to know, Jack pondered his certainties, even though he had no real proof beyond his own gut instincts.

Mel had known they were going to crash in France. He realized that now, looking back at the things she'd done and said. In that light, he could understand her reluctance to tell him who she was. It was dangerous enough what she must know, and the odds of them making it to England were a million to one—if that good. He and Larsen were most likely going to sit out the war in a prisoner of war camp, but first they'd be interrogated. If the Germans suspected Jack had information...well, he didn't kid himself that he could hold out against concentrated and determined torture.

And still he longed to know, would she make it back to the future? What time did she come from? How well did they know each other? Was there any hope...

Mel stumbled again and Jack reached out to steady her again. Her arm, through the heavy jacket, was strong and supple. If she weren't a woman, he'd think he'd done a great job of choosing a time traveler. But she was a woman, an amazing woman, but a woman. If the Germans got their hands on her, torture would be the least of her problems.

Dear heaven, he hoped he'd arranged a way home for her. It was his turn to stumble, on the thought and on a rock lurking under the snow. Mel caught him, her slight frame absorbing his weight and standing firm. The future must be an amazing place, if it held women like her.

A soft order from their guide halted them. They crouched in the shadows of a hedge, but not far off, bathed in pale moonlight, Jack saw the steeple of a church.

Sanctuary, he thought with relief. Then, to his dismay, he realized they were turning aside...toward the cemetery next to it.

A crawl along a small ditch brought them close to crypts and tombstones, then they used the stony shadows to inch closer and closer to the church. Jack felt himself relaxing again, until they stopped in front of a large crypt. It seemed their guide turned a key, then noiselessly eased the iron door open just enough for them to slip in, one by one. Jack was only slightly relieved when their guide followed them inside and had to fight unreasoning panic when he pulled the door closed behind them. Even deathly cold, the place was noisome and stale and smelled strongly of death, rotting plants and rotting...other things. And in the enclosed space, he could smell them, too, their fear, their perspiration, their individual odors.

Their companion moved with almost eerie stealth. There was only the rustle of clothing until he heard the rasp of match and saw the small flicker pierce the darkness. This light was applied to a small, heavily shuttered lantern that faintly illuminated the grisly interior.

Jack felt Mel reach for him and he gripped her hand, hoping he could steady her, when he felt none too steady himself. The man knelt on cold stone and worked at the panel on the front of one of the stone coffins to one side of the crypt, then pulled it off. From it he abstracted more blankets and a pot.

"We're...staying...here?" Larsen had a tremor in his voice and Jack didn't blame him. This was definitely horror movie stuff. It was all Jack could do not, to wrestle his way out the door to clean, fresh air. Mel gripped his hand so tightly, the fingers were going numb.

"How..." Mel had to stop and clear her throat before she could finish. "...how long do we have to...stay here?"

"Someone will come when it is safe," he said. "You must not talk. When you need air, open the door—very narrow. No light, except when door is closed. And then only this much. No more."

He showed Jack how to light it, turn it down and off, and how to work the shutters.

"What..." Jack began, looking at the pot. Be tough to cook in it with no fire. Or food.

"It's a chamber pot," Mel said. "At least we got the room with a...view."

"A..." Jack stopped as realization struck him. "Oh." Glad to learn that before he tried to fill it with food. To his surprise, he realized he was grinning.

Their host looked amused, too. "We did not anticipate..." He jerked his head in Mel's direction.

"Neither did we," Jack said and got a slight, but pointed nudge from Mel.

"No light. No sound. Is clear?"

"Is clear," Jack said grimly. This place was making a POW camp look pretty good. He'd start digging out the white flag...if not for Mel. If they could get her away safe...

He looked down at her and found her looking up at him. "Don't even think about it," she said. "We're a team. We stick together...until..."

"Until...what?"

"Until we can't anymore."

And when would that be? She smiled suddenly. It lit her face. It lit their gloomy...quarters. It lit his heart. He loved her. It was the wrong time. It was definitely the wrong place. If she was who he suspected, she was even the wrong person. And still the knowledge filled him, catching in his chest, almost choking him with an odd, clearly out of place, sense of peace, of rightness. He loved her. It was that simple. He'd never expected it. Actually he'd expected to die without ever feeling it. He didn't mind being wrong, but it was crazy.

They were at the mercy of strangers. They were stuck in Occupied France. They were being hunted by the German army. They were hiding in a grave.

But they were together. For now, it was enough. It would have to be. They were fast running out of time...

December 22, 1942

MEL WOKE SLOWLY from a light, fitful doze. If she'd dreamt, she didn't remember. She was stiff and cold and as usual, she needed to pee. Just before dawn, someone had come and moved them into yet another cellar. In the dim light and half asleep, it was hard to be sure, but Mel thought it was the priest who came to pull them out of the crypt. There's been some hot soup in huge, wooden bowls and a trip to an actual, though ancient, water closet before being shut in again.

Larsen was either too dazed or too depressed to talk much. He'd retreated to a corner as far from them as possible and wrapped himself up in his share of the blankets. Mel had to keep reminding her self how very young he was, to keep from kicking his tush. She was, however, very tempted to spank him.

Jack, now he tempted her for a far different reason. Last night it had seemed as if she saw something in his eyes when he looked at her. She was hesitant to identify what she thought the flash might be. What if she were wrong? In this instance, it felt more terrifying to be wrong about that, than facing down the enemy.

His back was warm against hers. She'd suggested they all huddle for warmth, but Larsen had ignored her. Jack had seemed to hesitate, but it was both sensible and logical. And it wasn't as if they could get up to any mischief in their present circumstances. She wanted to roll over and wrap her arms around his middle and take comfort from his closeness. Instead, she sat up and wrapped her arms around her knees. They weren't even close to comforting and, like the rest of her, they stank. On the upside, they didn't smell as bad as their quarters in the crypt.

Just thinking about that chamber of horrors made her shudder all over again. If she had an ounce of gumption, she'd kick Jack for getting her into this. She felt, rather than saw, Jack stir and drew herself into a tighter ball. Nope, no gumption at all.

"Mel?" his voice sounded sleepy and yes, sexy. *Dang.*

"I'm right here."

She could almost feel him thinking. No question the lack of privacy was a problem...and a blessing.

"We need to talk."

She didn't ask about what. When she didn't answer, she heard him sigh.

"In the movies, people always find ways to be alone," Mel said, keeping her voice carefully light. "It's kind of funny, really."

"How so," Jack sounded ironic and amused.

"Well, we've hardly seen anyone or talked to anyone. We've spent at least part of a night in a crypt...we're so freaking alone, we might be the only people on earth...but we're not." It was ironic.

"It's...annoying."

That, too, she had to agree. She sensed Jack wanted to say more. That he didn't indicated impressive self restraint, in her opinion.

"I wonder how long until someone comes? Do you think the sun has gone down again?" She wished she could see. She needed to be moving, even if it was only calisthenics. She realized she was tapping her fingers against her knee. It mightn't have mattered, but her knees were bruised and didn't like it, so she stopped.

"I don't think I believe in the sun anymore," Jack said, ruefully. "How long since we saw it last?"

"That would depend on what day it is," Mel said. She was pretty sure it was Tuesday, but not enough to assert it with confidence. If it was, that left four days, four freaking long days until her date with the vortex. Assuming that hadn't changed, too.

"I think its Tuesday," Jack said, "but it's possible we slept through it—"

There was the sound of fumbling with the door, and it silently opened, sending light to stab into the room and into her dark-widened pupils. Mel couldn't speak for Jack's pupils, but hers were getting pretty pissed about the extremes of light and dark. She shielded them as best she could and heard a soft, kindly voice say, in excellent English, "I'm Father—"

He stopped. Mel didn't blame him. This was not a good time for too much sharing. "I'm the priest of this parish. I'm sorry I could not attend to you sooner. I had...business..."

Mel knew what business he had to take care of before attending them.

"We're very sorry about...Madame," she said. She slowly lowered her hands and saw an old man in a cassock standing at the top of the wooden stairs, holding a small lamp high above his head. Was that some kind of lamp etiquette? It looked tiring.

"Madame was a brave woman," the old man said, gravely bowing his head. "It is evening. I can take you out to wash and refresh yourself, but only one at a time. It is not safe."

"Larsen," Jack said, in his command voice. "—you go first. Do exactly what they tell you. Don't linger."

"Yes, sir." Larsen scrambled awkwardly to his feet and moved stiffly toward the stairs.

"Will you be all right for a bit longer?" Jack asked her in a low voice.

"Sure," she murmured, though she really wasn't. It kind of depended on how long Larsen took and how good her sphincters were. To her relief, the priest set the lamp on the edge of the stairs, before closing the door. It wasn't much, but it was better than sitting in the dark again.

This cellar looked much like the other, so Mel didn't waste much time examining it, instead, she turned her attention, and her eyes, in Jack's direction. Okay, so he didn't look as good as he had. He had several days' growth on his face and his lovely dark hair was matted and filthy. His clothes were stiff with mud and the blood of his dead comrades. He looked tired and worried. And still, somehow, cute. Or maybe it was just that her definition of cute had been revised down by circumstances.

He stepped close, gripping her elbows. She hoped her face wasn't as dirty as his, but suspected it was far worse. She'd been pretty heavy-handed with the mud.

"He won't be gone long."

She hoped not.

"We might not be alone again."

She hoped not again.

"So we should cut to the chase."

Still he hesitated. Was he wondering which question to ask first or unwilling to commit himself to the key question? Whatever his problem was, Mel decided it was time to help him out of it. He'd told her it was her call. From what she could tell, all Jack needed was confirmation now. He already knew the essential part. She didn't know how he knew it, well, she sort of did, actually. She wasn't the world's greatest liar. Or time traveler for that matter.

"Yes," she said.

"What?"

She knew what she needed to say, but it was still hard to say it out loud.

"Yes...you sent me here."

Neither of them were what she'd call shifting around, but it felt like he went still. Or stiller. If there was such a word.

"To this place. To this...time..."

He gave a great, shuddering sigh.

"It worked then. I did it." He sank down onto a handy barrel and shoved his hands through his hair. When he lowered his hands, hair was sticking up in several places. "I did it."

"Yeah, you did it." He wouldn't be so thrilled if he was the one doing the time traveling. She hooked a tush cheek over the edge of his barrel. "I thought you'd be harder to convince."

"Ever since I realized I knew how to do it, I've expected...someone...to come back." He looked at her. "But not..."

"A woman." He couldn't help being a chauvinist. Life hadn't taught him differently. Yet.

"Well, yeah."

She jumped to her feet and faced him. "You not only sent me...you chose me."

She realized she had her hands on her hips and her feet planted in a...pugnacious manner. She could be Mrs. Cleaver chewing out the

Beaver—only in camo and mud. Okay, so maybe she wasn't even slightly like Mrs. Cleaver. But she probably looked like someone pugnacious in camo, though please not Rockman...

"Why?" He rubbed his head again. "I don't mean to be...but why?"

Mel crossed her arms. "Well, I do have some rather unique qualifications. And a personal stake in the outcome."

She sat down again. It was warmer sitting next to him.

Jack's brows rose. "A personal stake? Who—" He stopped. His face cleared of puzzlement, not mud. "Norm? You're related to Norm, aren't you?" Mel nodded. "Wow, Norm's...daughter?"

She shook her head. "Not daughter."

Jack's blue eyes widened. "Not? Then what—"

"Granddaughter. That baby in his pictures from home? That's my dad."

Jack looked like he'd taken one to the stomach. "Norm's...granddaughter." He looked at her. "Then we weren't—"

He stopped and this time Mel knew exactly why. She leaned against him.

"No." She sighed and thought he did, too. "We met, we meet for the first time in about sixty years, give or take a few weeks..."

"Sixty years." Now he sounded winded-plus. "I'll be..."

"Pretty...octageneric," Mel finished for him. She didn't want to say old or make him do the math on his age. Seventy-plus sounded worse when you were young for some reason. "But you were still pretty sexy." She flashed him a smile and got a half grin in return. "I'd always been curious about you. None of the surviving crew seemed to know what happened to you. I used to look at your picture and...wonder where you were and what you were doing. The mystery hero who liked H.G. Wells...or so I thought."

"It must have taken me that long to work the kinks out of time travel." He still sounded shocked. He rubbed his face, but the frown stayed firmly in place.

"Either that or..."

"Or?" He half turned to look her.

"Or you had to wait for the same time..." she finished in a rush, "you sent me last time." She braced for more shock.

"The same time...so this is what, a second try?"

He was pretty quick, but then he'd had time to think about time travel and its ramifications.

"More like a fix. From what you told me, or will tell me, we messed things up and I had to come back and straighten them out."

"That must have been some meeting." Jack sounded and looked amused.

She gave him a mock jab with her elbow. "No kidding."

Jack rubbed his face again. "There're so many things I want to ask you, but there's no time." He kind of shook himself, like a dog getting rid of water. "So what happens next? What do we need to do to fix things?"

Mel glanced at him, knowing she was making a *brace for another shock* face.

"What?" Jack asked. No surprise he sounded wary.

"There's kind of a problem with next."

"Problem?"

"You said this might happen, but it was a theory and I feel I should insert here, that you shouldn't be messing with things when you only have theories about what will happen. But playing the blame game doesn't really help us right now. I know that—"

Jack grabbed her shoulders. "Mel, what's going on?"

"I..." she added in a rush. "—don't know what happens next."

There was a silence.

"You have to know what happens next. If you're really from the future. I would have told you everything I could."

"And you did." Mel was embarrassed to hear her self sounding like a first grade teacher reassuring a less than stellar student. "It was a very thorough briefing. It was outstanding. Only... things... have changed. I may have helped with a few things I accidentally did, but I didn't notice anything at first, but now time is fluxing, at least I think that's what it's doing. I feel it, but I don't know, I mean, this is my first time, even though technically it's the second time." Her eye twitched and she shook her head. "Anyway, some things are the same, but not quite." She turned and gave him an over bright look. "At least we are in France."

Jack rubbed his face some more, but it didn't look like it helped much. "A few things?"

"If you saw a spy running and you knew it and could do something, wouldn't you?"

Jack stared at her for several heart beats before chuckling. "Probably would. And I'm sorry I missed it—though I expect I've seen the physics lesson."

Mel smiled slowly. "Maybe. I have many moves."

Jack's chest expanded, then contracted in a breath that sounded shaky. "I'll bet you do." It was his turn to give himself a shake. "Okay, let's start with what's the same."

"Well, us. France. The war. And most of the people who died up in the plane were...kind of right."

"Kind of right? What's the short version of kind of right?"

"Ric was supposed to die, but not in the plane. He was supposed to be here with us. Larsen was supposed to die in the plane, but didn't. But none of us are supposed to be here. We weren't here, in this place. We were close to here, if we're where I think we are, but not...here. I know there weren't any priests in your briefing. But there were cellars. Just not this one."

"I'd hate to hear your long version." Jack sighed again. "And what about Norm?"

"According to you, he was supposed to be badly injured, but survive. Because of the poor medical care in the POW camp, he spends the last part of his life in wheelchair."

"But that's not what you remember?"

Mel shook her head. "I don't remember him at all. He died."

"So that's what we did wrong." Jack slid his arm around her waist. He started to pull her close.

Mel leaned slightly away. "Don't hug me too tight. I need to pee."

Okay, that was probably too much sharing, even if it was the truth.

Jack chuckled. His teeth were straight and white in his dirty face.

She leaned against him, her head right over his heart. He didn't smell that great, but neither did she. In this case, the two negatives didn't add up to a positive, but she didn't care. If they were so wrong as a couple, why did it feel so right? Why did she feel so at home with him?

"Do you know what's hardest for me to believe in all this?" Jack asked, his voice changing from exasperated to deep and sad.

"What?" Mel asked the question, even though she already knew the answer.

"Sixty years. Sixty years apart? It's really sixty years between...us?"

Actually it was more. "I'm afraid so."

Jack went quiet again. Mel was content to listen to his heart thump against her ear. "What I don't understand is why I started all this in the first place."

"It's because of Ric." Mel quickly told him what she knew. "I just wish I knew what happened to Norm. I didn't see him leave the plane."

"Larsen said he bailed out with the others."

Mel nodded. "I'm not liking Larsen all that much."

Jack chuckled. "I don't think he likes you either." He went quiet again. "When's your pick up time? I know I arranged a way out for you, right?"

Mel nodded. "Christmas morning, if—"

"So we just evade capture for four more days and you're home free?"

"Well..."

"What?"

"I think the underground wants us to help them do something."

"We can't—"

"I know. I thought that, too, but I just have this feeling we should."

"Mel—"

It was probably a good thing Larsen came back right then.

MEL WASN'T SURE who was more surprised when she stuck her head in the basin of water the priest's housekeeper had prepared for Mel to wash her face. The priest or the housekeeper. But that surprise was nothing to when she emerged from the mini-bath and was revealed as a girl. Luckily all this had been preceded by a visit to the water closet or she'd have breached bladder containment at the first contact with the cold water.

"You are a woman—" he stopped and tried again. "I have not observed such a thing."

Mel couldn't help it. She grinned. "Now I'm sure that can't be true, *mon pere.*"

She surprised a laugh out of the old man. His face was a kind one, but sad. The humor lightened and brightened his overall aspect and made him almost handsome—though no amount of laughing could restore his hair.

"The Americans send their women to fight this war?"

Mel almost told him, not yet, but managed to restrain her self. "No, sir. I'm a reporter. I was lent this gear so I could fly in a bomber." The housekeeper gave a disapproving sniff. "It's very cold up there. *Ice Station Zebra* cold." Oh, they wouldn't get that allusion, would they? The book hadn't been written yet. "North Pole cold."

She shivered, not entirely artistically either. It was very cold in the old kitchen with her head wet, despite the fire in the big fireplace. She rubbed her hair with the coarse towel that had been provided. The water in the basin looked brownish red in the flickering light. She wondered whose blood she'd washed off, and hoped it wasn't hers. She cautiously probed her scalp and found a gash that felt bad, but probably wasn't. As if it had forgotten its duty, but now remembered it, it now started to throb.

"You are injured?" the priest inquired.

"Apparently." At a word from the priest, the housekeeper moved over and examined it. "It's probably a shrapnel wound, from the flak."

"You flew in the American plane up there?" The housekeeper looked astonished.

"Not only flew in it," Mel said ruefully, "got shot at and had to parachute out of it. While I'm getting a great story, I'm going to have a little trouble filing it." On the upside, the relatively sedate parachute descent was much better than the non-parachute leap into the time vortex or the HALO drop, for that matter—though the landing was definitely the worst.

Mel got another smile from the priest, but a suspicious look and another sniff from the housekeeper. A change of subject seemed indicated. Mel looked around her.

"This is a wonderful room."

She had a feeling it was French Country décor, mostly because this was France and this was the country. That she knew the term was because of exposure to HGTV.

The curtains were pulled across the windows, but the cheerful, though modest, fire in the massive fireplace gave off a welcoming light. The air was filled with a delicious smell of something cooking in the pot suspended over the fire. Bright pots hung from the ceiling, as did some clumps of what could be spices. Mel wasn't up on anything that didn't come from a bottle, so she wasn't sure.

A big wooden table held center stage, its top scored with years of living and eating. On the end away from her washing basin, a bowl and a hunk of bread waited. Mel fingered her short hair into what she hoped was a semblance of order, then cast a hopeful look toward the food.

"Has mademoiselle been ill?" The housekeeper looked as if she'd like to stand between Mel and the priest.

"No." Mel was scared, tired and homesick, but not ill.

"You are very young." He looked grave as he exchanged glances with his housekeeper.

"I'm twenty-eight," Mel said, then smiled at her reflexive reaction.

"And not married." The housekeeper sounded disapproving.

The priest smiled at Mel. "I'm sorry we couldn't do anything about your clothes." He indicated a chair. "Please, sit and eat."

Madame shuffled away and Mel sat down. The food was slightly better, too. The bread was a welcome addition to her fluid diet, though...Mel looked at it, then at the priest.

"Is this your supper, Father?"

His gaze flicked away, giving her an answer.

"I can't take your food." She pushed it toward him, but he firmly pushed it back.

He gave her a flickering smile. "I can afford to miss one or two." He patted his round stomach. "My people make sure I don't go hungry...even when they do."

"You're only doing it because I'm a girl," Mel said. But she did pick up the spoon. This was better than the other soup. "It's wonderful. Your country's reputation for cuisine is restored."

He chuckled. "I am fortunate in my housekeeper."

"You are indeed." Mel ate quietly for a few moments, but couldn't resist the urge to just talk. "Your English is excellent."

"I spent time in England, as a young priest." He hesitated. "Your French is quite fluent. Have you been to France before?"

Mel shook her head. "I have a good memory, that's all."

Mel fingered the dry bread for a moment. Finally she looked up. "Do you take confessions from non-Catholics, sir?" His dark brows rose and Mel added hurriedly. "It's not a sin or anything. Well, I guess it could be if it was you, but I'm not a priest, not that I could be, but I'm not a nun—"

"My dear, what do you want to tell me?"

"Sorry." Mel gave him a rueful grin, but it faded off her mouth as she searched for the right words. "I just wanted someone...to know...something. About Jack."

"This Jack," he pronounced it the French way. "—he is one of the men in my cellar?" Mel nodded. "And you wish to tell me you love him?"

"Yes. How did you know? Am I that obvious?"

He smiled in a kindly way. "I did not know you were a mademoiselle until you dipped your head in the basin. No, when you said it would be a sin for me, it was, how do you say, the clue?"

"I guess that did kind of give me away." Mel nibbled at her bread, and sipped some soup before continuing. "It's just that...events will pull us apart. And even if they didn't, well, he's flier and there's a war. I don't want to burden him with how I feel, but I wanted to say it. I wanted someone to know that I love him."

"You think this will be a burden for him?"

"We have a dark and dangerous journey ahead of us, *mon pere.* He's already worried about me, though I can take care of myself very well, and well...it's complicated." She was tired of saying it, mostly because it was so true.

"Love is always complicated, but it is also a gift."

"Well, then our situation is more than complicated." She sighed and pushed her chair back. "And he's waiting for his supper. Thank for listening, *mon pere.*"

"It is what I do," he reminded her, with a slow, but still kind smile.

Mel started toward the cellar, with an inward sigh, when the housekeeper suddenly reappeared, her face white and twisted by fear. She said two words.

"The Boche."

Mel picked up the pace, but a knock sounded on the kitchen door before she could take more than a single step. She looked around the room, seeking a refuge. Then she looked at the priest.

"I have a plan. Sit down at my place," she ordered. "Clear the bowl I was washing with, then answer the door, but slowly, Madame."

"Slowly," the priest echoed.

As the housekeeper did as ordered, Mel moved quickly to a row of coats hanging from a rack right by the door. There was a row of boots on the floor beneath the coats. One coat didn't have boots with it, though. This was the coat Mel slipped into, sliding her feet back until she was neatly against the wall at the end of the row and partly in shadow. The coat was long, covering all of her but her feet, though she had to bend her knees slightly to keep her head below the neckline. Her position wasn't comfortable, with her knees bent and her breathing a bit confined, but at least it was warm. If she could have hooked her collar on the rack, she could have slept. At least until terror kicked in.

"Remarkable," the priest murmured.

The heavy coat somewhat muffled her hearing, but Mel felt the swirl of cold air as the door was opened and the housekeeper ushered in the unwelcome visitor.

"Colonel Thorhaus," the priest said, in French. Mel was familiar with the German colonel's dossier. He'd been assigned to oversee this district shortly after the occupation began. Following the massacre here, he'd been assigned to another district, where he refused an order for a mass execution—and been executed with the occupants of a

French village. However, his delay had enabled some of the people, and all of the children of that village, to escape. One of those children had grown up and was something important in the study of immune deficiencies. History recorded Thorhaus as, if not an honorable man, then at least a redeemed one.

While her brain produced facts about the German colonel, she heard a chair pushed back and the shuffle of feet against the floor as the priest rose to greet his uninvited guest.

"I did not expect you this evening, Colonel."

That sounded odd. Was the Colonel a frequent visitor? That had to be awkward if the priest were part of the underground. Or perhaps it was a benefit? Who would expect the priest to be an active underground member?

"I felt...a need to talk to you after...the unfortunate accident at the Bouvier farm." His voice was also the cool, cultured voice from their landing site and from the farm. And now he had a name. "I did not authorize...action. Leutnant Kass has an unfortunate instinct for...haste."

"Judgment does not belong to me, Colonel," the priest said. "Will you sit?"

Through a slit in the coat, Mel could sort of see the Colonel look around. "You're eating in the kitchen? I thought you might be out when the only light was back here."

"It is an issue of warmth and fuel conservation," the priest said, quietly. "Would you like some soup?"

Mel could hear the reserve in his voice, though only because it was different from the way he'd talked to her.

"That is kind, but no. My supper will be waiting." Another pause. "I could arrange for some men to cut you firewood."

"It is a kind offer, but unnecessary. My parishioners take excellent care of me."

"If you change your mind, please let me know."

The priest must have offered him a chair, because Mel heard chairs creak as the two men seated themselves. The German had his back to her, so Mel carefully straightened her trembling legs, grateful for the respite. Thankfully the rough stone wall offered some support as well. She could see his crisp, German profile. His hat and gloves were on the table in front of him and he sat rigidly erect in the old, wooden chair. He didn't look comfortable and Mel felt oddly sorry for him.

Mel had to admire the way the priest waited quietly for the German to speak.

"Don't let me interrupt your meal," the Colonel finally broke the silence.

It seemed to her that the Colonel was troubled about something, though it was more sensed than seen in the flickering light from the fireplace and her limited view.

"I'd just finished when you came in," the priest said. "We could repair to my study—"

Thorhaus shook his head. "As you said, it is warmer here and I won't stay long."

To Mel it seemed he still hesitated.

"You've no doubt heard of the missing fliers?"

"I do hear...many things," the priest said carefully.

"I...hope your people won't...assist them. Kass is...eager to flex his muscles, as is *Herr* Ullstein. The outcome could be most...unfortunate. They would do well to stay as neutral as the church."

The priest didn't say anything, but Mel could see him looking attentively at Thorhaus. Silence fell again.

"Was there something else, Colonel?"

Mel could feel something change in the room.

"These fliers, they come from a bomber called *The Time Machine*."

"A whimsical name, to be sure."

Mel could see a slight frown between the priest's brows, as if he were puzzled and a bit uncertain.

"Did you hear how they eluded us?" The priest shook his head. "I don't suppose you would. It's not generally known. They are clever and resourceful. But they are in France. It is a long way to any place safe for them. If they were to turn themselves in, I would do my best to shield them as much as possible. I am a soldier, not..." He stopped and pushed his chair back, causing Mel to shrink back into her coat. "I must go."

He stood up, his movements a bit too crisp, for Mel's taste. She'd spent a lot of time around military men, but this was military-plus. Of course, she could be prejudiced.

He half turned toward the door, but stopped. "Have a care. There are dangerous currents about."

"And you, my son. Have a care for..." the priest stopped.

Thorhaus waited for a moment, then prompted, "For...?"

"Your...soul. To lose your life is nothing to losing your soul."

He began to pull his gloves on. "I'm not a religious man."

"Because you don't believe in God, does not mean He does not exist." The priest sounded slightly amused. "And if you don't believe in...anything, what draws you here, my son?"

The German paused and Mel felt her stomach clench. He was looking right at her, or so it seemed. The moment seemed long before the German looked at the priest.

"It's quiet here. And you don't...want anything from me."

It was a surprisingly honest answer. In another place, another time, she might have liked him.

The priest smiled slightly. "I leave expectations to God."

Thorhaus laughed lightly, a pleasant sound and unexpected for it.

"Then please give him my compliments...and my thanks."

He spun briskly on his heel and strode past Mel and her hiding place. At the door he paused once more. To Mel's discomfort, it seemed he was looking right at the row of boots, a frown between his chiseled brows.

"Please, think about my warning. There is grave risk at this time."

There was another swirl of cold air, then the door snapped closed and he was gone. Mel didn't move. In the movies, dangerous people always popped back in unexpectedly. Maybe the priest had seen similar movies. He didn't move either. Just sat there quietly. When Mel's legs were trembling again from the effort of staying bent, the housekeeper came in.

"He is gone."

Mel straightened her legs with relief, though was reluctant to leave her warm cocoon. The room felt even colder when the folds fell away.

"So, how did you elude capture in the field?" the priest asked.

Mel sat next to him at the table, a grin pulling at the edges of her mouth.

"Well, *mon pere*, there was this ditch full of snow and our parachutes were white..." She stopped, to let him fill in the blanks. "He's no slouch if he figured it out."

The priest's brows rose. "Slouch?"

"He's not stupid."

"No." the priest looked grave. "He's not stupid." Now he looked at Mel.

"I sense you are an unusual young woman."

Mel grinned ruefully. "If true, it's a curse, sir."

That surprised a chuckle out of him, but he sobered quickly. "You must hurry."

She held out her hand. "Thank you. I hope we haven't..." But they had put him in danger. "I'm sorry."

"You don't put us in danger, mademoiselle. It is the Boche that are the problem."

"I thought," Mel hesitated, and then went with it, "I thought the church was supposed to remain neutral?"

"Each of us must choose the path our conscience directs."

"You're no slouch either, sir."

She could almost see him filing the slang term away and hoped it wasn't too much an anachronism to the time.

THORHAUS STOPPED BESIDE his command car, turning to study the fine, old church, so peaceful in the moonlight punching through the cloud cover. He'd sent Kass off to search areas in the direction of Spain and was enjoying the sense of peace he felt at not being under his observation. He was not Catholic, but he respected Father Mesuirer.

Something about the visit troubled him, though he couldn't put his finger on exactly what it might be. All had seemed the same, except for the priest being in the kitchen. That hadn't happened before. On the other hand, it was cold and he knew food and fuel were scarce in the village.

It was odd that the old housekeeper had left so quickly after admitting him, but that could have been because of who he was. She was respectful, but her eyes told of her hate for the invaders. But usually she hovered over the old man.

He rubbed his temples and sighed. He was an old soldier, not a... manager. There were too many emotions and nuances to managing French territory and its people. If he'd had any real power, he'd have brought in a real liaison from among the French, not the scaly collaborator who paid lip service to representing French interests during the occupation.

He found his thoughts drifting back to the plane and the unusual art on the fuselage. He'd asked the American sergeant about it, but all he could tell him was that the pilot liked the book. A book title painted on the side of a plane of war. H.G. Wells was a pacifist, from what Thorhaus had read of his work, though the titles of his books didn't sound pacifist. He'd been thinking about the cone or triangle and was wondering if it might be representation of a tornado. He'd never seen one, but had read of such things in America. But why link a book and a weather event? It was odd and interesting, though he couldn't have explained why, not even to himself. Maybe it was the mind behind it that really interested him. He had no proof the captain of *The Time Machine* was the brain behind the clever trick with the parachutes, but he felt sure he was.

He leaned back, closing his eyes and letting his thoughts drift. In another time and place, he would have looked forward to meeting him. A pity.

Chapter Fifteen

December 23, 1942

IT WAS JUST after daylight when Mouy returned, soon after the curfew ended. The old priest had supplied them with reading material, though his selections of English books were severely limited. Mel had occupied the time by alternately exercising to keep flexible, trying her hand at translating one of the French books for her and Jack and taking a couple of trips to the bathroom. They couldn't leave the cellar once it was light. Thank goodness it was winter with its shortened days.

Larsen surprised her by joining in the calisthenics and staying awake for her halting reading. Perhaps Jack had also had a chat with him while Mel was upstairs hiding in a coat. Or maybe Larsen was adapting.

Jack had looked relieved when Mel returned from her turn upstairs, but that could have been because he needed to pee. He didn't ask her what happened, so she didn't tell him. She spent the time while he was gone pulling up from her memory what used to be true about Thorhaus and the area. It couldn't all be changed, she concluded, more in hope than with any certainty.

"Do you really think we can get to England?" Larsen had broken into her thoughts to ask. He sounded young and scared and hopeful. And since she didn't know for certain they couldn't get to England, she gave him a positive answer. Gran always said it was important to think positive and Mel felt it couldn't hurt.

Mostly Mel had to keep reminding her self how young they all were. When she'd known the crew, they were old men, full of that fifty-fifty hindsight. At this point in their lives, they just thought they knew it all.

Mel stood off to one side, waiting for the Frenchman to speak. He looked reluctant, but whether it was about starting or including them in his plans, she didn't know. They must have looked young to him, too, she thought, feeling a sense of awe at what had been...or would be accomplished by the young men of this generation. And even with a couple of washes behind them, they still looked pretty scruffy. Speaking for her self, the lye soap was negatively impacting her hair.

Last time she'd seen it, it looked as defeated as she felt.

Mel considered breaking the silence, except it seemed what Mouy wanted. It was his call whether to trust them or not. It's not like she was dying to get involved in his adventure in sabotaging. Jack glanced at her and Mel shrugged.

When the silence got so tight, it seemed it had to snap, Mouy finally spoke. From nothing to a deluge, words rushed out in a flood of excited French. His arms got in the act, too, gesturing so violently all three of them took a step back. He spoke rapidly, shooting words out like a automatic rifle. It was lucky Mel couldn't forget. When he finally went mercifully silent again, Jack and Larsen looked at her. She mentally edited it for content and clarity and produced, "They've been asked to paint a target for the RAF."

She examined her own conclusions. Yeah, that was really it, though Mouy's version was more entertaining and physical.

Jack looked at Mouy, then back at her. "That's it?"

Mel did a quick recap of what Mouy had said. "Yeah, minus the detail..."

"Paint? Paint is..." Mouy mimicked painting. "We are to explode..." He made a sort of explosive motion with his hands. "This is not paint." He spat the word at her.

What she wouldn't give for some laser-guided missiles at this moment. And some SEALS...and maybe a clue...as in, get one...

"They want us to paint something?" Larsen entered the discussion. "Or not paint something?"

"Not paint, paint," Mel said. "Paint as in light it up." She used her hands, too. Maybe it would help with clarity. Or something. "It's some kind of secret facility that needs to be bombed. But it's hidden, so we have to go in and start some fires so the bombers can find it in the dark. Paint it with light, so to speak."

She stopped, pleased with this analogy.

Mouy stared at her for a few moments. Finally he gave a slow nod. "To paint with light." He grinned. "We will paint the masterpiece, no?"

"At least get someone's attention," Mel agreed.

Jack was frowning. "Why does he need our help? Sounds simple enough."

"Well, technically, it's me they need. Because I speak German. They need a German speaker to get inside. The outside perimeter is too heavily guarded for them to get close enough. And they need to mark the bunker entrance."

This didn't remove the frown. In fact, it might have deepened it. It was hard to say in the seriously murky light.

"Did the infiltrator know about this plan?" Jack wanted to know.

Mouy shook his head violently and beat one hand on his chest. "Only I. No one else."

And still Jack's frown didn't clear. "Do you really think you can do this? Do you really think you can talk your way in?"

She didn't think she could, but she didn't tell him that. She didn't think she could do any of the things she'd done. She was just too stubborn to admit it. One thing she'd learned in her many adventures. Never admit anything. And then, too, the SEAL thing may have given her delusions of competence. Or maybe not. Maybe she was competent. No...if you were competent, you wouldn't be in freaking Occupied France, her brain shouted at her. She told her brain to shut up and shrugged on some SEAL attitude. In the end, it was all about the bluff and always had been.

"Of course." If she ever got out of this, she was going to have to rethink her career choice. She had the feeling bluffing wasn't going to work for her anymore. She looked at Mouy, because she didn't want Jack to see any of the stark fear that might have leaked into her eyes. "When do we go?"

They must have some way of contacting the Brits, because they'd need a night with clear skies. Unlike the Americans, the Brits flew at night. That made it harder for the Germans to shoot them down, but it also made it harder to find and hit anything. And Mel had a date with a vortex on Christmas day. She hoped.

"The signal, it will come soon," Mouy said.

But would it come soon enough?

"What if it isn't clear enough to fly?" Jack looked worried now. "We can't hang around here for too long." And he knew about her date with the vortex.

"Two days only. They move on Christmas. Move to Germany," Mouy explained.

Mel had a feeling there was a back-up plan in place, if the bombers couldn't get through. She wished they'd go straight to it, but there was that stupid, insistent feeling that she needed to do this.

"Do you have a map of the compound?" Maybe she had some inside info on it.

He produced a map and spread it out, moving the lantern so she could see it. It was rough, but had the key landmarks, enough so Mel could pull up one of the post war maps she'd seen and mentally placed it over the top of this one. She'd looked at data from the Allies, the French, and the Germans. She'd seen maps and enough documents to fill a library, but she had nothing in there on this target. That fluxing feeling made a sweeping appearance again. It was worse than the last time, like free falling without a chute. The map spun in a circle and she had to close her eyes, fighting back a wave of nausea. She was leaning on the barrel top they were using for a table, or she might have fallen. It slowly subsided. She opened her eyes. No one seemed to have noticed.

"Here, we meet," Mouy marked a spot on the map. "You drive truck—"

"Whoa, me drive a German truck? I don't think so."

Mouy frowned and switched to French. "You could ride as passenger, but it is more risky. They will question the driver."

"How big is the truck? Could I hide behind the seat?" In her bag of tricks, Mel had some skill as a ventriloquist. She'd done a story about one, early in her career. She moved her lips, but she had learned to throw her voice. The lip thing wouldn't matter if no one could see her. She explained this to Mouy. Jack shifted restlessly beside her. It was a pain neither he nor Larsen could understand her...she quickly brought them up to speed.

"You can throw your voice?" Jack's voice sounded odd.

Mel said she could, throwing the words so they came from Larsen's direction. All three of them jumped slightly. Larsen looked around, then at Mel.

"How did you do that?"

She didn't have time for a lesson.

"You are...an unusual woman," Mouy said.

Mel smiled slightly. "So I hear. And it's not a gift."

"I'd like to more about what happens once we're inside," Jack said.

"The compound is here." His finger stabbed the map. "There is an aerodrome here, slightly more than a mile."

He went on to explain, pausing to let Mel translate. The plan was actually pretty simple. They had their stolen German truck and some uniforms, and they also had forged orders getting them inside as a supply truck. It was her job to answer any questions posed by the men at the gate and get them inside. Once there, they would plant four explosive charges in each corner of the perimeter and one close to the bunker entrance. Once the charges were planted, they would leave before the bombs started falling. No problem—if nothing at all went wrong.

And as she listened, commented and translated, Mel kept staring at the map, searching for a memory, any kind of memory of anything there besides trees and fields...

Only she couldn't. Surely the small disruptions she'd made in the time line couldn't result in such a huge change? Unless...

She could only think of two things that would explain it and she didn't see how either one could be a good thing for her or the time line she was attempting to restore.

MOUY LEFT THE map with them. It was a safe as any place at this point. Jack noticed that Mel kept looking at the map with a troubled expression. The usual lack of privacy was seriously inhibiting the necessary exchange of information.

"Anything wrong?" he asked, besides, oh, everything. Her gaze lifted to meet his, confirming that she was worried.

"That aerodrome is really close to the compound," she said. "Slightly more than a mile, that's...close."

"So?" What was she thinking? He may not have known her that long...yet, but he knew she was thinking. She never seemed to stop.

"Do you want to paddle to England?" Mel paused. "Or fly?"

Larsen straightened. "Are you seriously suggesting we...steal a German plane and fly to England?"

"It is better than walking. Or paddling." Jack slanted a quick smile at Mel, before looking at the map again. If they could get in the air, and keep from being shot down by their own guys, or the Germans, until they got close to the coast, they could ditch and get picked up. It was risky, but not more so than anything else they were contemplating doing. It would also depend on what aircraft there was. Larsen wasn't a pilot. With a stab of guilt, Jack thought about Mel's statement that Larsen was already supposed to be dead...

He'd thought it would be amazing to know the future...and it was...but it did have a down side. What must it be like to be Mel, to be moving through this time knowing it all, not just knowing who lived and died, but unable to forget?

And he'd done it, not because he should, but because he could. He'd sent her back the first time, to change an outcome he didn't like, to assuage his own guilt—and locked them both into repeating this time until they could get it right. If he had to do this again, he should send someone back to eliminate himself. What had happened last time that had forced him into sending her back again, instead of stopping it once and for all? Was it because of how he felt about her, or something else?

He'd have had a good reason. Surely he hadn't changed that much?

In Larsen's face, Jack saw his own mixed feelings about Mel's bold suggestion. They both wanted to get out of France. Based on what he'd seen and heard, an unpleasant time lay ahead of they were captured.

Unpleasant would be an understatement if the Gestapo got involved. So, torn between hope and disbelief, they both chose hope and agreed to try.

Larsen waited a bit longer, but when no one said anything, he retired to his corner and soon began to snore. It was fairly obnoxious, but it meant he was asleep. They were kind of alone.

Without spoken agreement, Mel followed him to a spot as distant from Larsen as was possible in the cramped cellar. Jack snagged their blankets on the way and folded them into cushions against the chill of the packed, dirt floor. Jack put his arm around her, for warmth, so they could hear each other, and because he wanted to.

The setting wasn't romantic and the girl smelled of lye soap. He almost smiled at this...parody of romance that they presented. She was huddled deep inside her clothes, so deep he could barely feel the outline of the slight, strong figure he knew was there. Her face was clean, but looked pinched and cold and tired. There were also cuts and scratches in varying degrees of healing scattered across the surface.

All this, he'd done to her, or at least he would be doing.

Only her eyes seemed the same as he remembered from their first meeting. The wide, purple pools were a mix of wary and surprised and anxious, all of it over laid with a careful neutrality.

He wanted to tell her he was sorry, but instead he whispered, "What's wrong?"

Did she sag against him? Did she shiver as she leaned into him, her hand on his chest to steady herself so she could whisper in his ear? Warmth flooded him. It felt good to finally be warm. Felt right to have her close.

"Jack, that facility wasn't in any of the material you gave me before I came."

That killed warm dead. He wished he knew more about time travel than how to do it. He hadn't had time to learn more. All he had were theories...

"You didn't tell me a lot about...travel..." Mel cast a quick look in Larsen's direction. There were still muffled snores coming from his direction, but he was glad she was being careful. "But you had concluded that there weren't alternate realities, or if there were, your...technique wouldn't result in inter-dimensional travel, just single dimensional."

Dimensions? Jack tried to look like he knew what she was talking about. He saw her lips twitch and suspected he hadn't succeeded all that well.

"That leaves only one other explanation..." She trailed off.

"That someone else is traveling, too," Jack said it for her. Which lead to the next obvious question? Were they inadvertently changing things? Or deliberately attempting to alter the future? "If that someone were...tinkering..."

That sounded better than tampering for some reason.

"Tinkering? A whole secret facility is tinkering?"

"Even an irresponsible traveler would most likely start small. Because a minute change could be catastrophic to the point of wiping out the future." Of course, it was irresponsible to tamper at all...as he was coming to realize. But if someone else were here, it would explain why Mel's attempt to restore the time line wasn't working.

"Like *Back to the Future*."

"What?" Jack looked at her, his brows arched.

"Sorry. It's a movie. The flux capacitor movie, actually."

She smiled impishly, turning her face from tired to...amazing and turning up the temperature again.

He rubbed his face, to distract himself from her. "I'm the one who is sorry. I should never have started this."

"It wouldn't have been so bad if you'd let me bring my own shoes."

He found himself grinning back at her, surprised he could. "They must have been some shoes."

"Never come between a woman and a pair of comfortable shoes."

He chuckled, the sound surprising and a bit loud in the enclosed space. Over in his corner, Larsen snorted a bit. Jack stiffened until he started to snore again.

"I'll try to keep that in mind," Jack promised.

Her head drooped to his shoulder, but he wasn't sure she realized it. Maybe because it felt as natural to her as it did to him? She was quiet for a time and he was content to wait. Finally he felt her sigh.

"We probably need to get a look at what they are guarding inside that facility," Mel said. "If someone is tinkering with time, it might indicate who. Or is that whom?"

Jack chuckled again, careful to keep it soft. "Either way, it's a good idea. How we make it happen, on the other hand..."

"It is a bit of a problem," Mel conceded.

A bit of a problem? Just what exactly what was she, or what would she be in the future? The thought gave life to the words and he felt her tense. She was silent for a time before slowly looking up at him, their faces mere inches apart.

"I'm a reporter."

"Mel—"

"It's the truth."

"A reporter...with your skills?"

"It's—"

"...complicated. Can't you uncomplicated it for me?"

A smile flickered on her face. "Mel's life for dummies?"

"What?"

"Sorry. It's kind of a future joke. There's all these books on how to do everything, called the Dummies..."She blinked a couple of times. "I guess you'd have to be there."

"I guess so." He tried to stay offended, but it was hard with her eyes, well, twinkling like that. Purple twinkles, even. Deep pools of purple twinkles. He could almost dive in and swim around in there. Diving for twinkles—

"You've heard of television, right?"

He knew a bit about it. "I saw it demonstrated at the New York World's fair."

"Really, well cool beans. Let me just say, it's come a long way. And I work in television."

She explained the concept of her show and the things she'd done. It would be easier to eye dive for twinkles than believe it, but with the twinkles, there was truth in her eyes.

"And you've never cried uncle?"

A wry smile curved up the edges of her mouth. Her lips were dry and cracked in spots, but he still wanted to kiss them.

"Not until now."

He could see how appealing she'd be visually, though maybe not as this moment. And like him, the men she'd deal with would tend to underestimate her spirit and determination. He still thought he was crazy to have sent her, but he understood better why he had.

He felt, rather than heard her sigh.

"What?"

"I'm torturing myself with what I'd be doing if I were home."

He didn't mind the distraction. "What would you be doing?"

"Well, first up, I'd take a bath. A long, hot bath. I don't think I've ever been this dirty. No, I haven't. I'd remember." Her smile flickered across her face like a light bulb that hadn't quite made the electrical connection.

Mel in a tub. Probably shouldn't think too much about that. "And then?"

"Pajamas. Soft, flannel pajamas and warm slippers." Her voice was rich with longing. "And than a real bed to lie on. I'd sleep and sleep and sleep. I might not ever get up."

"Not even to eat?"

She glanced up at him. "I'm trying not to think about food, because that might depress me."

Jack chuckled and smoothed a sticky, lye scented piece of hair off her smudged, tired face. His heart...clutched was the only word he could find to describe the feeling. It hurt, but in a good way and squeezed out the words he hadn't meant to say to her because he hadn't the right. Even if time didn't divide them, what he'd done to her should...

"I love you." He saw her flinch and tears filled her eyes. "I'm sorry, I shouldn't have—"

"Oh, Jack." Her hand came to rest against the side of his face. "I shouldn't either, but I do. I love you." She looked rueful. "I think I always have. Captain Jack Hamilton, the hero of *The Time Machine*. And now here you are."

"Not a hero."

"No, you're still that." Her gaze teased him gently. "But a man. Oh my." She leaned against him. "A bit ripe, but definitely a man."

He laughed lightly, his chin resting lightly on her head, wishing everything were different. Well, almost everything.

Gently, carefully, his hand found her tucked down chin and raised it until he could see her mouth. He lowered his head to hers their mouths connected. There was no passion in the contact. He didn't have the energy and he figured she didn't either. It was enough just to hold her and pretend they had a future. He eased back and hugged her closer.

"Why do you taste of mint?" he murmured, feeling vaguely surprised.

"I kind of brought back some breath mints with me from the future. Do you want one? Of course, I should have brought my toothbrush. I hope I have some teeth left when...you know..."

He knew.

There was silence for a few more minutes.

"Jack..." Her voice sounded dreamy.

"Hmmm..." He was tired of thinking. All he wanted to do was rest his soul in her arms.

"Will you marry me?"

That got his soul's attention. "Excuse me?"

She grinned. "Commitment issues, Captain?"

"It's more accurate to call it a situation issue. Otherwise, I'd already be down on one knee." It was the truth. He didn't want to lose her. He wanted to keep her, but there was this war going on, not to mention the fact they were hiding in a cellar being vigorously hunted by the enemy. And that he was sixty years older than her, or he would be.

"I know this priest...and there's a church just across the cemetery. It wouldn't be legal, of course but anyone who read the register would know that Melanie Morton loved Jack Hamilton and he loved her. "

"Why wouldn't it be legal?"

Mel sat up, partially pulling away from him. "You have to have a civil and religious ceremony in France."

He blinked. "How do you know that?"

She grinned. "A movie. Called *I was a Male War Bride*."

He didn't want to know. And she knew it. Her grin widened into a cute smirk.

"He might not do it, but if he will...will you marry me, Melanie Morton?"

"Why Captain Hamilton," her drawl was full of the South, "I'd be honored."

December 24, 1942

TIME SEEMED TO race forward again. It was funny how it worked—well, not really funny, but interesting in a sucks-dead-toads kind of way, Mel decided.

The priest wasn't hard to persuade, since the marriage wouldn't be legal, and for the same reason, it didn't really matter that neither of them was Catholic. Mel could see in his eyes that he understood what they were trying to do. Love wasn't just a gift, it was a light in the heart. There'd been a lot of dark since they were shot down. A lot of dark.

So, in even more dark, in that deepest, darkest part of the night, just prior to the unkind dawn over a hostile land, he led them past the dead to the old chapel for a living, though illegal ordinance. By the light of a single candle, that lit up the dark only enough to reveal their clasped hands, he married Melanie Morton to Jack Hamilton—in the eyes of God and each other, but not in the eyes of man or the law.

When Jack kissed her, only their mouths touched. Passion was out of place in this here and in this now.

She signed the register after Jack, wondering if it would still be here if, or when, she made it back to the future. Neither of them knew what effect the time flux was going to have on the future or this past. There was no time to linger and savor the moment. Only a moment to look at the two names and wonder, would she ever come here again and know what she knew now? Even if she didn't remember, she hoped they'd always be here, a mute witness that they'd been here and loved each other.

They had to race the dawn back to their noisome cellar. The brief burst of fresh air reminded her nose it could smell and she went through another painful adjustment period. There was, she had found, either too much to smell, such as their body odors, or too little, which included the food. Despite this, Mel found that happiness gave new clarity to her mind and new energy to her weary body and soul. Joy was more potent even than chocolate—though she wouldn't have said no to a shower, pajamas and a bed if any of it had been offered. And some cake. No, she'd never again say no to a piece of cake.

Mouy sent word, just after a meager lunch, that the signal had been given.

"We should all rest," Jack said. "It's going to be a long night."

Mel looked at Larsen and saw in his face a new maturity and sense of purpose. Sometime in during the dark, waiting hours, he'd come to terms with where they were and what they had to do.

Mel sat with her cheek against Jack's shoulder and tried to sleep, but like the night before they flew to France, sleep eluded her. Unlike that night, this time she didn't waste any of it wrestling with her conscience. Jack knew the truth. For good or ill, the burden had now been shared.

"Jack," she leaned up to whisper, "if you need to prove to me that this happened, just tell me, I went before I left the plane. And I'll know we really met."

"That's it? What does it mean?"

"In sixty years, maybe I'll tell you." Though she really hoped not.

THE GERMANS CAME BACK just after sunset. Mel was in Madame's room off the kitchen, changing from her uniform to black clothes provided by Mouy. Bad enough she now lived in the dark, now she was dressed to hide in it. She'd just gathered up her muddy uniform when she heard the bang of an angry fist against the door and almost dropped the bundle.

Her spider sense didn't even have time to tingle a warning. Her heart rate went from normal to racing between beats and her adrenaline kicked flight or fight into overdrive. The end result, she froze as the tramp of boots and sound of angry voices filled the next room. One in particular, she recognized.

Kass. Leutnant Thug.

Crap.

She looked at her muddy uniform and then around the room. No hiding place was safe for her hosts. There was a window. She doused the light and tossed it out, then quietly secured the window again. It was, she knew, a delaying tactic. Now she needed another one.

Kass was yelling at Madame. A slap, then a sharp cry. The priest's voice joined with the others, calm and reasonable. Kass's voice got louder, more aggressive...

Think, Mel, think fast...

The best defense is a good offense.

She didn't stop to think about it. If she thought about it, she wouldn't have the nerve to do it. She did take a moment to find her inner SEAL. Yes, there it was. If she'd been a cat, she'd be puffed.

She wrenched open the door and stepped right into the middle of the fracas. Her sudden appearance couldn't have been more startling than a grenade tossed in to their midst. Silence spread out in a wave that lapped the edges of the room. Before it could rebound into noise, Mel looked scornfully at each man in his turn. She could have sworn she was channeling Rockman.

"Who is in charge?" She snapped in precise German, her voice as harsh as she could make it. She looked at Kass and dismissed him with her eyes. Only when she'd looked at each man in his term, did she let her gaze find its way back to him. A slight, scathing lift of brow asked her question yet again.

Surprise had tilted the control balance her direction, but it wouldn't last. She could see Kass gathering himself together, fighting against the uncertainly clearly visible in his piggish gaze.

She marched up to him, stopping just out of arm range. She hoped. He was a big, bruiser of a thug with fat, pink lips and arms that almost brushed the floor.

"On whose orders are you here, Leutnant?" she both asked the question and sneered his rank. Rockman would have been proud of her.

He puffed up like the bag of hot air he was, though he was still a dangerous airbag. "Who are you? Show me your papers."

Mel took a couple of steps closer, forcing him to take an involuntary half step back. "I will be...delighted to show you my papers." It was implied that he would not be delighted to see them.

He licked his fat lips nervously. Now that she knew she had his attention, she lifted the edge of the black sweater, exposing a line of smooth skin to the half-leering, half scared men. She made herself slowly remove the sheaf of papers. It was an awful feeling and if things went wrong, it was going to get a lot worse, but her goal was for all the thinking to be on her side. Reversing blood flow elsewhere seemed like a good idea.

The papers weren't a forgery, though they were sixty years old. With a single flick of her hand, the pages crackled and unfolded so he could see the signature at the bottom.

Herman Goring.

The color visibly drained from his ruddy cheeks.

"You have inserted yourself here without orders and put at risk a most secret and important operation. Explain yourself."

His mouth moved a couple of times, but nothing came out.

Mel took another step toward him, until she was close enough to smell his sour body order. She didn't wrinkle her nose in distaste, but it wasn't easy. At least she knew she still had a sense of smell. She'd been starting to wonder.

He cleared his throat. "We had no information—"

"Do you seriously expect Berlin to notify *you* when they launch a top secret mission? Perhaps," She took another step toward him, so that they were almost nose to nose now, "you don't quite understand the concept of secret?" She waited for two heartbeats and added, "I do think my dear, Herman, would have mentioned you...if you had the necessary clearance to even talk to me."

Temper flared in his eyes and she wondered if she'd pushed too hard. She could see him balance on the knife-edge of control. Out of the corner of her eye, she could see the whites of his men's eyes. He'd get no support from them. They just wanted to leave.

"Did you want me to tell Herman something? The *Herr* and I are scheduled to speak with each other later tonight. He insists on hearing my voice every night. Of course, he trusts me completely, else why would he have given me unlimited authority." Mel paused. "Unlimited."

That pushed him toward control, but only barely. His meaty fists were still clenched. He stepped back, one step, then two.

"My apologies." His mouth worked a couple of times before he was able to add, "What are your orders?"

Now Mel stepped back, grateful for some fresh air. She clasped her hands behind her back, and looked around, her gaze stopping on the two men still gripping the housekeeper's arms. Her brows arched and they stepped hastily away from her. Madame rubbed her bruised wrists, casting Mel a suspicious look. The priest stepped forward and placed a comforting hand on her shoulder. Mel gave him a quick, hopefully reassuring gaze, before turning back to Kass.

She sighed. "I'm sure you are a good enough soldier, in your over enthusiastic, and doltish way. I have no wish to eliminate you. Bodies are so messy and difficult to dispose of." Another pointed pause. "Though maybe not so difficult this near a cemetery."

Kass swallowed with difficulty, the sound harsh in the weighted silence. He seemed to shrink in size.

"If I might suggest," the priest entered the discussion in stilted German. Mel wondered how much of the conversation he'd followed or guessed. "I doubt they have been seen here. If they were to withdraw and never speak of it..."

The four men looked her hopefully as she appeared to consider the suggestion.

"Very well." She stepped close to Kass again. "But if I learn you have broken your word, you will wish you were on the Russian front."

He stepped back and saluted sharply, giving her the standard, "Heil Hitler."

Mel echoed the move, though abbreviated it as much as she dared. There was a bad taste in her mouth and not just from lack of proper brushing. The four men shuffled out, one of them even pausing to close the door behind them. No one spoke in the room until the sound of their vehicle faded into the distance. Mel was afraid to even sigh. She stood rigidly in place, praying Kass was too stupid to start thinking again. Her story had more holes than the kid's book with the same name.

"See if they are gone," the priest asked his housekeeper, "then see to your...injuries."

She cast a suspicious, resentful glance at Mel, but did as she was asked.

"Who are you?" he asked, his voice still gentle, but with a thread of iron running through it.

What, she wondered, would he have done if she'd really been Herman Goring's mistress? Tough choice for a priest. And she hoped she wasn't about to find out. All he really had to do was tell Mouy. That sent a chill down her back and reduced SEAL attitude to almost zero. She turned to fully face him.

"I am who I was before those thugs came, *mon pere*." She was shaking inside, and it was starting to spread out. She stepped forward and dropped onto one of the table's wooden chairs. She looked up at him, hoping he could see in her eyes she was telling him the truth. "I'm not an agent of the Gestapo."

"And yet you carry identity papers convincing enough to scare Kass, who does not scare so easy."

His words were combative, but he did sit down across from her. Mel handed him the papers.

"They are very convincing." He looked troubled.

"I hope so. They had to be. And I might remind you, they just saved all our lives." Mel leaned toward the old man. "And I am not that person. Nor can I explain how I came to have them."

He fingered the pages, with a slight frown. "They look very...old, mademoiselle."

She couldn't lie to him. He'd know it now.

"If I could tell you, I would. But I promise you, you don't want to know. I don't want to know." The tension in the room was easing. She could feel it. "I just want to go home." Her shoulders sagged slightly and it embarrassed her how forlorn her voice sounded. She forced her shoulders back and lifted her chin. If she convinced him, it wouldn't be by being a girl.

There was a long silence, as she was weighed and judged.

"You are fortunate that I am a priest. Against my reason...I believe you. But I wouldn't mention these to...anyone else."

"Yeah, I was actually thinking the same thing myself." She gave him a shaky smile. "I will never forget your kindness and your trust. I won't let you down. I promise."

He patted her hands now. "It is only God that you must please. Only He can get you home, my child."

Mel sobered. "Well, I hope He has mercy on us both."

They were going to need it.

KASS DIRECTED HIS men to return to the base, trying to disguise his anger and humiliation from them. He was not, he well knew, popular with the men. He didn't care. It was not his job to be liked or theirs to like him. But these three, he had made them come out and they would rejoice in this set back.

But would they dare speak of it? As angry as he was, he didn't dare go back. Somehow, he must turn defeat into victory. If only he could capture the three fliers, it would not matter so much. He hated returning like a spanked little boy. But if he interfered in a Gestapo operation—no, he was not that angry. Nor was he a fool. What he wanted to do was get every man in the barracks out of bed and make them beat the bushes until they fell over or turned up the fliers. And if they didn't find them in the bushes, then tear each and every house in the district apart, piece by piece.

Tonight would be perfect, with the Oberst out to dinner. Out to dinner, while enemies of the Third Reich ran free. He was beginning to wonder where the Oberst's real loyalties lay...and how he could use the Oberst's weakness to his own advantage...

THORHAUS LEANED FORWARD as his car halted at the entrance to the compound, and presented his papers to the guard. It was clear they were expected. The guard merely glanced at them and handed them back, then waved at them, directing them to go the right, after passing through the raising barrier.

He was glad he'd accepted the invitation to dinner from his old friend. Like himself, Dieter Trump was a colonel of the old school. Thorhaus, never the less, reminded himself to be careful. In these dangerous times, confiding, even in friends, was a dangerous luxury he could not afford.

It was also a relief to be away from Kass. Usually they took the evening meal together, but even he couldn't force himself into this situation. Before he left, Kass had informed Thorhaus he'd be following up a lead on the missing fliers. Thorhaus was too weary to object and merely nodded. They'd all have to look out for themselves for the evening.

He had a feeling his friend the priest knew more than he should about the missing fliers and the underground. He hoped he'd be careful. Thorhaus could barely protect himself. If the priest were found aiding the enemy, only his God could save him.

He thought about his last visit with the old man. Was it just the kitchen meeting that had been odd? Or something else? Almost idly he replayed the scene. The kitchen had been a pleasant place. Reminded him of his mother's kitchen when he was growing up. The spices hanging from the rafters. The fire. The boots by the door—

Boots by the door. Something about the boots...one pair had been muddy. It might be that the housekeeper hadn't gotten around to cleaning them...but they had been smaller than the other pairs. And different...he wished he'd looked more closely at them. And he wasn't sure what their presence meant, though he could see the stern housekeeper making even a fleeing flier remove his muddy shoes. She made him feel like he was back in school again.

As his car slid to a slow stop in front of what he presumed to be Dieter's living quarters, he had an impression of a building both temporary and slapped together. What was his old friend guarding here?

His driver clambered out and opened the door. Thorhaus felt the cold air bite through his clothes as he left the protection of the car. There was the scent of wood smoke, German sausage and the dangerous one of real Kaffeebohnen, made from real coffee beans, instead of the Ersatzkaffee that smelled of nothing at all.

How did Dieter dare flaunt what had to be a black market purchase? His taste buds watered as he climbed the short steps and he inhaled deeply. It had been a long time since he smelled real coffee, let alone drank any.

"Eugen," Dieter's voice came from the shadow of the small landing. His hand was gripped strongly and he was steered between the black out layers into the lighted room beyond. "I'm delighted you could come!"

Now the elusive scent of cooking apples teased his taste buds, too. This was danger indeed.

"It's good to see you, Dieter." Thorhaus gripped his friend's hand, looking into his eyes, hoping to find them the same, hoping his friend hadn't changed. But his eyes showed only facile pleasure at the sight of an old friend. He sighed. Perhaps his gaze was also guarded. A pity there wasn't some secret mark they could wear, only recognized by those who didn't love Hitler and were only doing their duty.

THERE WAS A THIN, cold silver of moon hanging in the deep blue-black sky. Stark branches threw ominous shadows at their feet as they milled around the German truck, preparing to move out. A slight breeze lowered the temperature a few more degrees. There was a hint of wood smoke in the wind and a touch of petrol and a bit of truck smell, but not much else. Winter air had a different scent from other seasons. It was devoid of richness, almost sterile. Even their human scents were whisked somewhere else, it seemed. Or maybe it was just that Mel's nostrils were so cold, it reduced her smelling capacity. It was cold enough that her nostrils felt crackly and each inhale made her lungs ache.

In any event, it felt colder than last night or even their first night in France, though the cold factor could be bumped up by fear. It was hard to say, without any way to measure the level of cold or fear. It was, as she'd previously noted in memos to herself, ironic that her adventure in time had been so short on sensory detail, particularly since she'd landed in a country that should have been rich in it.

Mel stamped her booted feet and thumped the sides of her arms, trying to keep the feeling in them. When the time came, she needed to be able to move and move fast. Hopefully that moving would be away from danger, not toward it.

There was another reason for her enhanced chill factor. Her Gestapo ID had gone from a security blanket to a hot potato in her money belt, though she knew the analogy didn't really work, even inside her head. If it really were hot, wouldn't she feel warmer?

Would the priest keep his word and keep her secret? What if he had second thoughts, once she was out of sight? He was a most unusual priest to even be involved with the underground. Maybe he wasn't even a priest?

With so many question and no answers, the only thing Mel could think to do was check the Luger pistol the underground had provided. It was a pretty sweet weapon and it even had a silencer. Silent was good, though this launched another round of questions, ethical ones this time. Could she shoot an actual person, even one trying to shoot her? With so much riding on this operation, she hoped training would kick in when she needed it. This was not the time to hesitate and debate ethics and morals with herself.

In actual fact, it felt good to be armed, particularly after the incident with Kass. Hopefully he'd go home and be a little more careful in future, but she doubted it. She'd humiliated him and he wasn't the kind to take that lying down.

Mouy had brought two men with him, because Jack insisted he go with her to do the drop by the bunker. Mel had backed him up, because they needed to get inside and that would take both of them. They'd already agreed Jack would go in. Since Mel spoke German, she needed to stay outside.

Mouy and his men were dressed in complete German uniforms, but Jack, Mel and Larsen had dark pants and sweaters on under German great coats, which could be quickly shed if things went south and might even prevent them being shot as spies. The boots and helmets were also authentic. Her dark pants weren't sassy or tight fitting, like on the TV shows.

They were over large and cinched on with a belt that fortunately did fit. Hopefully she wouldn't lose the pants if things got physical. The sweater and coat were pretty warm and she had a knitted cap hiding her hair that fit under the helmet.

There was also a little tin of boot blacking, in case they needed to disappear into the night. At least it was a change from mud, though possibly not as good for the complexion.

It had been agreed that Mel would ride behind the big seat of the truck and speak for Jack, who would be driving, and Larsen, riding shotgun. They were in the cab, since they'd be less likely to be recognized or remembered later, not being locals. The tricky part, of course, was how to let Jack know what he needed to do. They'd come up with some simple thump signals. Risky, but then the whole thing was loaded with risk, so why not that, too? Hopefully the truck's engine noise would cover any glitches.

It was only when she climbed into her hiding place behind the seat that she realized she was in for a rough ride—and one without a view. A real pity she was going to miss seeing more of France at night. She'd so enjoyed the views so far. She'd get some unexposed film developed if she needed to bring back the memories when she got home.

She sighed. Sarcasm in your own head wasn't nearly as satisfying. She'd become much too used to an audience.

Mouy, in a surprising moment of gallantry, had put some blankets behind the seat for her. It was sweet, and she was touched, even though they didn't help much. There was something about the space that vigorously resisted comfort. Maybe it was a truck thing.

First the engine fired, with a truly hideous roar, assaulting her senses from all sides. Then Jack put it in gear and released the brake, adding a bone jolting element to the mix. Mix was the right term for it, too. Now she knew what it felt like to be ice cream and milk in a mixer. Not that she'd ever wanted to know that. Only a couple of life times later, the truck came to a jerking, jolting halt at what she presumed was the gate. A few moments after the truck stopped moving, Mel did, too—though there were a few aftershocks.

The engine was so freaking loud, Mel didn't hear anything until a gruff voice asked for their papers. She was crouched just behind Jack, but was pretty sure she could throw her voice far enough in Larsen's direction to sound convincing. And the engine was so freaking loud.

After a brief exchange with the guard, Mel thumped the seat to let

Jack know he needed to proceed. It was almost ridiculously easy getting in. She had a feeling getting out might be the hard part.

Their cover was a delivery to the Oberst's private quarters. Mouy had had a rough sketch of the compound that helped Jack steer a path to those quarters, only to the rear, where there was a small storage room off an equally small kitchen. The trucks headlights were hooded, for the blackout, and cast light only a few feet ahead of them. Jack braked once, sharply, throwing Mel into the seat back. A new bruise for her collection. She needed to get a new hobby...

Mel couldn't see her watch, but it didn't matter. She could feel time passing. It was like a tingling stream flowing over her skin and through her body. Mel flexed her fingers and it felt as if time flickered and flexed with her. If this time flux had a center, this felt like this was it. The feeling had increased the closer they got. Now she felt like she'd shock anyone who touched her. Was there such a thing as being time-charged?

The truck lurched to a stop, adding at least one more bruise to Mel's shoulder. He pulled in parallel to the building, so they could use it for cover. Mel slipped out after Larsen and immediately smelled coffee, sausage and apples. Sweet heaven. Real food. Her mouth watered and her stomach muttered a complaint. After days of liquid diet, she didn't blame it. Neither of them had ever been this hungry before. She waited with Jack and Larsen, her back pressed against the rough wall, while Mouy and his companions cautiously approached the kitchen.

Someone in white opened the door, a darker rectangle against the blank wall. Clearly great care was being taken not to break the blackout.

"You are late. Unload it in here." Mel projected an appropriate greeting and watched as Mouy followed him inside, his head down and face turned away from the man. When he came back out, he was alone.

"He's taking a small nap," Mouy explained, softly. "We must hurry. One is serving food to the Oberst. It seemed unwise to disturb him."

They quickly moved their charges into the storeroom, working silently and as quickly as they could. The RAF had dropped them the charges, five of them—one for each corner of the compound and the last for the middle and as close to the opening of the underground bunker as possible. They were long, gray cylinders and a bit on the heavy side.

"It won't be easy," Jack said, grimly. "The perimeter looked well patrolled, from what I could see."

"Look," Mel pulled open the German overcoat. "Have one arm inside the coat, holding onto it, and then stroll, like you're out for a smoke. Once you're as close as you can get, let it drop and slip your arm back in the sleeve. If anyone approaches, cough a lot, like you have a cold." She looked at Mouy. "And if anyone gets persistent, you'll have to give them a little nap."

And pray the bombers come. Otherwise they were kicking the equivalent of a fire ant's nest. As Mel had cause to know, that was not good.

"At least three must go, for the bombers to see," Mouy said. He looked at Mel and Jack. "Yours must go off as close to bunker as possible."

"I know." She tried to look tough and competent. "If you can get them close to something that will burn...it will help with our painting project."

Mouy and his comrades went first, slipping quietly out the door one at a time. Behind them, through the closed door between the storage room and the kitchen, they heard the clink of dishes and cutlery. And the smell of food, it was enough to make long her kick the door down and jump on the food.

Jack went with Larsen to the doorway. Now that they were to the point, Mel sensed Larsen was pretty freaked out. Not that she could see anything, but she sensed his restless movements and felt his agitation.

She didn't blame him. They were in the middle of an enemy camp, armed with explosives and dressed as spies. He didn't speak German. They were tired. They were hungry. They all wanted to go home. And it was dark. Really, really dark.

Mel moved close to the two men and said, softly, "Jack, why don't you walk with him, at least part of the way? I'll meet you at the bunker."

Jack was torn, she could feel it. He felt responsible for them both.

"I'll be fine," Larsen said.

He didn't sound too convincing.

"I'll wait a bit, to give you time, then head that way. We can hook up on the North side?"

"What if he comes in here?" Jack nodded toward the closed door.

"I'll give him a little nap," Mel said. "With a physics lesson."

Jack's smile cut the darkness briefly. "Right, north side in three minutes? Let's move out, Larsen."

Before they slipped out, his hand found hers. A brief squeeze and he was gone.

She was alone. And that wasn't the worst part. She was surrounded by food and there was nothing she could do about it. She didn't dare make a noise that would bring the other cook out here.

How much time had passed? The fluxing thing was interfering with her sense of time. She tried not to think about what happened last time she was here...though not here. What if fate's wheel had a locking mechanism and her death was determined? What if Jack died and she didn't get picked up? What if...stop it, Mel, she ordered herself.

She didn't know what to do except press forward and try to do her best and hope. It was, she realized, all anyone could do, in peace or war. At this moment, more than any other, she thought she understood Norm and Jack and even her father. The fine line between a brave man and a coward was a step forward...or a step back. Like them, she hadn't started out brave, she just started out and now she had to finish what she'd started, no matter the outcome.

There were people all around, but she felt terribly alone. It was if she stood at the center, while the world spun past...

She heard the clank of plates in the kitchen. Well, not quite alone.

KASS CLIMBED OUT his vehicle, but before he could dismiss his men, a figure stepped out of the shadows. *Herr* Ullstein of the Gestapo.

"*Herr* Leutnant, you're out late. And without the Oberst?"

Kass licked suddenly dry lips. What if the woman had complained about him? Was he about to be arrested?

"He is dining out with a...friend."

"He and Oberst Trump went to school together," *Herr* Ullstein said, strolling toward Kass from the shadows. "One hopes the old friends will resist the urge to...do more than reminisce."

What did Ullstein mean? Kass had not known who the Oberst was dining with or where, but clearly Ullstein did. Rather than expose his own ignorance, Kass remained quiet, settling for a slow nod instead.

It was cold and he wished they could move inside. Behind him, his men shifted uneasily.

"So, you are in charge?"

"Yes, *Herr* Ullstein."

"Please assemble every available man. I have information that the underground is...busy tonight. We will need to be busy as well."

Kass hesitated. Surely the *Herr* knew about Goring's agent in the area? Or perhaps she was his contact? Whatever his questions, he couldn't afford to do other than comply with *Herr* Ullstein. He snapped a salute and gave agreement, then turned to the waiting men.

"Are you deaf? Have the men fall out. Now!" The three men jumped and almost ran from sight. Kass turned back to the *Herr*. He wanted to ask questions, but wasn't sure he should.

Herr Ullstein made it easy for him. He signaled for him to follow him into the Oberst's office. The warmth was welcome, particularly if he had to go out again.

Ullstein opened a rolled up map and laid it on a desk. "Your orders are to secure this section of ground, between this point and the aerodrome. Detain any and all personnel, including our people, until their identity can be confirmed by me—unless you personally know them, naturally."

"Yes, *Herr* Ullstein."

"You understand, *Herr* Leutnant, you are not authorized to question anyone or remove any...material from anyone except weapons. Do I make myself clear?"

"Perfectly," Kass said woodenly. He was reserving the right to interrogate them himself. It was a pity Kass didn't work for Ullstein. Thorhaus kept him on a very short leash.

As they headed back outside, he also wondered what it was Ullstein was afraid the underground was after.

THORHAUS LIFTED HIS wine glass in a mute salute to the excellent meal. Dieter had always liked his food and it showed in his waistline. What was less clear was how he got it. This type of meal was more typical for Hitler's inner circle than a meal for an obscure Oberst in an obscure compound in France. Did that mean Dieter wasn't that obscure? Or that he was just good at finding food? Or was there something much more important than was readily apparent going on here?

He looked around. Dieter's quarters were Spartan, even factoring in the war and the location. Other than the food, there was no sign of privilege. He'd scrapped together some china for them to eat on, but none of it matched. The chairs were shabby and the corner of a military cot was visible through the slit of the bedroom door.

"I could believe I'm back in Germany." Before the war, he could have added, but didn't. It wasn't wise, even with an old friend.

"There is no reason to live like savages in this benighted country. These French are not pleasant to live with, though they do produce a good wine. I will be happy to return to Germany."

"You are leaving then?" He'd mentioned he might be, when he

pressed the dinner invitation.

"Christmas day. Too late to spend it with my family, but we take what we can get, do we not?"

Thorhaus hesitated, wondering if he dare ask what he was doing here, but he found he didn't have to. Dieter was in the mood to talk. It was not unexpected.

"When we have finished, I'd like to show you what we've been doing here. As an old soldier, like me, you'll find it...most interesting and most puzzling. And most rewarding." His thick face looked strangely intent for a moment and then he smiled. "I know you were wondering if I'd started dealing black market. I'm sorry to worry you old friend. They are...perks for dealing with these primitive conditions. Let's have our dessert and then I'll show it to you." He lifted a bell and shook it pointedly. "It's your favorite. *Apfelstrudel mit Sahne.*"

Thorhaus smiled his pleasure. Apple strudel with real whipped cream. It had been a long time. He'd almost forgotten what it tasted like. But along with the pleasure there was a tiny chill of worry. What could Dieter be involved in that would produce such rarities as real coffee and cream? And was it safe for someone like him to know about it?

Chapter Sixteen

MEL SLIPPED UP next to the outside door of the storeroom and peeked out, then pulled back as two soldiers strolled by, smoking quietly, their rifles hanging off their shoulders. It was so like a scene from *Hogan's Heroes* it was almost freaky. She kept expecting Corporal LeBeau to pop out and offer her some of the delicious food she could smell. She heard the muffled sound of a bell and footsteps. It was awfully late for a dinner party, wasn't it? Of course, it lacked a couple of hours to midnight and this was Europe...

Mel padded quietly toward the door. It was ill-fitting and a small sliver of light cut the darkness. Mel applied her eye to the gap and saw the non-napping kitchen guy bent over a tray. Two plates of something delectable were being prepped. Mel's mouth watered again, just looking at it. Plates with the remains of dinner were stacked to one side. It looked like the kitchen staff had eaten well, too. But she wasn't jealous. Really. Two more servings were set aside. One was most likely for the napping guy.

He stood back from his handiwork, apparently satisfied, lifted the try and moved to another door and went out, giving Mel a brief glimpse of Oberst Thorhaus sitting with another man.

Thorhaus?

Mel leaned against the wall. What was he doing here? If he died here, what ripple effect might that have on the future? What about the people he'd saved...or would save, or was supposed to save? Mel rubbed her aching temples, trying to think of what she could do about it, but there's wasn't anything. It wasn't a lack of creativity, but options. At the moment, she had something else to do. She used the patch of light to check her watch. Less than twenty minutes until the bombers were due. She needed to get moving.

Mel padded quietly back to the doorway and took a quick look out. Nothing. The clouds had mostly cleared out overhead, which was good for the bombers, but bad for them. The light from the sliver of moon seemed sullen in this grim place, but it was brighter than was comfortable. That made her smile. Comfortable? She'd left comfortable in another century.

The bunker was almost dead center in the compound, with the

various support buildings forming a rectangle around it. This wasn't a POW camp, so from what they could observe, the security efforts were focused mostly on the perimeter—with one notable exception. There were two guards posted at the entrance of the bunker at all times.

Mel moved left, following in the fading footsteps of the two guards, straining for advance cues to any danger in her path ahead. Around her she could hear the small sounds of the living, drifting on the cold, night air. The shuffled of booted feet, a cough, even a soft laugh. She'd done a night op on a compound not unlike this one, though it was simulated, with the SEALS. Boy, did she miss them now. They could have taken out the whole camp without a sound.

Look for the little things, Rockman had instructed. *The glow of a cigarette, someone shifting their feet in the dark, the sound of breathing or just the lift of the hairs on the back of your neck giving warning that something is wrong.* Well, she was looking, but it would have been nice to have night vision goggles or even a scope.

As Mel padded forward, she realized there were footsteps approaching her six. She sped up, landing lightly and silently on her toes, thankful her coat muffled the charge banging against her leg. She sure hoped it was stable or she'd be a spot on the ground.

At the corner, she took a quick look. It was clear for the moment. She darted from one shadow to another. From her right she heard a noise and a soldier came around the corner, passing within inches of where she pressed into the wooden wall.

Peripheral vision was the most dangerous and she didn't dare breathe until he'd passed from her sight. She let the pent-up breath out in a rushing whisper. Oh how she missed the soft sound of comrades in her ears. Radios would have been such a huge help.

Mel summoned Rockman's voice to fill the void as she moved like a well-trained ghost through the shadows until she could see the bunker entrance ahead of her.

As predicted, two guards marched a path in front of it. Mel watched them, timing their movements, noting they passed each other precisely in front of the entry point, then marched away for about thirty seconds, give or take a few. Thirty seconds to cross the space undetected and get inside. It would be close.

And if there was an alarm?

There'd be trouble in River City.

Where was Jack? Surely it had been longer than he'd asked her to wait? Yes, they needed a look inside the compound, but it was more important to set the charges and make sure it was destroyed.

She gripped her charge and her Luger, and then counted silently as the men marched away from each other. The trick was to move across the space without triggering their peripheral vision.

She took one, quick look around, but didn't see any sign of movement. She didn't dare wait...

She walked smoothly and lightly toward the entry point, counting in her head. Danger could come at her from any other direction, but there was nothing she could about that. She had to be out here...she reached the edge of the bunker and leapt down into the hollow that surrounded the entrance, dropping below the level of the sand bags just before the men made their turn. Her heart was pounding as she listened to their dual approach. The footsteps stopped and Mel tensed, easing the Luger clear of her body...until she heard the scrape of a match, another pause and then the footsteps resumed again. She pushed up with hands, just enough to see the glow of a cigarette retreating into the darkness. She let out another silent, relieved sigh. When her heart quieted its pounding, she eased the charge out, set the timer and tucked it back in the shadow of the sand bags.

Ten minutes until it blew. She couldn't wait for Jack. She was almost out of time. She'd have to go in herself. Then out of the darkness, she heard someone softly call her name...

JACK WALKED BESIDE Larsen and they set their charge without incident, tucking it under the chassis of a large, parked truck. It should burn nicely once the charge went off. Now all they had to do was get to Mel.

At first he was surprised how quiet it was, but they weren't trying to keep anyone in, just intruders out. Silently, afraid to talk, they made their way toward the center, moving between dark buildings and almost silent night. As he passed one building, he heard the low murmur of voices and figured it must be a rudimentary barracks. The whole place looked pretty make-shift to him. What was it hiding and why was it so important for one side to protect, the other to destroy it?

They were on east of where they were supposed to meet Mel. Across from them, he could see the two guards making a path in front of the bunker. Where was Mel? They were fast running out of time before the bombers were due. And the charges would blow. As he watched the men walk away from the entrance with measured beats, a shadow emerged from the shadows and strolled quickly between them, then dropped down behind the sand bags.

It had to be Mel. Dang, why hadn't she waited for him? Larsen was right, though. The girl had guts. Well, if she could do it...

Larsen leaned close.

"Did you see her go in? Dang."

Jack had an idea. He grabbed Larsen. "We could take out the guards and take their places. We look just like them."

Larsen didn't hesitate. "Let's do it."

Jack patted him lightly on the back. "Good man."

They silently separated, moving in opposite directions, and toward where the men would make their turn. Jack approached his man, and waited, crouching in the darkness, for the heel spin. It came and Jack made his move. The guy went down like a rock and without a peep. Jack dragged him into the shadow of near by jeep, took his gun and his place. It wasn't easy to match the slow, but deliberate steps of the replaced guard when he own heart was pounding like a piston. There was a tense moment when the other guy approached, but Jack relaxed when he realized it was Larsen. They both grinned at each other, but once past, Jack tried to look, without looking at where Mel was hiding.

"Mel." It wasn't easy to be both quiet and insistent, but he must have got her attention. He saw her head poke cautiously up.

Like a wisp of breeze, he heard, "Excellent."

"Change places with me." Did she hear him? He moved out of her sight line, wondering just how much time they had now. When he made the turn and return, he was relieved to see she hadn't gone in. Like a wisp of smoke, she rose from the shadows and fell in beside him, matching her steps to his. He handed her the rifle and then stepped around her, so that he was marching in her shadow. At the entrance to the bunker, he dropped down, crouching behind the sand bags and listening for any sound of alarm.

All he heard was the sound of Mel and Larsen's boots hitting the ground. He turned to the door. The lock securing the door had already been breached. The girl was good. He eased the door open, bracing for some kind of alarm to go off, but only silence greeted him. He pulled the door closed and pulled out a flashlight. He pointed it first at his watch.

Five minutes. He'd better hurry. They were almost out of time.

MEL PACED SLOWLY toward Larsen, feeling possessed by the spirit of Sergeant Shultz. I see nothing, she mouthed. The funny part, she couldn't see much of anything. There was a faint shimmer of light from that sullen moon. It was a good thing she was living this and not writing about it. There were only so many ways to say, it was dark. She could have seen more with night vision goggles, but then it would have been green dark, a luminous green dark, but green and still dark.

And she was starting to think to herself. She'd have talked to herself, but it wasn't an option. Too bad she didn't have more to think about to herself—other than how freaking scared she was to be in the middle of an enemy camp. And here was the other funny part—funny ironic, not funny, ha, ha—at the moment it was kind of boring.

She walked past Larsen, yet again, wondering how long Jack had been gone. It felt really, really long, but she had a feeling it had only been a couple of minutes. She did her six paces into the darkness and time seemed to slow and stretch again. For a brief moment she felt almost elongated, but then snapped back to normal, the sensation broken by the sound of voices—and voices that sounded like they were coming toward the bunker, toward them.

Boredom was immediately replaced with adrenal driven panic. Clearly, she needed to be careful what she thought. A little mental whining about boredom and wham...peril gets you right in the kisser.

"Larsen," Mel hissed at him as they passed again. "Duck out of sight this round." Mel shortened her pass in front of the entrance, turning it into four steps each way as the voices resolved into two shadowy figures approaching her position. Quickly, too quickly she began to hear bits and pieces of their conversation.

"...only temporary while we assess the value...moving it to Berlin...knew you'd find it interesting..." The speaker kind of reminded her of Sergeant Shultz, only one who knew something.

One of them carried a hooded flashlight that danced across the ground almost playfully. Clearly they weren't worried about tripping over anything. Slowly they drew close enough that the wind didn't snatch away chunks of their conversation. Their figures grew more distinct.

"And for this, you get coffee and apple strudel, Dieter? I can not wait to see it."

It was Thorhaus. Again? She'd think he was stalking her, only he didn't know she was here. Actually, she was might be the stalker in the piece, even if it was inadvertent.

No way to know who this Dieter was in the larger picture of the war without more information. She pulled her helmet low, checked her posture for ramrod-ness, and turned to face the approaching men, doing her very best Shultz impression.

From under the metal rim of her helmet, she saw the taller

Thorhaus walking beside a rotund figure. Rotund abruptly halted.

"Where is the other guard?" His voice was more querulous than sharp. "The orders are for two at all times."

Mel produced a snappy salute. "He is relieving himself, *Herr* Oberst." This talking gruff was killing her throat.

Thorhaus chuckled. "It is cold, Dieter. Remember when we had the night watch?"

Dieter hesitated, then a rumbling chuckle erupted from a tiny, dark slash of mouth. They were both smiling and relaxed, as near as she could see, clearly old comrades enjoying a reunion. It took them from television cliché to real as he clapped Thorhaus on the back. It was an odd, unsettling sensation. If the first step of dehumanizing someone was to distance your self from their reality, then the reverse was also true. Trouble was, she needed a bit of distance from them to complete her mission.

"I try to forget, my old friend, but always you remind me." He was still smiling when he turned back to Mel. "We're going inside. Open the door and wait for us out here."

Mel saluted again and stepped down the two, shallow steps with what she hoped was the right amount of brisk, trying to push the sight of his very charming smile out of her mind. Keep your detachment, she reminded herself as she rattled the lock to warn Jack.

"What is taking so long? Open the door." Dieter came down the steps with short, impatient struts. He struck Mel as a small man trying to look big. In another place and time, he would have been amusing. In the circumstances, it was a little sad.

Mel cracked the door. "Sorry, *Herr* Oberst. The cold has made the lock stiff."

There was no light inside. Mel breathed more easily. It must be driving him and Larsen crazy, not knowing what was happening. She held the door wide and stepped back to allow Dieter to enter. She could see Larsen moving quietly in from behind. Thorhaus was still outside the perimeter, but had moved to the top of the steps. No sign his spider sense was tingling. He gave off vibes of relaxed content. And why shouldn't he? Based on the supper she'd smelled, he was in clover.

Mel kept her chin down, while trying not to look like she was trying and also trying to watch both men without looking like she was doing that either. A lot of trying going on and no clue if there was any succeeding. The only thing she knew for sure, they didn't have time for this delay. Mouy would leave without them if they didn't make it back to the truck in time.

Mel started to ease her rifle forward.

Thorhaus stepped down the first step.

The air raid sirens went off.

And just when she thought it couldn't get anymore complicated.

INSIDE THE MAKE-shift bunker, Jack shone his light around, moving cautiously forward until the came to a small and dreary open space. He'd had no sense of descending, but he must have. Dirt walls were about half his height, the rest some kind of temporary dome, with sand bags visible through the slats. The floor was packed down dirt. A single bulb provided light, the wire stretching back toward the entrance. It reminded him of something. Maybe a modified air raid shelter? Clearly someone's comfort wasn't high on the necessities list when this place was pulled together.

It was not only cold, it was dank and smelled of dirt and mildew.

Dead center, there was a forlorn table, covered with a cloth of some kind. Jack pulled it back and stared at what had brought them all to this place and this time.

A pair of binoculars?

But was that what they were? It looked like binoculars, but...not. He picked them up. They were rubberized and sleek. And very light. It was too dark to look through them, but his gut told him they were wrong somehow, for this time. Mel might know, but she was outside. Was there time to show them to her and bring them back? They needed to be destroyed, that was clear.

He hesitated, then slipped the strap around his neck and tucked them inside the heavy coat. There was a small metal box, with a lock, probably waiting to be transported with the binoculars. He broke it open, using the butt of his Luger and found it filled with pictures and papers, all written in German, naturally. He took those, too. There didn't seem to be anything else of interest.

He started toward the entrance, but heard Mel's voice, speaking in German, followed too quickly by the rattle of the door's lock. He snapped off the light. Now he could hear another voice speaking. He wished he knew what they were saying.

Note to self, send someone back further in time to tell him to learn German. Make that freaking tell him to learn freaking German.

Then he heard the air raid sirens start up.

That wasn't good.

THORHAUS STOPPED AND glanced up. Mel almost looked up, even

though they both knew the bombers couldn't possibly be up there yet. Dieter turned and looked up, too, giving Mel the opening she'd been looking for. She used Thorhaus's momentary distraction to affect an introduction between Dieter's skull and her rifle butt. It was too noisy to tell if he went down quietly. All that mattered is that he went.

She half crouched by the slumped figure, hopefully giving off an impression of concern. Out of the corner of her eye, she saw Thorhaus turn back and see his friend down. He immediately came to him. Mel took him down, too, though a bit more gently. He had to survive. Even as she thought this, she felt the strangeness of the thought. She might be from the future, when Germany was an ally, but in this present, he was the enemy. If she'd had the time, both eyes would have twitched. She grabbed Dieter's flashlight and looked at her watch. They should already be gone. Make that long gone.

"Jack!" She had no compunction about shouting, with the sirens so loud. She saw a bobbing circle of light rapidly approaching. When he was close enough to hear, she shouted, "Did you find anything?"

"Just this." He pulled a pair of binoculars from under his coat and handed them to her.

Mel hefted them, then turned them over. There was something—

Larsen jumped down into the sand bagged perimeter.

"We need to go!"

"We should put them back," Jack said.

"There's no more time. We'll take care of them once we're clear of the compound." If they were from the future, and if she returned to the future, it would help if she could trace them to their source. Mel hooked the strap around her neck and tucked them inside her coat.

"Take these, too," Jack said, stuffing some papers in her pockets.

Mel pointed to Thorhaus. "Grab his arms."

"What?" Larsen looked at her like she was crazy.

Mel looked at Jack. "We need to get him out of here." She hoped Jack understood what she was trying to tell him, without actually telling him.

He did. He moved to the other side of the slumped man. "Grab his arms, Larsen. Mel, you lead the way."

Mel hooked the rifle over her shoulder, pulled her Luger and started off across the open compound. The sirens had startled the place into activity that was still fairly controlled and orderly. Their blackout was complete, so the odds were slim the bombs would find them, except by an accident. They didn't know about the charges and the change that would bring to their life expectancy. She just hoped they hadn't missed their ride.

Figures moved in the darkness around them, but no one appeared to pay them any particular attention. They blended in with the flow of people, who were most likely responding to some sort of air raid protocol. They moved with them as long as they could, and then fell out of the stream when they neared the kitchen where the truck had been left. They rounded the corner and stopped.

It was gone.

At that moment the first charge blew.

When lady luck turned on you, she didn't do it by halves.

KASS STOOD NEAR THE checkpoint, directing the movement of his men, but paused when he heard bombers heading this direction. It would complicate the hunt—then some kind of explosion or flare lit up the line between wood and sky in the distance. That was odd. He'd thought the bombers still too far away. And—

"I thought the aerodrome was further west," he said to a check point guard. It was a fairly small airfield, hardly worthy of the RAF's attention he would have thought. Had *Herr* Ullstein known about the raid? Was it something at the airfield the underground was interested in? Or someone coming to the airfield?

"It is, *Herr* Leutnant," the man said. "That is not the aerodrome." He frowned. "It could be the secure compound."

Kass didn't know there was a compound there, but then he was a mere Leutnant, as that bitch had been so happy to point out earlier tonight. "Can you raise them on your radio? Do they need assistance?"

The man tried, then shook his head. The radio crackled and he turned back to it for a few minutes. After a moment he looked at Kass, his face puzzled. "They say the bombers have not arrived, *Herr* Leutnant. The explosions are on the ground."

"It must be sabotage." That's why *Herr* Ullstein wanted him here with his men. But surely they could have stopped the sabotage—unless the *Herr* didn't want to compromise the woman? Or he hadn't known what form the sabotage would take? Whatever deep game was being played out, he must do his duty. He turned to his sergeant.

"Tell the men to move out." *Herr* Ullstein had said nothing about Oberst Thorhaus. Should he notify him? He didn't know exactly where he was.

"Do you know how to contact Oberst Trump?"

The man looked wary and uncertain.

"*Herr* Oberst Thorhaus is dining with him this evening. I wish to inform him—"

"They are both at the compound, *Herr* Leutnant. He was cleared past this checkpoint by the *Herr* Oberst Trump personally."

That was...unfortunate for the Oberst, Kass thought. A pity he would not live to learn who was the better hunter. Thorhaus was supposed to be a soldier, a career soldier, but what good was a soldier who baulked at the kill? What else was there in war, but blood?

THE DETONATION OF charges and the sympathetic detonation of the various objects they were next to, rocked the ground and almost knocked Mel off her feet. There were buildings between them and the perimeter, but the flash of the explosions was bright and painful against the horizon. The sound was quite frankly terrifying. She'd thought it was bad in the bomb shelter, but this was much worse. In addition to the explosions, debris started thumping the ground all around. She thought she counted all five charges, though two of them were close enough together for doubt. She couldn't see it, of course, but it seemed that the perimeter of the compound had been well and truly painted for the incoming RAF.

It was a pity they were caught inside the lines. It was bad now and would get worse when the bombs started falling.

They crouched where the truck had been, in deep shadow caused by the flickering fires on the other side of the building.

On either side, they could see figures, running now. Some trying to bring order and put out the fires, others who just wanted to get away. The noise was intense and very German. Oaths, orders, and shouts of pain. And through it all the growing rumble of the approaching bombers. She realized that one voice was shouting Thorhaus' name.

"Do you hear that? That's probably his driver."

"Driver. A driver would have a car," Jack said. "Answer him."

Mel moved partially out of the shadows and called out, "The Oberst is here! He is injured!"

A man detached himself from the melee near a command vehicle, all of it back lit by a raging fire. Mel was glad they hadn't set the vehicle on fire. He must have cared a lot for his commander to run toward her. It felt like the bombers were on top of them.

"Quickly!" Mel called.

The man didn't hesitate when he saw his commander. He knelt by him just in time to hear Thorhaus groan.

"He is alive. Help me get him to the shelter," the driver ordered.

"Can't you see that saboteurs have marked this compound? It is suicide to remain." Mel kept her head bent away from the man.

The man hesitated. "They won't let us out the gate."

"We'll figure something out." She turned, as if she had the right to give orders. "Here, you two, help us with this man."

She gestured in Jack and Larsen's direction, hoping they'd understand. They moved toward her and grabbed Thorhaus, propping him between them and dragging him forward.

"This way," the driver said. Mel jerked her head and the two men followed her fast as they could across the open ground to the vehicle. Debris continued to hit the ground around them as gravity reasserted its control. The flames were hot here and bright. Figures and shadows moved together and apart. It was hard to tell which was which.

Jack and Larsen shoved Thorhaus in the back seat. Before the driver could climb in after him, Larsen clubbed him with the butt of his pistol. Mel bit back a protest. This was a war. She climbed behind the wheel and cranked the ignition. There was too much noise to tell if it caught, but she thought she felt the seat rumble. Jack scrambled in next to her and Larsen, after an almost unnoticeable hesitation, climbed in next to Thorhaus.

Between the explosions and the roar of the approaching bombers, it was hard to think. She didn't bother to tell anyone to brace themselves or to hang on. If they couldn't figure it out on their own, they were too stupid to live. She slammed the engine in gear and stomped on the gas pedal. They shot forward, straight at the perimeter fence. She almost turned, but then thought, why not the fence? At least it wouldn't argue with them.

At first she wasn't sure, but then she knew it she was hearing it. It was the whistle of incoming bombs. She tried to put more pressure on the gas, but it was already all the way to the floor.

The fire spread along the perimeter, leaping from vehicles to buildings, as if racing to cut them off. Time slowed again. Mel had the odd feeing they were stopped and it was the fence rushing toward them.

The fire leapt to close the gap. They hurtled forward, trying to beat it. The race was a draw. Flames flickered and danced across the hood, obscuring her view. She felt, rather than saw, the impact with the fence.

There was a jolt. Not as much as she expected. Fence poles banged against the sides. At some point they fell away. They burst clear of the flame field. The fires threw light on the field ahead of them for a few yards. But the car quickly out ran its reach.

It seemed darker, as she waited for her eyes to adjust to the change. The vehicle jolted over and through unseen ruts and bumps. It was terrifying, but it didn't occur to her to ease up on the gas. Not with the bombs incoming.

The sirens wailed louder.

The whistle of the bombs grew closer.

Flames danced in the rear view mirror, as if mocking their escape attempt.

They raced forward into a wall of dark.

The first bomb connected with the ground behind them. The earth wrenched from the force of it, but there was no recovery time between it and the next impact. Then she couldn't tell them apart anymore. The ground beneath the vehicle seemed to ripple and dance from the concussions. They swerved and might have left terra firma briefly. At one point, it felt like the car was swatted forward by the force of the explosions.

The field wasn't nearly as smooth as it looked in the brief glimpse she'd have of it.

Teeth jolted.

Bones rattled.

Terror crawled out her gut and tried to burst out her throat. It couldn't, but only because her throat was too dry...

It wasn't dark behind, which made it harder to see ahead. The shadows moved and shifted unpredictably. It was like a freakish carnival ride, only one that could kill.

A tiny voice in her head suggested she ease up on the brake. Most of her brain was shouting, not yet. You're still too close...

More lurching.

More jolting.

Lots of banging the under carriage against the ground.

Some slipping.

Lots of sliding.

The further they got from the compound, the less light there was, though the painted compound still messed with Mel's night vision. She remembered there were headlights, of a sort, and tried them out. Oh yeah, that worked. Now she could see a couple of inches to—

A ditch! Only an instant to think. Not enough to ease up on the gas, let alone take evasive action. There was a slight, a very slight ramp on their side. She hoped that's what she'd seen. The vehicle went up the slight rise. A brief sensation of flight. A bone crunching landing. The vehicle bounced, bounced again. Mel's head connected with the roof. Stars wheeled across the horizon inside the car. Her feet briefly left gas and brake. The car slowed abruptly.

She had a vague impression they were at cross purposes with the road. She cranked the wheel to the left. The rear wheels spun—the whole car might have spun actually—before they gripped the dirt road again. Wheels hooked into the ruts and shot forward again. Road wasn't a whole lot better than the field.

In her rear view mirror, she saw the field explode into an expanding succession of dirt clouds. That was a little too close. She quickly shut off the headlights and floored it. No reason to shout, come get us.

Chapter Seventeen

MEL DIDN'T CHOOSE to slow down. The vehicle did it all by itself. The engine gave a grinding, gasping cough and then ceased making any sound at all. They rolled forward a few feet, and came to a slanted, lurching stop that seemed to indicate they'd ended in a ditch.

"Why have we stopped?" Thorhaus's voice was weak.

"Engine trouble, *Herr* Oberst. And a ditch," Mel admitted. She palmed her Luger and took a quick peek at Jack. He was white as a twentieth century sheet. Why...oh right. Woman driver. Tough gig for a forties male.

"There is an aerodrome near by," Mel added. "We'll go for help."

Mel looked at Jack again, wishing she could tell him what they were saying. It had to be way worse for him and Larsen. She made a slight motion toward the door and opened hers, as an additional nudge. Before she could slip out, Thorhaus spoke.

"What has happened to Dieter, Oberst Trump? He was with me before the sirens started."

"He was still in the bunker when we carried you out, *Herr* Oberst. I didn't see him come out." It was true.

Jack and Larsen were both out of the car, clearly waiting for her to join them. They had to be as nervous as she was, only in a guy way, as she waited for Thorhaus to respond.

The silence seemed over long. Did he suspect them?

"And my driver?"

Mel tensed. "He was...unable to leave." Also the truth, mostly.

"He is dead?" He sounded...sad.

"He was down, *Herr* Oberst. We...the bombs were falling. We barely got clear." Again a mostly true statement. Mel really didn't want to outright lie. She was so bad at it.

"Of course. I am grateful..." his voice trailed off.

"We will try to hurry, *Herr* Oberst," Mel prompted. She really didn't want to have to whack him again. And it was better, if someone came along, for him to think they were good German soldiers.

"Will you be all right?" Mel had to ask.

He seemed to rouse himself. "Of course." A pause. "You should hurry."

Mel felt him staring at her, was he willing her to look at him? She felt time ripple softly past her again.

Outside Jack cleared his throat.

"Yes, *Herr* Oberst." Mel gave an awkward, seated sort of salute, then scrambled out. Just before she turned to leave, she gave into the impulse to glance his direction, one she couldn't seem to fight. Thorhaus was a shadowy figure in the rear, but she felt him trying to pierce the dark of the night and see her. Not that he knew she was she. At least she hoped he didn't. She turned sharply away and followed Jack and Larsen down the road and out of his sight.

KASS STIRRED IMPATIENTLY as the truck took a ponderous and jolting course toward the aerodrome. He hadn't been ordered there and was a bit uneasy about deviating from the plan, but it was a miserably cold night. His men were doing the job as ordered, pressing slowly through the country side in the direction of the compound and aerodrome. They had some dogs, too few for the job, but all they had. The jaws of the trap were tightening. His men knew they'd pay a heavy penalty if anything larger than a squirrel got past them tonight.

Their headlights were hooded, to comply with the blackout, though it seemed pointless with the horizon lit up like a cabaret show. The road had many twists and turns, adding to the difficulty for his driver, but Kass didn't care.

He'd brought a squad of loyal men with him, in hopes of encountering the underground. If he could impress *Herr* Ullstein...

The truck swerved and almost left the road. The driver managed to straighten it, but he looked shaken.

"If I could slow down, *Herr* Leutnant. It is most difficult to see."

It was true that the bright horizon made the shadows deep. He had no desire to die or be injured in an accident. He gave permission.

The next blind turn, they almost hit a truck coming the other direction. Their truck swerved to the right, that one to the left. They passed each other so closely, Kass thought he saw the whites of the other driver's eyes.

Something else about that driver, made him uneasy. Something...

"Halt!" He twisted and looked back, but the other truck had already rounded the corner. "Turn around!"

"I can not. There is no where to turn a truck this size, *Herr*—"

"Out, out!" Kass leapt out and ran back to the corner, pulling his service revolver free of the holster. "With me! Come with me!"

His men leapt out the back and ran after him. As soon as they rounded the corner, Kass saw the other truck, parked crookedly across the road, the doors hanging open. Kass halted, holding his hand up to halt his men. It had to be the underground. This was his chance. But...

Were they watching, waiting in the shadows? Or fleeing like the dogs they were?

He signaled his patrol to divide and check the truck, while he visually examined the surrounding terrain.

His men approached the truck silently. Not that it mattered with the sound of distant explosions covering up any stealthy sounds the enemy might be making. The leader of his squad approached, saluting sharply.

"The truck is empty, *Herr* Leutnant."

Kass was quiet. His first impulse was pursuit, but which direction? And any direction they fled, it would be into a search line.

"Return to the truck," he ordered.

They marched back around the corner and—found the hood of the truck ominously raised.

"See if it will still start," Kass ordered, trying to control his rage. These upstart French would pay a heavy price for this night's work.

The driver tried the starter...and nothing happened.

"We are not that far from the aerodrome, *Herr* Leutnant," one of the men ventured to point out. "The road should be only a few meters ahead."

Kass sighed, knowing none of them would see it. He hated walking. He particularly hated walking in the dark.

"Stay alert and let's move out." Kass nodded to the one who'd spoke.

His squad formed up automatically. They were used to walking. He fell in at the rear.

When this night's work was finished, the first person he'd be talking to would be the priest. And this time, no one would stop him.

JACK CALLED A BRIEF halt several hundred yards into the woods. Overhead, the sound of the bombers was beginning to fade into the distance, or so it seemed. Mel stared up, wishing they were on one of them. The Luftwaffe still buzzed about, but it was hard to tell how the air battle had gone. The occasional flash of weapons fire gave the impression of a dry thunderstorm and, while it helped cover any noise they were making, it also disguised hostile noise.

"I can't see anything," Jack said, his voice a thread of sound in the night. "The fires are messing with my night vision."

His words triggered an *aha* moment. Mel pulled the binoculars out from under her coat. Were they...the tips of her fingers found the switch that turned them on. Now if they still had battery power...she raised them to her eyes.

Night vision binoculars. Dang. There it was, that neon green night. At least it was a change from the black night—though not nearly enough of a change to satisfy. She took care not to raise them above the tree line.

The ramifications were, of course, huge, but no time now to ponder them. At least she, who needed them, had them and not the Germans...but that could change at any moment. A pity they didn't have a self-destruct button, like the chip in her tush.

"We've got a bogey about one hundred yards, around eleven o'clock, maybe eleven-fifteen," Mel murmured. She'd never been that good with her o'clocks. She continued her scan. "Another at two-ish o'clock."

She lowered the glasses and sensed, rather than saw, scrutiny by both men. "You can look if you don't believe me."

"Now you're seeing in the dark?" Larsen asked. "Who are you? What are you? What are those?"

She almost said, your worst nightmare, but he wouldn't get it so why bother? She decided to answer the one question, she sort of could.

"These are what the RAF was trying to blow up. We keep these out of German hands at all costs." She looked at Jack, then at Larsen. "They are more important than you or you or me."

It sounded important and mysterious, and it had the added benefit of being the truth...for once. It made a nice change. She was better at the truth. Gran had made sure of that.

"Uh," Jack said, "isn't the air field that way?"

Mel knew which direction that was and looked—and saw the horizon ahead ominously lit. Stupid. She'd been stupid and arrogant. And stupid. Mouy had mentioned the aerodrome. Of course the RAF would target it. They'd know almost exactly where it was, once the compound was painted. Why not take out the air field at the same time?

"Well, bang goes our ride." She looked at Jack. "I'm sorry. This is my fault. We could have been well out of the area by now."

"We might still be able to get something in the air," Jack said. "I don't think going back is an option anyway."

Mel didn't need the night vision glasses to see what he meant. She could hear the crash of bodies through the undergrowth, maybe half a mile behind them, not to mention the shout of orders at almost every o'clock and the occasional barking dog. All of which were getting closer.

"Okay." Mel did a survey with the goggles. "It's clear in a straight line, this direction."

THORHAUS WAITED FOR what seemed a long time, after the three men left. As time passed, he began to feel better, though his head ached. He rubbed the back of his neck, wondering how he'd been injured. His last memory was starting down into the bunker. Then the air raid sirens going off...and nothing more.

It was miserably cold. He'd be better off moving, he decided and climbed out. He could see the lightened horizon back in the direction of the compound. And he'd worried that his excellent dinner would be his last meal—if anyone found out about Dieter showing him what they were working on. It would be a miracle if anyone came out of there alive. It was a miracle he'd made it out.

Off to the west, toward the aerodrome, there was also a glow. So the bombers had hit there, too. It was still the closest place of refuge and more appealing than returning to the compound. And it sounded like the bombers were retreating. He could hear dogs barking now, off toward the North and shouts. A search? Was more going on than a bombing raid?

He pulled his coat tighter, got his bearings, and plunged into the woods. The road might be easier, but it was longer...

KASS AND HIS patrol walked silently along both sides of the narrow road, scanning from side to side. Kass walked down the middle, still in the rear. If the underground were waiting and watching in the dark, he didn't want to make it easy for them. He didn't have to tell his men to be quiet. They were nervous and jumpy as they marched cautiously toward the ominously lit horizon. His ears told him the bombers were retreating, and he hoped the damage wasn't as extensive at it looked. With the heavy rumble fading into the night, he could better hear the sounds of the search patrols moving through the area. They could wait for a patrol to find them, but men were jumpy in the dark. He'd rather be in a well-lit place before such a meeting.

They had to be close to the aerodrome. It wasn't that far from the road, though this road did wind in and out. A French road, poorly constructed, he thought with disgust.

His gripped his revolver tightly and he looked from side to side as they pressed forward. Every few steps, he glanced back.

Was that a flicker of movement in the hedge to his left? He stopped, and had to stop himself calling out to his men and alerting the watcher. Before he could decide what to do, his men had passed silently around a bend in the dirt road.

His first impulse was to hurry after them. He didn't like the dense darkness or the isolation. But what if it were the underground? He'd miss his chance to capture them himself. He slipped quietly into the shadow of a large hedge, hardly breathing as he strained to hear anything that would confirm his impression of someone there. A twig snapped, still to his left, but further away than he'd expected.

He hesitated. There was still time to catch up with his patrol, though why the idiots hadn't noticed he wasn't with them...

If they were too stupid to look back, they deserved to miss out on the glory of the capture. With one last look back at the road, he eased quietly through the brush in the direction of the sound.

Only a slight rustle reached his ears. And the Oberst thought he couldn't hunt...

"WE WON'T BE flying out of here," Jack said. He could taste it. He could smell it in the smoke that the wind brought into their faces. He could hear it as the sound of the hunt drew steadily nearer. And he could see what was left of the aerodrome.

From where they crouched, it seemed like more than the air field was ablaze. Deep in the flames, he saw the skeleton of a hanger until it collapsed. Fuel trucks and planes added to the inferno. As they watched, the control tower swayed, and then crashed to the ground, sending dark figures running in all directions. A flaming figure burst out of a building and ran screaming for several feet before falling to the ground.

Mel turned away. In the flickering glow, Jack saw her clenched fists. He realized his hands were in fists, too.

"We need to move," he said. "Someone might spot us." It sounded like the search was closing from the north. Maybe they could circle the aerodrome and strike out for the coast again.

The other two followed him deeper into the undergrowth that bordered the field. He struck due east for several yards, and then turned south, but they hadn't gone far when it became apparent that searchers were moving in from that direction, too. The Germans hadn't known everything about tonight's operation, but it seemed obvious they'd known something.

Jack quietly called a halt. Mel and Larsen crouched on either side.

They had to know it was over. He knew it was over, but his mind kept searching for an out—not for himself, but for Mel. From what she'd told him, they were still several hours short of her pick up time. It wouldn't take that long for the searchers to converge on their position.

"Look, Larsen and I can draw them off. You speak German. Once they pass, you mingle with them. In the dark, they won't know the difference. That should buy you enough time—"

"You'll be shot as spies." Mel's voice sounded odd and flat.

"We'll get rid of this gear—"

"That won't be enough." She was silent for a moment. "You'll be turned over to the Gestapo. You'll hold out for a while—but you won't be able to hold out forever."

"What could we tell them anyway? Besides, the Geneva Convention—" Larsen began a protest.

"It won't protect you." Her voice remained flat, but still intense. "You do not want to be questioned by the Gestapo."

Jack felt a cold chill track down his back. Larsen looked like a scared kid, in the flickering light passing intermittently over his face.

"And what if they don't capture you? What if they shoot you? Bang, goes my ride."

"I know what's at stake. I'll stay alive until..." he stopped. Larsen must think they were insane.

"Until what? Jack, what's going on?" Larsen looked at Jack, then at Mel. She almost smiled, or so it seemed.

"There's no time to explain." Something about her expression sent a colder chill down his back.

"There's another way out." She paused. "There's a fail safe. If my heart stops—"

"What?" Larsen said.

Jack ignored him. "No."

"It's the only way and you know it."

"What's the only way..." Larsen tried again.

"That might have been the way it went down before."

"Before..." Jack sucked in his breath sharply. "You mean, you already..."

"You didn't tell me much, but you did tell me that."

Jack felt like he'd been gut punched. She'd died?

"It was the only way then." A pause. "It's the only way now."

The scientist in Jack knew she had a point, but the man didn't want to admit it. How could he live with her death for sixty years? How had he lived with it?

"I can't do it."

"You don't have to. I arrived fully equipped."

How could she sound so calm? As if she read his mind, her mouth curved into a wry shadow of a smile.

"I did it once and, oddly enough, it didn't kill me."

Jack grabbed her hand and gave a half laugh, half snort. "You're crazy."

An odd sort of peace filled him. There'd never been any hope anyway. They weren't meant to be together. But how to wait sixty years to see her again—

And then they'd have to start all over again.

"You're both crazy," Larsen said. "And we need to move—"

"Move where?" Mel looked

A dog barked, closer than Jack expected.

"We're running out of time," Mel said.

KASS HAD MAYBE taken twenty steps when he began to reconsider his hunting tactics. The darkness around him seemed filled with shadows and sounds. And eyes, eyes watching him, waiting for him to get far enough from his men and then, what? A knife to the throat? His body buried. If he disappeared who was to say how and why? He stopped. Maybe he should turn back.

He turned in a circle and realized he wasn't sure which way that was.

He was in a wooded area, and while there was a glow, it was against much of the night sky. He couldn't tell what direction, down here in the trees. He'd never been alone in the woods after dark, he realized, with rising uneasiness. He was from the city, not from the backward country. It wasn't panic he felt. Help was only a shout away, unless...

What if the enemy were closer than his men? He could hear the searchers getting closer, or did he? What if the underground were mimicking searchers? If Oberst Thorhaus had done his job like he was supposed to, there'd be no trouble from the locals. They'd know their place and stay in it. It was his fault that their enemies thought they could venture out in the dark.

Now it seemed like there was stealthy movement off to his right. He edged forward. It was his turn to step on a twig. The snap was loud. He tried to step back. His foot caught on something and he went sprawling. His hand clenched on his revolver and it spat the waiting bullet with a large snap.

Immediately someone opened fire in the night. There was a cry ahead of him, then silence.

THORHAUS HEARD THE shots and dropped into a crouch that made his aching head take a few stomach lurching spins. It might have been better for him to stay in his freezing vehicle. He'd forgotten what the night can do to imaginations and trigger fingers.

He'd been enjoying the walk, the sense of being almost alone. The glow of the fires could almost be a sunset at home. The air was brisk, the sounds could be shut out if one thought about the happier past, when he'd slipped out with his brother to watch the moon come up or to star gaze.

Fritz had died in the invasion of Poland. He'd loved to fly, but they were both too old for this war.

His legs started to cramp. The thrashing around and shouting seemed to have died down, but he wasn't eager to run into a patrol in the dark. They'd be even more jumpy now. What had set them off, he wondered? As near as he could tell, they were closing in from all directions, with Dieter's compound and the aerodrome as the center points.

Who was directing the search? As commandant of the area, they should have informed him, unless this was a power play by Ullstein or Kass. What had happened to them that they turned on each other and the world? The Russians were our friends, then they weren't. We invade England, now we don't. The American's enter the war because of the Japanese. It was insane. The whole world seemed to have gone mad and the Fuhrer with it.

The glow of the horizon seemed greater than just the compound, which made sense, actually. Why not target the aerodrome? If that glow were any indication, it had been a good night for the RAF. And a bad night for them.

He started quietly forward again, but keeping low. Didn't hurt to keep his profile smaller against horizon. Actually, it did hurt...his back. He paused to rub the aching spot and realized he could see, or was that sense, movement just ahead of him? Was that also the murmur of voices?

WHEN THE FIRST shot sounded, Mel, Jack and Larsen threw themselves to the ground. There were way too many people thrashing around in the dark, Mel decided. How ironic if they got plugged by accident. At least it would take the decision out of her hands. It was one thing to contemplate activating her dead man's watch, a whole other thing to actually do it.

"What if that's the underground they are shooting at," Jack said. "If they catch them, they may be satisfied they've gotten who they came for."

It was a nice thought, but it was hard to believe that Mouy and his friends, who knew the countryside, would be more easily caught than them. She pointed this out and heard Jack sigh. For a scientist, he sure resisted the logical.

Mel, she was trying to resist thinking too much. Maybe if she joked enough, she wouldn't notice the moment...

She shook her head.

"We can't wait any longer. We don't know how long it will take to form."

"The presence of three people could make it unstable," Jack objected. "If we knew more..."

"Well, we don't." Mel sat up and looked at Larsen. "This is going to sound strange..."

"Stranger than what you've already been saying?"

"Actually...yeah." It hard to keep her voice matter-of-fact, "Once I'm... gone...you need to both hang on to me as tight as you can. And as long as you can. It won't be easy."

Larsen was quiet for a moment. "You're right, that is more bizarre. What's going on?"

"There's no time to explain," Jack said. "Just trust me when I say, we're going to take a ride."

His gaze bored into her. Mel could feel it, even though she wasn't looking at him. She didn't dare. She might not have the courage to trigger the device and leave him.

"Let's get this gear off, Larsen." Jack's voice sounded tight. "We won't need it where we're going."

"Should I take mine off, too?" Mel asked. It would lessen their overall weight, though she had no idea if that mattered to the vortex. It wasn't a stall. There wasn't time for it...

Jack hesitated. "Maybe you better."

Mel shrugged off the heavy coat, shivering as the night air made an immediate assault on what was left. A crackle of papers reminded her they were in her pocket. She wished she could burn them, but it probably wasn't a good idea in their current circumstances. Instead, she stuffed them between her money belt and her body, hoping they'd make it all the way with her.

The two men's movements were slow and almost awkward as they undid belts and buttons and straps. Helmets and coats were case aside.

That just left the goggles. Almost absently she lifted them for one last look—

"Bogey at three o'clock," she hissed, dropping to her stomach. She didn't realize how good her SEAL training had been until she realized she was holding the Luger, with her free hand, the goggles still pressed to her eyes. "And another one at seven."

KASS STOPPED, USING a tree for shelter as he listened intently. He'd heard voices first and now he thought he saw three soldiers, only why were they removing their coats and helmets? With rising excitement, he realized it must be the underground.

He eased forward, moving as quietly as he could, his weapon ready. Suddenly one of the figures dropped to the ground. How had they spotted him? He raised his weapon, took aim at one of the standing figures and pulled the trigger. His shot had an echo—

One of the figures fell, even as something punched him in the chest, knocking him back a step. He tried to call out, but he couldn't inhale for some reason. He looked down, but it was too dark to see...

Weakness spread out from his chest. His fingers opened. The gun dropped to the ground as his knees buckled...

MEL SAW THE man's arm lift, sighted and fired, her shot almost on top of his. The neon green figured staggered once, stood there for a moment, then sagged to his knees and fell forward on his face. He didn't move again. There was an exclamation from the other bogey. She turned that direction and saw a figure crouched about twenty yards away. He was partially behind a tree. Not a good shot.

"Larsen's been hit," Jack said.

Mel dropped the goggles. Jack, in a crouch, was half supporting Larsen. Mel closed the brief distance between them, pulled off her glove and felt for a pulse. Even in the uncertain light, Mel could see the dark line trailing from his slack mouth.

In the distance there were more shouts and the crashing of bodies through the underbrush, heading their direction.

"He's gone." And she'd just killed someone. It didn't feel real. More like a simulation than anything, except this had been a man, not a cut out figure. Maybe later she'd think about that. But there was no time now. Only time to act and hope—

"I've got to do it now. They're coming."

"Actually, I am here," a courteous voice said from the direction of the last bogey. He looked exactly like a cut out, against the deeper dark of the foliage. She mentally cursed her self for getting distracted from him.

Thorhaus. And he just had to be the one guy she knew she couldn't shoot without impacting the timeline. Great.

"You speak English," Jack said, sounding shocked.

What was he doing wandering around in the woods? They'd left him safely in his car. He'd be lucky if he own guys didn't shoot him.

She had to die...and hope it would be enough...

She dropped her Luger and eased the goggles inside her sweater, hoping he wouldn't notice her movements in the darkness—though it might actually be easier if he shot her...

"Hang on to me," she said, her voice pitched for Jack's ears alone. She felt for the button that would release the cyanide—

Jack's hand clamped on hers.

"Jack—" she started to object, but he cut her off.

"Look."

At first she didn't understand, then she realized it was getting...lighter. She looked up. The stars were twisting and thinning into silken strands of silver light that grew brighter with each passing second. Slowly, almost painfully slowly, the strands started to form around a circle. A breeze ruffled her hair as the strands moved faster and faster.

"Is it my vortex?" Jack had to raise his voice to be heard above the building wind.

Mel wasn't actually sure. She hadn't seen it forming, but what else could it be? Was it early or was she late?

The dark center tightened and the silver part widened. Then, like a tornado reaching down to the earth, the center came toward her—or toward her tush, to be more accurate. The roar of it filled the air around them. It stirred up the dirt and brush. She couldn't see Thorhaus anymore. Or Larsen's body.

"Jack." She couldn't lose him now. She followed the hand that still gripped hers until she found his shoulders and threw her arms around his neck. "Hang on!"

His grabbed her back and she buried her face in his shoulder. He held her so tightly she couldn't breathe. She didn't care. The howl grew louder, the wind wilder. She had to look up. She couldn't help herself.

Now it didn't look that different from the last time, except that it was inverted.

"This is going to be rough," she shouted.

The tip was almost on them. Debris pelted her face. She hid her face again, unable to watch.

Wind swirled around them and she felt her feet lift off the ground, and they were in the heart of Jack's creation.

THORHAUS ROSE TO his feet, staring at the sky as it began to twist and deform like some mad dream. He'd never seen anything like it. It was beautiful and terrifying. Perhaps it was God's wrath on them all for making war...

As the tip came down, he realized it was heading right for the two men. They clutched each other, like embracing lovers. It was odd, but nothing compared to the whirling, silver sky.

He tried to push his way to them. They needed help. But the wind threw him back like he was a small toy.

He lay on his face, trying to burrow into the icy ground as the freak storm raged over him.

It howled.

It roared.

Branches and bits of dirt pelted him. It was the end...

There was a sudden rushing sound that seemed to drag the wind away from him. He rolled over in time to see it turn in on itself and then the sky closed again and only the stars twinkled, as if it all been in his imagination.

He struggled to his feet and staggered toward the spot where he'd seen them...and tripped over something. Something soft. He finally remembered he had a flashlight and pulled it out, letting the small circle of light play over the face.

Kass.

He felt for a pulse, but was not surprised there wasn't one. He should be angry or even sad, but all he could think was the trouble this would cause for the locals...

Even as he looked down at his dead aide's surprised face, the area began to fill with his men. There was a shout.

"There another body, *Herr* Oberst."

Thorhaus rose wearily and walked over to the man. His light showed a young face wiped clean of everything but surprise.

One of his men searched the body. With an exclamation of surprise, he handed Thorhaus the man's identification tags.

"It appears they have shot each other, *Herr* Oberst," the man said.

"Is he one of the missing fliers?"

"Yes," Thorhaus said. His thoughts still whirled like the anomaly he'd just seen. "Did...you... see...anything...else?"

The man jumped to attention, saluting smartly. "In addition to the three members of the underground, *Herr* Oberst? *Herr* Ullstein is most pleased."

I'm sure he is, Thorhaus thought, but did you see that great, big silver...thing? Only it was clear they hadn't. How could that be? It almost seemed as it if...it had cleaned up after itself.

The couple he'd seen was gone. And if they were two guys, well, he wasn't Eugen Thorhaus. If this dead boy were one of the three fliers, then was that the other two from *The Time Machine*?

With a jolt of shock, he realized what he'd seen looked something like the artwork on the plane's fuselage. Time machine. Time machine? Was it possible?

It couldn't be...and yet...something had happened here, something only he had seen...or could remember seeing? Had his proximity to that thing affected him differently than the men?

His headache turned into a raging throb. He wanted to return to his quarters and think, but this situation could spin terribly out of control. Ullstein had been waiting for something like this to use as a *lesson* for the locals. There'd be reprisals for sure.

Thorhaus knelt by the young man, while the soldier's flashlight played over his face. So young. So brave. He fooled me, he through wryly, remembering him sitting so calmly next to him in the car. And where are your companions? The driver, the one who spoke such excellent German. He'd looked back at him and Thorhaus had caught a glimpse of...what? Had that been a woman and not a man? He had the other crew members. He could ask them if a woman had been on the plane. Whether they'd tell him...he shrugged mentally. No matter what else happened here, he would never tell Ullstein.

"Is anyone else...hurt?" Thorhaus asked. He reached out and closed the young man's eye lids. He hoped someone had done this service for his son...

"Only the Leutnant, *Herr* Oberst," one of the men said.

Thorhaus swept his flashlight over the area. It didn't even looked wind blown. "We're through here. Where is *Herr* Ullstein?"

"He is at the aerodrome, *Herr* Oberst."

"Then we will take the bodies there," Thorhaus decided.

It wasn't as far as he'd thought it would be and was a sobering sight, even with most of the fires extinguished. I'm old and tired.

Thorhaus rubbed his face wearily as he directed one of his men to find Ullstein.

He returned very quickly. "There has been an..." he stopped, a look of uncertainty on his face. "The men we captured attempted an escape. They were all killed, but—"

"But what?" Thorhaus was too tired for any more drama.

"*Herr* Ullstein has been killed."

It was almost too much to take in. His head ached and his body felt buffeted, but there was also a sense of...reprieve. Berlin would send someone to replace him, but for now...

Thorhaus straightened his shoulders wearily. "Is anyone in charge here? We will deal with the...loss later. For now we need to restore order."

There would be reports to write, but for now, there didn't seem to be anyone left to tell him how to write them. Ever since he'd seen Kass, he'd feared what would be required of him. Now, finally, he knew what he had to do...

...and what he'd never do, no matter what.

JACK HUNG ON to Mel with all he had, but it wasn't going to be enough. He knew it, even as he struggled against it. She'd said it would be bad and she was right. The wind ripped at him, trying to wrench her away from him. He could feel her fingers digging into him—and he could feel them sliding—across his back. He dug his fingers in so hard, he knew he must be bruising her, but still the distance between them increased.

From her back, his grip slipped to her shoulders.

Then to her upper arms.

...he had her by the wrists.

He wouldn't let go of her hands...but he did...

...fingers tried to twist and grip...

...finger tips...

"Jack!" He heard her call out.

He didn't have time to say her name before she was gone.

Chapter Eighteen

Present Day

"Jack..."

The sound of her voice jerked her awake. She opened her eyes. Where...she was lying on her stomach. She spread her fingers across the surface. It was soft. And she could see Sunbonnet Girls. She was home in Wyoming.

She rolled onto her back, her breathing a bit rapid. Man, that was some dream. It had been so vivid...she felt...disoriented.

Daylight streamed in through the windows, bathing her in comforting warmth. She rolled to her side, then sat up, her feet hanging off the side of the bed. Her booted feet. And she was dressed in black...

She looked up and saw a reflection in the mirror of the vanity opposite...that could not be her.

She touched her face and saw the mirror reflect the movement. She moved her shoulders and those shoulders moved. Okay, so it was her, but...what...

It wasn't a dream. It happened. She'd been there. Now she was here.

Home. She was home.

She'd been in the vortex with...Jack.

Jack.

She couldn't think about him right now. She couldn't deal with—

She was home. Focus on that.

Home.

Home had plumbing. She could pee. She could take a bath...

Boy, did she need a bath. And look at that hair. Helmet hair. She had helmet hair, quite possibly the worse case in the history of the world.

The black sweater felt coarse and stiff against her chin and it bulged strangely out from her chest. The goggles. And the papers—she felt around and found them still there, too. Amazing. She removed both and stuffed them in the bedside drawer. She'd think about them later, too. She noticed her hands trembled and curled them into fists.

Right now she just wanted to be home.

She stood up, swaying slightly. Hungry. She was so hungry. But a bath first. She couldn't stand to smell herself for one more minute.

Tears welled up in her eyes when she saw the tub. The tears were for the tub and not...other things. It was a beautiful tub. She knelt and stroked the cool surface and laid her face against it. It was cold and smooth and soothed her hot, aching eyes. Water, it had hot and cold running water.

She rubbed her eyes and reached out to turn the taps. It started cold, because that's how it was, but soon steam rose to swirl in the air around her. No lye soap either. She peeled off her clothes and slid in with a sigh as it embraced her, hot and clean...mercifully clean...

She emptied it twice before the water quit turning dingy, first from her body, then from her hair. When everything but her head was a whitened prune, Mel finally climbed out, wrapping her self in a large, fluffy, heavenly soft towel.

Her hands still shook, but that was because she was hungry...

Focus. She had a truly impressive collection of bruises, but they would heal—at least the ones that could be seen...

Don't go there...

Her tattoo was still a faint shadow on the inside of her arm. It seemed like years...sixty years, actually, since she'd been afraid of a HALO drop. Perspective really was everything.

She finger styled her hair, luxuriating being clean. And lotion. She'd almost forgotten the wonders of lotion. Her dry skin soaked it up like a sponge. She kept applying it until the white flakes were mostly gone. Her hands were reddened and rough, the nails a mess. It felt shallow, it probably was shallow, but it was heaven to be clean and warm. Her suitcase was in the bedroom and inside it she found a modern bra, modern skivs, modern jeans, modern sweater, socks and shoes. She almost wept again, as she hugged them, before pulling them on. The fabrics were soft and smelled like fabric softener. Good old spring breeze.

She'd never take any of it for granted again. This time when she faced the mirror, the person looking back was actually familiar. She was Mel of the twenty-first century, back where she belonged...except...maybe her heart. It felt stuck between the two centuries...lost in time...

The clothes she'd worn were so stiff she almost couldn't stuff them into the laundry bag. She'd figure out what to do with them later.

Her stomach rumbled, a pointed reminder there were other delights in the twenty-first century besides clothes and baths. She turned toward her closed bedroom door. Dual memories jostled inside a head, inside a brain that couldn't forget anything. Which of the memories were real? Was Norm dead or alive? And Gran? And...no, don't go there. Not yet. Later she'd deal with the past, but not now. Later.

It was so quiet in the house, she could hear the hum of her electronic clock. She might be alone in the world, not just in the house. She eyed the door knob. Why the hesitation? She'd leapt out of planes and out of time and here she was balking at opening a door.

The sun from the west facing window slanted across the floor and across her feet. Dust motes hung in the beam. Mel put her hand in it. Warmth stroked her skin and the bruises in the shape of a hand print...where...

No. She couldn't go there. The girl who couldn't forget would have plenty of time to remember...

And still the door waited. Not to mention, her impatient stomach.

Mel gripped the knob and turned it. As always, the door resisted slightly, then creaked a soft protest, before swinging wide. Mel stepped through the opening into a murky future, looking around for clues.

There was Gran's chair, where it had always been, a book lying on the side table with her reading glasses close by. Gran. She knew that chair and she remembered another chair, a shabbier one. She remembered a funeral. She remembered her...here. Which was real? She could feel grief and loss as acutely as she felt security and peace.

The room was a bit shabby, but bright and cheerful and familiar. But it too had another overlay inside her head, another version of reality—one where the past stopped with Norm's death...

Mel turned toward the kitchen—she didn't need to do this on her present food deficit—but stopped when she saw the television.

"Oh." She touched it lightly. It was pathetic, but since she was alone, she went for it and just hugged it, resting her chin on the slightly dusty top. "HGTV."

Okay, this was getting embarrassing. She straightened and headed into the kitchen. For this place, she also had two memories of how it was supposed to be. This one was the best one. It was bright and modern. Mel remembered when they'd added on to the small, frame house, extending the kitchen into the back yard as more kids came to this happy home, and creating a master suite. Mel looked to the right as she entered, seeing the breakfast nook as it was now, with a large and cheerful country table, and the other memory of a built-in nook.

Family here.

Family not here.

She felt a rising hope she was afraid to embrace. All the memories jostled inside her head, like two puzzles mixed together. Which memories went with which reality?

She needed a Diet Dr. Pepper. The refrigerator waited, another door to the past to be opened to...what? She could see empty shelves with a six pack of Diet Dr. Pepper and a couple of nearly dried up condiments...and a place of great bounty—but both had Diet Dr. Pepper. It seemed to be a constant and it was the thought of it that got her hand on the handle. It had been, well, either five days or sixty years since she'd had a cold one and boy, was she ready for it. She pulled it open with a prayer in her heart...

Bingo.

Thank you, she mouthed, her hand sliding around a cold can. It also had all the other things a refrigerator was supposed to have. Eggs and milk and a cake. An actual cake. Mel put the soda on the table, went back for the cake. Then cheese, some pickles, milk, a banana, a bowl of hard-boiled eggs. Bread, there had to be bread and butter. She found it on the counter, under a cover and shifted all of it to the table. And jam, home-made jam. Sweet.

She popped the top of the soda, first, and took a long drink. Now she knew she was really back. She pulled out a chair and looked at her bounty, not sure where to begin—remembering a bare wooden table with a bowl of soup and a hard piece of bread...

No. She clenched her hands, her body hunched around the pain. Slowly, very slowly, she straightened again. I have to be here. I have to be now. I have to find a way to let go...

And she needed some protein...she hacked off a hunk of cheese, chewed it a couple of times and sent it down for her stomach to work on, followed it with a banana chaser. Okay, enough nutrition. Now for some cake. She pulled the cover off.

Rich, dark chocolate frosting rippled across the surface of what she knew would be an outstanding base. No one could make cake like Gran...

She wanted to bury her face in it. And why not? If anyone deserved to dive into a cake—

She heard the front door open with a familiar creak and voices.

Voices. Two voices. His and hers.

"Mel?" Gran. "You awake yet, you lazy girl?"

"Oh, let her sleep. She looked tired last night." Norm.

Both here.

Both alive.

A blurry halo formed around the cake as her memory knitted a few of her memories into the right order. There were still a lot of loose ones to tie up, but one thing was clear.

You did it, Jack. She let his name burst free of the restraints inside her head. He had the right. You got me home. You got him home. You gave me my family back. I'll find a way to forgive you for not giving me you...

Faces popped in her head like an out of control camera flash. Cousins. Aunts. Uncles. Family. She was part of a family. This bounty would have to be enough.

"Mel?" Gran called out again.

"Gran?" The first try was a weak one. "I'm in the kitchen."

"I'll bet she's in the cake. Don't you eat that cake. That's for the party tonight."

"I hope she is in the cake, then I can have some, too."

"You behave, old man." Her scolding tone was heavily laced with love and it beamed into the room ahead of them, followed quickly by the real thing.

First in was Gran, her frame filling the doorway. She stopped, her faded blue eyes widening as she took in Mel's feast scattered across the table top.

Gran wasn't huge, but she wasn't tiny. She was, in Mel's opinion, just right for hugging and Mel needed one of those more than she needed cake. She jumped up and wrapped her arms around her. Her powdered skin had a papery look and was as soft as a baby's against Mel's cheek and she smelled of her current favorite Avon™ fragrance.

Norm came in behind Gran, a grin expanding across his mouth as he looked at the moveable feast.

He looked so dear and familiar, though a bit wrinklier than her last sight of him a few days...and sixty years...ago.

Their shapes blurred and wavered. Mel reached past Gran to take his sturdy hand and bring it to her cheek.

"I missed you both so much." She buried her face in Gran's cushiony, safe shoulder, soaking up the feel of her usual, cool and crisp, apron against her cheek.

"What's wrong, honey child?" It was her pet name for Mel. A hand stroked her hair. She was still cold and fresh from being outside.

"Gran..." She wanted to sob and her body shook with trying not to.

"Has something happened?" Worry sharpened her tone and broke up the log jam in Mel's throat.

"I...had a dream that you...died. And Norm, too."

"Norm? Since when do you call your grandpa Norm?" Gran pried Mel's face from the nest and studied it, worry the predominant theme in her dear eyes.

Mel didn't know what to say, so she sniffed.

"Tears?" A tissue came out of an apron pocket and stroked the moisture from her cheeks. "That must have been some dream."

Mel managed a shaky smile. Mel took the tissue and blew her nose. When she could speak, she managed a, "Yeah."

Right now it seemed like a dream, except for the ache where her heart had been...

"She needs her grandpa, Elaine." He eased past Gran and took her in his arms.

This hug was different. It was a guy hug, for one thing, and reeked of guy security and Old Spice. She leaned against him, the way she'd wanted to back in time. Memories broke inside her head, wild waves against a rocky beach. Her knees buckled and she'd have fallen if he hadn't been holding her so tightly.

"It was just a dream, honey girl. It was just a dream."

Honey girl. That's what he called her, what he'd always called her. When he wasn't dead...

"You sit down," Gran said, "and I'll cut you a piece of cake. You, too, old man."

Mel could almost see the glance they exchanged over her head. It brushed against her like the lightning bolt that missed her one night while she was out not crying uncle a few years back. Many such glances about her had passed between them through the years—through these new years. She remembered them all as clearly as she remembered not having them. It was seriously freaky.

She dropped back onto her chair, wiped her eyes again and managed a shaky smile. It became less shaky when Gran placed a generous piece of rich, chocolate cake in front of her.

"Oh, wow." Mel almost whimpered and had to again fight the impulse to bury her face in it. Chocolate couldn't cure what ailed her, but it couldn't hurt.

"You're looking at that cake like you haven't seen one before." She set a piece in front of Norm. "Here, don't let her eat alone."

She smiled at him and he grinned back. It was worth it. *It was worth it.* Tears did a come back in the corners of her eyes. She gave a tiny shake, pushed back her sleeves and grabbed her fork. The cake gave no resistance and was better than it looked, which didn't hardly seem possible.

"Oh, wow." Mel couldn't find words. It was hard not to feel a little shallow, but it was here. She was here and dang, it was good.

"Having a choc-gasm in front of the grams? Not cool, coz."

Mel looked up, then jumped up and fell on his neck. "Jimmy?"

Her cousin. She had a cousin, Jimmy. Her favorite cousin. She had a favorite cousin. He was a taller version of Norm at that age, she noted with pleasure. She hugged him again. And he liked to be called Jim, but she always pretended to forget, even though they both knew she couldn't.

"It's so good to see you." She wanted to cry again, but managed not to.

He thumped her affectionately, though a bit painfully, on the back. "Yeah, that was a long...twelve hours apart."

Mel's brain coughed up a memory of him picking her up from the airport last night. Perhaps she should just shut up until she finished connecting the dots of her past.

"She had a bad dream," Norm offered, a bit thickly through the bite of cake.

"Must have been a doozie if it made you forget something."

He plopped in a chair and reached out to snatch Mel's piece of cake. Mel used her fork to drive him off. No one, not even a favorite cousin was coming between her and cake today—or tomorrow for that matter.

"Have your own piece, Jimmy," Gran said, hacking off another chunk and sliding it expertly onto a plate. "Milk?'

"I'm sure Mel will share some," Norm added, shoving the carton Mel had pulled out of the refrigerator in his direction.

"How can I share what I haven't had yet?" Mel asked, plaintively, as she pushed her empty glass toward Norm. He poured her some, too.

Jimmy took his fork, with a charming smile for Gran, then turned back to study the food spread.

"Interesting breakfast, coz. Maybe what you eat is giving you nightmares?"

"Or I could just be hungry." Mel picked up her fork and renewed her acquaintance with her cake.

The other brow arched. "I've seen you hungry, Mel. This is way past that." He ate a huge chunk of his cake, swallowed it, and then washed it the rest of the way down with half his glass of milk. "You might consider my feelings. I told Frank you were a cheap date because you didn't eat much."

Frank. Mel froze. From stem to stern. This time she had the sense to think before she spoke, though it was a near thing. If she hadn't had cake in her mouth...

"You're such a liar," Mel quipped while she frantically searched her memory until she found one where she did agree to the blind date. Tonight. Oh man..."I've always been high maintenance and expensive. I'd end this now, before it's too late.

"Don't even think about trying to get out of it. I've got witnesses that you agreed to it willingly." He glared at her, the effect somewhat marred by the chocolate on the tip of his nose.

Mel handed him a napkin from the holder in the middle of the table and flicked the end of her own nose to let him know where to use it. "Too bad Blanca isn't here to lick that off for you."

Of course, this whole set up was so she could meet Blanca, who was something in fashion, without being an awkward third on their date. With a name like that, Mel wasn't sure Jimmy would be enough in common for them.

Jimmy grabbed her chin and studied her face critically. "Those SEALS sure beat up on you. Wear some make-up, okay? Frank thinks you're a looker. He watches your thing, you know."

"You're not giving me any incentive here," Mel said, surprised at how easily she fell into bantering with him. It was a comfortable fit...even though she felt like she was dancing on the head of a pin and could fall off at any moment.

"I'm going to put some laundry in," Gran said. "You got anything for me to wash?"

Gran must be worried if she was offering to do her laundry. Mel thought about the stuff in her laundry bag and shook her head.

"I'm good."

"You do her laundry? I thought you didn't play favorites?" Jimmy looked down at his cake, then at Mel's. "She got more cake, too."

"Behave yourself," Gran said, fondly, before disappearing in the direction of the laundry.

Norm...grandpa grabbed her arm. "Those are some nasty bruises, honey girl."

If she could think grandpa a couple of times, maybe she could say it.

He went on, "It was a bang up show, but I sure wish you wouldn't. It worries your grandma, you know."

"I...don't think I will anymore." As she said, Mel knew there really was no thinking about it. Her contract was up and after what had just happened, she couldn't take her own life so lightly anymore. She owed more than that to both her grandparents, and to Jack and herself. "They're trying to send me up in the shuttle. It's so last century."

"That'll get Gran dancing a jig," Jimmy said, though Mel noticed his gaze sharpened.

Mel chuckled. "Not a jive?"

Norm looked alarmed. "I think our jiving days are over."

He turned her hand over and traced the fading Uncle Sam tattoo on her arm. "It looks like its fading."

"It's a temporary tat," Mel said, not just feeling deja-vu, but living in the state of.

Norm looked almost startled but all he said was, "Good. I guess I'm old fashioned about girls and tattoos."

"You mean you didn't tell him about the one on your—" Jimmy stopped and grinned at her, the smart Alec grin.

Mel shook her head. "You keep it up, I'm going to give you a physics lesson you won't soon forget."

Norm jerked slightly. Mel looked at him, but he was eating his cake like it was the only thing in the world.

"And just for the record, no tattoos anywhere, except for this one—" She tried to squeeze out a grandpa or even a gramps and couldn't do it. For the moment, he was Norm.

Jimmy pushed his chair back, his expression lacking the proper repentance. "We'll be here at seven. Make sure you have your glad rags on and a properly compliant attitude."

He was almost out the door, when Mel said, "Jimmy?" He looked back. "What?"

"Just how blind is my blind date?"

Jimmy looked skyward. "Why do I even try?"

"That's what I was wondering." Mel stuck her tongue out at him.

The door banged and he was gone.

"Frank is nice enough," Norm said. "You'll have a nice time." He hesitated. "I'm surprised you didn't run this morning."

In a way, she'd been running for days, but she couldn't tell him that.

"I'm taking a break, at least for today."

"How do you feel about walking? I need to do my mile."

Mel smiled. "Walking I can always do, if it's with my favorite g—uy."

Still couldn't manage a grandpa.

THE STREET OUTSIDE looked almost eerily similar to her last homecoming, though in some ways more...alive. There was still the odd Halloween bat blowing from the odd tree and there was the nip of an incoming snow fall in the air, but like Gran and Norm's house, the street looked more modern, less dead-end than it had. Mel had checked her cell phone and now knew she'd landed home a day before her meeting with Jack in the future-past. Or was that past-future?

She'd checked the mail, while she waited for Norm to get his coat and hat on, but there'd been no *private and personal* envelope for her this time. And since she now lived in New York and visited here, that made sense.

Norm had had the film with the pictures in his foot locker. Had he ever gotten them developed? Gran was almost finished with the bomber group history. She didn't have a lot of time to work on it, since they paid regular visits to their children, scattered across the country.

But, she realized, no one had ever mentioned a female reporter being in the plane when it went down. And she couldn't ask him about it, because she wasn't supposed to know about it.

On the front step, he offered her his elbow. With a feeling of delight, Mel accepted the offer. It was how they always walked, but it felt like the first time, too. The little street went two ways, but they always walked toward the park.

Norm was silent and Mel didn't mind. There were all sorts of mine fields in talking until she got the two pasts sorted out. And she was suffering from another case of *time shock*. Just like her arrival in England, she felt...whammed. She was happy. She was heart broken.

She didn't want to go on a date tonight.

It didn't take long to reach the little park. It still surprised her how small it looked, now that she was all grown up. The park looked drab and forlorn, all done in brown and yellow. There was a breeze, but it had nothing to ruffle but the edges of Mel's hair as they strolled along the exercise path. They did one complete circuit in silence, before Norm broke the silence by clearing his throat, a prelude to speaking.

"Did I ever tell you about the reporter I met in the war?"

Mel couldn't stop a slight jerk at his words. "No, you didn't."

"She had a *tat* just like yours. A temporary *tat*, that's what she called it."

Mel didn't know what to say, so she didn't say anything.

"Funny, haven't thought about her in a long time." His gaze turned distant and reflective. "Her name was Melanie, same as yours.

Fact is, I suggested your name to your dad and mom. She had guts, that one and lots of sass. Like you."

"Really?" Where was he going with this?

"She flew with us the day we were shot down...and I never saw her again after that." He reached inside his coat jacket and pulled out...a photo...and handed it to her.

Mel knew what it was, but she looked down at the faded picture anyway, a lump rising large and painful in her throat. There they all were. Jack, Ric, Lours, Fitz, Bennie, Larsen, Harry and Roy, Sam, and the Ram, And there she was, in the corner. He had saved the film. He had gotten it developed. She wanted to touch Jack's face, but she didn't. And she still didn't know what to say. The only thing she did know, she couldn't lie to him.

"Why...didn't you ever say anything about...her?" That was a nice, neutral question.

"I'm not really sure." He frowned a bit. "At first, it was to protect her. We saw three chutes come out after us. I figured one of them might be her. The Germans didn't know she was a woman. We thought it might give her a chance to get away. This colonel asked me a lot of questions right before we were transported to our camp. Never could figure out what he wanted, but he wasn't getting it from me."

He sounded so fierce and Mel had to smile. He was quiet for several steps and Mel thought maybe that was it, but it wasn't.

"I half expected to see her after the war, but, well, after a while I figured she hadn't made it. Not her or...Jack."

Mel couldn't stop her body jerking again.

"Always had the feeling they...had feelings for each other." He stopped walking and looked at her for the first time. "Always thought you had a bit of a crush on him, too."

Mel managed a smile that felt a bit on the lame side. "Yeah, I guess I kind of did. He..." she had to swallow that lump to finish, "saved your life up there."

"He was a good man."

They started walking again.

"I still miss him."

I do, too, she wanted to say. She clamped her lips tight.

Mel thought about her tat. Five days of lye soap had almost erased it from her skin. Almost...she wished the same for her memory...almost...

But he deserved to be remembered. Maybe, eventually, instead of blocking her from caring about anyone else, her feelings for him could be a spring board to a relationship that was actually possible.

In the olden days, women had one year of strict mourning. She'd allow herself the year and no more. She smiled half-heartedly to herself, because that was all that was left of her heart. No one dies of a broken heart, she reminded herself, except her mother, or at least, that was the way the story went.

She'd been angry about it, she realized, almost her whole life. Why hadn't her mother loved her enough to live? Her chin lifted. You took your knocks, but you kept going, like Gran...at least that's how she'd done it when she'd lost Norm.

Mel couldn't say she'd never love again, but right now, it didn't seem possible. Jack...had dominated the horizon of her heart since she was a little girl, one way or another. She thought about the way he'd looked the first time she'd seen him back then. He'd be a hard act for any other man to follow.

"I've been having," Norm broke the long silence, almost abruptly. "—the... strangest thoughts."

Mel opened her mouth, but closed it again. She couldn't even say grandpa, let alone ask him what he meant. He might just tell her.

"Why would you and she have the same tat? How is that possible? They didn't have temporary tats back then."

"Really?" The word squeaked out her throat. Grandpa seemed to be firmly stuck there. Grandpa. Grandpa. Grandpa. Grandpa. Norm.

Mel peeked at him. He looked worried. She knew what he was feeling, like he'd gone crazy. He knew...but he didn't or couldn't believe it.

"Maybe it's not really like mine..." Mel said, when the silence got too long.

"Well, let's see." He pulled out more photos, this more recent. It was a blow up of just her, with *The Time Machine's* nose art by her head. The other was of her tat.

He stopped, staring at her with a kind, steady gaze. Mel didn't want to expose her wrist, but she'd been doing what he told her all of this life. She pulled her sleeve back and held it up. He held the photo up next to it.

"Exactly alike." He held the photo up next to her face. "She looks like you, too."

She stared at him. She didn't have to say anything. He knew her, he'd helped raise her this time around. He could read it in her eyes.

"How is that possible?" He suddenly looked so frail. She led him to a bench.

"It's all right there," Mel said. "On the fuselage of Jack's plane."

Norm stared at it for some more long beats of her heart. "Not a book?" Mel shook her head. "An actual...?" Mel nodded. "But...why—" He stiffened. "Not a nightmare?"

"Not a nightmare."

He looked pale and drawn. Gran was going to kill her. Mel covered his gloves hands with hers and gripped them.

"I'm glad I can finally tell you." Her voice shook a little. "How very proud I am of you. Thank you for what you did for me, for everyone. You were... amazing."

"Me? You could have been killed."

Mel twitched and hoped he didn't notice. He did.

"Honey girl..." His tone was an order.

She shrugged. "Apparently it did kill me...one time."

"How many times have you done...it?"

Mel shrugged. "Only twice, that I know of, but I only remember the one time."

He took a few minutes to process this.

"Makes my head ache thinking about it."

"No kidding." She was quiet for a minute. "I...killed someone, Norm. A German officer. I just...shot him."

"It was war. You did what needed to be done."

"But it wasn't my war. And I keep wondering what it changed."

"You can't change it now, honey girl. Can't put spilled milk back in the carton."

Not without doing it all over again, she amended, not something she really wanted to do.

He shivered slightly. Mel patted his arm.

"Let's go home. You'll catch a chill and Gran will blame me."

He nodded and got to his feet, offering his arm again. Mel took it and they headed for home. They were almost there before he spoke again.

"So...you and Jack...?"

Mel sighed. "Yeah."

"Do you know...?"

"I don't know where he is."

Another silence.

"I'd like to see him again."

"Yeah...me, too."

Chapter Nineteen

One Year Later

MEL FINISHED WITH her earrings and stepped back for a last look in the oval mirror affixed to the vanity. She still felt those so glad to be wearing moments, even after a year in the twenty-first century. The jeans were soft and supple and the bright, red cashmere sweater a make Mel happy self-gift, was amazing. Mel was almost back to normal, if she didn't look too deeply into her own eyes—which she mostly didn't.

But today was an anniversary of sorts, the self-imposed end of her mourning period. And, just like a year ago, she had a blind date, courtesy of Jimmy. She didn't feel ready, but feelings could change, she reminded her reflection.

She'd come a "long way, baby," since being flung back into her life. There'd been a lot of rumors when she chose not to renew her contract with *BrightLine Weekly*. Her producer had resorted to weeping, wailing and even gnashing his teeth, but Mel stood firm—and then found her self adrift in a sea of uncertainty as she tried to figure out what she did want to do, now that she'd grown up. She closed her New York apartment and moved home. Since she'd spent most of her time working, she had the money set aside to take a year off. But too much free time left her vulnerable to thinking and out of thinking came longings.

She had a couple of offers from news organizations still on the table, but if she waited much longer, she'd be older than old news

While she tried to decide what to do, she'd tried to keep busy. She'd helped Gran with the bomber group memoirs and worked with some of their sons in restoring an actual B-17 bomber. They were almost finished and hoped to take to some air shows next spring. That had been the best, being back inside a bomber. It didn't make sense. It's not like her time in the air had been fun, but Jack felt closer during those times, just out of her reach...but there.

It was still a struggle and not just because she still yearned for Jack. She'd become, she'd gradually realized, a bit of an adrenaline junkie. She missed the excitement and the variety of not crying uncle. And she missed the company of this new generation of heroes, but she kept her promise, to her self and to Norm. The most dangerous thing she did was learning to snow board with Jimmy and Blanca.

Norm, the only one who knew the truth, had done what he could to protect her from the match-making efforts of her large and loving extended family, but she'd made her self go on a few dates. She didn't enjoy them and she was pretty sure her dates didn't either.

She still couldn't call Norm "grandpa." Gran had finally quit commenting on it and, since some of the great grandkids had picked up the habit, it wasn't as noticeable as it had been.

She didn't know if her inability to fix on a new career was real indecision or that part of her still hoped she'd run into Jack. It was probably the latter, she admitted to herself. She'd been waiting for him her whole life. What was a year? Just an eternity to the waiting heart...

It might have been easier if she'd seen him die, instead of just disappearing. There was a tiny part of her that kept hoping she'd catch up with him somewhere, but for all she knew, he'd be flung back in time.

Hope. The truth was, she'd lived on it for the past year, but it was probably time to put that particular hope in her hope-less chest and get on with the rest of her life. How long could she wait for an out-of-time man to find her? Her heart said, forever. Her brain wanted her to get a life.

Hence the blind date with Jimmy's friend. Luckily, this time she wasn't dreading the whole Blanca thing. They weren't destined to be bosom buddies, but Mel didn't dislike her and could see why Jimmy did like her. Gran had warmed up, too, which was a good thing, since they'd started talking about making it official.

Mel didn't begrudge them some nuptials. She'd kind of had hers. She even had a copy of the wedding register they'd signed. She'd gone back to that little village in France, hoping to see something familiar, but sixty years and a daylight view had left her wishing she'd left well enough alone.

It was great to know that the village survived. The old priest had died peacefully in his bed, close to the end of the war. Mouy and his friends hadn't survived that night, but they had accomplished their mission. She was pretty sure the man she'd killed was Kass, which helped some.

Thorhaus had more than lived up to his place in history. This time, instead of presiding over a massacre, he'd saved many lives. He'd still died by a firing squad, but without the asterisk by his name.

Mel had tried to find out more about the night vision goggles she'd brought back with her, but had quickly out run her contacts. She wasn't an investigative reporter and couldn't explain why she needed to know who had purchased the low tech goggles. So they were also tucked away in her hopeless chest.

She sighed. She really didn't want to go out tonight, but life was full of things you did, because you should, not because you wanted to. Wisdom from the book of Gran.

A light tap on the door was a welcome distraction from her tangled thoughts.

"Come on in."

Gran entered, moving stiffly. This winter had been harder on her aging joints than the last and Mel was glad she'd been around to help. Gran lowered herself onto the bed and then gave Mel a thorough once over. Mel turned in a circle for her benefit.

"You look nice," she finally pronounced. "I'm glad you're getting out."

Mel looked at her more closely. Was there a question in there? Mel could remember a time when it had only been her and Gran. Had she reveled so much in having Norm around that she'd left Gran out?

Mel sat down by her, looping an arm around her shoulder. "Am I wearing out my welcome?"

Gran gave her an affronted look. "This is your home."

"Yeah, but it was yours first. I've just...loved being here with you and Norm, while I figured things out."

Gran started to open her mouth, then closed it firmly.

"Then what is wrong?"

Her gnarled hands moved restlessly for a few moments.

"You're a grown up. I vowed I wouldn't pry."

Her feelings were hurt, Mel realized. She'd thought about telling her what happened, but it was such a wild tale, she didn't know how to begin.

Norm tapped on the door, and then peeked around it. She met his gaze with a question and got a slight, but decided nod in return. He came in and shut the door, settling in the chair across from them.

"I should have told you, Gran. I've been...a bit clueless."

"More than a bit," she said, tartly. "There's nothing you could tell me I wouldn't understand. Or that would change my love for you."

Mel looked at Norm. He was trying not to grin. She gave him annoyed look and he tried a little harder not to look amused...but not enough.

"I guessed some of it, of course," Gran said. "I'm not a fool or blind." She hesitated, worry written large across her face and in her eyes. "Was he...married?"

"No!" Mel didn't hesitate, because she didn't have to.

Gran looked relieved. Then she looked mad. "If he didn't have the sense to love you, honey child, then he's not worth grieving over."

"Oh, Gran," Mel leaned against her. "I do love you."

"Maybe you should just tell her who you're pining for. That would speed things up."

Or give Gran a heart attack.

Gran got an "I thought so" look. Then her eyes widened. "A...another...woman?" She tried to look PC, but she was from the wrong century for it.

Mel smiled. "That might actually have been easier to deal with." Mel looked down, took a deep breath and looked Gran directly in the eyes. "I'm in love with Jack Hamilton, Gran, you know, Norm's Jack. The Captain of *The Time Machine*."

Gran leaned back a little, a slight frown pulling her brows together. She looked at Norm, who nodded encouragingly.

"You're in love with a...dead...old guy?"

Mel kind of shrugged. "Actually, he might not be dead. Or old." She'd merged with her life the way she was in the past. It was possible, if Jack had been hurled into the future, that he had, too. She had no clue what effect his disappearance in the past, would have had had on the future. The day he had showed up before, had been the longest day of her life. She'd been heart broken and relieved. And gone to bed with a headache because of it.

Silence. Gran blinked a couple of times, but it didn't look like it helped any. Finally she looked at Norm.

"What is she talking about?"

He got up and came to her, taking her hand in his and saying tenderly, "She's trying to tell you that she time traveled into the past, met Jack—and me, by the way—and they fell in love."

"Oh." Her lips thinned. "Now that you've had your fun, suppose you tell me what's really wrong?"

Mel got up and dug in her hopeless chest, removing the picture of her in the past and the copy from the marriage register. She handed both of them to Gran and sat in the chair Norm had vacated.

Gran studied them in silence. A couple of times it looked she was going to say something, but she either she decided not to or she couldn't.

Finally Mel had to break the silence. "The marriage wasn't legal, but it meant something to us to do it. We thought I'd return to the future and he'd...live his life. But we were trapped and the only way out was the vortex."

"You..." Gran cleared her throat and tried again. "You've never lied to me, so of course I believe you. Mostly. Actually, I'm having a little trouble with this. How—"

So Mel told her, everything except that it was a fix trip and about the night vision goggles. No sense worrying either of them about illegal time tampering when they couldn't do anything about it. Even Norm had never heard this much of the story. Mel didn't cry, though it was a near thing a couple of times.

If she'd had time for the swelling to go down before her date, she'd have let 'er rip. But she didn't. Vanity and grief were an odd and uncomfortable mix, but apparently not mutually exclusive.

"That's not a tornado on the plane?" Gran sounded dazed.

"It's a flux capacitor, or at least Jack's version of it." At least they'd both seen Back to the Future.

Gran finally let out a huge, shaky sounding sigh. "I can see why you didn't want to talk about it."

Mel saw her grip Norm's hand tightly and kind of bump his shoulder with hers. Telling her Norm had died hadn't been easy...

"And you don't know what happened to Jack?" There was an odd note in her voice.

Mel shook her head. "The vortex could have hurled him anywhere, any time, I suppose. I know he worried about making it unstable, but he, the future Jack, didn't tell me a lot about the actual process, since I can't forget anything. And Jack in the past didn't know yet. Or something like that."

"Did he...have family?"

"I know he had a sister," Mel said, "and his parents were living then." She hadn't felt like she had the right to contact them and if she'd known they were around...it would have been hard to stay away.

"No brothers. You're sure?"

Now it was Mel's turn to turn the bright gaze on Gran. "What's going on?"

She fidgeted. "I...met your blind date for tonight. He came over with Jimmy a couple of days ago. You were both out...somewhere, but he said, he said, he was the spit of Jack and he said he was Jack's nephew—but his last name is Hamilton, so that would be from a brother, not a sister." She looked at Mel. "His name was Jack..."

Mel was on her feet without realizing she'd moved. As if to a movie cue, she heard the outside door open and Jimmy calling out.

"Hey, we're here! Present yourself, coz!"

She looked at Norm and Gran. She could feel the color drain from her face. It was probably a mess on the carpet around her feet. The edges of the room when dark and she felt herself sway, as if pushed by a breeze...

Norm scrambled up to steady her. "It might not be him, honey girl."

"I know." Her voice was a thin thread of sound because her throat felt like it had almost closed.

"Just a minute, Jimmy," Gran called. "She's not quite...dressed."

"I can't go out there. If it's him...not in front of Jimmy..." Mel clutched their hands. "If it's not him, I'll ... cry uncle." She managed a weak grin that faltered, then faded. "Why didn't he...?"

"It was Jimmy's idea to surprise you. Don't think he, Jack, knew about it," Gran said. "Jimmy knew you had a crush on Jack." She stopped. "This is confusing."

"Tell me about it," Mel said, the sentence breaking in the middle.

Mel realized Norm was looking toward the closed door, too. Jack had been his friend first. They could hear a murmur of voices, but she couldn't tell. She couldn't tell...

"I'll get Jimmy and Blanca into the kitchen. Norm—if it is him, well figure it out before they—"

Gran went out through the bathroom, emerging into the living room through the other bedroom door. Distantly, Mel heard Gran asking Jimmy and Blanca to come look at something in the kitchen. She heard her door open and was conscious that Norm had left the room, pulling the door to behind him. More murmuring voices. Now footsteps, heading toward her door.

Jack or Norm? She stared at the closed door, afraid to hope, afraid to breathe.

A light knock, then a gap appeared between frame and door. It grew wider and wider. She couldn't look. She spun around, but she could see the door in the mirror. She closed her eyes.

Norm or...Jack...

JACK STOOD IN NORM'S living room, pretending to look casually around, his heart beating so hard, he was surprised Jim and Blanca didn't hear it. Where was she? Surely she'd figured out who he was? She had to know that he'd come as soon as he could. Unless...

Maybe she'd had longer to wait? He didn't know when she'd

emerged with her life? What if years had gone by? Actually, he didn't know she had emerged into her life. What if the vortex had thrown her ahead of him?

What would he do if she didn't know him? He turned, half ready to just leave, but Jim was between him and the door.

When he'd lost his grip on Mel in the vortex, there'd only been a moment to process it, then everything had gone...blank. When he opened his eyes, he was in the hospital. His future self had been in coma, he learned, once he could get his staff to believe he was really Jack Hamilton.

He was still working on a theory for how his memory had updated. He did know he'd merged with himself. He had both sets of memories. It had taken some doing to fit the right ones together—and that had helped convince people he was himself. For a week, he'd been a lab rat caught in a maze. They didn't want him to contact Mel or anyone else. But then he remembered their last mission and the night vision goggles. Even they could see the importance of tracking down someone tampering with the wrong side of history.

They'd wanted to send someone neutral, but Jack told them he'd told Mel to only release them to him. A pity he hadn't thought about that, but luckily they believed him. It wasn't like they could approach her and ask her if she'd traveled through time recently.

They'd set up an identity for him and allowed him to meet Jim Morton, Mel's favorite cousin. Once he'd made the connection between their grandfathers it had been easy to get Jim to suggest a blind date between him and Mel, though Jim had warned he wasn't sure he could get Mel to agree. She'd never been wild about blind dates, Jim told him, but she'd really been down on it lately. Jack didn't dare ask why or press too hard.

But she'd agreed. He'd alternated between hope and wondering what she was thinking of, to go out with someone she didn't know.

He finally decided to just go to her house, but she'd been out...with Norm.

It was clear Elaine didn't know what had happened to Mel. She'd been kind and interested to find he was related to...himself...but only in a normal way, not in an I'm-going-to-pin-your-ears-back way he'd expect.

As each day passed slowly in his new history, he came to understand more of what Mel had gone through while traveling through time. Was it her? Did she still love him? That was the essential question. She had every right to hate him, he knew. He'd gotten her into this mess, fallen for her, sort of married her, and then disappeared.

Against the odds, they had a chance to be together...if...

Elaine emerged from a bedroom beckoned Jim and Blanca into the kitchen, giving him a long, almost worried look. Did she look a little shell-shocked? He was afraid to hope...

And where was Mel? Why didn't she come out? It didn't take that long to dress, did it? It never took her long in the past, but maybe she was different in this time?

Another door opened, closer to him, giving Jack a brief glimpse of a dresser, before Norm closed it behind him. Norm. Old, but still Norm. Of course he was old. It had been sixty-plus years...but dang.

Would his old friend know him? He looked at Norm and didn't know what to do but wait while he was studied with wary hope.

"Jack?" Norm was older, but the grin that spread across his face was just the same.

"You look like crap, Norm." They pounded each other on the back, stopped and looked at each other, then pounded each other again. "What you been doing to yourself for the last sixty years?"

Finally they stopped pounding and did some looking and Norm the buddy changed into Norm the grandfather. He crossed his arms across his chest.

"Just what are your intentions toward my grand daughter? And what were you thinking to send her—" He stopped.

"You should kick my butt," Jack said. "Right out the door."

"I would, but then she'd kick mine." He nodded toward the closed door. "She's in there, waiting for you."

Relief shook him. "I was afraid—"

"Afraid of what?"

"What if she hadn't...gotten here yet?"

Norm grinned. "That might have been a bit...interesting." He frowned. "How long have you been here?"

"A couple of weeks. Took me a while to convince everyone I was...me."

Norm kind of twitched. "I think I'm too old to even think about this stuff."

Jack grinned. "What about me? I turned eighty-five last week."

"Well, go put my girl out of her misery, old man," Norm said. "We can catch up later...as long as you don't wait too long. That wedding wasn't legal."

Jack put out his hand and they shook, gaze meeting gaze.

"Thanks, Norm."

"You're not out of it yet, you know. Elaine hasn't really had time to think about it. She'll probably be gunning for you when she does."

Jack chuckled and turned to the door. Sixty years were supposed to separate them, but instead there was a single door.

Mel...

Jack grabbed the knob and turned. He pushed and it stuck. Oh no, you don't. He pushed harder and it gave, swinging wide.

Mel...

She was standing with her back to the door, her fists clenched at her sides. In the mirror, he could see she had closed her eyes and her body was braced. He stepped through and closed the door. She looked so different in her modern clothes, almost unfamiliar. He felt...uncertain. He didn't know this Mel.

"Mel?" It was a question, though he wasn't quite sure what he was asking her.

Her lashes lifted, slowly but not stopping until her eyes were wide and wondering. She spun slowly to face him.

"Jack..." The answer was in her voice.

One step by each brought them together. Full body contact. For the first time in this century, he felt at home.

"You smell...good," he said shakily as her head burrowed into his shoulder. She chuckled and looked up, her amazing eyes swimming with tears.

"You smell better, too."

He pulled out a handkerchief and gently stroked the tears from one eye, then the other. Her smile started slow, but expanded to maximum and almost rocked him off his feet.

"I was afraid..." Jack started, then stopped.

"Of what?"

"That you wouldn't feel the same. That you'd found someone else. That you, the you I knew, wasn't here yet. Of losing you again..."

Mel's brows arched. "I never thought of that."

"What would you have done, the you before, if I'd come calling?"

"Well, duh. I've been in love with you my whole life. What do you think I'd have done?"

He laughed and hugged her again. She cupped his face with her hands and looked at him for a long moment.

"Welcome to the twenty-first century, Captain."

She still had a smart mouth, he thought a bit dazed. Best thing to do with a smart mouth is shut it, and since that's what he wanted more than anything, he did.

JIMMY LOOKED AT Mel suspiciously, when she and Jack finally emerged from the bedroom. Since they weren't legally married, it seemed like a good idea. Blanca looked amused at the turn of events. Norm looked content and Gran looked...like a magician whose magic trick turned out to be real magic.

"We explained to Jimmy that you already knew each other and had a misunderstanding," Gran said, quickly, a bit too quickly. "When Jack found out Jimmy was your cousin..." She stopped. She'd done a good job with the cover story, but it could easily develop holes with embellishment and she seemed to realize that.

"We need to...talk..." Mel said. "Do you mind if we bail on dinner with you and Blanca? We promise we'll make it up to you."

Blanca looked delighted. Jimmy still looked suspicious, but let himself be led out of the room. Only when they were sure they were alone, did they all look at each other.

"Well..." Gran began, but Norm cut her off.

"Elaine, I'd like you to meet my best friend, Jack Hamilton."

Gran took his proffered hand, looking at his face with understandable wonder.

"Then you really are from..." She couldn't say it. Mel didn't blame her.

"I'm afraid so, but I'm delighted to finally meet the light of Norm's life." He raised her hand to his mouth and lightly kissed it.

She smiled a little, then took her hand back and put both of them on her hips. "Yeah, well, be that as it may, what you did, sending Mel back in to a war, I ought to spank you or something."

"Yes, ma'am," Jack said, meekly. "I was completely out of line."

"Well, what's done is done and I'm glad you've come to put it right—" she stopped. "You have come to put it right?"

"Yes, ma'am." This one sounded like it came with a salute.

Mel bit back a grin. If Gran knew Jack's idea of putting things right, she'd kill him on the spot.

"We want to make our wedding anniversary official," Mel said. "Think you could pull together a small wedding on Christmas Eve? We could web cam it for those in our family who can't make it."

Gran opened her mouth, whether to object or agree, Mel wasn't sure.

"No big deal, Gran. Just something quiet and simple. I know its short notice."

Norm grinned, but Gran said, "Are you sure...you can? You're not supposed to be here...young. Can you...marry? What if you suddenly got old again or something?"

She wouldn't worry about that, if she'd seen him old, Mel thought. "It won't change anything if it did, Gran."

She smiled up with Jack, because she still couldn't believe he was finally here.

Jack shrugged. "I'm still me, as far as they can tell. My staff still need to finish running some tests and they'd like to interview Mel about her experiences. But we'll be back in time for the wedding."

"Sixty years and some change...that's got to be some kind of dating record," Gran said. She walked up and hugged Mel, then Jack. "If you keep our girl looking like this, you'll have no trouble with us."

Hugs all around, then Mel said, "I'm going to take Jack for a ride in my SUV to get some fast food."

"Are you sure he's ready for that?" Gran asked.

"If you thought war was hell." Norm rolled his eyes.

Mel felt a bit guilty about pulling him away. She knew Norm wanted time with his friend, too, but now there was time, almost all the time in the world. With his arm securely around her, Mel led him toward her SUV.

"So you really think we can take care of the time tampering?"

Jack nodded. "They think they've narrowed it down to the week it happened. With your memory of how things are supposed to be, we should be able to narrow it even further. And now that I've got the goggles and paper work the Germans had, we might even know who we're looking for before we go back in time." He squeezed her shoulders. "Don't worry. We'll be back in plenty of time for the wedding."

Mel stopped and looked at him. "Both of us? At the same time? Forgive me if I'm a little skeptical..."

Jack pulled her into his arms. "I have this theory about that..."

At the moment, Mel decided, she wasn't interested in his theories, but he'd better have more than one before she was jumping in a vortex again, and she'd tell him so when they finished kissing. If they ever did...

The End

Pauline Baird Jones

Pauline Baird Jones is the award-winning author of six novels of romantic suspense. After an abrupt, work-related move from New Orleans to Houston, she's re-adapting to life in a Western environment and settling into her new digs. For updated news about Pauline and to check out her free stuff, visit: www.paulinebjones.com.

Also by Pauline Baird Jones:

Do Wah Diddy Die
Pig in a Park
A Dangerous Dance

Lonesome Lawman Series:
#1 The Last Enemy
#2 Byte Me
#3 Missing You

Special 5 year Anniversary Issue:
Lonesome Lawman Omnibus

All available directly from

Hard Shell Word Factory
www.hardshell.com

Printed in the United Kingdom
by Lightning Source UK Ltd.
124386UK00001B/63/A